Remembering Betsy Gray

By John Dowds

...The tree of liberty must be refreshed from time to time with the blood of patriots and tyrants. It is its natural manure...
(Thomas Jefferson - 1787)

Introduction

Set in Ireland during 1795-98, **Remembering Betsy Gray** tells the story of a young Irish couple who met and fell in love and set out to achieve their dream of overcoming centuries of sectarian hatred and violence and build a new Ireland. Throughout the eighteenth-century the main complaint by Presbyterians, Catholics, Jews and Quakers was that they were treated like second class citizens in their own country. Membership of the Church of Ireland was compulsory for anyone who wanted to become involved in the management of the country. Political, judicial and financial power lay in the hands of a few rich, landowning Anglican aristocrats, who controlled the selection and election of the three hundred representatives of the Irish government, notorious for corruption and self-interest. The only checks on the politician's extravagances was by the English parliament, which was primarily interested in protecting British jobs, subsequently, their actions helped destroy the Irish woollen trade, crippled Irish shipping, and introduced prohibition of exporting Irish cattle and sheep. The Irish population also paid a tithe for the upkeep of the Church of Ireland along with taxes on their homes and goods. Farms were held on short-term leases, the cost of which was normally increased upon renewal. When the new leases could not be paid whole families were evicted without compensation or allowed access to any lawful protection. These financial and social inequalities lead to the emigration of over three hundred thousand Presbyterians and their families to America throughout the eighteenth century.

Following America's war of independence in 1775, and the revolution in France in 1789, new ideas challenging traditional political values spread throughout Europe eventually reaching the shores of Ireland where they were picked up and championed by a group of Presbyterian clergymen and businessmen in Belfast who believed political reform in Ireland had now become a vital issue. In 1791, under the guidance of Dr William Drennan they helped form the Society of United Irishmen to bring about the changes by peaceful means. The group's liberal ideas quickly spread throughout the whole of Ireland and soon membership of the United Irishmen exceeded over two hundred thousand Irishmen of all religions.

3

However, when France declared war on Britain in 1793, the Society of United Irishmen was banned because by seeking political reform of the Irish government the Society was deemed to be committing a treasonable act. The government's actions forced the organisation to go underground and begin secretly plotting for an armed revolution to bring about the political changes they were seeking.

...all men are born equal, and with equal natural right, in the same manner as if posterity had been continued by creation instead of generation...
(Thomas Paine - The Rights of Man 1791)

...The opinions of men with respect to government are changing fast in all countries. The revolutions of America and France have thrown a beam of light over the world, which reaches into man...
(Thomas Paine - The Rights of Man 1791)

...For a'that, and a'that
It's coming yet for a'that,
That man to man, the world o'er,
Shall brothers be for a'that...
(Robert Burns - A man's a man for a' that 1795)

Chapter 1

Lost in the mists of time, there is a story about a young Irish girl who dreamt it was possible for the people of her beloved country to overcome centuries of sectarian hatred and violence, and build a new society, in which everyone was able to live in harmony and peace no matter what their religion was. Her name was Elizabeth Gray, or Betsy as she was better known to her friends and family.

Betsy was raised along with her younger brother George, by her parents, Daniel and Ruth Gray on their thirty-acre farm, in the townland of Gransha, County Down, Ireland. With her long dark hair, sparkling brown eyes, and quick, pleasant smile, Betsy was well known, and liked by everyone in her small rural community.

Betsy lived in a single storey, thatched roofed farmhouse. The outer walls were built with local stones and whitewashed using crushed shells gathered from a nearby beach. There was a doorway in the middle of the front wall that led into a large spacious kitchen with an earthen floor. Dominating the gable wall there was a large open fireplace with a broad chimney that seemed to push its way up through the roof. Above a generous peat burning hearth, there swung a black metal rod, that had various lengths of metal hooks dangling from it upon which several types of cooking pots could be hung. To the right of the hearth there was a small wooden cupboard where the cast iron pots, and a large blackened kettle were stored.

The rest of the furniture in the kitchen was practical and basic in design. A large pine table with six chairs sat in the middle of the room. To the rear of the kitchen, beside a second doorway leading out to the back of the building, stood a tall wooden cabinet with six drawers in the base and four shelves filled with plates and mugs nestling on the top.

To the left of the front door there was a long narrow corridor that led from the kitchen to three separate bedrooms completing the generous living space in the cottage.

When Betsy was growing up, her father was very active around the farm, growing their own potatoes and oats, plus a small crop of barley, which he sold to a brewery in Belfast. He also kept a few cows and pigs from which the family was able to produce milk, butter, and bacon, which they would sell at the local market in Bangor.

However, despite all their efforts her father realised that the produce they were selling from the farm was not able to generate enough income to meet all of his growing family's needs, and so he decided to go into the linen business.

Betsy's father started by growing flax on three acres of the farm. When the crop was mature the whole family, including Betsy, was involved in the back-breaking job of pulling the tough flax stems from the soil by hand, and soaking them in a water filled dam her father had dug in another one of his fields. The stems were left there for ten days when, with the stench almost unbearable, the whole family would help lift the softened stalks out of the water and spread them out on the grass to dry. Once dried, the stems were beaten with wooden mallets to separate and clean the flax fibres. The tangled bunch of fine fibres from the beating were then straightened by pulling them through metal combs of decreasing fineness to make the fibres soft and ready for spinning onto bobbins. This was a task often carried out by Betsy and her mother. Her father would then take the bobbins and weave the yarn into a brownish coloured cloth on a weaving loom he had installed in a new room built onto the side of the farmhouse. To fund all of this new activity her father had to borrow money from their land agent.

Once a week, Betsy and her mother would load rolls of the brown cloth onto their horse and cart and take it to the linen market in Belfast to sell. With the income from the farm products and new cash generated from their linen business, the family was able to live quite comfortably for a number of years.

On Betsy's sixteenth birthday her father presented her with a gift of a beautiful, bay Connemara pony.

'Happy Birthday,' he said handing Betsy the reins. 'He can help us around the farm, but he is yours to keep and look after. What are you going to call him?'

Betsy was overcome with joy as she gazed at the pony with his tan coloured body and black mane and tail.

'I think I'll call him Sandy,' she said. 'He's the most beautiful horse I have ever seen.'

Over the coming months Betsy loved taking Sandy out for a ride every day. With his large, kind eyes and gentle face Sandy would often gaze at her, and with a gentle nudge seemed to understand her every mood.

Despite her family's prosperity, Betsy was worried about her father's health. She could see that working on the farm during the day and spending every evening weaving cloth on the loom until late into the night was beginning to take its toll on him. Her concerns about his fitness increased when, following a very wet Spring and a dull, dank Summer, they had a poor harvest, which meant they had fewer products to sell at the local markets. As a result, the farm lost a lot of money forcing her father to go back to the land agent and ask him for another loan on top of the one he already had.

While all of this turmoil over money was going on her father received a letter from a minister in the Church of Ireland. Betsy casually watched him open the envelope and read the contents. She was surprised when she saw his head drop and his shoulders sag, and when he looked up at her, he despairingly shook his head from side to side.

'I don't understand these people. It's tough enough having to pay my taxes to the government and to the council, as well as pay the rent we owe on the farm, but I also have to set money aside to make sure I can repay the loans we owe to the land agent. On top of all that I mustn't forget to buy feed for the animals and pay all the other farm bills… and now this nonsense.'

Her father paused, before putting the letter back in the envelope and holding it up for her to see. 'The mighty Church of Ireland has just sent me a bill demanding I pay for their upkeep,' he said wearily shaking his head. 'The people who worship in the Church of Ireland have nothing to do with me. Why are they persecuting me? Where are my rights as a worshiper in a Presbyterian church?'

With a final shake of his head, her father walked over to the kitchen table and placed the envelope on top of a stack of other letters containing final demands and went outside to bring his cows in from the fields.

As far as Betsy knew her father didn't look at the letter again, and a few days later, while ploughing the meadow field, he collapsed and died. The doctor said his death was due to his weak heart. Betsy wasn't so sure; she was convinced his death had been caused by the stress brought on by the financial pressures of running the farm.

After her father's funeral, Betsy's mother took over the financial management of the farm. She turned out to be quite an astute businesswoman and within a few weeks she started to restructure the farm business. The first change she introduced was to sublet twenty acres of their land to one of her neighbours. She also stopped growing and spinning their flax yarn. Instead, she bought spun yarn from a Bleach Green in Belfast that was sourcing good quality yarn from top quality spinners in Donegal. The linen cloth she produced on their loom was considered to be of the highest quality by the buyers at the linen market in Belfast. This meant she was able to demand a premium price for her fabric. The changes she introduced meant she was able to cope with the financial demands she faced on the farm.

One night, a few months after her father's death, Betsy was invited by Gina Russell, her best friend, to go to a meeting in the church hall to listen to a talk that was to be given by two local Presbyterian ministers. Reverend Warwick and Reverend Porter were going to speak about the need for political and social reform in Ireland. Betsy quickly agreed. She knew both speakers well, having attended several church services where they were preaching. When Betsy and Gina arrived at the hall it was already packed but they still managed to find two seats.

Reverend Warwick was the first to speak. He gathered his notes and walked to the podium in the centre of the stage.

'Thank you, my friends, for turning up in such great numbers tonight. Reverend Porter and I are going to talk about the need for political and social reform in Ireland. Last week one of my parishioners, his wife and their four children, were forced out of the farm they had been living and working on for the last ten years by the bailiffs. His crime? He could not repay money he had borrowed from his land agent to build a new milking shed. His builder had gone bust. Another parishioner broke his leg in an accident on his farm and was unable to work. When he fell behind with his rent the land agent sought a court order to remove him and his family from the farm. The whole family, including a baby of six months, were forced to sleep in a ditch until we managed to find someone who would help them. When new tenants moved into their farm the land agent took the opportunity to increase the rent. I could go on all night quoting examples of financial hardships our people are experiencing because of policies introduced by the corrupt politicians in the Irish government. They are only concerned about looking after the interests of the wealthy landowners who got them elected. Five years ago, in 1791, a small group of enlightened Presbyterian businessmen met in a coffee shop in Belfast under the guidance of Doctor William Drennan. Their intention was to create a Society of United Irishmen. One of their key demands was that reform must include Catholics and Protestants because they believed when people are liberated from poverty, tyranny, ignorance and superstition through access to education, the common citizen's moral sense will promote civic benefits and general happiness. The Irish government eventually decided to ban the United Irishmen when France declared war on Britain in 1793, on the grounds that by seeking political reform the Society was committing a treasonable act. But we say we are not traitors and we refuse to give up. We say to the Irish government, if you will not give us our basic human rights, we have the right to take them by force if necessary.'

Everyone in the audience cheered and roared their approval as Reverend Warwick paused to take a sip of water.

'We Presbyterians, Catholics, Jews, and Quakers are treated like second class citizens in our own country. We are collectively identified as dissenters, mavericks, or rebels. We are banned from taking part in the public life of our communities, and now the Irish government demands we pay a financial tax to the Church of Ireland, to pay for the upkeep of their buildings and to maintain the wealthy lifestyle their ministers have become accustomed to. What has the Church of Ireland got to do with any of us? I say we should not be paying a tithe to them, and when we get into government it will be the first tax we shall abolish.'

There were times during the Reverend's speech that Betsy was convinced he was speaking directly to her.

'The Society of United Irishmen tried using peaceful methods to gain political changes in the past. But when the Irish government banned us, we were left with only one alternative to win the political reforms this country so desperately needs, and that was to fight for them. Fight for our liberty just as the unarmed French peasants did when they united and brought down the French government, and created a more democratic society where they no longer have to pay homage to their land owners, and where they were able to remove privileges from the French aristocracy, and the Catholic church, which they had been enjoying for centuries. If they can do it, so can we.'

'Yes, we can,' shouted someone from the audience.

'Underlying all of these momentous changes are three basic beliefs. The first is equality... the second is personal freedom... and the third is the creation of communities where people are encouraged to work for the common good of everyone.'

The Reverend Warwick removed a piece of paper from his waistcoat and placed it on the lectern in front of him.

'As you know, sadly our great Scottish poet Robbie Burns passed away recently. Robbie was a great champion of the ordinary man. I would like to finish with a quote which I believe sums up what we are trying to achieve.

'For a'that, and a'that;
It's coming yet for a'that,
That man to man, the world o'er,
Shall brothers be for a'that.'

'God bless you my friends and let us hope when the time comes, we shall be brothers, and we will unite together no matter what our religion, and we will put an end to the oppression and the sectarianism that has blighted the people of this country for far too long.'

The crowd rose to their feet to enthusiastically applaud his speech. After a few moments Reverend Warwick collected his papers from the lectern and sat down.

Reverend Porter stood up and walked over to the lectern where he set his notes down before gazing around the audience in the packed hall. He was a tall imposing man, with long, fair hair. He closed his eyes briefly and muttered a prayer before he began to speak softly.

'When the people of America took up arms in 1775 to fight for their freedom from the British Empire, and when the peasants of France rose up a few years later in 1789 to oppose the rule of absolute monarchy and the dogma of the Roman Catholic Church, they did so because they believed they had a fundamental right to oppose tyranny. They also believed that all men are born free and equal, that rulers don't have a divine right to their authority, and that the church and state should be separate. The man who developed the philosophical principles underpinning these ideas was an Irishman, born here in Saintfield one hundred years ago. His name was Francis Hutcheson, the same man who influenced Dr Drennan's thinking when he set up the United Irishmen. He was one of us. A Presbyterian who believed in liberty and in the rights of the ordinary man. His writings have encouraged people throughout the western world to seek changes in how they are governed and how they should be living.'

As the Reverend Porter spoke Betsy noticed some of the people in the audience leaning forward in their seats as though they were straining to hear what he was saying, but as she watched she noticed the Reverend was beginning to raise his voice and wondered if it had just been a ploy by him to get their attention.

'Robbie Burns and other great poets were also inspired by Hutcheson's ideas. As was Thomas Jefferson, one of a team of men who were involved in writing The American Declaration of Independence. Jefferson questioned the power of the church, and laws that established the power of great families to rule. For Jefferson there would be no assumption that a given class of people was born to rule. And if there was to be an aristocracy, it would be one based on talent, and not on an individual's birth. But above all, Jefferson recognised that ordinary people must have a say in how their government was constituted. The people must be able to take part in elections and use their vote to decide which politicians will represent them. Hundreds of thousands of our people have emigrated from here to live in America. Thousands of them took up arms to fight for what they believed in and now they live in a land where they and their children are able to enjoy unbounded freedom. We dare to ask, if this can be so in America, then why can't we change things here?'

'Yes, we can,' roared the audience as they jumped to their feet and began cheering.

'We demand to be allowed to vote in the election of the politicians who represent us in the Irish government,' bellowed the Reverend Porter.

The audience remained standing, clapping and cheering his every word.

'Our aim is to build a new and better Ireland,' Reverend Porter shouted. 'An Ireland that recognises all men are born equal. Where political power is based upon the ballot box in a free election, and the consent of people of every religious and political persuasion. Will you join us and help build this new and prosperous Ireland?'

'Yes,' roared the audience.

'Thank you,' shouted Reverend Porter. 'Thank you, my friends.'

As the audience began to settle down Reverend Warwick walked back onto the stage and stood beside Reverend Porter.

'Will anyone who wishes to join the Society of United Irishmen please remain standing.'

No one sat down.

'To become a member, the next thing you must do is swear an oath of loyalty. If you don't want to take the oath, I would ask that you leave the hall now.'

Everyone stayed where they were.

'We will administer the oath to everyone at the same time,' suggested Reverend Warwick as he picked up a pile of paper copies of the oath. The two ministers began distributing them. When they finished, Reverend Porter went back up onto the stage.

'Before I start administering the oath, I would like to make sure everyone has a copy of it,' he said holding his aloft.

A couple of people held their hands up. Reverend Porter waited until everyone confirmed they had one.

'Good, before I start administering the oath to everyone, there is something I want to point out. The oath starts, In the presence of God, I ...... , and there is a space. When you are swearing the oath, I want you to add your own name in the space. So, if everyone is ready, please raise your right hand, and repeat after me.'

Reverend Porter looked up and waited until everyone's right hand was raised before he began reading the oath out loud.

Betsy repeated every word he said.

'In the presence of God, I Betsy Gray do voluntarily declare that I will persevere in endeavouring to form a brotherhood of affection among Irishmen of every religious persuasion, and that I will also persevere in my endeavours to obtain an equal, full and adequate representation of all the people of Ireland. I do further declare that neither hopes, fears, rewards or punishments shall ever induce me directly or indirectly, to inform, or give evidence against any member, or members, of this or similar societies, for any act or expression of theirs done or made individually or collectively in or out of this society, in pursuit of this obligation.'

As Betsy uttered the oath out loud each word seemed to bury deep into her mind, leaving her with a feeling she was one with the audience.

When everyone finished Reverend Porter held up his hands. 'Welcome to the Society of United Irishmen. You are now part of an organisation whose aim is to remove the corrupt Irish government and bring peace and prosperity to all of the people in the country we love.'

Betsy was eighteen years old. She felt as though she had just discovered a new purpose in her life. A purpose that was much bigger than anything she had ever dreamt of before, filling her with determination to use everything in her power to achieve her ambitions.

Gina was just as excited. 'This is the biggest thing I have ever done,' she said. 'I feel as though I'm buzzing.'

'I know, I feel the same,' added Betsy. 'I can't believe I'm actually doing something for my country. I never thought I would be able to say that.'

They left the hall full of excitement about what the future might hold for them.

Over the next few months, as the United Irishmen increased their preparations for an uprising, the Irish government reacted with venom. They suspended trial by jury and gave local magistrates a range of new extensive powers. Homes of those suspected of being involved in the United Irishmen were searched and the inhabitants detained or punished on little or no evidence. Curfews were imposed in some parts of the country. But more importantly, the government declared that anyone found guilty of administering the oath of the United Irishmen would be sentenced to death.

The reality of these new measures was harshly brought home to Betsy one day when she went to Newtownards to collect some dress material for her mother. When she arrived in the town, she noticed a crowd of people gathering outside the entrance to the local courthouse. When she asked a woman what was happening, she told her, a United Irishman was about to be flogged for stealing several ash saplings. A few minutes later Betsy watched as a group of soldiers escorted a slightly built teenage boy from the court building and marched him across the road to a small grassy area where a large 'A' shaped wooden frame had been erected.

Betsy watched in horror as a couple of soldiers tied the boy's arms and legs to the wooden struts on the frame before tearing the shirt from his back exposing his bare skin. A court official stepped forward and read a short statement declaring fifteen-year-old Samuel Jones had been found guilty of stealing ten ash saplings that were to be used in the making of pikes for the United Irishmen. His punishment was to be 500 lashes. There were gasps of astonishment and revulsion from some of the people in the crowd at the severity of the sentence.

To one side of Samuel Jones, Betsy saw a soldier begin limbering up as he practiced swinging the cat o' nine tails whip which she assumed he was going to use to administer the court's punishment.

The crowd was silent as the soldier delivered the first lash on the boys bare back.

'One,' shouted the tallyman as the multi-tailed whip seared into the skin on the boy's back leaving long red swollen lines.

The people at the front of the crowd tried to step backwards but quickly realised they were being hemmed in by a ring of soldiers forcing them to watch and listen. As the count increased the tallyman's voice was often drowned out by the piercing screams and pleas for mercy by Jones as the cat o' nine tails began to rip the skin from his back.

By the time the tallyman called out, 'Five Hundred,' most of the people in the crowd were openly sobbing.

The ring of soldiers, in their military correctness, stood to attention allowing the crowd to disperse while the blood-stained ropes which had held Samuel Jones's arms and legs were cut allowing his bloodied body to collapse to the ground. Betsy watched as a middle-aged man stepped forward. Her neighbour whispered he was Samuel's father. Betsy heard him ask one of the soldiers if he could take his son home. Mr Jones was weeping as he bent down and gently gathered his son's bloodied body into his arms and stood up, tall and straight, before he slowly walked away with the broken body cradled in his arms.

As the silent crowd began to disperse Betsy didn't move, she was still shocked at the brutality she had just witnessed. She felt frightened and complicit as though she had been involved in hurting the young boy. A soldier shoved her in the back with the butt of his rifle and ordered her to step aside. With the image of Samuel Jones's tortured body burning into her mind Betsy walked away.

When Betsy arrived home with the roll of fabric, she told her mother what she had seen in Newtownards.

'That's terrible,' her mother said. 'I don't know what this country is coming to. At church last Sunday they were talking about a man from Holywood who was caught with some saplings they said he was going to use to make pikes. How do they know what he is going to do with them, they are only pieces of wood?'

'I wonder if he was the same man, they whipped this morning,' said Betsy. 'The only thing is he wasn't a man; he was nothing more than a child. I saw his father there. The soldiers made sure he watched the whole punishment. When they finished whipping the boy the militia told him he could take his son home. The poor wee mite's body was a mess and covered in blood.'

'God bless him,' her mother said softly. 'We can't go on living like this. Killings, and beatings like that one this morning are happening all over Ireland every day. Only yesterday I heard about a village in Wexford where the army ordered the people to billet a company of soldiers in their houses and farms. The army officers refused to hand over any money to pay for their soldier's board and said they had to let them sleep in their beds. They say the soldiers raped the women they were staying with.'

Betsy reacted angrily. 'That would never be allowed in any other country. This government is immoral, the sooner we get rid of them the better.'

'I know,' her mother said wearily. 'But you need to be careful Betsy. If they find out what you are doing for the United Irishmen, they will throw you in prison with the rest of them.'

Betsy sat down in a chair beside the hearth. 'I know, I promise to be careful. Maybe there will be some good news in this week's Northern Star. Has James dropped our copy in yet?'

The Northern Star newspaper was one of the main sources of information the leadership of the United Irishmen used to keep their members up to date with what was happening throughout the country. Various writers, including Reverend Porter, contributed articles to the weekly newspaper. Some of their pieces were humorous, often ridiculing rich landowners and their clerical friends, while others were on a more serious note describing the hardships Irish people were experiencing. The radical ideas described in the newspaper were dissected and eagerly discussed by members of the United Irishmen at their weekly meetings. The Irish government was also aware of the importance of this newspaper in inciting people to rebel and as such were determined to disrupt its circulation in any way they possibly could. They ordered their soldiers to arrest and punish anyone who was found to be involved in the newspaper's distribution. However, despite the risk of being flogged or sent to prison, some people were still prepared to deliver the newspaper. One individual who did this on a regular basis was Bangor man, James Armour. Each week Armour would collect his allocation of newspapers from the printing office, located in an alleyway near the centre of Belfast called Wilson's Court, and deliver them to the various addresses he was allotted in the County Down area.

Betsy's mother shook her head. 'No, I haven't seen James yet. He's normally here by now. I hope nothing has happened to him.'

'I hope not,' agreed Betsy wearily. 'It has been a long day. I'm going to bed after supper.'

Next morning Betsy was cooking porridge in a pot suspended on the swinging crook over the hearth for their breakfast when there was a knock at the door. When she opened it, she was surprised to find James Armour standing there with their copy of the Northern Star in his hand.

'You're late,' she said mockingly as she took the newspaper from him. 'Come in, you're just in time for breakfast.'

'Thank you very much,' replied Armour willingly accepting her invitation. 'I'm so hungry. I promise you I didn't plan it this way. I tried to deliver the papers yesterday, but the soldiers were everywhere. I had to keep moving around and hiding in the hedge rows until I couldn't go home because of the curfew and had to catch some sleep in a barn down the road.'

Armour set his bag of undelivered newspapers on the floor beside him and sat down at the breakfast table where Betsy had placed a bowl for him. Her mother and George soon joined them. While they were eating, Pip their Jack Russel began barking excitedly and running to the front door. Betsy went to let the agitated dog out and as she opened the door, she spotted a horse and cart that was packed with red coated soldiers stop on the main road at the end of their lane. She closed the door quickly and called out to Armour.

'Quick, the soldiers are coming. We had better hide you. George will show you where to go.'

Armour lifted his bag of newspapers and ran after George. Once outside George stopped by a pile of logs and removed several wooden blocks to expose a trapdoor hidden underneath. He raised the door to reveal a small pit, just big enough for someone to hide in.

'Quick, get in,' demanded an anxious George. 'They won't find you in there.'

Armour leapt into the hole and squeezed down as George closed the trapdoor and swiftly replaced the logs before running back into the farmhouse and joining Betsy and his mother at the breakfast table. A few moments later they were startled by a loud banging at the front door. Betsy's mother calmly rose and went over to open the door.

An army officer wearing a spotlessly clean, red jacket and white pantaloons was standing outside. 'Good morning,' he barked. 'I'm Lieutenant O'Leary of the Monaghan Militia. We have received a report that a man was seen delivering the Northern Star newspaper in the district last night. Have you seen any strangers around the farm?'

'No,' she replied adding a shrug of her shoulders. 'We haven't seen anyone for days, and anyway, we don't read the Northern Star.'

O'Leary shrugged his shoulders. 'It doesn't matter. I have orders to search all the buildings in the vicinity anyway,' he quipped before turning to his sergeant. 'Check the outbuildings.'

As the sergeant and some of the soldiers headed off to search the barn the lieutenant and two of his men entered the farmhouse. 'Search those rooms,' O'Leary ordered, nodding in the direction of the bedrooms and weaving room.

'But you will find no one there,' appealed Betsy's mother as she picked up Pip and held him in her arms.

'We will know soon enough if you are speaking the truth,' scoffed the lieutenant.

As the soldiers rushed into the rooms Betsy spotted her copy of the Northern Star lying beside the fireplace. She feared it was only a matter of time before the lieutenant also saw it. As she was trying to

17

work out what to do, they heard a loud scream and high-pitched squealing coming from the yard outside. The commotion was quickly followed by a single rifle shot. O'Leary shouted to the other soldiers to follow him as he ran outside. Betsy grabbed the newspaper and shoved it down her dress before joining her mother and George outside in the yard where she was expecting to find soldiers standing guard over Armour. Instead she saw a soldier lying on the ground, his white linen gaiter trousers were badly torn and bloodied from a couple of ugly looking slash wounds on his legs.

'Private Carron, what the hell happened to you?' exclaimed O'Leary.

The wounded soldier stopped trying to stem the blood from the cuts on his legs and scrambled to his feet. 'I climbed into the pigsty to check if anyone was hiding inside the hut and that fucking pig attacked me, sir. It tried to eat my bloody legs. It was trying to kill me.'

'Did you shoot the pig?'

The soldier seemed surprised. 'No sir.'

'But I heard a shot.'

'I'm afraid my rifle went off accidently when I smashed the butt onto the pig's head,' he replied as the other soldiers began to gather around him, unable to supress their laughter at his discomfort.

'She was only guarding her babies,' Betsy shouted angrily at the soldier. 'You shouldn't have gone in there.'

O'Leary glared at the wounded soldier. 'Get back on the wagon you bloody idiot,' he snapped before turning to the other soldiers. 'Well, did you find anything?'

'No sir,' they replied.

O'Leary turned to follow the limping soldier. 'Okay, we are done here. We've other work to do.'

Betsy felt angry at their behaviour. 'But, what about the damage your soldier did to my pig and the pigsty?'

O'Leary stopped and slowly turned around. He gazed at her for a few moments before quickly walking over to the pigsty where he stopped and removed his pistol from its holster. He took aim and shot one of the small piglets.

Betsy rushed over to the pigsty.

O'Leary turned and glared at her. 'Now the bitch has one less baby to worry about,' he said sarcastically before walking away. 'And, if you don't shut up, I'll shoot the rest of you.'

'Get back on the wagon,' the sergeant barked to the soldiers.

A stunned Betsy watched them leave.

'Bastards,' muttered George.

'I know,' his mother replied softly as she stooped to set the dog down. 'But there's nothing we can do. You'd better go and get Armour out of that hole before he suffocates.'

A few miles away, farmer David Johnston was sitting in his farmhouse with his wife Martha, discussing their plans for lifting this year's potato crop. David was the third generation of his family to live on their two-hundred-and-thirty-acre farm. He was proud of his position within his community as both a farmer and good landlord to the thirty weaver tenants who lived on his land. He was also very proud of his family history, epitomised by stories of his great grandfather, Robert Johnston.

One story that David liked to tell was about when his grandfather first arrived from Scotland. He had come to Ireland in search of religious freedom and had just enough money with him to purchase the tenancy on the farm. He moved onto the land immediately and over the next few months built the single storey dwelling that was still in use today. He used local stones that he cleared from his fields for the walls. He cut several branches off a large Irish oak tree that was growing near the house and shaped them into rafters and then gathered enough straw from his first harvest to cover them making sure the roof was watertight. His grandfather also built a low wall to enclose the farmyard he had laid, giving easy access to the nearby stables and cowsheds. He worked hard for months clearing the land himself and digging several ditches to improve the drainage and encourage the first crops he sowed to grow. That desire to continuously improve the farm had been handed down through the generations to David. He also saw it as his duty to do his best for the local community and those who depended upon him.

David was the eldest of four boys. When he was in his mid-twenties, his parents, like many other families that attended the same small Presbyterian church in nearby Bangor, decided they were going to emigrate to America. They were fed up with being treated like second class citizens, and the constant struggle to make a livelihood. They dreamed of having a better life in a new country. Three of David's uncles had already made the journey to the new world and would often write to his father, telling him about the many opportunities in America for hard working families. They would talk of a country where there was no religious discrimination, and how people were free to practise their religion without fear or prejudice. When his parents told him about their plans to go to America, David decided he would remain in Ireland and manage the farm. Although he had found being on his own a bit of a struggle at first, he gradually became used to being his own boss.

David was thirty-eight years old when he married local girl, nineteen-year-old Martha Madison two years ago. Despite their age difference they were very much in love.

While David tended to the animals and the crops Martha maintained a large kitchen garden at the rear of the farmhouse from which she collected their daily vegetables.

'I need to get some more peat and logs for the winter,' said David as he reached over to the wicker basket they kept beside the fireplace and lifted out a couple of blocks of peat before tossing them onto the dying embers of the fire. As the sparks settled, his collie dog began to bark.

'Someone is out there,' Martha said glancing towards the door when she heard male voices out in the yard.

David looked at her. 'I'm not expecting anyone' he said, turning to look out one of the windows.

They heard more shouting and before they could move there was a loud banging at the farm door. David stood up and walked over to open it.

'Good morning. I'm Lieutenant O'Leary. Are you David Johnston?'

'Yes. I am.'

Suddenly several armed soldiers pushed past the lieutenant and rushed in through the door pushing Johnston and pointing their rifles at him.

Johnston raised his arms as he stepped backwards.

'Keep your hands up,' the soldiers shouted.

'Stay where you are,' one of the soldiers ordered Martha.

She noticed blood on his ripped trousers as she sat back in her seat.

Lieutenant O'Leary followed the soldiers into the kitchen and walked over to Johnston.

'My understanding is that you joined the Irish Volunteers in 1789. Is that correct?'

Johnston hesitated.

'Come on sir, I asked you a question,' snapped O'Leary.

'Yes, I did.'

'Good… I want the rifle you bought when you enlisted.'

Johnston looked surprised at his request. 'But I don't have a…'

O'Leary pulled his pistol from its holster and pointed the gun at David's head. 'I said I want your fucking rifle sir.'

Martha stood up. 'Please, please don't hurt him,' she pleaded before being shoved back into her chair by one of the soldiers.

'Don't worry Martha,' Johnston said reassuringly. 'I'll be alright.'

O'Leary paused and looked across the table at her before he smiled. 'Okay Martha, will you tell me where his rifle is?'

Martha shook her head. 'He just told you, he doesn't have one.'

O'Leary glared angrily at her. 'Very well… Sergeant,' he barked.

'Yes sir.'

'Take Johnston outside and hand him over to Corporal Jones.'

Martha began to fear for her husband.

'No,' she screamed as she flung herself across the table, her arms outstretched as she tried to grab hold of her husband. But before she could reach him one of the soldiers smashed the butt of his rifle into the back of her head.

As Martha's unconscious body slumped to the floor an angry Johnston leapt to his feet and tried to punch the soldier who had hit her, but he was quickly grabbed from behind by a couple of the soldiers and dragged kicking and shouting, outside to the farmyard where a tall, muscular man was standing. The soldiers dragged Johnston over and dumped him at his feet.

'Lieutenant O'Leary said he is all yours Corporal Jones,' panted one of the soldiers.

Johnston saw that Corporal Jones held a short length of rope in his hands with a noose at one end. The corporal bent down and slipped the noose over Johnston's head before turning around and quickly pulling the rope over his shoulder lifting Johnston up onto his back. Jones was much taller than Johnston and the noose quickly tightened around his neck. Jones began to walk around the farmyard with a choking Johnston dangling from his back. As Johnston fought to try and breathe, he heard the other soldiers clapping and cheering. Johnston was convinced he was going to die.

'Stop,' roared Lieutenant O'Leary a few minutes later, when Johnston's face began to turn a sickly purple colour.

Corporal Jones let go of the rope immediately and dropped Johnston's semi-conscious body to the ground, where he began frantically tugging at the noose around his neck. He eventually managed to loosen the rope enough to allow him to suck in some precious air.

Lieutenant O'Leary stood over Johnston's prone body. 'Now will you tell me where you have hidden your rifle.'

Johnston shook his head as he gasped for more air and waved his hand from side to side indicating he didn't have one.

Lieutenant O'Leary whispered into his ear. 'Very well then… we will hang your wife.'

Johnston's bravery vanished in an instant.

'No, no,' he babbled, shaking his head vigorously as he reached out for the officer's arm.

Lieutenant O'Leary shoved his hand away. 'Sergeant,' he hollered. 'Bring the wife out and give her to Corporal Jones.'

Johnston watched in horror as two of the soldiers ran back into the farmhouse and re-emerge a few moments later carrying Martha's unconscious body.

'No, no, no…' pleaded Johnston as they dumped Martha at the feet of Jones. 'Okay… okay,' he wailed. 'I'll tell you where it is.'

Lieutenant O'Leary smiled as he looked down at Johnston. 'Well, where is it?'

'The rifle is buried in a peat stack at the back of the farmhouse.'

O'Leary turned to a couple of soldiers. 'Go around the back and search the peat stack.'

'Yes sir.'

A few moments later they returned carrying a rifle and a metal pike blade.

The soldier handed the rifle to O'Leary.

'Have you anymore weapons?' the officer demanded as he inspected the rifle, noting how clean and well-oiled the barrel was.

'No. That's all I have.'

Taking the pike blade from the soldier he asked. 'Have you taken the oath of the United Irishmen?'

'No. I haven't.'

'Have you ever been a member of the United Irishmen?'

Johnston shook his head. 'No, never.'

'Then, why do you have this pike blade?'

'I found it in one of my fields. Someone must have dropped it there. It's not mine.'

O'Leary studied Johnston's face for a long time as he tried to make up his mind about him. Sworn membership of the United Irishmen was a capital offence and carried the death penalty. One option he was considering was to hang Johnston here and now, no one would care a jot. However, there was always the chance he might be of more use to them. Making his mind up he handed the pike blade back to the private before turning to the sergeant.

'Cuff him. We'll take him back to Newtownards with us, we can question him there.'

'Yes sir.'

'And Sergeant.'

'Yes sir.'

'Let the people around here see what happens to anyone who tells us lies. Burn the farmhouse.'

'No,' screamed Johnston. 'Please don't do that. I told you where the rifle was. You have it, I have no more weapons.'

'Come on,' bellowed the sergeant. 'You heard the lieutenant. Burn the farmhouse.'

Soldiers rushed inside the house and grabbed pieces of smouldering peat from the fire and began stuffing the glowing embers into the thatched roof. As thick, grey smoke began to bellow into the sky the sergeant marched his men and Johnston back to their horse and cart and left.

Betsy was hanging out some washing when she noticed a column of smoke rising into the sky. The smoke was coming from the direction of her friend Martha Johnston's farm. Betsy quickly carried the rest of the washing back inside and ran to the stables where she saddled Sandy and within minutes, she was galloping along narrow country lanes towards the smoke.

When Betsy arrived at the Johnston's the scene that greeted her was one of utter mayhem. Flames were shooting up from the thatch on the farmhouse roof. Scores of people had climbed onto the roof and were trying to tackle the fire with buckets of water, while others were dousing the nearby cowsheds and barns with water in a bid to make sure the flames didn't spread to them. A neighbour of the Johnston's, Henry Poulter, shouted over to Betsy to join a line of people transferring buckets of water from the farm well to the men on the roof.

As Betsy slotted into the line, she glanced up at the men and noticed one in particular, he was about six-foot-tall, with fair, reddish hair, which had been cut short, in the new 'croppy' French style. As she gazed at the man, he suddenly turned around and stared at her for a few seconds before he smiled, waved and turned back to fight the fire. Betsy felt herself blush as she continued to pass buckets of water along the line, glancing occasionally at the man on the roof. With the help of more neighbours who had arrived they were able to extinguish the fire.

As wisps of white smoke and steam drifted into the sky an exhausted Betsy sat down beside Martha to grab a much-needed rest and to share in a glass of water.

'What happened Martha?' asked one of the neighbours.

Martha sighed as she sipped the water. 'The soldiers were here this morning. They were looking for a rifle David was given when he joined the Volunteers in 89.'

'Did he still have it, I thought they were all handed back?'

'No, he still had his. He kept it because he said he paid for it. He hid it out the back in the peat stack. I've already checked. It's gone. He only used it to shoot rabbits.'

'So how did they know he had one?'

Martha shrugged her shoulders. 'I don't know. The lieutenant in charge of the soldiers kept asking David where it was.'

'Why didn't he just deny he had one?' someone suggested.

Another neighbour leaned over and added, 'He should have told the lieutenant it was a long time ago and that he had given it back.'

Martha glanced up at the speakers, she knew they meant well. 'He tried all of that, but the lieutenant was adamant David still had it.'

'How did they find it?' someone else asked.

'I don't know. All I remember is the lieutenant saying something about taking David outside and I tried to stop them. The next thing I know I was lying in the yard totally confused about what was happening. When I looked up and saw the smoke, I thought it was coming from our chimney. It took me a few minutes before I realised it was actually coming from the thatch on the roof. That's when people started arriving.'

'Was the lieutenant called O'Leary?' asked Betsy.

'I don't know. David answered the door. I did hear him saying something, but I can't remember what it was.'

'Did he have a county Monaghan accent?' asked Betsy.

'Yes, he did,' replied a curious Martha.

'And did one of his soldiers have torn trousers with blood on them?'

Martha looked quizzingly at Betsy. 'Yes. How did you know that?'

'They were at our farm this morning, before they came here. Lieutenant O'Leary and his soldiers were looking for James Armour. Someone must have told them he was seen delivering the Northern Star to farms in the area. James had arrived just before the soldiers came. He told me he had tried to deliver his papers last night but there were soldiers everywhere and he had to keep moving around and hiding in the hedge rows. When it passed curfew time it was too late for him to go home, so he crept into one of our neighbours' barns and slept there. James was having his breakfast with us when the soldiers arrived. We hid him out the back and told Lieutenant O'Leary we hadn't seen anyone. But while his soldiers were searching the farm one of them climbed into the pigsty and our pig Milly attacked him and bit him on his legs.'

'She would have been trying to protect her young,' said one of the neighbours. 'Pigs are very protective.'

'Yeah, they do that sort of thing,' said another neighbour. 'What did the soldier do when Milly attacked him?'

'He hit Milly with his rifle and when I complained, Lieutenant O'Leary shot one of Milly's piglets and told me that if I didn't shut up, he would shoot all of us.'

'Bastards,' someone muttered.

While Betsy had been speaking, an elderly, grey-haired minister rode into the farmyard. Betsy had met him before, the Reverend William Steel-Dickson was in charge of the United Irishmen in the whole of County Down. She watched as the Reverend stopped to talk with the young man who had smiled at her earlier. The two men were deep in conversation before the young man turned away and left the farm. The Reverend Steel Dickson walked over and joined them.

'Hello Martha,' he said. 'I'm very sorry for your troubles, tell me what happened?'

'The soldiers were here this morning looking for David's gun,' said one of the neighbours.

'Someone told them about the rifle David was given when he joined the Volunteers,' said Martha as she raised her hand and began rubbing the back of her head.

The Reverend tutted in disgust. 'They're a law onto themselves.'

'They can do whatever they want,' said Martha.

As she removed her hand from the back of her head Betsy noticed there was blood on it.

'Have you been cut?' she asked.

Martha stared at the blood. 'I don't know.'

'Come here, let me have a look,' said Betsy moving over to inspect the back of her friend's head.

'Where's David now?' the Reverend asked.

'I don't know,' said Martha. 'The soldiers must have taken him with them.'

The old minister nodded his head. 'They will probably take him to their barracks in Newtownards and hold him there,' he said. 'Before taking him to court.'

'What would they charge him with?' asked one of the neighbours.

'They will probably charge him with not declaring the gun,' said Reverend Steel Dickson. 'Who is your solicitor?'

'We normally use Hugh Atkinson, in Bangor.'

Reverend Steel Dickson nodded. 'I know Hugh. I'll go and talk to him this afternoon and see if we can get in to see David before they transfer him to Carrickfergus castle.'

As he was speaking one of Martha's neighbours, Henry Poulter joined them. Poulter was Betsy's commanding officer in the United Irishmen.

'Good morning Reverend.'

'Hello Henry. Well, what is your assessment of the damage?'

'I'm afraid there has been a lot of smoke and water damage, but we managed to save most of the thatch on the roof. The heavy rains last week left it damp and soggy, which helped slow down the spread of the flames. None of the rafters were damaged and the house is structurally okay. But we are going to have to remove all the damaged straw and replace it with fresh bundles. I know where we can get some. Unfortunately, most of the furniture will have to be replaced and the walls repainted. We will be looking for volunteers to help us. As for the barns and cowsheds, they are relatively undamaged. We were very lucky so many people were able to get here quickly.'

'I know. I'm very grateful to everyone,' said Martha. 'When I realised the roof was on fire, I thought we were done for. Davy has been planning for months to knock the house down and replace it with a two-storey building with a slated roof. Maybe this was meant to be.'

'I was talking to him yesterday,' said Poulter. 'He mentioned that your potato crop was ready to lift. Don't you be worrying about that; I will get the potatoes dug up and stored in the barn. We can even take some of them to the market in Belfast for you.'

'Thank you,' said Martha as Betsy continued to examine the back of her head.

'There's a cut here,' Betsy said. 'It looks quite deep. We'd better get it cleaned and put something on it.'

Betsy left to go and look for a clean piece of cloth and some fresh water.

'It would be impossible for you to live in the house until we can get the roof repaired, Martha,' said Henry Poulter. 'You are welcome to stay at our farm for as long as you like. Jessie and I have a spare bedroom since our James emigrated to America. It would be nice having someone using it for a change.'

'Thanks Henry,' said Martha squeezing her friend's hand as Betsy returned with a cloth and some fresh water and began cleaning her wound.

Later, as Betsy was getting ready to go home Henry Poulter stopped to talk to her.

'Reverend Steel Dickson wants us to call the whole district out tonight and come back here to harvest David's potato crops. He thinks we should put on a show of strength to send a message to the militia that we will not be pushed around or intimidated. Will you tell the members in Gransha to gather at the Six Road Ends crossroads at five o'clock tonight and be ready to join the main group when we arrive? We will march to the farm together. There should be six or seven hundred of us, that will be a good show of our strength.'

On Betsy's way home she rode around her neighbours' houses and farms telling them what Poulter and the Reverend Steele Dickinson had asked them to do.

Shortly before five o'clock Betsy and her neighbours began to gather at the crossroads. After a while someone said they could hear singing, and a few minutes later three large columns of people appeared over the hill singing La Marseillaise. As they marched past Betsy guessed there must have been around five or six hundred people. Some had young children with them. Betsy quickly formed her members into three groups and seamlessly joined the tail ends of the columns as they continued their march to Johnston's farm.

When they reached the farm Henry Poulter and several men quickly allocated everyone into various small working groups. Betsy noticed that the leader of her group was the same tall, good-looking man she had spotted on the roof of Martha's farmhouse. As she gazed at him, she thought he was the most handsome man she had ever seen, and when he started walking towards her, she felt a tingle of excitement. She tried to stay calm, pretending to be surprised when he stopped in front of her.

'Hello,' he said in a soft, clear voice. 'I was hoping I would see you here tonight.'

'Oh,' said Betsy her mind not offering her anything else to say.

The young man continued. 'Do you mind if I ask your name?'

Gina had been standing beside her listening intently to their conversation. 'She's called Elizabeth Gray,' she stated quickly. 'But we call her Betsy… What's your name?'

Betsy blushed at the boldness of her friend.

'I'm William Boal,' he replied. 'But my friends call me Billy.'

Gina eased herself in front of Betsy. 'Well Billy, it's so nice to meet you,' she said flashing a broad smile. 'I'm Gina. I'm Betsy's best friend. What would you like us to do for you?'

'Gina,' exclaimed an embarrassed Betsy.

Billy smiled at Betsy. 'I was just going to ask if you would take your friends to that corner of the field over there,' pointing to where he wanted them to go. 'And start gathering the potatoes from the last three rows. We have forks and spades over there for digging, and some bags to put them in.'

Betsy could feel her face glowing red. 'Of course, we will,' she smiled. 'Come on everyone.'

As they walked over to the rows Gina grabbed hold of her arm and leaned in to whisper in her ear, 'I think our Billy fancies you.'

Betsy tried to ignore her but couldn't stop herself from glancing back to see what Billy was doing and was a little disappointed to find he was already involved in giving instructions to another group.

Betsy organised her team into diggers and collectors as they began gathering the potatoes and storing them in the hessian sacks that had been left for them. It took about an hour for them to complete their allocated rows, by which time most of the other potato pickers had finished. Dozens of sacks full of ripe potatoes were carried from the field and placed inside a large barn. When all were stored away Poulter ordered everyone to line-up in front of the damaged farmhouse to listen to the Reverend Steel Dickson.

It was starting to get dark when the old man climbed onto the back of a cart in the farmyard to address them.

'Thank you everyone for giving up your time and coming here tonight,' the Reverend Steel Dickson called out. 'Your hard work has helped save the Johnston farm from ruin. I was reminded earlier that it was only two years ago that I had the honour of celebrating Maratha and David's wedding. A number of you also attended the ceremony. It was a day of great happiness and hope. But, all of that has changed. You don't need me to remind you that we are living in terrible times. The Irish government has imposed their vile cruelty and terror on every village and farmhouse in Ireland. They want to destroy the United Irishmen, but they will never defeat us. Today, General Lake sent his soldiers to the Johnston farm to inflict havoc and spread fear amongst our community. His soldiers tortured David and physically attacked Martha. They did their abhorrent acts because David had not handed in the rifle he was given when the citizens of this parish joined the Volunteers to defend Ireland from the threat of invasion. When the Irish government disbanded those loyal men because they were asking for constitutional reform; Dr William Drennan called several ex-volunteers together in Belfast to lay the foundations of the Society of United Irishmen to continue the fight for political reform, but when France declared war on England, the Irish government used that as an excuse to outlaw the United Irishmen and began arresting its leaders. They can arrest and imprison as many of us as they want but, they will never diminish our drive for freedom, and just like the American people and the peasants in France, we will never give up our struggle to live as free men and to elect our own politicians. We demand equality for all Irish citizens. Be they Protestant, Catholic, Jew or Quaker. We believe in a society where all men are born equal and where everyone has the right to live in peace, and we will never give in… But I have to warn you to be on your guard, because the Irish government and their secret agents are trying all sorts of dirty tricks to provoke us into a reaction. We will not respond to them. We will decide when the time is right to fight. Until then, I urge each and every one of you to continue with your preparations for war and be ready to fight when you hear the call to arms.'

As everyone cheered someone in the crowd called out. 'What about the French, are they coming to help us?'

Reverend Steel Dickson raised his arms to quieten the crowd.

'Someone has just asked me, if the French army is coming?' he shouted. 'They will come, but they will only stay until we have gained our freedom and elected Irish people to an Irish parliament. Be reassured, we will never replace a corrupt Anglican aristocracy propped up by London with another regime from Europe, be they from Paris or Rome, no matter how good they may appear to be. We will be our own masters in Ireland.'

'Our pikes will not be enough against guns and cannons. We need more modern weapons,' shouted another man.

Reverend Steel Dickson nodded in agreement. 'Don't worry my friend. When the time comes to fight, thousands of soldiers currently serving in the Militia and in the Yeomanry will leave their barracks and come to join us. They will bring their rifles and cannon with them. When the army of the United Irishmen take to the streets, no government force on this earth will be able to withstand the fury we, the free people of Ireland will unleash upon them.… Until then, I urge you to stay strong… Now let us pray.'

Everyone in the crowd bowed their head as Reverend Steel Dickson's voice boomed out loud and clear in the still evening air.

'Oh Lord, we call upon you to help Ireland in its hour of need. We ask that you guide our leaders along the righteous path to victory. Help us dear Lord, gain our freedom from this tyranny. Strengthen our hearts and our minds so that we can overcome the hardships we will surely face and help lead us to your promised land. Let us never forget the words that Jesus Christ taught us, as we say the Lord's Prayer.'

Every one of the several hundred men, women and children joined in, 'Our father who art in heaven….' before finishing with a loud, 'Amen.'

As Reverend Steel Dickson was helped down from the cart Poulter began ordering his officers to start preparations to move off. A large, heavily built ex-army man from Comber known as Sergeant Major John White, walked to the front of the ranks.

'Companies,' he roared. 'Companies…. Attention.'

There was a shuffling of several hundred feet as people moved into position.

Sergeant Major White waited until everyone was silent. 'We will march from the field in three columns,' he roared. 'By the left… quick march. Left… Right…Left…'

As the first marchers began to leave the field, their bodies swaying in harmony, someone began to sing.

'Arise children of the fatherland
The day of glory has arrived...'

Soon everyone was singing the La Marseillaise as the weary United Irishmen made their way home.

Chapter 2

When Betsy awoke, she lay in her bed as the dark grey light of nights end slowly evolved into the bright morning colours of another day. She listened to a blackbird singing outside her window while watching several golden, sunlit images, perform a silent dance on the smooth white bedroom walls. She was thinking of Billy Boal, with his eager smile, his bright sparkling eyes and the soft gentle tone in his voice whenever he spoke. She hoped she would see him again.

Betsy was stirred from her thoughts by the sound of her mother softly singing along to the rhythmic clicks of the shuttle next door as she weaved a new fabric on the loom. Betsy recognised the tune. It brought back happy childhood memories of when her mother would hold her in her arms, and hum to her while her father worked on the loom.

Betsy slipped out of bed and pulled the bedroom curtains to one side, allowing the bright sunshine into her room. She stood taking in the scene from the window, the cows grazing in the fields and a flock of crows flying overhead on their way to their feeding spots on the coast. As Betsy watched the hens busily scratching around in the dirt for something to eat, she felt warm and relaxed. After a few minutes she went to the dressing table and poured some fresh water from a jug into a bowl. As she began washing, she heard her mother call out.

'Betsy, are you awake.'

'Yes mum.'

'Will you get George out of bed and fetch me a glass of water.'

'Yes, I will,' she answered quickly drying her face before pulling the sheets back on her bed to air the mattress.

'George,' she called out as she passed his bedroom. 'It's time to get up.'

'Alright Betsy' he answered sleepily.

When Betsy walked into the kitchen, she was glad to see that her mother had already lit the fire. She put water and oats into a pot and left them to soak for a few moments while she filled a large mug with water and carried it into her mother.

'Thanks Betsy.'

Her mother sipped the cool liquid. 'There are two linen pouches over there with money in them. The red one is for the land agent Garfield, he was due to call yesterday to pick up the rent, but he never showed. Give it to him if he arrives. And be careful, I don't trust that man.'

Betsy picked up the pouch and placed it in her pocket. 'I don't like him either. Why can't you give him the money?'

'I would if I could Betsy, but I have to go over to the Knox's farm this morning. Daniel Knox wants me to measure Rachel for her wedding dress, and we need the money.'

Betsy's mother was a gifted seamstress and was often hired by her neighbours to make their clothes or, as on this occasion, their daughter's wedding dress. Betsy and her friends felt a little tinge of sadness about Rachel's marriage, because she and her husband to be were leaving the country the day after the wedding, joining hundreds of thousands of Presbyterians who had already emigrated to America where they believed there were more opportunities and they would be free from persecution and religious discrimination. Their leaving was going to be hard on the loved ones they left behind, because everyone knew they would probably never see them again.

'It shouldn't take me long,' Betsy's mother said. 'But I don't want to miss a payment. You can't trust these agents; they are always looking for an excuse to evict people like us and get new tenants in so that they can charge them a higher rent. Make sure you are here to pay him.'

'Yes, I will. What's the other pouch for?'

'That's for some bobbins of spun yarn I've ordered from the Bleach Green. They should be delivered today. There will be a new man bringing them. It should have been Clifford Peters, but he was arrested in Belfast last week, and was accused of hiding arms for the United Irishmen. The court sentenced him to five hundred lashes. They took him straight out of the courthouse and started whipping him, but the poor man was too old, and he died after about three hundred lashes. They knew that would happen. It was a death sentence. His widow and family must be going through hell.'

'Damn the government.'

'Don't swear Elizabeth,' exclaimed her mother. 'These are hard times for people like you and me, but they will pass. I have a couple of rolls of fabric that are to go to the bleach green to be dyed,' her mother said pointing to rolls of linen cloth neatly stacked on a shelf over by the wall. 'If I'm not back before the new man arrives, make sure he gives you the agreed price for the cloth. And make sure you check the quality of the yarn on the bobbins that he gives you. I don't want any weak filaments. They tried that on me once before. I couldn't weave the yarn, it just kept breaking. It was a waste of money.'

Betsy stuffed the second pouch into her pocket. 'Maybe you'll be back before they come.'

'I might be, but just in case make sure you are here,' her mother said. 'I'll finish this roll and then I'll go over to see Rachel. Is George up?'

'Yes, he should be, I'll get his breakfast.'

'And don't forget you need to make some more butter this morning for the Bangor market. I left some milk out yesterday, it should be set by now.'

'Okay,' Betsy called out as she went back into the kitchen.

A few minutes later a weary George joined her and sat at the table as Betsy quickly made a large pot of porridge and gave him some. When he finished, he gathered his tools and left to walk the short distance to the timber yard in the village where he was employed as an apprentice carpenter.

Betsy went out to the dairy at the side of the farmhouse and checked the three large basins her mother had filled with milk the previous day. The milk had settled. She began skimming the cream from the top of it into a large churn. As she began agitating the soft liquid in the churn with a large heavy plunger, she heard her mother leave. She raised and lowered the plunger. It was a monotonous activity, but she was soon into a steady rhythm concentrating on the up and downwards movements of the plunger.

Suddenly she became aware of someone behind her and quickly turned around to see their land agent, Oliver Garfield, standing in the open doorway staring at her. He had a broad smirk on his face. She stopped agitating the cream.

'You frightened me Mr Garfield.'

'I've told you before Betsy, please call me Oliver. I'm sorry if I startled you, I didn't mean to.'

Betsy moved towards the door. 'You'd better come into the kitchen Mr Garfield. Your money is in there.'

'Oh, don't stop working just for me Betsy. Please carry on. I was enjoying watching you,' said Garfield stepping in front of her, and blocking her way. 'You don't have to go just now. You could stay here with me for a while. You know I like you a lot.'

Betsy glared at him defiantly.

'Come on now. We can be friends.'

Betsy pushed him out of the way and walked out of the dairy. 'My mother will be back shortly. Your money is in the kitchen.'

As she walked back to the farmhouse, she could feel Garfield's eyes ogling her body. Once inside the kitchen she quickly found the linen pouch and handed it to him.

'Here's your money.'

Garfield took the pouch and emptied the coins onto the table and began to slowly count them, gazing up at Betsy every now and then. 'What do you think of my new waistcoat? A friend of mine brought it back from London for me. Blue waistcoats are all the fashion over there, and I only like the best,' he said as he provocatively stared into her eyes. 'Do you like it?'

'I need to get back to my work,' Betsy replied defiantly, ignoring his question.

'I heard you have been a naughty girl Betsy,' Garfield said smugly. 'I heard you were selling your own butter, as well as your vegetables in Bangor market last week.'

Betsy shrugged her shoulders. 'So what, there's nothing wrong in doing that,' she said boldly. 'I had some surplus that was all.'

Garfield shook his head as he sneered. 'I don't think it is as easy as that Betsy. You see according to the lease on the farm you are only allowed to sell the vegetables you grow. It does not mention butter. My understanding is that if you increase what you have to offer, we would have to raise your rent to allow for your better income,' Garfield smiled as he stacked the rent money in front of him. 'It's only fair we all share in your good fortune Betsy, don't you think.'

'But what I sell at the market has nothing to do with the lease,' said Betsy in her defence.

Garfield leered at her. 'Oh, I don't think so.'

Betsy felt annoyed by his behaviour.

Garfield mocked hurt. 'Do you want me to tell the landlord what you have been up to and run the risk of him increasing your rent?' he said staring expectedly at her.

Betsy ignored him and started walking towards the door. 'You have your rent money, I want you to leave now,' she said defiantly.

Garfield moved quickly and grabbed hold of her arm, swinging her around to face him.

'That's not what I want to hear.'

Betsy pushed him. 'Get away from me,' she said defiantly.

'Come here,' said Garfield as he went to grab hold of her.

Betsy put her hands up and pushed him backwards as she tried to defend herself.

Suddenly there was a loud knocking at the front door and a man's voice called out, 'Hello, is anyone at home?'

Garfield stopped as Betsy rushed over to the door, and quickly opened it. To her utter relief Billy Boal was standing there.

'Oh,' he said when he saw her. 'I'm looking for a Mrs Gray. I was told she lived at this address. I have brought some bobbins of yarn for her.'

As Billy was speaking, he glanced into the room and saw a man standing in the shadows behind Betsy, and for some reason he sensed that something was wrong. He looked back at Betsy.

'Is everything okay?'

Betsy felt elated.

'Yes, I'm fine now, Billy. You are at the right address, I have been expecting you,' she replied quickly, before turning around. 'Mr Garfield was just about to leave,' she stressed as she glared at the irate land agent.

Garfield's annoyance was written all over his face as he grabbed the rent money from the table and stormed out, shoving Billy out of his way as he did so.

'Don't forget Betsy Gray, if you continue selling your butter at the market, I'll increase your rent,' he shouted back angrily as he stomped down the lane.

Billy watched Garfield until he reached the main road.

'What was all that about?' he exclaimed as he turned to look at Betsy.

'That was our land agent, Oliver Garfield,' Betsy said. 'As you can see, he's not a very nice man. Please come inside.'

'Did he hurt you?' Billy asked as he stepped into the farmhouse.
'No, I'm okay.'

'What did he mean about having to increase your rent?'

'Someone told the bugger I was selling butter at the markets, and he reckons that gives him licence to increase the rent. But he made it very clear it wasn't more money he was looking for.'

'What!' Billy exclaimed angrily.

Betsy shook her head. 'Don't sound so surprised, I'm not the only woman agents like Garfield have tried to abuse. Everyone around here is struggling to make ends meet, and people like him know that. I've heard about other women Garfield has approached and told them he would look after them if they would agree to his sexual demands.'

Billy was incensed. 'That's the sort of corruption we were talking about at our meeting in Donaghadee last week. We heard about greedy landowners who had given license to their agents to raise their tenants' rents so they can make as much money as they can from them. With the price of land going up all the time there is nowhere else for people to go. I didn't know it was actually happening around here and that brutes like Garfield were trying to exploit a bad situation for their own ends.'

'They always do,' said Betsy. 'The only way to stop this sort of abuse is to have our own parliament where we can pass laws to protect us from unethical landowners and corrupt agents like Garfield. The Irish government doesn't care about ordinary people, it is our responsibility to sort things out. You don't have to believe me; it's what Thomas Paine says in his book The Rights of Man. We've been reading extracts from it at our meetings.'

'I heard it is an excellent book, but I'm afraid I missed out when they went on sale. Did you know that Thomas Paine was arrested in England and indicted for treason by the British government? When his trial came to court he was sentenced to death. The British government accused him of trying to destroy the state. Fortunately, he managed to escape to France. I think he's living in America now, but at least he's safe.'

Betsy shook her head. 'I didn't know that, but it doesn't surprise me, the English are very wary of changing the status quo, especially here in Ireland.'

'There was another idea of Thomas Paine which I liked. He said that ignorance is only the absence of knowledge. It is possible a man may be kept ignorant but he cannot be made ignorant. That's why I agree with him when he says it is so important that everyone has access to education and the information that affects our lives. I wish I'd read his book; do you have any spare copies?'

'I don't have any here, but I'll see if I can get you one. Maybe you could pick it up the next time you call.'

Billy's face reddened slightly. 'Thanks, that's a good idea. I have to collect some fabric from a farm down the road next week. Would it be okay if I called then?' he said quickly.

'That would be wonderful,' Betsy felt her face blush.

Billy smiled. 'Good. Do you read the Northern Star at your meetings?'

'Yes, our branch gets a copy every week. Some of our members can't read or write. I read the important articles to them and we discuss them.'

'That's a great idea. You must have seen the stories by the Reverend Porter about Billy Bluff and Squire Firebrand. They're very funny.'

'Yes, I did. Everyone loves them.'

'I heard Lord Castlereagh hates the Reverend Porter; but there's nothing he can do about it, because he can't prove it's him.'

'It's a wonder the government hasn't tried to shut him up.'

'It's the sort of thing they do.'

'They're probably biding their time, but at some stage in the future they'll arrest him to deter other people from poking fun at the aristocracy.'

Suddenly the front door opened, and Betsy's mother walked in. 'Oh, hello,' she said stopping to look at Betsy and the strange man in her house.

'Mum,' Betsy offered quickly. 'This is Billy Boal; he's from the Bleach Green. Billy has taken over from Clifford Peters.'

Mrs Gray studied Billy and shook her head. 'I thought it was awful what they did to poor Clifford, anyway, nice to meet you Mr Boal.'

'How was Rachel?' asked Betsy.

'She's very excited about the wedding, but sure aren't these terrible times we're living in, her father was just telling me about a man who was shot dead by the soldiers down near Saintfield at the weekend. Apparently, the poor man was working in one of his fields when the soldiers killed him. An officer said the man ran away when they tried to question him. But everybody else is saying the army murdered him for no reason.'

'These are terrible times,' said Billy. 'Innocent people are being murdered every day.'

'Is there to be no end to it,' said Mrs Gray. 'Daniel Knox was telling me about a woman who lived up in the glens of Antrim. The soldiers accused her of hiding guns in her house for the United Irishmen. She told them she wasn't but when the soldiers searched the house, they found an old pistol hidden under a floorboard in her bedroom. She told them she didn't know it was there. The soldiers didn't believe her. They dragged her out of her house and hung her from a nearby tree in front of her five children.'

Billy shook his head as he listened.

'And, sure wasn't Jenny Bodley's boy arrested on some made up charge of stealing lead from one of Lord Castlereagh's buildings to make bullets for the United Irishmen. When he went to court, the judge found him guilty, and ordered him to be sent away to Russia to join the English army. The wee boy was innocent. They've left his poor mother totally distraught. Ever since the death of her husband she had been depending on the boys' wages to buy food for the family.'

'People don't feel safe in their own homes anymore,' added Betsy.

But her mother wasn't finished. 'Our neighbour, Jimmy Couthers, he lived just down the road there. He was arrested last week and thrown into jail because the soldiers found him outside his house after curfew. But he was only going to fetch the doctor for his sick wife. They kept him in prison for a week and when he went to court the judge ordered him to be sent away. He's in the navy now. The poor man will never see his wife again; she died shortly after he was arrested.'

'The land he was farming is up for rent,' said Betsy.

'There you are,' said Mrs. Gray. 'I don't know what's going to happen to us all if we carry on the way we are going. Did you offer Mr Boal a drink, Betsy?'

'No, not yet,' she replied. 'Would you like some milk or tea perhaps?'

'A glass of water would be fine,' Billy replied before turning back to Mrs Gray. 'I've brought the spun yarn you ordered.'

'Good, let me have a look at it.'

While Betsy went to get some water, Billy opened his bag and began placing the bobbins of spun yarn on the table.

'How many have you brought?' Mrs Gray enquired. 'I thought I'd ordered more than this.'

'You did, I've another bag outside. I'll fetch it in a minute, but they're all as good as these.'

Mrs Gray picked up the first bobbin and unravelled some of the yarn, running the fine filaments through her fingers. 'Good,' she smiled. 'This is excellent.'

'I was told you had some fabric for me to collect.'

'It's in the loom room. Go and fetch the rest of the bobbins, and I'll see you in there.'

Billy went outside and lifted the heavy bag from the back of his saddle and carried it into the loom room, where Betsy was waiting with a glass of water for him.

'Here's the fabric,' said Mrs Gray placing her hand on one of the rolls. 'Mind you, I'm expecting to get the same price I agreed with Clifford. It's very good quality.'

Billy went over and unravelled a short length of cloth, running his hand over the cool fabric. He smiled. 'Now I know why Clifford said you were his best weaver. This is the best cloth I've seen by far.'

Mrs Gray smiled as she looked at Betsy. After they exchanged payments Billy carried the fabric out to his horse. Betsy followed him. He tied the fabric onto the back of his saddle and turned to her.

'It was lovely seeing you again Betsy,' he said softly as he gazed into her eyes. 'Would it be okay if I called to see you on Sunday afternoon around two o'clock rather than waiting until next week?'

'Yes, I would like that, and I'll have that book for you. We could go for a picnic. I know a nice little spot down by the coast.'

'I look forward to that Betsy,' said Billy as he climbed onto his horse. 'See you Sunday,' he called as he rode down the lane. When he reached the main road, he stopped and waved back at. Her mother smiled at her when she walked into the house.

'Billy seems a nice young man,' she said. 'Will he be calling to see you again?'

'He's coming on Sunday; we're going out for a picnic.'

Her mother embraced Betsy warmly. 'I'm so pleased for you. I noticed you never took your eyes off him the whole time he was here, and I could see by the way he was looking at you that he felt the same. I know young love when I see it.'

Betsy hugged her mother and as she closed her eyes, all she could think about was Billy Boal.

Chapter 3

In a small, damp prison cell in Newtownards, David Johnston was trying to come to terms with what was happening to him. He had never been in trouble with the authorities. He certainly never imagined he would spend a night locked up in a prison cell. He hadn't slept. His imagination was running wild, thinking about what might happen to him. He knew death was a reality and that his severed head might soon be joining those of other United Irishmen impaled on spikes on top of the courthouse roof. He regretted he hadn't heeded warnings from some of his friends about becoming too deeply involved with the movement. It had been too easy being a rebel. Talking about political reform and armed rebellion, and of which constituency he might stand in as a candidate in elections to a new parliament. But those thoughts of bravado were long gone, shrivelled up into nothing, as he considered how close he was to the hangman's noose. His future looked bleak. All optimism gone.

He was acutely aware of every sound and movement outside his cell as he lay on a straw mattress, grieving over his predicament.

He sat up when he heard one of the jailers call out.

'The new prisoner is in cell three.'

That was his cell number. A few moments later he heard a key being inserted into the lock on the heavy cell door. He stood up when one of the jailers walked in through the partially opened doorway.

'You have visitors,' he declared.

Two men strode confidently past the jailer and into the cell. Johnston recognised them immediately. Both were considered to be the arch enemies of the United Irishmen and had been the subjects of many heated debates at several recent meetings. They were believed to be the instigators behind the increased hostilities by the army against them.

The first man was local magistrate, the notorious Reverend Cleland known to members of the United Irishmen as the Hanging Judge. Johnston personally knew several people who had been tried by him on charges relating to membership of the United Irishmen. The Reverend Cleland showed none of them any mercy, sentencing many to death by hanging or to an excessively long prison sentence.

The Reverend Cleland's colleague was none other than Viscount Castlereagh. He had been Johnston's commanding officer when he served in the Volunteers in the late eighties.

Castlereagh nodded to the jailer. 'Thank you, that will be all,' he said, indicating he wanted him to leave.

Castlereagh waited until the cell door was closed. 'Good morning David. I must say I never thought we would be meeting in a place like this. But then again, these are exceptional times.'

'Hello, your Lordship,' Johnston muttered dejectedly. 'Neither did I. Do you have any news about my wife, Martha? The last time I saw her she was lying on the ground in the yard at the farm after one of the soldiers had knocked her unconscious.'

'Your wife is safe and well,' replied Reverend Cleland.

'And what about the farmhouse? Why did the soldiers have to set fire to it?'

Castlereagh cleared his throat. 'I'm sorry about that David,' he said before turning to look at Reverend Cleland. 'Well, what do you have to say about the fire?'

Reverend Cleland seemed surprised by the question. 'The lieutenant in charge of the troops who carried out the arrest has been reprimanded. There was no need for him to set fire to the farmhouse.'

'Good,' said Castlereagh before turning back to Johnston. 'My understanding is that your neighbours quickly rallied around and managed to put the blaze out before any serious damage was caused. So, you can stop worrying about it.'

Johnston felt a surge of relief. 'Thank you, your Lordship. I don't know why I've been brought here. There has been some misunderstanding, …'

'David…' snapped Castlereagh. 'Stop lying. You know exactly why you are here. Do you see that pile of papers?' he said pointing at the paperwork Reverend Cleland was holding in his arms. 'They are records of everything we know about you. For instance, we know you are a General in the United Irishmen. We have scores of sworn statements from people who attended several United Irishmen meetings where you were present. We even know which Masonic hall you were in when you were heard stating that you would be willing to take part in a rebellion supported by French troops, to overthrow the government of Ireland. I'm sure you are aware that what you were advocating at those meetings is a capital offence, which is punishable by death... as any traitor should expect...'

'I'm no traitor,' declared Johnston.

'I'm glad to hear you say that,' said Castlereagh. 'But Britain and Ireland are at war with France; and if you deal with our enemies then you will be treated like a traitor. So, let us have no more pretence David. Can we at least agree upon that?'

Johnston lowered his head.

Castlereagh sensing his despair cleared his throat before continuing. 'Good David. I'm glad you are beginning to see sense. We have been watching you and your friends for some time. We know everything about your plans for an uprising.'

Johnston didn't lift his head as he muttered. 'There was a time when you were one of us. You must know that our only aim is to make things better for everyone.'

'Oh, but I do know,' Castlereagh replied softly. 'And that's precisely what I want to do.'

Johnston glanced up at him. 'When I served alongside you in the Volunteers, I often heard you say the Irish government had to change their ways, and that they needed to be reformed. What has changed your mind?'

Castlereagh moved closer to Johnston. 'David, I still think the Irish government needs to be reformed. But what you and your friends in the United Irishmen are advocating is wrong. You will destroy everything you want to achieve. If you instigate an uncontrolled uprising of the Irish people, you will be responsible for releasing a sectarian monster that will result in the deaths of thousands of innocent Protestants. Believe me, I know. I was in France when the revolution started over there. I saw the blood of innocent people flowing down the streets of Paris. Those people were slaughtered because the leaders of the revolution lost control of the monster they had unleashed. The rioters went on the rampage. They murdered anyone they thought held a position in the government or had been part of the French aristocracy. The mob could not be controlled. The people were a merciless rabble, and that's what will happen in Ireland if your colleagues continue in their quest to call for an uprising. Many innocent Irish people will die. Many old families will be wiped out when deep-rooted religious hatred is unleashed. Don't you see that the Catholics want our land?

Your land. They want to make Ireland a Catholic state. Ruled from Rome by bishops and their priests. They do not want Protestants like you and me living here. If you don't believe me, I can show you reports I receive daily of sectarian murders that are constantly taking place in the southern counties. Imagine the slaughter there will be when the restraints placed on these killers by the British army are removed because of the actions of people like you in the United Irishmen.'

Johnston lifted his head. 'None of the sectarian killings you talk about are being carried out by members of the United Irishmen,' he replied defiantly.

Castlereagh shook his head as though in despair. 'Oh David, if you honestly believe that, you are a naive fool. The whole world knows there is bad blood between Catholic and Protestant in Ireland. It's guileless people like you and your cronies in the United Irishmen who are encouraging old hostilities to surface once again.'

'We're not doing that,' declared Johnston.

'Look my friend,' said Castlereagh. 'I know you believe the answer to the world's woes is to treat everyone as though we are all equal but I'm sorry, Irish history, and what I saw in France tells me that you are wrong in your thinking. The actions by the United Irishmen will unleash wave after wave of sectarian killings. You will not be able to stop them until every Protestant in Ireland is dead or has been burned out of the homes their families have lived in for generations.'

'That's not our intention,' offered Johnston weakly.

Castlereagh shook his head wearily as though he was dealing with a young child. 'I know it isn't David, but that's the reality of what will happen because of the actions of a group of about seventy misguided Presbyterian ministers and their followers,' he stressed. 'Do you know that you have people in the United Irishmen who are also members of the Catholic Defenders? People who recently murdered an innocent Protestant weaver and burnt his house to the ground.'

Johnston shook his head and shrugged his shoulders.

'And, are you aware that some of your members are also in the militant Protestant Peep o' Day Boys? Another gang that recently hung a fifteen-year-old Catholic boy because he was in the wrong district.'

Again, Johnston did not answer and shook his head.

Castlereagh continued. 'Those two groups detest each other. They hate the very ground the other walks on. They are constantly involved in fights in which people have been murdered or badly maimed. What do you think will happen when the army is no longer around to keep them apart because they are trying to quell a rebellion that was started by the United Irishmen? Who would stop the Catholics and Protestants from killing each other then?'

'That will not happen,' said Johnston quietly. 'The United Irishmen is a non-sectarian society.'

'You can be so naive David. Did you know that Wolfe Tone was in Paris last week? He was trying to muster support for a French invasion fleet. The very force that you and I joined the Volunteers to protect Ireland from. The French are a Catholic nation. Who do you think they will support when they come here?'

Johnston didn't answer.

'They will join forces with the Irish Catholics, and when they do, their armies will slaughter all of the Protestants in Ireland. Is that what you want?'

'No... No, you are wrong. That's not what will happen,' Johnston said. 'The Irish people want to live in peace. They don't want religious conflict. They want everyone to be treated as equal. We believe that everyone wants to work together to make Ireland a better place for all its people to live in.'

But even as he spoke Johnston could see by the look on Castlereagh's face that he did not believe him.

Castlereagh shook his head. 'No David, that will never happen. You trusted me when I was your commanding officer. All I ask is that you put that same trust in me again, because I believe there is another way for you to achieve your aims,' Castlereagh softened his voice. 'If you agree to work with me, I promise, you will achieve everything you are after. Peace, harmony and prosperity for everyone. We will reform the Irish government in such a way that there will be no need for any bloodshed. We can do this peacefully David. What do you say?'

Johnston was still thinking about Castlereagh's offer when Reverend Cleland began to speak.

'David, I want to make it quite clear to you about what you are facing over the next few days, and what your options are. You will

46

be taken from here into the courthouse where you will appear before me. You will be charged with being a member of the United Irishmen, and of being a senior officer in that organisation. I have statements from witnesses who will testify that they saw you at several meetings of the United Irishmen, and that they heard you plotting to overthrow the Irish government. That, as you well know, is a capital charge...'

Reverend Cleland paused and nodded his head. 'You will be found guilty. I will sentence you to death by hanging, and because of the severity of your offence, you will be treated like a traitor. Your head will be removed from your body and will be impaled on one of the spikes on top of the courthouse. Do you understand?'

'Yes,' mumbled Johnston.

Castlereagh placed his hand on Johnston's shoulder.

'It doesn't have to be like that David. If you decide to work with us, I will make sure the witnesses don't testify and the Reverend Cleland will find you not guilty of any offence due to a lack of evidence. You will be released immediately and free to go home to Martha and enjoy the rest of your life with her by your side. The decision as to what happens at your trial is entirely up to you.'

Johnston listened intently to Castlereagh. He wasn't surprised they wanted him to become an informer. He and his fellow officers in the United Irishmen were convinced the organisation was riddled with spies. He looked long and hard into Castlereagh's eyes before he made his decision. Johnston felt a wave of relief flood through his weary body.

'Tell me what I have to do.'

Castlereagh slapped him on the back. 'Good man David, I knew you would see sense. You will give Reverend Cleland a weekly report on what is happening within the United Irishmen. I'm particularly interested in any news about where and when the French invasion force is planning to come ashore.'

Reverend Cleland was also very pleased with the outcome. 'Good man. I will talk to you again about how to contact me. You have made the right decision.'

Johnston did not answer him.

'Before we go,' said Castlereagh. 'Who is the overall commanding officer of the North Down Division?'

Without hesitation Johnston answered him. 'Brigadier General, Reverend Steel Dickson.'

Castlereagh nodded his head and smiled. He already knew the answer. 'And who is his second in command?'

'My neighbour, General Henry Poulter,' Johnston answered coldly.

'When was he promoted?'

'We held an emergency meeting shortly after Clifford Peters died whilst receiving his sentence of five hundred lashes. We voted for Henry to take his place immediately.'

Castlereagh smiled unenthusiastically. 'That explains why Poulter was able to muster so many people to stop your farm from burning, and why he was able to bring a lot more back that night to gather your potato crop. You owe him a lot, but don't let that cloud your judgement. We need to keep an eye on Henry Poulter. He could be a dangerous man.'

Johnston felt a pang of regret when he heard what his friends had done for him.

Reverend Cleland walked over to the cell door. 'Jailer,' he called out. 'We're finished in here. Let us out.'

Castlereagh turned to Johnston. 'Your solicitor, Hugh Atkinson is waiting to see you. He does not need to know about this meeting. When he comes in tell him you are going to plead not guilty to all of the charges.'

Johnston thanked him as the heavy cell door opened.

Castlereagh smiled and nodded at him. He thought Johnston would be a good asset. He wasn't the only informer he had within the ranks of the United Irishmen, but he was the most senior. At last he would have someone at the top table who would be able to keep him informed about what Reverend Steel Dickson was up to. Castlereagh had worked with Dickson in the past and had been impressed by his ability to organise people and to get things done. He felt reassured that he would now finally be able to stay one step ahead of his main adversary.

'Goodbye David,' Castlereagh said as he left the cell. 'You're doing the right thing.'

As the door closed behind them Johnston began to feel physically ill by the thought of what he had just agreed to do. He was still contemplating the horrible consequences when the cell door was reopened and Hugh Atkinson, his solicitor, was ushered into the cell by the jailer.

Chapter 4

Sunday was a strict day of rest on the Gray's farm at Gransha, just as it was in every other Presbyterian household, and as such it had its own slow routine. Betsy's mother, as normal, rose at seven and lit the fire before preparing breakfast. The early rise also gave her enough time to make sure the clothes they were going to wear to church later that morning were clean and ironed.

Around eight o'clock she woke Betsy and George telling them to get out of bed and get dressed for breakfast. Betsy arrived in the kitchen a few minutes later, but despite many requests, George was slow and reluctant to leave his bed. When he eventually made his way to the breakfast table he looked completely dishevelled. As he sat down beside Betsy, she could see there was something wrong.

'Are you alright?

George shook his head. 'No. I'm not feeling well.'

His mother studied him for a few moments and put his malaise down to growing pains. She poured him a glass of milk before serving the porridge. George took a long drink of cool milk.

'I didn't hear you come in last night,' said his mother.

'It was very late. I don't know what time it was.'

Betsy studied his face. 'Have you got a hangover George Gray?'

George glared at his sister. 'Shut up,' he demanded, before putting his head in his hands.

His mother reached over and placed her hand on his forehead. 'You have a temperature. Well, were you drinking?'

George raised his head slightly before replying rather sheepishly. 'Yes… and I feel awful.'

His mother shook her head more in despair than anger. 'I've told you before, you are not allowed to drink alcohol.'

'I know Ma,' pleaded George. 'And I'm sorry, but we were at a ceilidh in O'Halloran's barn last night, and one of Robert's friends brought some poteen with him.'

'Don't tell me you were drinking poteen,' said his mother disapprovingly.

'Yes, I did, and it tasted awful. I don't know how people can drink that stuff.'

'Where did he get it from?' demanded his mother.

'Ma you can get poteen from any farmhouse except ours. Everybody is making it. We drank it because the whiskey and porter they were selling in the barn was too expensive.'

'I thought you said you didn't like drinking.'

'I don't.'

'So why did you do it last night?'

'It was a special occasion.'

'What do you mean by that?'

'It was special because Robert and I joined the United Irishmen.'

'Why did you do that?' his mother asked without looking up from her breakfast.

'Maybe you should tell us what happened George,' suggested Betsy.

George shrugged his shoulders as though it was no big deal. 'We were at the ceilidh, and around midnight a group of men came into the barn and ordered the band to stop playing. One of the men, a big man with a beard, jumped up on to the stage and said he was from the United Irishmen. He said there was going to be an uprising soon, and they were looking for volunteers who were prepared to fight for the ordinary people of Ireland.'

Betsy nodded her head. 'What else did he say?'

George paused for a moment. 'He mentioned something about revolutions in America and France and said it was Ireland's turn to fight for her independence. He said the whole world was changing and corrupt governments were being overthrown. We put our hands up when he asked for volunteers.'

'Why didn't you come to me if you wanted to join the Society,' said Betsy. 'I could have taken you to one of our meetings.'

'I know, but I have to do it my own way. I am fifteen years old. I'm in charge of my own life. I don't need my big sister to do things for me. Anyway, Robert and I have been talking about joining the United Irishmen for ages, sure everybody is in it.'

'Did Martha Johnston know Robert was thinking about joining them?' asked Betsy

'I don't know, Robert told me he rarely sees her ever since she married David. She is always up at her farm.'

'Did you know the United Irishmen were going to be recruiting at the ceilidh Betsy?'

'No, I didn't, but there is a big push going on to get new members especially young men. Reverend Steel Dickson is telling everyone the uprising could happen any day soon.'

'There you are,' added George triumphally. 'I have to go to a meeting on Tuesday night in the church hall to start my training.'

'Training for what?' asked his mother.

'Somebody said they would be training us in how to use muskets and pikes.'

Betsy nodded her head. 'It's all changed. When I first joined the Society, the meetings I went to were like Book Clubs. We were encouraged to read newspapers and political pamphlets by writers like Drennan. The Reverend Warwick ran education classes and introduced us to the writings of great philosophers like Paine, Voltaire and Rousseau. He would talk to us about the thinking behind the United Irishmen and what it is that we are actually trying to achieve. Now, all the talk is about preparations for an uprising.'

Betsy's mother didn't say anything as she listened to their conversation. She was worried. She knew what the consequences would be if either of her children were caught by the soldiers. 'Just take care of each other,' she eventually said. 'I'm relying on you to look out for him, Betsy.'

They finished their breakfast in silence. As soon as Betsy finished her chores she changed into her best dress and joined her mother and George to walk the short distance to their Presbyterian church for the eleven o'clock service. The theme for the sermon that morning was about building a fair and just society in which the importance of accepting religious and ethnic differences were seen as fundamental building blocks.

After the service Betsy called in on one of their neighbours, Hugh Higgins to borrow his copy of the Rights of Man. As they walked home Betsy told her mother she was going on a picnic with Billy in the afternoon and would miss dinner.

When they arrived home, Betsy went into the stables. While she was saddling Sandy, she heard Billy coming down their lane. As she went out to meet him, she thought how handsome he looked.

'Hello,' she said when he stopped his horse beside her.

'Hello, you,' he replied as he gazed down before he suddenly jumped down and gathered Betsy in his arms and gently kissed her.

It was the softest, sweetest kiss Betsy had ever experienced.

'I've not stopped thinking about you,' he whispered. 'I've been dreaming of that kiss ever since the first time I saw you. I think I'm in love with you.'

Betsy pulled him towards her and returned the kiss. 'I think I'm in love with you too, William Boal,' she whispered.

Billy smiled. 'I've never been so happy. I feel as though you make my whole life complete.'

They kissed again and Betsy eventually said. 'I've prepared food for a picnic this afternoon. There's a place I know near the coast. I often go there. It is so peaceful, in the middle of beautiful woodland with a stream and a waterfall.'

'That sounds wonderful.'

'I've managed to borrow a copy of that book you were looking for from a neighbour.'

'The Rights of Man?'

'Yes, it's in my bag.'

'Great. Let's go.'

They mounted their horses and trotted down the lane watched by Betsy's mother from the farmhouse. She was happy for Betsy and sensed that Billy Boal was a good man. She hoped they would find happiness together.

With Betsy leading the way, they rode at a steady canter for the next thirty minutes until they reached the coast where they slowed and walked their horses along a narrow pathway that followed the rugged shoreline and sandy beaches for a few miles until they came to the mouth of the river that flowed out from a densely wooded valley. They turned and followed the river upstream, riding along a narrow dirt track, until they reached a tumbling waterfall. They stopped and dismounted at a small flat grassy area.

Betsy rolled out a blanket and sat down with her basket of food. After Billy secured the horses, he sat down beside her. Betsy offered him a sandwich and a glass of elderflower water. As they enjoyed their food, Betsy gazed at the water cascading down over the steep rocky face. At the foot of the falls there was a deep, clear pool where the water seemed to rest a while before continuing the journey towards the sea.

'I wish we could stay here forever,' she murmured.

'Me too,' Billy echoed as he gazed at her.

She smiled at him. 'I used to come here a lot after my father died. It's my sanctuary. I feel so peaceful here,' she said as she lay back on the blanket.

Billy leaned over and gently kissed her.

Later, Betsy asked him if he had heard any news about David Johnston's court case.

He shook his head. 'No, I haven't. I've been away for a couple of days.'

'Where did you go?'

'I was down in Armagh. I went to see some weavers and dyers the company wants to do business with. That went very well and on my way back, I went to Lisburn to meet some United Irishmen.'

Betsy was intrigued. 'So, what exactly do you do in the Society?'

Billy laughed at her question. 'I'm a go between.'

'What's that?' she queried.

'I pass messages between Reverend Steel Dickson and the rest of his leadership team. He used to write letters to each of them, but he had to stop when some were intercepted by the soldiers and several people ended up in jail. He has been using me as a messenger ever since. I've a good memory, which means I don't have to carry any notes. I can quote word for word what the Reverend says to me and pass it on to someone else. I'm also able to use my job as a linen products supplier as a cover, which means I can get into any townland or village without any trouble from the soldiers.'

'Do you respond directly to the Reverend Steel Dickson?'

'Yes. He was a friend of my father. I was born near Cotton...'

'That's not far from us,' said Betsy quickly.

'I know. My parents died when I was very young, and I was brought up by an aunt in Armagh. I lived there until Reverend Steel Dickson asked me to come back and help him last year. He fixed me up with this job and a place to stay. The family I'm living with are actually distant cousins of my mother.'

'So why did he want you to go to Lisburn?'

Billy looked at Betsy. 'I'm not supposed to tell anyone.'

Betsy smiled and kissed him. 'I promise you I won't tell anyone else.'

'Reverend Steel Dickson has heard that a French fleet, carrying thousands of soldiers, is coming to Ireland before Christmas, and he wants us to be ready to fight alongside them.'

Betsy was shocked at the news. 'So, does that mean we might be at war by Christmas?'

Billy nodded. 'Yes, it could be. But the French will have to get past any Royal Navy ships first before they can land, and if they don't manage to do that there will be no uprising.'

'There were men from the United Irishmen at a ceilidh my brother George was at last night looking for recruits. Is that related to this?'

'It could be. But we're always looking for new people, and that was another reason why I was in Lisburn. Reverend Steel Dickson told me to go there to see a shopkeeper called Henry Munro and ask him to set up a meeting with a schoolteacher called Magennis. He's in charge of the Defenders in County Down. Reverend Steel Dickson wanted to see if they would agree to form a pact with the United Irishmen.'

'Why is he so keen to sign a treaty with the Defenders?'

'That was the same question I put to him,' said Billy. 'I thought they were only interested in looking after the welfare of Catholic farmers and weavers.'

'So did I. That's why they're always fighting with the Protestant, Peep o' Day Boys.'

'That's exactly what I said to Reverend Steel Dickson. But he disagrees with that idea. He thinks Protestants and Catholics fight each other because powerful, rich landowners and their agents are using religious differences to play one side off against the other, so that they can make as much money as possible out of their tenants.'

'I agree.'

'Reverend Steel Dickson detests terms like Catholic and Protestant. He believes the rich and politically powerful use them to segregate us into camps. And once we are divided, they rule us. He wants to unite everyone under the one name, that of being an Irishman. He says we should keep religion out of government, and firmly believes that better education for everyone along with laws preventing exploitation would stop the fighting.'

'So, what happened?'

'I went to Lisburn and met with Henry Munro and his leadership team. I told them what Reverend Steel Dickson wanted. Several of Munro's men were very wary about trusting the Defenders because of the bitter fighting there had been between Protestants and Catholics over the years.'

'So, did they agree to a meeting?'

'Yes. Munro managed to persuade them to go along with what the Reverend was proposing. He then contacted Magennis immediately and said he wanted to set up a meeting with him and his senior officers. Next day Magennis sent a message saying he would meet with him, but he would decide where it would take place. Apparently Magennis is paranoid about his security. Munro agreed and Magennis sent one of his men to escort us to an old barn, way out in the countryside. The Defenders had guards and lookouts on every part of the journey. There was no chance of the soldiers sneaking up and surprising or capturing any of us.'

'It sounds rather scary.'

'No, it wasn't really. When we got to the barn everyone was introduced to each other. Most of the Defenders were very pleasant people, but there was one man in Magennis's leadership team who wasn't so nice. He was called John McMullin. He was a very bitter man and kept calling us things like Planters and Protestant bastards. He would say we had no right to live in Ireland, and that we should go back to England or whatever hellhole it was that our ancestors came from.'

'He sounds horrible. How did Munro deal with him?'

'Munro let him rant on for a while, and then he looked him straight in the eye and said, your opinion is different to mine. My aim is to build a bond between Irishmen of every religion, and for all the people in Ireland, to take part in the election of a new parliament in Dublin. That's why I am a United Irishman.'

'That's just like our oath… What did the man say?'

'He had no reply. He shut up after that. He was just a religious bigot, and let's face it Betsy, we have them on both sides. Thankfully they're in the minority, but as the Reverend pointed out they can be very dangerous. Henry was a brilliant negotiator. I was really impressed how he managed to negotiate an agreement with Magennis and his men. They agreed to stop fighting with local farmers and when the uprising comes, they agreed to fight alongside us. But, and this was a very important point, they would fight as United Irishmen.'

56

Betsy smiled. 'Good for you,' she said as she leaned over and kissed him. 'I'm sure Reverend Steel Dickson was very happy when you reported back to him.'

'He was, but there's something else going on that he is very worried about.'

'What's that?'

'The soldiers arrested one of our senior men a few days ago.'

'But they are always doing that?'

'I know, but this time it's different.'

'Who is he?' asked Betsy.

'He's called William Orr. He's married with five children; his wife is expecting their sixth child soon.'

'So why is the Reverend Steel Dickson so concerned about him?'

'William Orr is a member of the Northern Committee of the United Irishmen and was very active in the organisation. He was also a contributor to the Northern Star and submitted many articles to the newspaper about the need for political change.'

'Do you know him?'

'I've done a lot of work with him. He's a very successful businessman and owns a farm near Farranshane, just outside Antrim. But he's also a friend of mine. I met him about three years ago when I joined the Masons. He was very supportive and helped me settle in. I've been to his house on many occasions, and I've heard him speak at several United Irishmen meetings. He is a great orator.'

'What were his talks about?'

'Mainly about the political situation in Ireland. When he speaks, everyone listens. He's a tall man, just over six feet, and very athletic looking. I think he's about thirty years old. But he has a great way with people. Everyone thinks the world of him. He has a little quirk when he dresses, he always wears something green, like a tie, or even a ribbon around his hat. He thinks we should be able to get the political reforms we need without seeking assistance from the French or anyone else. He wants Ireland to be able to build its own commercial links with countries around the world and sell our goods wherever we want. He firmly believes the politicians in England and their friends in Dublin Castle were deliberately preventing us from doing so because a prosperous and successful Ireland was not in England's best financial interests.'

'What's Orr accused of?'

'They are saying he presided over a meeting of United Irishmen last April and administered the oath to two serving soldiers.'

'Is it the same oath I took when I joined?'

'Yes. The same. But it's a crime to administer that oath now.'

'And did he swear in the two soldiers?'

'No, he didn't. It's true that he chaired a meeting of United Irishmen. It was in a barn belonging to his neighbour, Jack Gourlay. I know several people who were there, and they told me that during the meeting two soldiers from the Fife Fencibles, Hugh Wheatley and John Lindsay, were brought in and introduced to everyone as sympathisers. It was a man named William McIvor who administered the oath to them. When the meeting finished everyone went their own way, but apparently the two soldiers went straight to the home of George McCartney, the vicar of Antrim and the local magistrate and gave sworn statements that William Orr had administered the United Irishmen's oath to them.'

'But that was a lie.'

'I know. McCartney sent their statements to Castlereagh in Dublin castle. He sat on them for months until a few days ago when he ordered William Orr to be arrested.'

'Why the delay?'

'We're not sure, but Reverend Steel Dickson thinks it's all part of some scheme thought up by Castlereagh to destroy the United Irishmen. William Orr was charged with High Treason. That carries the death penalty. Reverend Steel Dickson hopes Orr's counsel will be able to get the charges dropped or reduced, but he's not very confident.'

'Why not?' asked Betsy.

'He thinks the politicians in Dublin Castle are determined to hang William Orr.'

'But that would be murder. Orr's an innocent man.'

'The government doesn't care about that as long as they win. It means none of us are safe.'

'I feel safe with you,' murmured Betsy as she nestled into Billy's arms.

It was late in the afternoon when Betsy and Billy returned to the farm. After feeding and watering their horses Betsy invited Billy to stay for tea. When they went into the farmhouse, she was surprised to find Rachel Knox trying on her new wedding dress.

'Hello Rachel,' said Betsy.

'Hello,' said Rachel as Betsy's mother adjusted the hem on her dress. 'And who is this good-looking man?'

'I would like to introduce you to William Boal,' said Betsy. 'Otherwise known as Billy. Billy this is Rachel.'

'Hello.'

'Nice to meet you Billy. Where have you two been then?'

Betsy smiled at her friend. 'We rode over to the waterfall for a picnic. It was a beautiful day. We had a wonderful time... I like your dress.'

'It's nearly finished,' added her mother. 'Can you make something for our guests to eat. There's that new packet of tea you bought in Belfast the other day; we could have some of it.'

'Of course,' said Betsy as she put the kettle on the fire and started buttering some bread. 'I was telling Billy about you and Hugh going to America after the wedding.'

'Yes, Hugh's uncle has offered him a job as a senior accountant in his manufacturing business. I think they make farm machinery. It all sounds so exciting... Betsy, you must bring Billy with you to our farewell party and to the wedding.'

Rachel turned to Billy. 'Please say you will come. It would be so nice to see you there.'

Billy was a little taken back by the suddenness of the invitation. 'Yes, I would love to. Thank you very much. When is the party?'

'It's three days before the wedding. We want to give everyone the chance to sober up before they have to go to church.'

'Where is it being held?'

'We have booked O'Halloran's barn. We are going to have a group of musicians and singers for the night. Hugh has even arranged for several pony traps to bring guests and to take them home afterwards. We want everyone to really celebrate our wedding and us going to America.'

'Whereabouts in America are you going?'

'We are going to Philadelphia, in Pennsylvania. Hugh has been writing to his cousins over there for months about joining them. They say there are so many opportunities for people like us. Just think, no more fear of being thrown out of your home because there is no work. America is such a wonderful country. Everyone has been telling us about the sense of freedom you get as soon as you arrive there.'

'That reminds me, did you get your sailing tickets sorted out?' asked Betsy. 'I remember you saying that you were having some trouble with the booking agent.'

'Yes, Hugh has managed to sort everything out. There was a misunderstanding about the sailing date. But we are fine now. We sail from Larne the day after our wedding on a ship called Condor.'

Betsy was surprised. 'Gosh that's a bit of a rush. You'll need to have everything packed and ready to go before the wedding.'

Rachel nodded at her. 'We will. Unfortunately, my father can't go to Larne; his doctor says he is too ill to travel that far. Jenny won't be able to come either she has to stay on the farm to look after him. Will you come and wave me off Betsy? It would mean so much to me to see someone from my side in the crowd when our ship finally pulls away from the quay. All of Hugh's family will be there. Oh, please say you will.'

'I will go with you Betsy,' said Billy. 'If you want to go.'

Rachel had always been so positive about her decision to emigrate and the pain of leaving her friends and family was the price she was willing to pay for a new life in America, but lately, Betsy was beginning to detect some doubt in her friend. She wondered how Rachel really felt about leaving.

'Of course, I'll go with you. But you must promise to write to me every month and tell me the truth about your life in America.'

'I will, I'll write every month, I promise,' begged Rachel. 'So, you are coming?'

'Yes. We'll be there to wave goodbye to you and Hugh.'

Chapter 5

It was almost two weeks after David Johnston's arrest before a date was finally set for his trial. Martha had tried on several occasions to visit him in prison, but the jailers told her they were under strict instructions that Hugh Atkinson, his solicitor was the only person allowed to see him.

During that time Betsy had called at the farm daily to help Martha clean and redecorate the farmhouse. Martha's neighbours also helped by giving her new linen sheets and curtains to replace those destroyed by the smoke during the fire, and it didn't take long for Henry Poulter and some of the local men to strip the damaged straw from the roof and replace it with fresh new thatch.

On the day of the trial, Betsy rose early and rode over to Martha's farm to wait on the pony and trap she had organised to take them to Newtownards. Martha had insisted on that mode of travel because she was convinced David would be released and she wanted to make sure she could bring him straight home with her. When they arrived in Newtownards Betsy was surprised at how many of Martha's neighbours had come to offer their support. As they walked to the court, Betsy was shocked to see soldiers standing guard around a new set of gallows that had been erected close to the courthouse building. Several people had started to gather around the scaffold and amongst them she spotted the brother of James McKay who had been arrested a couple of weeks ago and charged with stealing a rifle from a local manor house and of membership of the United Irishmen. Betsy stopped to ask him what had happened to James. His brother told her that his trial had just finished, and James had been found guilty by Reverend Cleland and condemned to death. His sentence was to be carried out immediately.

As they spoke the courthouse doors suddenly opened and soldiers began pushing their way past them. Betsy felt ill as she watched James being frogmarched from the courthouse to the gallows. The last time she had talked to him was at a meeting of the United Irishmen. He had told her about the birth of his new baby daughter and why it was important he took a stand for her rights as a citizen of Ireland. She watched as James was helped onto the gallows where he climbed up a short set of steps. She could see him looking around the crowd as though searching for a friendly face. Suddenly everything seemed to happen quickly. The hangman slipped a noose over James's head and kicked the small set of steps James was standing on, out from underneath him. Betsy closed her eyes, the crowd gasped, everyone could hear the grief-stricken screams and cries of James's family and friends.

Betsy could still hear the sobs when a few minutes later she and Martha were ushered into the courtroom. They quickly found a seat where they waited for a few tense moments before Johnston was eventually escorted into the dock. Betsy thought he looked tired and drawn as she watched him gaze around the packed courtroom. She saw a weak smile on his face when he spotted Martha.

Betsy could sense Martha's apprehension when they saw the Reverend Cleland walk in and sit in the judge's chair. After the jury was sworn in, David Johnston was asked to stand up as the clerk of the court read out the charges.

'David Johnston you are charged with concealing weapons belonging to the United Irishmen. You are also charged with being a senior officer in that organisation, in which capacity you administered the oath of the United Irishmen to others. You are also charged with plotting with others to overthrow the Irish government.'

'How do you plead to these charges?' said Reverend Cleland.

'Not guilty your honour,' Johnston replied immediately, his voice sounding weak and shaky.

'Very well. Will the prosecutor present the evidence against the prisoner?' said Reverend Cleland.

Lieutenant O'Leary was the first witness to be brought to the stand.

The prosecutor stood up. 'Lieutenant O'Leary will you tell the court what happened on the day you went to the accused's farm.

'Yes sir. I received information that David Johnston had been in the Volunteers and that he had been issued with a rifle upon enlisting. I and a platoon of soldiers went to Johnston's farm to retrieve the weapon, but when we arrived there Johnston denied ever having received one.'

The prosecutor asked the lieutenant to continue.

'Mr Johnston kept denying he had been given a rifle, but I had documentary evidence to prove that he had. I continued to question

Mr Johnston until he eventually agreed to tell me where it was. When we retrieved the rifle from a stack of peat at the back of Mr Johnston's farmhouse, we also found a pike blade hidden with it.'

The rifle and pike-head were then shown to the court.

Lieutenant O'Leary continued. 'When I asked the accused about the pike blade Mr Johnston claimed he had found it on his land. I then asked him if he was a member of the United Irishmen. He said he was not. I did not believe him. I think he is.'

'Thank you,' said the prosecutor. 'No more questions.'

Hugh Atkinson stood up to question the officer. 'Lieutenant O'Leary, was the prisoner tortured to get any of this information?'

The lieutenant shook his head. 'No, he was not.'

'So how did you get it?'

'We used a form of aggressive questioning.'

'Did this involve half-hanging?'

'Yes, it did. I had to get the prisoner to talk.'

There were gasps of astonishment and some ironic laughter from those sitting in the public gallery.

'Lieutenant O'Leary I would like to point out to you that half-hanging is a form of torture in anyone's view,' said Atkinson before continuing. 'Lieutenant O'Leary you also accused my client of being a member of the United Irishmen. On what grounds are you making that accusation?'

'I don't have any proof, but in my judgement finding the two weapons together was clear evidence of a link to the United Irishmen.'

'So, you have no evidence that my client is a member of the United Irishmen?'

'No Sir.'

'Thank you, Lieutenant. I have no further questions for this witness your honour.'

As O'Leary left the witness box Hugh Atkinson remained on his feet.

'Your honour I would like to request that the statements given by Lieutenant O'Leary be struck from the record as torture was used on my client to obtain some of it. I would also contend that the opinion of Lieutenant O'Leary's about my client's membership of the United Irishmen is not proof of any crime.'

The Reverend Cleland agreed with the solicitor's view but said the lieutenant's evidence would still stand. At this point Betsy was expecting another witness to appear to give evidence supporting Johnston's link to the United Irishmen and was somewhat surprised when the prosecutor stood up and said they had no more evidence to bring before the court.

Atkinson immediately jumped to his feet to ask that the charges against his client be dropped for lack of evidence.

The Reverend Cleland shook his head in disbelief as he studied the notes in front of him for a few minutes before looking over at the prisoner.

'It's my decision that this case has not been proven. I therefore find David Johnston, not guilty of the charges brought against him. Mr Johnston, you are free to go. However, I suggest the next time you are asked a question by a member of his Majesty's military forces you give your answers immediately and truthfully.'

Johnston's head dropped and his body swayed as he began to sob. Martha rushed over to him and threw her arms around his shaking body. The rest of the people in the court stood as Reverend Cleland left the chamber.

Martha helped Johnston to walk from the dock. 'Come on I'm taking you home,' she said as she ushered him out of the courthouse to where some of his friends where gathering.

Across the street the crowd had already dispersed. The gallows were empty.

'Speech,' someone called out when they spotted Johnston.

Johnston raised a hand in recognition. 'Thank you all for coming. You have no idea how wonderful it feels to be among friends again.'

As he was speaking Betsy ran down the street to tell the driver of their pony and trap that they were ready to leave. A few minutes later Martha and Johnston boarded the carriage.

'I'll see if I can get a lift home with someone else,' said Betsy.

'No, you will not,' replied Martha firmly making room beside her. 'You're coming with us.'

'Walk on,' called out the driver to his horse as soon as Betsy was on board.

As they headed down the street Johnston waved to his friends and called out, 'Thank you again, for coming.'

'How are you feeling?' asked Betsy when they reached the edge of the town.

'Tired and drained,' replied Johnston wearily.

Martha hugged him. 'It's so wonderful. I couldn't believe it when the prosecution said they had no more evidence to offer. I was sure they were going to produce some lowlife witness who was going to swear his life away. They have done that so many times in the past.'

'I've heard that too,' said Betsy. 'I was particularly worried when they wouldn't let you visit David before the trial. That's normally a bad sign... What was it the prison guards kept saying to you?'

'They would stop me from entering and say, your husband is charged with high treason and will not be allowed to see anyone until after his trial,' Martha said in a mock southern Irish accent. 'But they were so wrong. It's a miracle,' she shouted as she squeezed Johnston tightly.

Johnston smiled weakly as they headed out of town.

Betsy was also excited with his unexpected release. 'Did you honestly think you would get out today, David?'

'No,' he said and shook his head as he looked away.

For some reason Betsy felt slightly disturbed by his reply and would often look back at that moment and wonder what it was that made her feel uneasy about David's response.

Chapter 6

On the night of Hugh and Rachel's farewell party, Billy left his horse at Betsy's and they were picked up in a pony and trap and taken to O'Halloran's barn a few miles away. By the time they arrived a large crowd had already gathered. Betsy was amused by the boisterous behaviour of some of the guests as it was obvious several them had been drinking for some time.

Inside the barn, the music was loud and fast. A band, consisting of three fiddlers, a man with a tin whistle and another on a bodhran, were playing reels and jigs continuously. As the night wore on, the intensity of their music increased, encouraging the revellers to dance even more passionately.

Around midnight, during a short break, a troop of skilled dancers performed several traditional Irish and Scottish dances. When the dancers finished Henry Poulter was invited onto the stage to sing. Henry only knew one song, which he often sang at parties for friends who were leaving for America, it was called The Parting Glass.

With the band supporting him, the crowd sang along.
'Oh, all the money that e'er I had
I spent it in good company…'
When they reached the last few lines of the song, everyone sang as loud as they could…
'Come on then fill to me the parting glass,
Good night and joy be with you all.'
When the song ended and Henry had taken a few bows, the leader of the band announced a short break. He invited everyone to help themselves to the food being laid out on long tables at the back of the barn by a team of caterers. There were several large bowls filled with Irish stew, plates stacked with different types of roast meat, dishes loaded with potatoes and various types of vegetables, numerous slices of buttered bread, and to help wash it all down there were ample supplies of bottles of stout, glasses of wine and tumblers filled with whiskey.

After most people had helped themselves to some food the band began playing again. They started with a few slow ballads and a couple of waltzes before gradually picking up the pace with more jigs and reels. Around five o'clock in the morning, the band stopped playing as a lone piper entered the barn followed by Hugh and Rachel. He led them up onto the stage where Hugh addressed the crowd.

'My wife to be and I,' said Hugh to loud cheers and whistles from the crowd. 'Would like to thank you for coming here tonight. You have helped make this an unforgettable farewell party. It goes without saying that we will sorely miss you all. But the good news is you can come and visit us any time you are in America.'

Someone in the audience shouted, 'Three cheers for Hugh and Rachel. Hip, hip.'

'Hooray... Hooray... Hooray,' shouted everyone in the crowd.

'Thank you,' said Hugh and Rachel.

A few moments later Hugh indicated he wanted everyone to be quiet. 'I would like to invite a very special friend onto the stage to sing the last song of the night. You all know him well, so ladies and gentlemen please put your hands together for Rachel's father, Daniel Knox.'

The feeble old man was helped onto the stage by Rachel's sister Jenny. As he was too weak to stand a chair was brought out for him to sit on.

'I'm going to sing a beautiful song by the wonderful Scottish poet, Rabbie Burns, called Auld Lang Syne. Please join in and we'll sing the first verse and the chorus. But before we start, we need Hugh and Rachel to go down and stand in the middle of the dance floor, and for the rest of you to gather around them in a circle.'

Daniel waited until everyone was in position. 'Now if everyone will please cross their arms, like this,' he said demonstrating what he wanted them to do. 'And grab hold of the hand of the person on either side of you.'

He waited until everyone had done what he asked.

'Good,' he called out. 'And while you're singing, please think about Rachel and Hugh, as we say goodbye to them.'

Everyone in the hall joined in as he began to sing.

'Should auld acquaintance be forgot,
And never brought to mind
Should auld acquaintance be forgot,
And auld lang syne.'
For auld lang syne, my dear,
For auld lang syne.

*We'll tak a cup o'kindness yet,
For auld lang syne.'*

When they finished, many people in the crowd were weeping as they ran towards Hugh and Rachel to wish them farewell.

A few moments later people began to leave, and the musicians began putting their instruments away. The party was over. It was almost eight o'clock in the morning by the time Betsy and Billy were dropped off at her farm. After saddling his horse Billy kissed Betsy goodnight before riding home.

Three days later on the day of the wedding, Betsy rode in a four-wheeled trap with Billy, her mother and George to the neat, little Presbyterian church in Greyabbey. When they arrived, they found the church was already packed with neighbours and friends. Betsy admired the beautiful flower displays of roses and sweet pea on the windowsills as they were shown to their seats. When she mentioned them to the usher, he told her they had been arranged by Hugh's mother. He also pointed out a large display at the front of the church, close to where a nervous looking Hugh was sitting with his best man and the Reverend Porter as they waited on Rachel's arrival.

Suddenly Betsy heard the piercing skirl of bagpipes as a piper announced the arrival of the bride and her father. The congregation stood as Betsy glanced behind her to watch Rachel walk down the aisle. Betsy thought she looked absolutely stunning in her blue dress and matching bonnet, carrying a beautiful bouquet of flowers. When they reached the chancel Rachel's father stopped and said a few words to Reverend Porter before he passed Rachel's hand over to Hugh. Betsy saw a loving smile pass between the couple.

'Welcome friends,' said Reverend Porter to the congregation. 'On behalf of Hugh and Rachel I would like to thank you all for being here on this very important day.'

Betsy enjoyed the entire wedding service, often imagining herself standing beside Billy one day as they committed themselves to each other. She would turn and smile at him occasionally and he would smile back.

When the service ended Reverend Porter looked at Hugh and Rachel and said. 'You may kiss your wife.'

A few moments later they walked back down the aisle together. The entire congregation followed them to the community hall next door where refreshments had been set out by an army of helpers. Hugh and Rachel stood inside the doorway thanking each guest personally for helping to make it a very special day for them. A harpist began playing softly while people searched for their seats. Once everyone was seated, several waiters began serving the hot food.

A couple of hours later, after the best man's speech, there were tearful goodbyes as Hugh and Rachel left to board the carriage waiting for them outside the hall. It would take them to a hotel near the port of Larne where they were staying one night before boarding the ship that would take them to America tomorrow afternoon.

Next morning Billy rode over to Betsy's farm and after breakfast he and Betsy left to ride to Larne. It was almost midday when they reached the ivy-covered hotel on the outskirts of the small seaside town. Several members of Hugh's family were already there, and Rachel was very glad to see Betsy and Billy when they arrived. After a quick lunch everyone left the hotel to travel the short distance to Larne harbour.

As they approached the docks, it was easy to spot the Condor, it was the largest ship in the harbour. They stopped near the harbour office while Hugh and Rachel went inside to finalise their boarding arrangements. As they waited Betsy noticed anxious parents nervously watching excited children playing around their luggage on the quayside, while a middle-aged man argued with one of the ship's officers at the gangway onto the ship, about why he shouldn't have to wait to go on board.

For some of the people the realisation they were about to finally part with their loved ones was too much for them. There were tears and grief-stricken hugs as people said goodbye knowing it would probably be for the final time. The mournful cries of seagulls circling above the ship seemed to provide an appropriate backdrop.

While Betsy was watching the people on the quayside, she noticed a familiar looking carriage stopping at the edge of the crowd. As one of the carriage doors opened Betsy glanced over to see who was inside. To her surprise she saw Rachel's father and her sister Jenny. She ran over and helped the old man step down from the carriage, and as she was helping him through the crowd, she saw Rachel emerge from the office.

'Rachel,' she called out. 'Look who's here.'

Rachel turned around. 'Daddy,' she cried as she ran over and threw her arms around him.

'Oh, I'm so pleased you were able to come. I was really missing you. Thank you so much.'

'Daddy insisted we come,' said Jenny. 'He wanted to see you.'

'Thank you, my dear Daddy,'

'I had to come Rachel. I knew you would be upset. But please don't be. You belong in America. That's where your dreams are taking you. You have to live your own life, and not worry about me. When your mother and I got married, my uncle John offered to pay our boat fares to America. He said we could stay with him until we found our own home. I desperately wanted to go. But your mother wouldn't leave her parents. I have always regretted that decision. We must give our children the best opportunities we can in this life. I'm so proud of you for what you are doing.'

Daniel Knox held his daughter close as the Harbour Master called on all remaining passengers to board the Condor. Several porters arrived and began carrying their suitcases on board.

Rachel kissed her father's cheek and thanked him before she turned and walked up the gangway. Betsy could see that she was weeping when she joined Hugh on the deck of the ship.

A gang of dockers quickly removed the gangway and untied the large heavy ropes that had been securing the Condor to the quayside. As sailors pulled the ropes back on board the ship others climbed the rigging and began unfurling the large canvas sails.

Passengers on board the Condor began to wave frantically as the sails caught the wind and the ship eased away from the quayside. The grief-stricken cries from those watching on the dockside reached a heart-rending crescendo when the ship reached the middle of the lough and headed for the open sea. Some of the people on the quayside became inconsolable and had to be virtually carried from the docks. Betsy was left with a terrible feeling of sadness as she watched the Condor sail into the distance.

'That was heart breaking,' she said softly to Billy. 'I've never witnessed so much sorrow before.'

'I know,' Billy said. 'Did you notice how many people were onboard the Condor?'

'Yes, it was packed,' she replied. 'It's so sad that so many people want to leave Ireland. I'll miss Rachel and Hugh. I wish they could have stayed. They are good people.

'I know,' said Billy. 'I have often wondered if I would have enough courage to risk everything and leave. When I think about the many hundreds of thousands of Irish people who have emigrated from here, I try to imagine what this country could have been like if only they had stayed.'

'That's why we are chasing our dreams of a better Ireland,' said Betsy. 'And we must never forget that.'

Daniel Knox watched until the Condor reached the open sea before he turned to walk back towards his carriage, but after a few steps he stopped and slumped to the ground.

Betsy heard Jenny cry out and saw her trying to lift him. She ran over and tried to help along with several members of Hugh's family. One of the men said he was a doctor, but after a quick examination of the old man he looked up at Jenny and shook his head.

Jenny looked stunned. 'No, he will be alright, we just have to get him to the hospital. They'll be able to help him there.'

The doctor stood up. 'No Jenny. It's too late for that. I'm sorry but your father is dead.'

'No, no,' she sobbed. 'No, that can't be true. He was fine just a few minutes ago.'

The doctor nodded his head. 'There is no doubt.'

'But what can I do. Rachel is gone, she doesn't know he is dead. What will I do?'

'We have to take him home,' said the doctor. 'There is an undertaker close by. I'll talk to them.'

'Thank you,' sobbed Jenny as Betsy held her.

The Doctor returned with an undertaker who, after a final check of his paperwork placed Daniel Knox's body in a coffin and lifted it onto the back of his hearse.

Betsy joined Jenny in her carriage as their sad convoy headed back to the Knox's farm. Billy rode behind bringing Sandy with him.

It was almost midnight by the time Betsy finally arrived home in Gransha to find her mother had waited up for her.

'I've made you some supper,' she said as Betsy walked in.

'Thanks mum, you shouldn't have stayed up.'

'You know I can't sleep if you or George are not home. It's easier staying up.'

'I'm glad you did. I've had a terrible day.'

Her mother looked anxiously at her. 'Why, what happened?'

Betsy stood before the open fireplace, her head bowed slightly as she raised her hand to her forehead and stroked her taut skin for a few moments. She struggled to speak, and when she finally managed to get some words out, she began to weep, and her body started shaking.

Her mother quickly wrapped her arms around her. 'What's wrong Betsy?' she asked as she held her close. 'It's all right,' she whispered. 'It's all right.'

'Rachel's daddy died this morning,' said Betsy as she continued sobbing.

'Oh no. How awful,' her mother whispered softly. 'What happened?'

'He came to Larne to say goodbye to Rachel. It was so wonderful to see them together, mum. He told her not to be worrying about him. Poor Rachel looked so pleased to see him. But as he watched her boat sail away, he had a heart attack and collapsed. Jenny and I tried to lift him, but I think we knew he was already dead. There was nothing we could do.'

Betsy's mother held her close. 'Shush,' she whispered. 'It's alright.'

It was a few moments before Betsy had calmed down enough for her mother to let her go.

'One of Hugh's brothers is a doctor,' said Betsy as she sat down in a seat by the fireside. 'He arranged for an undertaker to bring Daniel's body home. Billy and I travelled back with Jenny. When we arrived at her farm some of her neighbours were already there. I don't know how they knew.'

'Bad news always travels fast,' said her mother.

'The neighbours were so good. They helped us carry the coffin into the house and set it up on a couple of trestles in Daniel's bedroom. Some of them are staying the rest of the night with Jenny. Daniel's funeral is going to be held on Tuesday morning.'

Her mother sighed as she sat down. 'Poor Jenny. Her mum died just over a year ago, and now her father has gone. Jenny is the only one left on the farm. I don't know how she is going to cope. She wouldn't be able to run that place without someone to help her. Perhaps she will sell up and join Rachel in America.'

'Oh my God, I'd almost forgotten about Rachel, it will break her heart when she finds out,' sobbed Betsy.

'I know, but there's nothing we can do.'

Betsy's mother went over to the kitchen cupboard and lifted down two cups.

'I've made you some tea,' she said as she filled both cups and handed one to Betsy. 'Here have this it will help you to relax.'

Betsy took a sip of hot tea and held the warm cup in her hands.

'I went through a range of emotions as I watched Rachel's ship sail away from Larne harbour this morning. It felt so strange. There was a feeling of excitement when I thought about all those wonderful things Rachel would be able to do when she reached America. But this would be quickly followed by a deep feeling of sadness... the same sadness I felt when Daddy died, and I realised I would never see his face again... My heart felt as though it was going to break.'

'I know what you mean,' her mother said sadly. 'A person's death or someone emigrating can trigger similar emotions. When I was about fifteen, I remember standing on the dockside in Belfast harbour with my mammy and daddy. We were there to say goodbye to my big sister, your aunt Mary, when she emigrated. I watched her board a ship called the Anna Maria that took her to America. When I watched the ship sail away, I felt all those emotions you just described. I was left with a deep feeling of sadness. It was like being at her funeral. But even though Mary still writes to me every month, it's not the same. I miss her so much... and I often think about the years we could have spent together. I would have loved to share the joy I felt when you and George were born. She and I could have comforted each other at times of grief... I have always felt Mary's leaving put my daddy into an early grave. Mary was his favourite.'

'Why didn't you go to America mum?'

Her mother stared into the fire for a long time. 'I should have. We have more relatives living in America now than in Ireland, but I never felt like I needed to go. And when I met your father, that was it, I couldn't have gone without him, and he would never leave Ireland. He always talked about his dream that Ireland would become a place where we could all live in peace. He hated people talking about Catholic Irishmen and Protestant Irishmen. To him there was only one description of the people on this island and that was Irish. He always said, hatred will tear us apart, but it is love that will bring us together. I still believe in that, even though some people may think I am naive.'

'No, you're not mum,' said Betsy. 'I also believe it's love that will bring us together, and one day daddy's dream will come true.'

Betsy's mother smiled at her before looking up at the clock. 'It's late, what time are you going to the market in the morning?'

'I was going to leave about six o'clock. I get a better site if I'm early. I have to pick Gina up as well; she wants a lift to Bangor. She has to do some business for her father.'

As they left the kitchen her mother stopped. 'Oh, I nearly forgot. Martha Johnston called by this afternoon looking for you.'

'What did she want?'

'She didn't say, said she would catch up with you sometime.'

Betsy was puzzled. 'Oh well, it can't have been all that important.'

'No, I think it was just a social call.'

'Probably.'

'I made some meat pies for you to take with you. I'll get up with you in the morning and help you finish loading the cart. I've put some potatoes, carrots, a few turnips and the last of the cabbages on the cart. There are some dresses that I have made that I want you to take with you this time, to see if we can sell them. We could do with the extra money.

'Of course, I will,' said Betsy.

'And will you buy some of those bread rolls you brought back last week? They were very nice.'

'Yes. Goodnight.'

Chapter 7

Next morning, Betsy and her mother rose early and together they loaded the cart with everything Betsy was going to sell at the Bangor market. When they finished Betsy went to the stables to get her horse, Sandy. Although Sandy had been to Larne and back the previous day, he seemed alert and excited when she harnessed him to the cart.

As Betsy was about to leave her mother gazed up at the sky. 'It looks like it is going to be a dry day.'

'I hope so,' said Betsy. 'Walk on,' she added as she flicked Sandy's back with the reins and set off on her short trip to the market at Bangor.

On her way she stopped outside the tack shop where Gina's father sold saddles and bridles. Gina and Betsy had been friends since early childhood and attended the same school and church. In their early teens they were inseparable and had joined the church choir for a short time before being politely asked to leave because they chatted too much during the services. Gina came out of the shop and climbed up beside Betsy.

Once they were out on the main road Betsy joined a convoy of traders making the same journey to the market. After about thirty minutes they were stopped at a security roadblock on the outskirts of Bangor town. To Betsy's relief she saw that most of the carts were being waved through. As they approached the barrier one of the soldiers indicated he wanted her to stop.

'Where are you going?' he asked.

'To the market in Bangor.'

As the soldier quickly peered into the back of her cart Betsy heard someone call out.

'Well if it isn't the bad-tempered pig owner.'

Betsy looked over to her right and saw Lieutenant O'Leary standing amongst a small group of soldiers. He walked over to the back of the cart.

'So, what have we here?' he asked as he lifted a sheet Betsy had placed over the food she was selling.

'Do you have any bacon for sale?' the lieutenant asked as he started to laugh.

'No, I haven't,' replied Betsy.

'We've heard rumours the United Irishmen are going to try and move some of their weapons around the countryside today. Have you heard anything about that?'

'No, I haven't. Why would I?' she replied.

O'Leary studied the contents of the cart closely.

'Perhaps we had better check everything you have.'

He stepped back from the cart.

'Pull over to the side of the road,' he ordered.

Betsy could not believe what she was hearing. She was about to argue when Gina told her to do as she was told.

Lieutenant O'Leary followed them. 'Take everything of this cart,' he said to two soldiers. 'And search it thoroughly. Make sure they're not smuggling any weapons.'

'But,' protested Betsy as she jumped down from the cart. 'Why do they have to do that? I'll be late for the market.'

'Are you making a complaint?' the lieutenant asked.

Betsy didn't reply.

'Good. Now step back.'

The soldiers began to unload the cart, placing each item on the ground after inspecting it. Lieutenant O'Leary watched until the cart was completely empty.

'Well, nothing there,' he muttered before he turned and walked away. 'You can go now,' he called out.

Betsy stared at the lieutenant's back. She wanted to run after him, to confront him and tell him how rude and ignorant he had been. But she knew that was exactly what he wanted her to do. Instead, she turned away and began to reload the cart.

A soldier helped Gina lift a sack of potatoes.

'I'm sorry,' he whispered as they placed the sack into the cart. 'Lieutenant O'Leary can be a right bastard.'

Betsy realised it was the soldier who had been attacked at the farm, Private Carron.

'This is the soldier I was telling you about,' hissed Betsy.

'I'm sorry Betsy's pig attacked you,' whispered Gina. 'She can be very stubborn.'

Private Carron smiled as he lifted a sack of carrots and placed it into the cart.

'It was my own fault. What's your name?'

76

'Gina.'

'That's a nice name.'

'Where are you from?' asked Gina.

'I grew up on a farm in Mayo. I shouldn't have upset the pig. I hope you know we're not all like O'Leary. He shouldn't have shot the piglet. The lieutenant can be a right pain in the arse at times.'

Gina laughed as she placed Betsy's mother's dresses in the cart. 'Thank you,' she whispered.

'My name's Peter by the way. It's very nice to meet you Gina.'

'Thank you, Peter by the way.'

The private winked and smiled at Gina as they continued reloading the cart. They were almost finished when Lieutenant O'Leary came storming over to them.

'Private Carron, what the bloody hell do you think you are doing?'

The private set the jars of honey he was holding in the cart before turning to face Lieutenant O'Leary and quickly standing to attention.

'I was only helping the young ladies, sir. I heard them say they were going to be late for the market.'

Lieutenant O'Leary was livid. 'Get back to your duties Carron, we are not here to help these bloody people.'

As Private Carron marched away Betsy saw him grin at Gina as they climbed back onto the cart.

'Walk on,' she called to Sandy as she flicked the reins.

'I think Private Carron likes you Gina,' said Betsy as they trundled down the road.

Gina smiled at the soldier as they passed him by.

'Yes, he was very nice, wasn't he? Not like his lieutenant at all. He can stop me any time he wants.'

'Gina,' howled Betsy as they both burst out laughing.

When they finally arrived at the marketplace Betsy managed to find a secure spot to leave Sandy and the cart while she went in search of the market manager. Gina left saying she was getting a lift home with someone else and would see her tomorrow.

As Betsy walked through the marketplace she glanced at the extensive variety of products for sale. Bangor held one of the major markets in County Down. That was why she came here. There were stalls selling fresh fruit and vegetables, and others offering a fantastic range of fresh sea food, fish, lobsters, mussels and oysters, freshly caught locally in the Irish sea. In one corner of the market there was a group of stalls selling a variety of home-baked breads, fruit cakes and scones. Several other stalls were bedecked with seasonal flowers and an array of houseplants, shrubs and a display of fruit trees ready to be planted. One section of the marketplace was given over entirely to the sale of a wide range of clothing including shoes, boots, women's coats, dresses, and everyday shirts and trousers for men. A few of the racks displayed expensive dresses, and men's jackets, which their traders claimed to be the latest fashions from London and Paris.

Betsy eventually found the manager in his office at the rear of the market yard.

'Good morning, Thomas,' she said as she entered the small dank room.

Thomas Jamison was a tall, heavily built man, in his late forties with a large oval shaped face that instantly broke into a cheerful smile when he looked up from a paper strewn desk and saw Betsy. Jamison had been managing the market for several years and was considered by most of the traders to be a fair man to deal with. He had a reputation for looking after his regular stall holders and was rumoured to allow those going through tough times to set up their stalls at a reduced rate to help them get back on their feet.

'Well if it isn't the beautiful Betsy Gray,' he said as his smile broadened. 'Am I glad to see you.'

'I was hoping to get here earlier, but I was stopped by the army. I'm looking for a site, but I see most of the good ones are gone.'

'I heard you were having some trouble at an army roadblock on the Gransha Road this morning. What have you been up to then?'

Betsy shook her head. 'It was nothing. There was a Lieutenant O'Leary there who doesn't like me. He was just being stupid.'

'Well, not to worry, you're here now. I've held onto your usual site. I knew you would be along sometime.'

Betsy was surprised. 'Why thank you Thomas, I wasn't expecting you to do that,' she said as she opened her purse. 'Same amount as last time?' she queried.

'Yes, it is… I've just one favour to ask of you,' he said lowering his voice slightly.

'What's that?' said Betsy wondering what was coming.

'Those meat pies you said your mother made, are the best in the marketplace. I wouldn't mind taking a couple of them home with me tonight.'

Betsy smiled at him as she counted out her money and placed it on his desk. 'Don't worry about that, I've brought some with me, I'll keep a couple of them for you. Call over later and pick them up.'

'Great,' said Jamison as he lifted her money. 'There is another thing you need to know. I've heard a rumour there might be some trouble in the town this afternoon.'

'What's that all about?'

'There's going to be a protest march by the United Irishmen. It's all about the arrest of a man called William Orr. I think he comes from around Farranshane, just outside Antrim. Have you heard of him?'

'Yes, I have,' said Betsy. 'He was accused of administrating the United Irishmen's oath to two soldiers.'

'That's him.'

'Well, he's innocent you know. He didn't do it. I heard his counsel was hoping to have the charges against him dropped.'

Jamison shook his head. 'They weren't successful. The judge turned down the application for his trial to be dismissed and sent him back to his prison cell in Carrickfergus. He's due to go on trial soon. People are saying it doesn't look good for him.'

Betsy was genuinely taken aback, 'I was so sure he was going to be released. I've never met him, but my boyfriend knows him, and he says William Orr is a good, God-fearing man, who has never done anything wrong in his life.'

'That's what everyone is saying, but if he is found guilty, he will be hung.'

'That's terrible, my boyfriend said Orr's wife is pregnant with their sixth child. What will happen to them?'

'I don't know,' said Jamison gravely. 'There's a lot of unrest around at the minute. I've heard people say they think the poor man is being victimised and that's one of the reasons why there's going to be a demonstration this afternoon. The protesters are going to demand his immediate release from prison, as if anyone in the government will listen to the likes of us. I've heard the army is going to try and stop them.'

Betsy felt worried. 'But if they do that, there will be a confrontation.'

Jamison nodded. 'That's right, and people will get hurt. I've heard some prison cells in Carrickfergus jail have been cleared out in anticipation of large numbers of new inmates arriving from the march. The authorities are up to something. You would almost think it was them who were planning the protest. I've been advising the rest of the market stallholders that it might be best if they packed up and went home early.'

'What time is the march?'

'I'm not sure but most of the traders are leaving around one o'clock.'

Betsy turned to leave. 'Thanks for the advice.'

She went to get Sandy and the cart and took them over to the site she had been allocated. As she manoeuvred the cart into position, she heard a familiar voice call out from the stall next to her.

'Good morning Betsy.'

'Morning John,' said Betsy.

John Agnew was in his late twenties. He was part of a group of merchants who travelled around the countryside buying fruit and vegetables from several farmers who didn't have the time or resources to go to the markets themselves. John would then resell them at various markets around Counties Down and Antrim. Until a few years ago John had been an active member of the United Irishmen, often attending the same meetings as Betsy, but a disagreement a year ago with another member about admitting Catholics to the Society had resulted in him leaving and joining a new organisation called the Orange Order. John told Betsy he did so because their membership was pledged to defend his civil liberties and his Protestant religion. Betsy had argued with him because she thought it was too narrow an approach to resolving Ireland's problems, but despite their different political views she liked John and always looked forward to their discussions about politics and the current state of the country.

Betsy began setting out her display, making sure to leave a couple of her mother's pies under a piece of linen cloth in the cart for Thomas Jamison to collect later. As soon as she finished a few of the local shoppers began to arrive. Trade was slow to start with, but gradually began to pick up. Around ten o'clock an old friend stopped by. It was Martha Johnston.

'Hello Martha,' said Betsy.

'I called at your house yesterday, but your mother said you had gone to Larne to see Rachel off.'

'Yes, mum told me you called. Billy and I went but it was so sad. Jenny brought her daddy down to say goodbye to Rachel, but when her ship sailed away, he had a heart attack and dropped dead on the quayside.'

'I heard about it this morning. It's going to be dreadful for poor Rachel,' said Martha. 'She won't find out about his heart attack until she arrives in America. When's that?'

'In about two months.'

'Imagine not knowing for all that time that her daddy had died the day she left.'

'It's too awful to think about. Poor Jenny will have to do everything on her own. Thank goodness she has plenty of good neighbours around her.'

Betsy served another customer while Martha waited.

Was everything all right when you called yesterday,' said Betsy when the customer left.

'I came to tell you about William Orr. The application to have his case dismissed has been refused and he has been sent back to prison. David is organising a protest march this afternoon, and I was going to ask if you would like to join us.'

'Of course I will, but I need to find somewhere to leave Sandy and the cart.'

'Don't worry about that, there are stables down by the beach where you can leave him for a couple of hours.'

'Where are these stables?'

'They are called Smiths; they are down at the back of the old castle ruins. We use them all the time when we come to Bangor.'

'I know the place; I've used them before.'

'Good I'll see you on the beach around three o'clock. Everyone is very angry about the way they are treating William Orr. It should be a good turnout. Surely they wouldn't hang an innocent man.'

'They might try to, but we won't let them.'

They were interrupted by another customer asking how much one of the dresses on display cost.

'I'd better deal with this, I'll see you later,' said Betsy turning to her customer.

Around eleven o'clock, John Agnew wandered over to Betsy's stall. 'I've just opened a bottle of fresh Armagh cider; would you like a glass?' he offered.

'Yes please,' she replied picking up a small bundle containing her sandwiches and walked back with him to his stall.

'Thanks,' said Betsy when she sat down and Agnew handed her a glass filled with golden coloured cider.

'How come you were so late this morning?' he asked.

'Oh, it was nothing. I was stopped by the army at one of their security checkpoints. Unfortunately for me it was under the control of a Lieutenant O'Leary who doesn't like me. He ordered his men to remove everything from my cart and search each piece thoroughly.'

'What were they looking for?'

'O'Leary told the soldiers to make sure there were no guns or pikes in the cart.'

'The authorities are starting to panic,' said Agnew. 'They're clamping down all over the place. The United Irishmen have really put the wind up them. I heard a few other traders complaining about being held up at security road blocks this morning. There's something going on. You said Lieutenant O'Leary doesn't like you, why is that?'

'The lieutenant and his soldiers arrived at our farm saying they were looking for a man who they believed was delivering the Northern Star. Apparently, he had been seen in our area the previous night. The soldiers didn't find anyone but during their search one of them was attacked by our pig. When I complained about the damage, the soldier had done to the pigsty O'Leary became angry and shot one of the little piglets. The lieutenant said if I carried on complaining he would shoot all of us.'

Agnew shook his head. 'And you think he was still angry with you when he stopped you this morning?'

'Obviously. Why else would he tell his men to take everything off my cart.'

'You need to be careful Betsy. If the lieutenant finds out about your involvement in the United Irishmen, he will do more than harass you.'

'I know, and I will be careful.'

Agnew looked around to make sure they were alone. 'I've heard the United Irishmen are getting ready to take to the streets soon. Is that right?'

'Are you talking about the protest march this afternoon?'

'So, it's going ahead then?'

'Why not. William Orr is innocent.'

'That's not what I heard,' said Agnew. 'My understanding is that Orr tried to persuade a couple of serving soldiers to join the United Irishmen and made them take the United Irishmen's oath.'

'No, he did not,' said Betsy firmly. 'Orr is innocent. The soldiers he was supposed to have sworn in are government agents. They are telling lies. The real reason why Orr was arrested is because he criticised the government in a couple of articles he wrote for the Northern Star.'

'You should let the courts decide Betsy, we all have to obey the law.'

'But what should we do when the law is behaving badly?'

'That's your opinion Betsy. It's not mine. Be careful. There are people around here who want to destroy this country and will use this march to stir things up.'

Betsy sipped her cider. 'I'm sure there will be marshals on the march making sure everyone behaves themselves. Anyway, why don't you come back and join the Society. You will always be welcome.'

'No, I don't think I can do that Betsy. At least I know where I stand with the Orange Order. The United Irishmen have become too militant. All I want is to be able to celebrate my Protestant religion.'

'But what about Catholic emancipation? You were all for that at one time.'

'That was until I realised what the consequences of doing that would be for this country.'

Betsy shook her head. 'You shouldn't listen to the government's propaganda; they want to stir up the old sectarian hatreds.'

Agnew didn't answer her.

'Don't forget,' added Betsy. 'They're the same politicians who supported the United Irishmen when they were first formed. And then they dropped them when the membership started asking for equal rights for all. We believe everyone should have the right to vote. What's wrong with that?'

'I know things aren't perfect Betsy,' said Agnew. 'I supported William Drennan when he was asking for political reforms in the early days of the United Irishmen, but since his arrest more sinister forces seem to have taken over the leadership.'

'But that's not true,' said Betsy. 'Most of our leaders are either Presbyterian ministers or successful businessmen.'

'I'm only telling you what I heard. Now it looks as though they want to install a Catholic dominated parliament in Dublin. If that happens, Ireland will be ruled from Rome and all Protestants will be hounded out of the country because they don't want us here. Their priests hate us. They call us heathens. They say our souls are condemned to eternal hell. They preach that the only true religion is the Catholic faith and all others are followers of the devil. How can you deal with people like that? Don't forget what happened in 1641, when the Catholics massacred thousands of innocent Protestants.'

Betsy was surprised by his reference to an atrocity that had occurred over one hundred and fifty years ago.

'John, you know there's no chance of that sort of thing happening again.'

'No, I don't,' Agnew replied. 'And that's the problem. Everybody says the United Irishmen are waiting for French troops to land in Ireland so they can join forces with them and throw the English out of Ireland. Is that true?'

'No, and you know it's not. We want Ireland to be ruled by Irishmen and not by people from England. There is a difference. We are not talking about throwing the English out of Ireland.'

Undaunted Agnew continued. 'Well I heard it was, and the last time that happened was in 1688 when King James landed in Kinsale at the head of a French army. He was going to use Ireland as a base to help him regain his throne in England and establish the Catholic faith as the one and only religion in the country. But, the Protestants in Derry closed the castle gates against his army and refused to surrender to him despite thousands of them dying in appalling conditions. It was their sacrifices that gave King William the time he needed to bring his own army to Ireland and defeat King James at the battle of the Boyne in 1690. That victory has allowed Protestants the freedom to celebrate our religion ever since.'

'I know all that,' said Betsy feeling slightly annoyed with John's constant reference back to the past. 'But the political processes that

King William left in place to govern Ireland have become corrupt over the years and they are no longer fair. The politicians in the current Irish government have no interest in improving the rights of ordinary citizens, they are only interested in maintaining the privileges and wealth of its elite members.'

'I disagree,' said Agnew. 'It's the actions of the United Irishmen that are threatening to take away our rights.'

'No, we're not,' said Betsy defiantly. 'We want to build good relationships between people of every religion on this island. We're defending your rights, not threatening them. It's the actions of corrupt ministers in Dublin and London that you should be concerned about.'

'But,' demanded Agnew angrily . 'If you give Catholics the vote in the election of politicians then Ireland will be ruled from Rome. We will become a catholic state. Protestants will become second class citizens in our own country.'

Betsy shook her head vigorously. 'No. No. That will not happen. The Reverend Steel Dickson is adamant we will not replace London rule with a similar elite who are loyal to Rome.'

'I don't know how you are going to do that; you can't even protect innocent Protestant weavers in County Armagh from attacks by the Catholic thugs in the Defenders. More violent clashes like that will only spread throughout the rest of Ireland if the United Irishmen get their way.'

Betsy was adamant in her rejection. 'No, they won't John. And you know that. Can't you see that people like you in the Orange Order are being used by the Irish government to spread ideas that will only divide us. The government always does that when there is a threat to their rule. One day they will turn against you John, and deep in your heart you know you can't trust them.'

'No, I disagree with you. It's the leadership of the United Irishmen you should be worried about. Why don't you come and join us in the Orange Order? We're setting up a woman's section. You could help do that.'

Betsy smiled and shook her head. 'No, I couldn't, I truly believe in the aims of the United Irishmen. We can make a difference, but first we have to liberate Ireland from those corrupt tyrants in Dublin and make sure there are no more illegal persecutions of innocent people like William Orr.'

Agnew smiled at his friend. 'I admire your loyalty Betsy, but please be careful. I heard about a United Irishmen who hid his pike in the thatch on his cottage and when he went to court the judge ordered him to be sent away to join the Royal Navy. And that was not an isolated case Betsy. The courts are ordering prisoners into the army to serve in Russia, and China. They are also sending them to prison camps in New South Wales on the other side of the world. There are a lot of frightened people out there who don't know what is going to happen next and they genuinely fear for their lives. And when people are like that, they become unpredictable. You could get hurt.'

'Thanks John. I will remember that, but I will be fine.'

Agnew glanced over at her stand. 'It looks like you have a customer.'

Betsy's heart sank when she saw Oliver Garfield standing at her stall.

'Could I have some service over here,' Garfield called out to her.

'Thanks for the cider,' said Betsy as she rose and went back to see what Garfield wanted.

'I hope everything you're selling here complies with your rent agreement. If not, you are going to have to give me some payment,' he sneered. 'Where's the boyfriend then?'

Betsy didn't answer him.

Garfield picked up one of the bread rolls Betsy had bought for her mother. 'Have you any honey left?' he asked.

'The roll is not for sale.'

Garfield glared at her. 'I asked for honey.'

Betsy stared back. 'I have none.'

Garfield feigned disappointment. 'But I told you to keep me some,' he pleaded as he bit into the dry roll and walked round to the back of the cart and looked inside.

'Let's see what you have hidden underneath here?' he said lifting the piece of cloth Betsy had placed over the pies for Thomas Jamison.

'Ah, a couple of meat pies,' Garfield exclaimed. 'Sure, they'll do me rightly.'

He tossed the roll and cloth away and bent over the side of the cart and picked up the pies, but when he stood up someone grabbed hold of his shoulder from behind.

'What do you think you're doing?' demanded a deep male voice.

Garfield turned to see the frowning face of Thomas Jamison glaring at him.

Betsy smiled as she said. 'I was keeping them for you.'

Jamison looked down at Garfield's hands. 'Put them back,' he growled.

As Garfield hesitated, he noticed a crowd beginning to gather around them and quickly decided to do as he was told.

'I wasn't going to take them anyway,' he said apologetically as he placed the pies back inside the cart. 'I was only asking Betsy what she had left.'

John Agnew walked over from his stall and glared angrily at Garfield. 'No, you weren't. I saw what you were up to, you were threatening Betsy.'

'I've seen him here before,' someone in the crowd shouted. 'He's always harassing the young girls.'

'Why don't you just clear off,' another member of the crowd shouted at Garfield.

Jamison pulled Garfield closer to him. 'I think it's time you left. And don't let me see you in my marketplace again,' he ordered. 'Did you hear me?'

Garfield was feeling extremely sorry for himself and wished he was somewhere else.

'Yes... yes, I did,' he replied meekly.

Jamison shoved him away. 'Now get out of here.'

'Yeah clear off,' added Agnew. 'We look after our own here.'

Garfield turned and pushed his way through the angry crowd and started running towards the exit.

'Thank you,' said Betsy to Jamison and Agnew. 'He's becoming a bit of a pain. You'd better take your pies Thomas before someone else tries to steal them.'

It was shortly before one o'clock when Betsy began to pack up. There was very little left to put back onto the cart. It had been a good day, perhaps her customers had been aware of the protest march and made sure they finished their shopping early. She went and got Sandy and hitched him onto the cart.

John Agnew was also getting ready to leave.

'Bye,' she called out as she headed towards the exit.

Chapter 8

'See you next week, Betsy,' shouted Jamison when she drove past him at the market gates. A few minutes later she arrived at Smiths stable yard behind the old castle ruins. Betsy had been here before and knew the manager Albert Simms. Albert was an ex-army man and had the distinction of having only one front tooth left in his mouth. He liked to entertain those who would listen with stories about how he lost the rest of his teeth while fighting the Arabs in the Sahara Desert.

'Albert,' Betsy called out, spying the old gentleman as she entered the stables. 'Is it okay if I leave Sandy and the cart here for a couple of hours.'

'Sure,' said the old soldier as he ambled over to her. 'Just pull up over there. I'll sort everything out for you. I suppose you are going to the protest march.'

'Yes I am. Is that alright?'

'Of course, it is Betsy,' replied Albert pointing to a little banner pinned on one of the stable walls. On it he had written, 'Free Orr'.

'If I didn't have to work, I would join you. I was born in this country and I've fought all over the world for it. When they retired me out of the army, I thought I would be coming home to a peaceful land where I could enjoy my retirement. Instead I found a place being run by corrupt and self-centred politicians who couldn't care less about the ordinary folk of Ireland… I have seen the big houses some of these people live in; their women folk prancing around in their fancy clothes when they come in here with their expensive horses and carriages. But it's my tax money, these bastards are spending on having a good time. Look at the old rags I have to wear. They don't care a jot about the likes of you and me… I never met this man William Orr, but from what I have heard about him he sounds all right to me. He is a good Christian man. You go ahead Betsy, and don't be worrying about Sandy. I'll look after him.'

'Thanks Albert,' said Betsy jumping down from the cart and giving the old man a hug. Albert was quite embarrassed. It had been a long time since he had enjoyed the soft embrace of a young woman.

A few moments later Betsy walked onto the sandy beach where many protestors had already started to gather. As she walked through the noisy crowd searching for Martha she listened to people's arguments as to why William Orr should be set free. She eventually spotted Martha standing beside David Johnston and a group of men who were senior leaders of the United Irishmen.

'Good to see you Betsy,' said Johnston standing to one side so that she could join them.

'Hi Betsy,' added Martha as a few of the other men nodded towards her.

'Well it looks like we are going to get a good turnout,' said Johnston gazing around the growing crowd on the beach.

'Is it true Orr's appeal was turned down?' asked one of the men.

'That's what we heard,' said Johnston. 'But his legal team is going to try again. Although they are not very confident. That's why it's very important we let Orr know we all support him.'

'I think the authorities are determined to make an example of him,' said one of the men.

'Sure, everyone knows they want to hang a Presbyterian,' said a voice from behind Betsy which she recognised immediately and turned around to smile at Billy.

'William Orr is an innocent man,' said Martha. 'They wouldn't dare do that.'

'And we're not going to let them,' said Betsy defiantly.

'Free Orr,' shouted Martha as the rest of the crowd around them quickly joined in with one mighty, 'Free Orr.'

Betsy grabbed Billy's hand. 'I'm so pleased you came, I only found out about the march at the market this morning. Is the Reverend Steel Dickson coming?'

'No, unfortunately not, he has to preside at the funeral of one of his congregation. But he fully supports the protest.'

As Billy was speaking Henry Poulter joined them.

'Hello everyone,' he said as a large smile spread across his face. 'I've just been talking to a very special individual who would like to say a few words to you. He's sitting over in Kelly's Tavern.'

'Who is it?' asked Martha.

Poulter shook his head. 'I can't say. He doesn't want anyone to know he is here. But it's very important that you meet him. It's best if you just follow me.'

Some of the men shared inquisitive looks as they followed Poulter across the road to Kelly's Tavern and into a large room at the side of the public bar. Poulter closed the door once everyone was inside and walked over to a man sitting at one of the tables.

'Ladies and gentlemen, I would like to introduce you to Doctor William Drennan. One of the founding fathers of the Society of United Irishmen.'

Betsy was overjoyed. It had been Drennan's ideas that had helped her understand why it was important she dedicate her life to achieving political reform in Ireland. She had studied his political pamphlets and each of the newspaper articles he wrote for the Northern Star and felt as though she knew him personally. When Drennan stood up to shake hands with Poulter she thought he looked very handsome with his brown eyes and dark hair. She also noticed he was wearing a green neckerchief.

'Thank you, Henry,' Drennan said before turning to face everyone else. 'Thank you so much for coming to see me. It is a great privilege to be here.'

'And we're glad to see you Dr Drennan,' said David Johnston shaking his hand. 'Let me introduce you to my wife Martha.'

'Hello,' said Drennan.

'And this is Betsy Gray,' added Poulter. 'A very hard-working member of our Society. We couldn't do without people like her.'

'Hello Betsy,' said Drennan as he shook her hand.

'It's such a great honour to meet you Dr Drennan,' said Betsy. 'You have inspired me and so many people to fight for such a worthwhile cause.'

'Why thank you.'

Poulter carried on introducing the rest of those present.

'Please sit down,' he said when he finished. 'I know meeting Dr Drennan will come as a surprise to you, as it was to me when he contacted me last night and asked if he could join us today. I'm sorry I couldn't tell you earlier, but we could not take the chance of the authorities finding out. With the arrests of our members throughout the island we're all too aware of the need for secrecy. Dr Drennan is going to talk to us about why he feels it is right we take our people onto the streets to protest about the illegal arrest and detention of William Orr.'

Dr William Drennan stood up.

'Thank you. It's a great honour for me to be able to speak to you today. I'm also glad to see some of my old friends from our time together in the Volunteers when we, along with thousands of other Irishmen, swore an oath declaring our loyalty to King George. Some say this means we should accept the rule of the Irish government because this is how the King wants Ireland to be ruled. But I refuse to accept that because everyone of us have God given rights, which must be protected by our government. That's the role of government. But the politicians in Dublin have failed to do that for decades. The Irish government is more interested in pursuing policies that have helped to suppress jobs in farming and manufacturing here, but which have safeguarded jobs of workers in England. They have introduced policies to restrict our beef exports, and others which prevented our wool industry from being developed at the request of the English Parliament. There are many more examples of how their actions have kept the population of Ireland in poverty while helping people in England become richer. Ireland must take control of her own destiny. The Irish Parliament must have legislative independence. When the Irish government disbanded the Volunteers, we formed the Society of United Irishmen to continue our demands for political reform and Catholic emancipation. They are crucial to the future wellbeing of Ireland. The response was to ban the Society and arrest anyone suspected of being in a leadership position. Several people I know were incarcerated for long periods of time and spent many months rotting in a prison cell before the case against them was suddenly dropped by which time the accused were penniless and mentally and physically broken. I have had first-hand experience of this treatment, but the case against me was quashed after a few months. Everyone knows William Orr is no criminal. He is a decent man. He has worked for the good of his community and his family all his life. William Orr is innocent. His only crime is to love the land of his birth, and to speak out about the mistreatment of Catholics and Presbyterians. We must resist all efforts by the Irish government to divide us along sectarian lines. We must stay united. We must Free Orr.'

Everyone in the room stood to applaud.

'Will you address the crowd?' shouted Johnston. 'They must hear your speech.'

Drennan shook his head slightly. 'No. I can't do that. I know if I stood in front of the crowd on the beach and repeated what I have just said to you I would be arrested within days and this time I would be lucky to escape with my life. Thank you for your confidence in my abilities, but I can only speak about this in private where I'm sure I am in the company of trusted ears and hearts. I'm sorry but I must decline your kind offer.'

Henry Poulter shook Drennan's hand. 'Thank you very much Dr Drennan. It's good to know we have Irishmen in our midst who can guide us through these turbulent times.'

'Here, here,' was the cry.

Poulter turned to face everyone. 'Now it's our turn. When you get back start gathering your people together and prepare them for the march. We have a large banner with Free Orr printed on it, this will be at the front. If you could all line up behind the banner and remind everyone that this must be a peaceful protest. We must maintain our dignity throughout. Don't give the authorities any excuse to disrupt us. Do you have any questions?'

'Do you think the army will try to stop us?' asked Betsy.

'Yes… we think they will at some stage, but as long as we keep the march peaceful there is nothing they can do. Make sure you tell everyone not to provoke the soldiers… Are there any more questions?'

No one answered.

'Good let's go,' said Poulter as people began leaving the room.

'It was good to hear Dr Drennan confirm our suspicions that the government is using William Orr as part of their policy to try and weaken us,' said Betsy as she walked back with Billy.

'I agree,' he said. 'He was right to mention sectarianism in Ireland. I've been around Armagh and Tyrone and it's very bad down there. There have been several clashes between Catholic and Protestant weavers. It's all about land rents and the price people can charge for their cloth. The landlords have a lot to answer for. It's them who are stirring the hatred up. Drennan was right, we must stamp it out. A couple of weeks ago some of our members told me they were thinking of leaving the Society because we were letting too many Catholics in, but at the very heart of the United Irishmen is the belief that we are all equal and everybody must be involved in the talks about political reform. If we don't, sectarianism will be allowed to destroy Ireland. I should have tried to change their minds.'

'We will make sure we do that in future.'

'I agree,' said Billy. 'The Reverend Steel Dickson told me recently that we should remember to love our neighbours, and if we kept that thought in our head when we met someone it would influence our attitude towards them.'

Betsy leaned over and kissed him on his cheek. 'I'll always love you Billy Boal,' she said, causing him to smile and blush.

When they reached the beach, they found the stewards from the Gransha area and began helping them organise everyone into lines for the march. Betsy was surprised when George and Robert appeared carrying bundles of flags. Some of them had FREE ORR, or ERIN GO BRAGH, or IRELAND FOREVER printed on them.

'Where did you get them from?' asked Betsy as they began handing them out to the marchers.

'Mr Poulter asked us to hand them out,' replied Robert.

Martha seemed surprised to see Robert. 'What are you doing here?'

'Didn't he tell you, he and George have joined?' said Betsy.

'Joined what?'

'The United Irishmen,' replied Betsy. 'The pair of them did it a few weeks ago.'

Martha looked shocked. 'No, you didn't. Did you tell my Ma?' she asked directing her question to Robert.

'She knows,' he replied coldly before walking away.

Betsy knew there had been difficulties in Martha's family since she decided she was going to marry David Johnston. Her mother had made it quite clear that she was not very pleased with her decision because of the age difference between them. She had been so angry that she stayed away from the wedding in protest. Judging by the way Robert and Martha were talking to each other it didn't look like there had been any change in the relationship between them.

Meanwhile, over at the exit Poulter and Johnston were unfurling a large green banner with FREE ORR embroidered in golden letters on it. Two strong men raised the banner and walked out onto the road as Johnston and Poulter began organising the rest of the protestors into lines behind them. The beach emptied very quickly.

As the marchers walked along the road, they began singing the hymn Onward Christian Soldiers.

Betsy and Billy waved at the spectators lining either side of the street as they applauded and shouted Free Orr, when they passed. There was a feeling of excitement and goodwill amongst the marchers. However, the mood changed quickly when the people at the front of the march turned the corner onto Main Street and saw the army manning a roadblock ahead of them.

'It's a trap,' shouted one of the men carrying the banner.

'Keep going,' ordered Johnston. 'They can't stop us.'

'What about the soldiers?'

'This is a peaceful protest,' shouted Johnston. 'Just keep walking,'

Suddenly some of the marchers began chanting, 'Free Orr.'

The cry was quickly taken up by all the marchers and their pace picked up as they walked towards the waiting soldiers.

'Free Orr…Free Orr.'

As the marchers walked along the Main Street, the soldiers behind the roadblock began jeering and mocking them.

The men carrying the large banner at the front of the march stopped when they reached the roadblock.

An army officer behind the barricade shouted at the protesters. 'This march has been declared illegal. If you do not disperse immediately, you will be arrested.'

Henry Poulter stepped forward. 'This is a peaceful demonstration to protest about the illegal arrest and detention of an innocent man called William Orr. We respectfully ask that you remove your barriers and allow us to continue. We are not here to cause any trouble.'

The officer shook his head and repeated his threat. 'This march has been declared illegal. If you do not order your people to disperse immediately, you and they will be arrested.'

'But sir,' said Poulter. 'We are simply exercising our right to peaceful protest. We are not doing anything illegal.'

A few of the marchers behind him were becoming restless and began shouting obscenities at the army officer. Suddenly, one of the marchers threw a tomato at the officer hitting him in the chest and splashing its contents over his uniform. Another marcher threw a large stone that narrowly missed the officer's head. As more missiles were thrown the officer quickly stepped back from the barricade. At the same time his soldiers reacted to the stone throwing by raising their rifles and pointing them in the direction of the marchers.

Another officer ordered the soldiers to fire a warning shot over the heads of the marchers. There was an almighty explosion, as twenty soldiers fired their rifles. As bullets screamed over the heads of the protestors, panic quickly spread. Several marchers turned around and began running back down Main Street towards the beach. At the same time dozens of soldiers began streaming out from behind the barrier and seized several of the marchers. As the protestors began to scatter Betsy and Billy were split up in the mayhem that followed.

As Betsy ran down the street, she spotted a group of young men being chased into an alleyway by several soldiers armed with batons. To her horror she realised that George and Robert were amongst them. She followed them and saw a couple of soldiers grab hold of George and start kicking and hitting him with their batons. Betsy screamed as she charged and managed to push them away. As she stood over George several men from the march joined them to face the soldiers, who soon lost interest and turned away to run after other protesters.

George struggled to his feet.

'I have to find Robert,' he said. 'Do you know where he is?'

'No, the soldiers have gone after him,' said Betsy as she inspected a red swelling on his face. 'We need to get out of here they will be back soon.'

'But I need to find him,' pleaded George.

As he went to follow the soldiers, he was grabbed by Edward Donnelly one of the men who had helped rescue him. 'You won't be able to save Robert,' he said. 'The soldiers will be back soon with reinforcements. They've already arrested dozens of marchers. It's too late to save your friend. You should try to get yourself and your sister home.'

'Come on George,' pleaded Betsy pulling him after her. 'We have to get away from here.'

George hesitated for a moment before following her. They ran back out onto the Main Street where they saw several fights between soldiers and marchers. They passed an elderly man sitting on the side of the road trying to stem the flow of blood from a severe cut on the back of his head. As they ran down the street Betsy noticed a man standing in a doorway on the other side of the road. Although he was wearing a mask, she thought there was something familiar about him. As they ran past him Betsy saw the man raise a pistol and aim it at the soldiers manning the barricade. She saw a flash from the nozzle of the gun and heard a gunshot. The man shoved the pistol into one of his pockets before running down a nearby alleyway and disappearing.

Betsy and George heard more gunfire behind them when they reached the end of Main Street and didn't stop running until they reached the stables.

'Albert,' Betsy shouted as they ran in through the main entrance.

The old man came out of one of the stalls where he had been brushing down one of his horses. He looked surprised to see them.

'I heard gunfire,' he said. 'What's going on?'

'The soldiers stopped the march at a roadblock on Main Street,' panted Betsy. 'They attacked the marchers with batons and then started shooting at us. We had to run away.'

'It was a trap,' added George. 'They were waiting on us. They've arrested dozens of people.'

'That's what they will do,' said Albert in a matter of fact way. 'I was in the forces for thirty years; I have seen it all before. The core role of the army is to defend the state, and they must have seen your march as a threat. They're not finished yet. They will send the soldiers out to saturate the streets around here and will arrest anyone they suspect of being involved in the march. The best thing you can do is to lie low for an hour or so. The soldiers will eventually have to return to barracks to get something to eat. My advice is that you let things calm down before you try to go home. I've a small room upstairs where you can hide. They will never find you up there. Come with me and I'll show you.'

Betsy and George followed Albert as he climbed a couple of flights of stairs leading to the upper floors of the stables. When they reached the top floor, Albert showed them into a large room filled to bursting with saddles, bridles and other various pieces of horse tack.

'There's a room behind the bridles over there where I sleep sometimes when I have to work late,' he said as he began pushing several leather bridles to one side to reveal a doorway. 'You can stay in there for a while. I'll give you a call when it is safe to come down.'

Betsy opened the door and stepped into a long narrow room that was furnished with a single bed and a small round table with a couple of chairs. On one wall there was a large window that filtered light into the room through dirty glass panes that looked as though they hadn't been cleaned in a long time. The glass was so badly stained that it was almost impossible to look through. Betsy walked over to the window and scraped some of the dirt away until she was able to gaze out on the streets below. She could see small groups of soldiers chasing after some of the marchers.

'Looks like they're still arresting people,' she said when George joined her.

'What do you think will happen to Robert?' asked George, sounding frightened and worried for his friend.

Betsy looked at him. 'I don't know, but it will not be good George. The courts have been sending young men to serve in the army or the navy; some have even been sent to Van Diemen's land on the other side of the world. We won't know what punishment they're going to give him until he appears in court.'

'When do you think that will be?'

'Not very long. It could be in the next couple of days. The law courts can be very quick when they want to be. I'm afraid all we can do is to pray for him and the others who were arrested.'

'Why didn't Johnston stop the march when he saw the soldiers lining the streets. He should have seen it was a trap. The soldiers were just waiting on any excuse to attack us.'

'But it was a peaceful march,' said Betsy firmly. 'Henry Poulter told everyone on the beach to behave and not to react to any provocation.'

'But somebody did.'

'Did you see who threw the tomato and the stones?'

'No, we were near the back of the march. But we could hear the soldiers braying like donkeys. What was all that about?'

'They were mocking us. They were pretending to say Erin go bragh. Our slogan Ireland for ever. I have seen them waving flags with Erin go bray written on them. It was their way of trying to provoke us.'

97

'They were waiting for us Betsy. We should never have gone near that barrier...'

'...Shush,' whispered Betsy when she heard heavy footsteps climbing the staircase.

They both stood still and listened to men's voices and the sound of heavy boots walking on the floorboards in the room next door. The footsteps grew louder. Suddenly they heard a voice outside the door.

'You have a lot of tack hanging up here old man. Where did you say you learnt your trade?'

They heard Albert answer. 'I was in the army for thirty years son. They taught me everything there is to know about looking after horses. I only trained with the best.'

'So, what battles did you fight in?'

'I fought all over the world for the British army. I was captured in Egypt. That's where I lost my teeth.'

The voices were getting louder and clearer. Betsy held her breath when she heard the bridles outside the door being moved.

'What's in there?' asked the voice.

'Nothing friend,' said Albert firmly. 'You don't need to look in there.'

'Check every room,' ordered a voice from the room below.

Betsy looked around her. There was nowhere to hide. She could hear her heart beating loudly as she heard the bridles being pushed to one side.

'You have my word,' she heard Albert say. 'Soldier to soldier, there's nothing in there.'

Betsy waited for her world to collapse. She held onto George's hand as they watched the door handle begin to turn and the door slowly open. They braced themselves as a soldier's head peered into the room.

Betsy recognised him immediately. It was Private Carron.

There was a startled expression on his face when he saw Betsy and George.

'I told you there was nothing in there soldier,' said Albert who was standing behind him.

A voice from the floor below shouted. 'Well private, have you found anything?'

Private Carron nodded his head at Betsy. 'Nothing here sergeant,' he shouted and slowly closed the door. 'All clear up here.'

Betsy and George breathed a sigh of relief. They could hear Albert and Private Carron walking back down the stairs. They tried to follow another muffled conversation taking place in the room below, but it was too far away for Betsy to make out what was being said. After a few moments there was silence.

Betsy and George were still shaking from their experience when they heard footsteps coming back up the stairs. A few moments later the door was opened by Albert. He stood in the open doorway with a big broad smile on his face.

'Thank goodness it's you Albert,' said Betsy.

Albert walked into the room. 'I knew that soldier was a good one as soon as I met him,' he said.

'I thought we were done for. I was convinced I was on my way to Botany Bay.'

'No... I knew he wouldn't let me down,' said Albert. 'We soldiers stick together. We know when to be tough and when to show mercy. Give it another fifteen minutes and then I think it will be safe for you to come down and go home. I'll give you a call.'

Albert went over and studied the swelling on George's eye. 'You'll need to put something on that,' he added.

'I'll be fine,' mumbled George.

Betsy and George stayed in the room for another hour before Albert came back to tell them it was safe to go home. Down in the yard he had already harnessed Sandy to the cart.

'The soldier told me there would be checkpoints on the main roads out of the town. If they stop you, you might have some explaining to do when they see that bruise on his eye. The soldier said the coast road, should be clear. It might take you a bit longer going that way but at least you'll be safe.'

Betsy hugged Albert close to her. 'Thank you for everything. You saved our lives. If you hadn't looked after us, we would be in Carrickfergus jail by now awaiting deportation.'

Betsy kissed the old man on the cheek.

Albert coughed and stepped back. 'Now... now, young lady it was nothing. My good mother always taught me that a little kindness was an easy load to share with someone else. Good luck, you take care now.'

Albert walked into the nearby stall and began grooming one of his horses.

Betsy could hear him coughing as she climbed up beside George on the cart and told Sandy to walk on. Once out on the street Betsy was glad to join several other people on their horses and carts, all heading out of Bangor and onto the shore road. There were still small groups of soldiers milling around the streets, but thankfully none of them gave her or George a second glance.

After a while Betsy noticed that George was sobbing. 'What's wrong?' she asked.

George shook his head and looked away.

'Come on George, what is it?'

'I was just thinking about Robert. What's his mother going to do if he is sent away? She needed his wages.'

'Maybe the courts will be lenient with him, after all he didn't do anything.'

'The army arrested him because he took part in a protest march that was organised by the United Irishmen. The soldiers were waiting to arrest us. Of course, they'll send him away.'

Betsy clasped his hand. 'Let's wait and see.'

Darkness was falling when they reached the small fishing village at Groomsport where they turned inland on the final part of their journey. George lit the side lamps as they trundled along. After a few miles they heard hoofbeats coming towards them in the dark. As they came closer, they suddenly heard a man call out.

'Betsy... Betsy.'

She felt her heart would explode as she recognised Billy's voice.

'Thank God I found you,' he called out as he pulled up alongside them.

Betsy stopped the cart and climbed down as Billy dismounted. They quickly embraced.

'I've been going out of my mind with worry since I lost you on Main Street,' he said as he held her close to him. 'I thought the soldiers had arrested you.'

'They nearly did,' said Betsy as all the emotions she had been holding back burst forth and she started to sob. 'It all happened so quickly. When I saw soldiers chasing George into an alleyway I ran after them. I'm sorry you were worried.'

'Never mind,' whispered Billy. 'You're safe now. How did you get out of Bangor?'

'We hid in the stables where I left Sandy,' said Betsy. 'The manager is an old ex-soldier called Albert. He was wonderful. The soldiers came and searched the stables. One of them found us hiding in the top room but he didn't give us away. He and Albert saved our lives.'

'Have you heard how many people were arrested?' asked George from his seat on the cart.

'We're not sure, but we think it's around seventy.'

'What about Martha, did she get away?' asked Betsy.

'Yes, she did. She and David are safe and well. When the soldiers charged us, we managed to escape down an alleyway. I thought you were running behind me but when I looked around you weren't there.'

'I'm sorry,' said Betsy.

'What'll happen to the people they arrested?' asked George.

'Special courts are being held in Carrickfergus to sentence them. We've heard it's likely the men will be forced to join the navy or the army, and the women will be sent to Van Diemen's land.'

'For how long?'

'We don't know. We have to wait and see.'

'Is there nothing we can do?' pleaded George.

Billy shook his head. 'I'm afraid not.'

It was dark when they finally arrived back at the farm. Betsy's mother and some of their neighbours came rushing out to greet them.

George jumped down from the cart and hugged his mother.

'Praise be to God, you're safe,' she said.

While her neighbours took the horse and cart into the stables Betsy and George went inside the house where there were more people waiting to see them.

'Thank you so much,' said Betsy when she recognised some of the men who had helped her rescue George from the soldiers in the alleyway. 'If you hadn't been there, I don't know what would have happened to us.'

'It was nothing,' said Edward Donnelly. 'We're just pleased we were able to help.'

'Does anyone know what happened to Robert Madison?' asked George urgently. 'Has anyone seen him?'

Donnelly shook his head and looked around the room. No one said anything.

'We don't know what happened to him. The last time I saw him the soldiers were chasing you both.'

'Do you think he got away?' asked George urgently.

'I don't know,' said Donnelly sadly. 'When we were trying to get out of the town, we saw the soldiers marching a large crowd of people they had arrested towards their barracks. There must have been about thirty people. Someone said they were using other places to keep the prisoners in. They must have arrested a lot of the marchers.'

'They did,' added Billy. 'We think the number is about seventy.'

There were gasps of horror.

'We should never have walked up Main Street,' said Donnelly angrily. 'Once we reached the barrier we were surrounded by soldiers. It was like walking into a trap.'

'Eddie is right,' someone shouted. 'We should have stopped the march at the bottom of the road as soon as we saw the roadblock. More people would have been able to escape when the soldiers charged.'

'It was a trap,' said someone else.

'We heard several gunshots as we were running towards the stables,' said Betsy. 'Was anyone hurt?'

'Three marchers were taken to hospital,' replied Ferguson. 'I heard their wounds aren't serious.'

'Were any soldiers shot?'

'I don't think so. Why do you ask?'

'When we were running down Main Street, I saw a gunman,' said Betsy. 'He was shooting at the soldiers standing at the barrier.'

'None of our people were armed,' said Donnelly.

'Betsy's right,' said Joe Blair, one of her neighbours. 'I saw a gunman as well.'

'Me too,' added another voice.

Everyone looked towards Billy. He shook his head.

'I don't know who the gunmen were. I distinctly heard the Reverend Steel Dickson telling everyone it was to be a peaceful protest. Are you sure the gunmen were United Irishmen?'

'I don't think they were,' said Blair. 'I saw one of them talking to the soldiers when we were trying to get away. They seemed to know him; it was like they were having a friendly chat.'

'What did the man look like?' asked Billy.

Blair concentrated for a few moments. 'He was about your height. He was wearing a broad brimmed hat with a green band tied around it. I suppose that was to indicate he was one of us. He had a light brown jacket... but the most distinctive feature about him was the blue waistcoat, that he was wearing.'

'There was a man at our house a few days ago wearing a brand-new blue waist coat,' said Betsy.

'Who was that?'

'Oliver Garfield. He said his friend sent it to him from London.'

'Is he a member of the United Irishmen?' asked Donnelly.

'Who... Garfield, the rent collector?'

'Yes him. Is he a member?'

'No, I don't think so.'

Joe Blair raised his hand. 'Come to think of it, the man I saw firing a pistol at the troops was also wearing a blue waistcoat.'

'But, why would Garfield be shooting at the army?' queried Betsy.

'I don't know,' said Billy.

'We need to have a chat with this Oliver Garfield,' said Donnelly. 'He has some explaining to do.'

Throughout the night more worried neighbours arrived at Betsy's farm seeking information about their friends and family members who had taken part in the protest march. While everyone was sharing their stories, Betsy heard a gentle tapping at the front door. A hush descended on the room as she opened it to find several people standing outside. As candlelight from the farmhouse fell on their faces, Betsy quickly recognised some of the marchers who had been reported as being arrested.

'Come in,' she said quickly, ushering everyone inside.

There was an air of excitement and relief as worried relatives and friends spotted their loved ones and ran over to embrace them. But as George watched the returning marchers his heart sank when he realised Robert wasn't among them. Betsy saw the sad look on his face and went over to comfort him.

'Robert's not among them,' he sobbed. 'They must still have him.'

Betsy put her arms around him. 'Don't worry,' she whispered. 'It's still early; he will be okay.'

As the excitement began to settle, Edward Donnelly asked one of the new arrivals what had happened to them. Up until then, most people's stories had been about running from the soldiers and hiding until it was safe to get away. But when eighteen-year-old Thomas Sloane stood up to speak, his story was different.

'There was a time this afternoon when I didn't think I would see any of my family again. I was convinced I was going to be sent to prison or Botany Bay for ever…'

Brice Killen, another eighteen-year-old, interrupted him. 'Tommy, tell them how we were saved by Richard,' he called out.

Sloane raised his hand in recognition of his friend's intervention. 'Brice is right, everyone should know what Richard McClure did for us today. It was his bravery that saved us. But my words would not be good enough to describe everything Richard did and the gratitude we feel towards him. I think it would be better if you heard the story from the hero himself.'

Betsy noticed the embarrassed look on Richard McClure's face. After all it is not often your boss's son praises you in front of your peers.

'Tell us what you did Richard?' she asked.

'Yes, you must tell us,' encouraged Billy.

Betsy's mother reached over and gave McClure a glass of water. 'Here son, have a drink of this and tell us in your own time what happened tonight.'

A nervous and awkward looking McClure accepted the glass and took a couple of anxious sips before setting it on the table. 'I… I um…. I was on the march this afternoon, I wanted to show my support for William Orr. I think the government was wrong to arrest him. They should release him immediately… I was near the front of the march when the soldiers attacked. I ran into an alley to escape and kept running until I found myself up against a locked gate. For a minute I thought that was the end for me, but I managed to climb up it and, as I was about to jump down, I saw more soldiers shouting at me on the other side. The only thing I could do was to keep climbing. And that's what I did. I climbed onto the roof of the house

104

next to the gate and kept running across the rooftops until I found somewhere to hide. I was able to watch the soldiers on the streets below. I could see them running after the marchers. I saw them grab hold of Thomas and a couple of other people and march them off. I followed and saw the soldiers push them into an old building at the back of Main Street. Two soldiers were left to stand guard at the door into the building while the others went to round up more marchers. My first thought was to get Thomas out of there, and so I managed to climb onto the roof of the building without the soldiers seeing me. I prised open a skylight and dropped down into a room which I thought must be above the one where Thomas was being held. When I looked out a window overlooking the front of the building, I saw the soldiers coming back with more prisoners. I waited and heard them pushing the new prisoners into the room below me. When the soldiers left, I began levering up the floorboards and cut a hole in the ceiling of the room below...'

Brice Killen interrupted him. '...I was in that room thinking I'd never be seeing my family again when I heard a noise coming from above. I looked up and couldn't believe what I was seeing. There was a knife cutting a hole in the ceiling. I thought God had sent an angel to save us. And when I saw Richard poke his head through the hole and say he was going to get us out, I couldn't believe my luck.'

'Neither could I,' said Sloan. 'You should've seen the look on everyone's face when we heard Richard's voice. I think we all thought we were dreaming until we realised, he really was there, and going to help us. One of the prisoners was a Belfast man called Danny McCurdy, a big muscular man. He was able to lift each one of us up to the hole in the ceiling and then Richard pulled us up into the room he was in.'

'Danny was the last man left,' said Killen. 'We weren't going to leave him. We didn't know how we were going to do it, but we were determined to get him out. It was tough and took four of us to pull him up through that hole. I don't know how the sentries didn't hear us.'

McClure continued his story. 'Once we managed to lift Danny out, we climbed through the skylight onto the roof. I took everybody over the rooftops to where I knew we would be able to climb down. That's when we split up.'

Sloan picked up the story. 'It was very dangerous on the streets. The soldiers were everywhere, but we managed to slip past them,' he said. 'When we reached the fields on the edge of the town we just kept running until we arrived here.'

'Have the soldiers got your names and addresses?' asked Donnelly.

'That's a good question,' said Betsy. 'When the soldiers arrested you, did they ask you for your name and address?'

'No, they didn't say anything to me,' said Sloan.

'I heard one of the officers say they were going to process us later,' said Killen.

'So, did anyone give their details to the soldiers?' asked Billy.

'No, none of us were asked,' replied Sloane checking around to make sure he was right.

'How many got away?' asked Betsy.

'Richard pulled ten people through that hole,' said Killen. 'Four from here, the rest were from Belfast.'

'But there's only three of you here, who was the fourth person?' asked George.

'Robert Madison,' replied Killen. 'He wanted to go straight home to tell his mother he's safe.'

George breathed a sigh of relief. 'Thank God,' he whispered as Betsy squeezed his hand and smiled at him. 'I told you Robert would be alright.'

'I think we all owe Richard a big thank you,' said Billy as he began to clap his hands.

'Well done Richard,' shouted everyone as they joined in to applaud his bravery.

When the applause stopped Billy said. 'It's late, I suggest we all go home and try to get some sleep, the soldiers won't come looking for you tonight. Thanks to Richard you're still freemen.'

The room quickly emptied as everyone left to walk home. Billy was the last to leave.

'I'll call in when I can Betsy, but I think we need to lie low for a while, at least until the dust settles on this. I'll be seeing Reverend Steel Dickson over the next couple of days, I'll tell him about Richard and Garfield and that several people thought the march was a trap to arrest our members.'

'I agree with them. We need to find out what's going on,' said Betsy as she watched him climb on his horse. 'If they're right it could mean we've a traitor in our midst.'

Chapter 9

Next morning, while Betsy was in the dairy making butter for the Bangor market, she heard someone's horse trotting down the farm lane and stop in the yard. She looked out and saw Martha Johnston dismounting from her horse.

'Hi Martha,' she called out. 'I'm over here.'

A few moments later Martha joined her. 'Good morning Betsy, I just wanted to make sure you were alright. I was going to call last night, but David said it was too dangerous to go out. We could hear the soldiers calling out to each other as they searched through our fields for people who fled after the march.'

'Do you know if they caught anyone?'

'No, at least not on our land as far as I know.'

'How did you and David get home yesterday?'

'With great difficulty,' said Martha. 'When the soldiers rushed out from behind their barricade and began attacking the marchers everything seemed to go crazy, and when I saw them arresting some of the demonstrators, I didn't know what to do. I was frozen to the spot until David grabbed hold of my hand and dragged me down Paupers Lane and into McCaffery's pub. We hid in there for about an hour with dozens of people who had been on the march, and then David went out to make sure the soldiers had gone. We managed to collect our pony and trap and rode straight home. What about you?'

Betsy stopped churning the butter mix and wiped her hands with a piece of linen cloth. 'When the soldiers charged, I ran down the street, and when I saw some of them chasing our George and your Robert into an alleyway I ran after them. The soldiers were beating George when I arrived but thank goodness Edward Donnelly and a few of our neighbours had followed me. They dragged the soldiers off George and scared them away. George wanted to try and find Robert, but it was too dangerous. I managed to get him to go with me to the stables where Albert showed us where to hide. We stayed there until it was safe to come home.'

'What about our Robert did you see him?'

'The soldiers arrested him.'

'Oh my God,' said Martha. 'Is he in prison?'

'No,' said Betsy realising she had been a bit careless with her words. 'Don't worry he's safe and back at home with your mother.'

Martha closed her eyes briefly. 'Thank God. If anything, ever happened to him it would kill my mother... But you said he'd been arrested.'

'He was, for a brief while, but he was saved,' Betsy assured her. 'Did you know we have a hero in our village?'

'No, who are you talking about?'

'Do you know a young farmhand called Richard McClure?'

'No, I don't.'

'He works on the Sloane farm. Richard has been a member of the United Irishmen for about three years. Last night he managed to rescue Robert and nine other marchers the soldiers had been holding in an old building just off Main Street.'

'How did he do that?'

'Richard had been on the march. When the soldiers attacked, he climbed onto the roof tops to escape. He saw Robert and the others being put into a temporary prison after they were arrested. He climbed onto the roof of the building and broke in through a skylight window and was able to drop into the room above where they were being held. He cut a hole in the ceiling of the room they were in and pulled them all up through it. He managed to free all ten prisoners. He's a hero.'

'But the soldiers must have their names and addresses. They'll come looking for him. He'll have to leave the country.'

Betsy shook her head. 'No, he won't Martha. The soldiers hadn't taken his name, nor of any of the other prisoners by that stage.'

'So, do you think he'll be safe?'

'Yes. Robert will get away with it. I don't think there'll be any comeback.'

Martha sat down and sighed with relief. 'Thank goodness. Do you know that my mother is still angry with me for marrying David? She thinks he's too old for me. I was hoping she might soften her attitude when she saw how kind he was. But that hasn't happened yet. It's her loss. Anyway, I need to see this Richard McClure to give him some money and thank him for what he did.'

'I'm sure he would appreciate the money but unfortunately we'll never be able to thank him in public in case the authorities find out. They would hang him for what he did.'

'I heard the courts will be very busy. We had a commercial traveller call to see David at our farm this morning, and he was saying he heard over eighty people were arrested at yesterday's march. He said most of them would be charged with unlawful assembly and disorderly conduct.'

'Did he say what sort of sentences the courts will be handing out?' asked Betsy.

'No, he didn't, but David thinks most of them will be deported to Australia. We won't know what happened to any of them until later today. The traveller also said he heard that several houses had been set on fire during the riots.'

'I didn't see any fires. Did you?'

'No, I didn't.'

'Did he say where?'

'No, he didn't, but he did say there's a rumour going around that there's going to be a curfew in north Down from sunset to sunrise, and anybody found outside their house during these times will be sent to prison or deported. David thinks it will only be a temporary arrangement until things settle down.'

'But the march was peaceful. It was the soldiers who attacked us. We can't do anything about that. What does David mean when things are back to normal?'

Martha looked bemused by her question. 'I don't know.'

'Did you hear that Oliver Garfield was seen shooting at the soldiers,' said Betsy.

Martha was astounded. 'No, why on earth would he be doing that?'

'That's the question everybody was asking last night. Some thought he might be working for the government, so that they would have an excuse to go after the United Irishmen.'

'And is he?'

'We don't know yet, some of the men are looking for him.'

'He collects the rents from some of our tenants for David. I don't like him. There's something creepy about him.'

'I know, I feel the same way,' said Betsy without elaborating.

'I wouldn't like to be in his shoes when they catch him. But at least you are safe Betsy, that was the main reason I called... There is something else, David asked me to find out if the company George works for is involved in renovating houses?'

'I think they are. George was telling me about work he was doing on a house over in Donaghadee last week. Why do you ask?'

'Ever since David's arrest he has become very restless and edgy. He hasn't been sleeping well, and now he's saying we should spend any money we have on living for today instead of saving for a rainy day. He has decided he wants to convert the farmhouse into a two-storey building and put a slate roof on. I think poor David was traumatised by the ease with which the soldiers were able to set fire to our thatched roof. Do you think George's firm would do that sort of work?'

'I'm not sure; you should go over and ask them yourself. Daniel Torrance is the man in charge. He's the one you need to talk to. I've heard George say he does all the planning for the jobs the company takes on.'

'Thanks,' said Martha as she stood up. 'I'd better go. I'll call in and see Torrance on my way over to the Ballycopeland Windmill. I have to pay the miller for some work he did for David. Bye, see you later.'

'Bye,' replied Betsy as she went back to churning her butter.

Over the next few days rumours began spreading about what happened to some of the people who had been arrested, but it wasn't until Sunday morning when Betsy went to church that she heard the full extent of the punishment meted out by the courts. Martha had been right. Most of the prisoners were to be exiled to Australia for life. Several other young men were ordered to serve in the Royal Navy or the Army and were sent away immediately.

The minister also announced that the Irish government had introduced a curfew from sunset to sunrise claiming it was necessary to reduce the tension in the community that had been created by the Bangor march.

While Betsy was at the church Henry Poulter told her they had been searching for Oliver Garfield to ask him about his activities during the march, but they couldn't find him. Betsy heard from another friend that Garfield had fled to London.

Over the next few weeks, as autumn began to turn to winter and daylight hours became shorter, the curfew was gradually lifted as tensions receded allowing daily life to return to normal.

Although the United Irishmen continued to meet in the Gransha church hall, Betsy noticed the number of members attending was gradually falling. When she asked some of them why they thought people were staying away they told her it was because no one could see the need to prepare for an uprising that was never going to happen.

All of that changed one day in early December. It had been a normal day on the farm. Betsy was setting the table for the family's evening meal when her mother arrived home in a very happy mood.

'What are you so pleased about?' Betsy asked.

'I've heard some very interesting news.'

'What's that?'

'They say a French fleet with fifty thousand soldiers on board will be here by Christmas,' said her mother casually as she brushed snow from her overcoat and hung it up near the fire to dry.

'Oh yes I've heard that one before,' said Betsy as she carried on laying the table. Reports of an imminent landing by a French invasion fleet were very common. A few months ago, the gossip had even been about a Dutch fleet that was on its way and would be landing soon. But nothing ever came of it.

'So, who told you that?' she asked setting the knives and forks out.

Her mother replied coyly. 'I have my contacts. Wait and see. This is not a rumour, Betsy. The French are coming. Soon all of this mess will be sorted out. The British will have to negotiate, and we will finally get a government that works for the Irish people.'

Betsy nodded her head. She still did not believe her mother and continued setting the table. Nevertheless, something in the back of her mind kept asking, but what if it was true?

During their meal Betsy began questioning her mother about where she got her information from. But she refused to divulge her source, simply repeating that it was true. Betsy still wasn't sure whether to believe her or not.

Later that night when Billy arrived, she asked him if he had heard anything about a French fleet that was supposed to be on its way to Ireland.

'Who told you that?' said Billy, taken aback.

Judging by his reaction Betsy knew instantly there was some truth in what her mother had been saying.

'My Mammy,' she answered casually.

'But… who told her?'

'I don't know, she won't tell me. Well is it true?'

Billy shook his head in amazement.

'Yes, it is,' he eventually said, wondering how the news had leaked out. He had been told a few hours ago that it was top secret. 'Reverend Steel Dickson told me that Wolfe Tone has been in Paris for the last few months trying to get help from the French government and apparently, they have agreed to send a fleet of ships with thousands of soldiers and weapons on board. They'll be here around Christmas time.'

Betsy felt excited. 'Where are they going to land?'

'I don't know,' replied Billy shaking his head. 'Reverend Steel Dickson has to go to an executive meeting in Dublin tomorrow along with other leaders from all over Ireland, maybe we'll find out then.'

'Did he say how many soldiers were coming?'

'No, he didn't have that sort of detail… I can't stay long tonight. I have to go to Henry Poulter's farm and give him some messages from Reverend Steel Dickson about what he wants the Down leadership to do while he is away.'

Billy held Betsy in his arms and kissed her. 'This is the news we have been waiting years for. Soon we will be able to govern ourselves. I'm going to Dublin with Reverend Steel Dickson tomorrow and will be away for a couple of days. If anyone asks you where I am, tell them you don't know. Our trip is top secret.'

'I promise,' said Betsy.

When Billy left Betsy went to her bedroom and lay on the bed. For the first time in many months she felt a sense of relief and a growing optimism that the long years of expectation and fear were finally coming to an end. As she fell asleep Betsy's mind was full of thoughts about how wonderful the future was going to be.

Over the next few days, everyone Betsy met was talking about the French fleet. She was amazed at how people were able to describe how many ships were coming and the number of soldiers each ship would be carrying. They would also describe the different types of cannons and the numbers of muskets and pistols they would be bringing ashore with them. The only uncertainty seemed to be the actual location as to where and when the fleet would land.

There were daily sightings of French ships arriving in various harbours, loughs and beaches the length and breadth of Ireland, confusing not only the members of the United Irishmen, but those in charge of the British armed forces. Each rumour helped to create a general air of despondency within the Irish government as they realised the full extent of the threat facing them.

Government spies were busy reporting back to their masters on how news of the French fleet's imminent arrival was raising morale within the United Irishmen and that their leadership was telling the members to be ready to take up arms at a moment's notice.

Chapter 10

As Christmas day arrived there was still no word of the French fleet landing, and doubt was beginning to spread throughout the membership of the United Irishmen. It was a couple of days into January and the new year of 1797, before Reverend Steel Dickson was able to organise a meeting in the nearby town of Saintfield to explain what had happened.

Betsy was sitting beside Billy at the back of the Presbyterian church hall when the Reverend Thomas Ledlie Birch introduced the meeting.

'My friends,' he began rather gravely. 'A few weeks ago, our spirits were raised when we heard the news that the French government was sending large numbers of French troops and weapons here to help us bring about the political reforms we so desperately need in Ireland. We have called this meeting tonight to explain what happened to that fleet. I'll hand you over to the Reverend Steel Dickson.'

Reverend Steel Dickson walked slowly to the podium. He had just come back from Dublin where he had spent many days working long into the night trying to find out what was happening with the French Fleet, whilst at the same time making sure the United Irishmen under his command in County Down were fully prepared for battle. He looked tired and weary.

'Thank you all for coming,' he said quietly as he shuffled the papers in front of him. 'Much has been said about the failure of a French fleet to land here last month. Here are the facts as far as I know them. On Thursday, the 15th of December 1796 a French fleet, consisting of forty-five ships left the French port of Brest bound for Bantry Bay on the shores of Ireland. Onboard the ships were twenty-thousand French soldiers and extra muskets and cannons that were to be distributed amongst the United Irishmen. A week later, on the morning of Thursday, 22nd December, a few of the ships sailed into Bantry Bay, where they dropped anchor, but before disembarking they decided to wait on the ship carrying their leader General Hoche to arrive. Unfortunately, the General's ship had been blown off course and was lost, somewhere in the Atlantic Ocean. Over the next couple of days while the ships waited in Bantry Bay they found themselves in the middle of one of the worst storms the area has ever experienced in over one hundred years. After battling severe weather conditions for several days, what was left of the fleet was forced to abandon the mission and return to France.'

There was a hushed silence as the news sunk in. After a few moments the noise levels started to increase as members of the audience began discussing the implications of what had happened to the fleet.

'What about the uprising?' someone called out.

'What can we do now?' someone else shouted as a sense of unrest began to spread throughout the audience.

'There's nothing we can do,' came a reply.

'Does that mean it's all over?' a young man shouted.

Betsy looked around her at the people arguing with each other. Some were becoming quite agitated and angry. One individual wanted to call it a day, another said it was futile to carry on. She looked towards the stage for some guidance, but even the leadership were arguing amongst themselves about what to do next and seemed to be just as confused as everyone else.

'We must not give up,' said Betsy loudly.

But no one took any notice, her voice drowned in the confusion of noise as everyone in the hall put forward their own point of view.

'We must not give up,' shouted Betsy.

Some of the people sitting in the pews closest to her stopped talking and turned around.

'We must not give up,' Betsy shouted even louder as everyone else in the hall stopped talking and turned towards her.

'The French fleet was not defeated in battle by the British navy. They were forced back by the worst storm in one hundred years ... But the good news is they will return. And when they do, whether it's in the Springtime, or during the Summer months, we must be ready to fight... The membership of the United Irishmen is stronger than ever before. We have more arms than ever before. We are better trained than ever before... I heard someone ask, what can we do? I say, we go back to our members and tell them our struggle for freedom is not over. It's only just beginning. Tell them our enemies will have been shaken to their very core by the willingness of the French army and navy to come to our aid. Tell them, our friends who serve in the Yeomanry and Militia have not deserted us. Tell them they still stand with us. I say we should go back to our meetings and begin recruiting as many new people as we can. Start training them in the skills of warfare, so that the next time the French return, we are better organised and better prepared to join them in the fight for our freedom. Tell them our day is coming.'

There was a hush as Betsy finished. At the front of the hall a young woman stood up. 'Here, here,' she shouted and began applauding.

Others quickly followed her, and soon everyone was on their feet applauding and shouting their approval.

'Well done Betsy,' said Billy. 'You're so right. Our fight must go on.'

Betsy gazed around the hall and up at the stage where Reverend Steel Dickson and his leadership team were on their feet applauding her speech.

'Well done, Betsy,' Reverend Steel Dickson called out to her. 'Well done.'

As the applause began to subside Reverend Steel Dickson raised his hands. 'You all know what you have to do,' he called out. 'Betsy Gray has shown us the way. Our struggle for political reform goes on. We have not lost heart. We knew there would be dark days along the way, but now we can begin to see a glint of sunlight coming from over the horizon. Go back to your members and tell them the fight for freedom goes on.'

The Reverend Steel Dickson closed the meeting with the Lord's prayer before wishing everyone a safe journey home.

'I didn't know you were such a natural speaker,' said Billy to Betsy as they walked out of the church.

'Neither did I,' she confessed feeling slightly embarrassed at everyone's reaction. 'It was just a spur of the moment decision. I could sense some of the people in the audience were becoming disheartened with all the bad news and I felt compelled to say something. I believe we have so many good things going for us that it's only right we carry on.'

'You never cease to amaze me Betsy Gray,' Billy whispered as he pulled her close to him and kissed her.

Chapter 11

Betsy had been right when she told her audience in Saintfield that the Irish and British governments would have been stunned by the news of the arrival of a French fleet in Bantry Bay. A few days later Viscount Castlereagh organised a meeting in Dublin with his chief political and military advisors to discuss their reaction to the aborted invasion.

Castlereagh opened the meeting. 'A French assault force of forty-five ships recently anchored in Bantry Bay. They were prevented from landing their soldiers and thousands of extra rifles and cannons they had on board, by a severe storm which eventually forced every one of the ships to weigh anchor and return to France. We were lucky this time gentlemen, but unless we eliminate the threat to our internal security by the United Irishmen, we will not be so fortunate when they return.'

'If they come back, the navy will destroy them at sea,' sneered one of the army colonels. 'And if that doesn't work our soldiers will crush them as soon as they set foot on Irish soil. The French soldiers are no match for the British army.'

It was obvious by the scathing look on Castlereagh's face that he did not agree with the colonel's remarks as he stared at him for a few moments before continuing.

'I was in Bantry Bay when the French fleet arrived,' said Castlereagh coldly. 'I didn't have enough men with me to guarantee a victory if the French soldiers had been able to disembark, and that was because we had to keep thousands of our best trained soldiers in their barracks hundreds of miles away in Ulster in case the United Irishmen up there decided to take advantage of the French invasion and start their revolution.'

'But I thought the United Irishmen were a spent force,' said the colonel.

Castlereagh shook his head. 'I'm afraid you're wrong in your assumptions, sir. They're not a spent force as you suggest, and there is no doubt the arrival of French ships in Bantry Bay has helped to raise their morale. They're still recruiting. I have seen reports of hundreds of new members joining their ranks every day. The leadership of the United Irishmen in Ulster recently signed a pact with the Catholic Defenders, which means they will have a combined force in excess of one hundred thousand armed men in that province alone. I saw with my own eyes what happened in France when the rabble took control of the revolution. Innocent blood flowed freely on the streets of Paris, and unless we change our attitude towards the United Irishmen the same bloodletting will happen here. None of us will be safe. We will be slaughtered. Our homes will be destroyed. Our families thrown onto the streets to live in poverty.'

'So, what are you proposing to do?' asked the colonel.

Castlereagh turned to face him. 'Our priority must be to destroy the United Irishmen in Ulster. They're strongest in counties Antrim and Down. We'll disarm them and remove their command structure. We must break their will to fight.'

'How are you proposing to do that?' asked one of the officials. 'We are doing as much as we can. Our prisons are full to the brim, and our courts can't cope with any more trials. We simply don't have enough magistrates.'

'I agree,' added the colonel. 'I don't think the Ulster fraction of the United Irishmen will take to the streets to engage with our troops until the French return, but by then it will be too late to do anything. I was hoping this case against William Orr would provoke a reaction from them, but even that seems to have died a death. What is happening there?'

'It all became very complicated,' replied one of the officials. 'It was over the legal case against Orr. Our original plan was to charge him with High Treason, but we needed to have at least two witnesses who were prepared to testify against him. In Orr's case there was a problem with the evidence of one of the witnesses and so we had to change what we were doing. We are preparing a new charge against Orr. This time he will be charged under the Insurrection Act which means we don't need two witnesses to testify against him, one will be sufficient. Orr will be found guilty and will be hung. Hopefully then you will have your uprising, but just in case his hanging doesn't bring the United Irishmen out onto the streets we will be introducing several other measures which we believe will reduce their willingness and capacity to fight.'

'And what are these new measures?' demanded the colonel.

'Perhaps we should ask General Lake to describe them to you,' said Castlereagh.

General Lake had been sitting quietly listening to the conversations. He cleared his throat and began to speak.

'In a few weeks' time, in March to be more precise, we will be introducing Martial law in Ulster. The legislation will give our soldiers the right to act as judge and jury with any suspects they arrest. My officers will be allowed to use whatever force they think is necessary to extract confessions from the prisoners they arrest concerning the activities of the United Irishmen and the location of their weapons. Any punishment meted out by my soldiers will be swift and appropriate. Our priority will be to target the homes of anyone who has served in the Volunteers because we believe these ex-soldiers are currently hiding most of the United Irishmen's firearms. We are going to disarm the whole bloody lot of them. We will designate the nine counties of Ulster as a war zone. The good citizens of the province will find out what it is like to be our enemy. We are going to unleash a reign of terror aimed at the members of the United Irishmen and their leaders from which they will never recover. So that when the French invasion force returns to Ireland no Ulsterman will have the courage to step outside his home let alone join the ranks of the French army to take up arms against us.'

'Do you think we have enough troops to do that?' asked the colonel.

General Lake nodded his head as he continued. 'Several new regiments are on their way to help us. There is one Welsh regiment in particular which I think will be well suited to these sorts of duties. They are the Ancient Britons under the command of Colonel Williams-Wynn, they know how to deal with insurgents. Any United Irishman coming into contact with them will never forget the experience. To boost the number of soldiers available to us we are in the process of forming new Yeomanry and Militia regiments in Ulster to serve in their own localities. We will be able to use their local knowledge to help identify any potential targets.'

'But I thought large numbers of the local soldiers were sympathetic to the United Irishmen's cause,' added the colonel.

'You're quite right,' said General Lake. 'However, we believe a soldier's ultimate allegiance is to king and country, therefore, we are going to introduce a new oath of commitment whereby all soldiers will have to swear a new oath declaring their loyalty to King George.'

'That's not all that we are planning to do,' added Castlereagh. 'We are well aware that some of our serving soldiers may have already joined the United Irishmen, so we are going to give them the opportunity to denounce the Society and reaffirm their allegiance to the crown. Anyone who refuses this offer will be severely disciplined.'

Castlereagh stood up. 'Are there any more questions?'

'These are dangerous times,' said General Lake. 'We must do everything in our power to beat these bastards.'

'I agree. You will receive your orders before you leave. May God go with you,' said Castlereagh as he left the room leaving the army officers and officials discussing their next moves.

Chapter 12

Towards the end of March, Martha Johnston was working in her kitchen one day when she heard a horseman ride into the farmyard. Martha pulled her shawl over her head and went out to meet him.

'Hello, can I help you?' she asked the well-dressed man.

'I'm looking for Mr David Johnston.'

'What do you want with him?'

The rider ignored Martha's question. 'Where can I find Mr Johnston?'

Despite the man's boorish attitude Martha did not feel any sense of concern. Strangers often turned up at the farm looking for her husband.

'David is working in the barn. Shall I call him for you?'

'No, that will not be necessary,' said the rider dismounting from his horse. 'I will find him.'

Martha watched him walk over to the barn. She was tempted to follow him, but she had seen too many travelling businessmen and decided to go back inside the farmhouse. It was warmer inside.

David Johnston was spreading hay for his cattle when he heard the barn door being opened. He looked up as the stranger stepped inside.

'Hello, can I help you?' he asked.

'Are you David Johnston?'

Johnston studied his visitor. 'Yes, who wants to know?'

The man stepped forward. 'I have a message for you from a friend,' he said taking a piece of paper from his pocket and offering it to him.

Johnston took the note and opened it. His body tensed as he recognised the handwriting. It was from Reverend Cleland. He was ordering him to attend a meeting with him in the government buildings in Belfast at six o'clock that night. When Johnston went to put the note in his pocket, he noticed the man's outstretched hand.

'I am to return the correspondence with your reply.'

Johnston handed the note back. 'Tell your friend I will be there.'

The man turned and left, leaving Johnston wondering what Reverend Cleland wanted him for. The threat of losing everything had profoundly changed David's outlook on life. The experience had left him craving for security, and a realisation that the only way he was going to achieve this was by working as hard as he could for the Reverend Cleland and the government. Since his release he had sent him as much information as he could about the activities of the local United Irishmen. In his last intelligence brief, he had warned Reverend Cleland about the increasing number of new recruits joining the United Irishmen since the failed attempt by the French to land their troops in Bantry Bay. He had warned him about a drive to forge new pikes, and how some units had started to compile lists of houses where muskets were being stored and designating them as potential targets for places to attack in the event of an uprising. Johnston thought he had been doing enough. He finished spreading the hay and went back to the farmhouse.

'Who was that man?' asked Martha as Johnston pulled off his work boots.

'He is a United Irishman. I have to go out tonight. Reverend Steel Dickson has called a meeting of the executive in Belfast. He wants to update us on his plans for the uprising. I shouldn't be too long. You don't have to wait up for me.'

'Do you want me to make you something to eat?'

'No, I haven't time,' he said as he washed his hands and face at the kitchen sink. 'I'll get something in Belfast.'

Johnston went to his bedroom and changed out of his work clothes putting on his city suit and a heavy overcoat for the journey. A few moments later he kissed Martha and left. When he arrived at the government buildings in the centre of Belfast a doorman ushered Johnston into a room where Reverend Cleland was waiting for him.

'Ah, David,' he said getting up from his chair to shake his hand. 'I'm glad you could make it.'

'Hello,' replied a cautious Johnston. 'I was surprised to get your note. I thought I was giving you enough information. I hope I haven't done anything wrong.'

Reverend Cleland was quick to calm his visitor. 'No, no, David, your work is excellent. Viscount Castlereagh and I are very pleased with the information you have been providing.

'So why have I been summoned here?'

Reverend Cleland sat down indicating where he wanted Johnston to sit.

'First of all, David, I want to congratulate you. The information you have been sending in has been a great help to us. Some of our colleagues in government were convinced the threat from the United Irishmen was over, but thanks to your excellent work Viscount Castlereagh was able to prove to them that they were wrong. Through your briefings he was able to demonstrate that the United Irishmen, in Ulster, are stronger than they have ever been. Viscount Castlereagh has asked me to pass on his personal gratitude to you.'

Johnston breathed a sigh of relief. 'Thank you very much. I do try my best, but it can be very dangerous at times. Sometimes I think my colleagues don't trust me.'

Reverend Cleland smiled and nodded his head. 'We understand your concerns David, but let me reassure you, they do not suspect you. We have other agents working for us, and their information tells us that you are seen as one of the Society's most loyal officers. If that changes, I will warn you immediately, and we will move you and your family to a safe place. But I don't envisage ever having to do that.'

'Thank you, that's very reassuring.'

'Good. Now I want to talk to you about why I asked you here tonight. The Irish government is about to embark on a series of new tough actions designed to reduce the United Irishmen's fighting capability with a particular focus on Ulster. You will be pleased to know that the information you have been supplying us with has been central in helping us design our plans. We know the membership of United Irishmen has doubled since the failed French invasion in December which means we always have to maintain thousands of soldiers in Ulster to contain and suppress them in the event of an uprising. By doing that we are reducing our ability to respond if the French were to attempt another landing in the south of the island.'

'Do you think that will happen?'

'Yes, our sources in Paris tell us they will try again. That's why our first priority is to destroy the United Irishmen organisation in Ulster. We are going to take away their weapons and remove their leadership.'

'What do you want me to do?' Johnston asked.

'We want to know more about where and when the leadership meet? Who is in attendance? What they discuss, and who the main characters are? It is common knowledge there are over seventy

Presbyterian ministers in counties Antrim and Down who are actively involved in the United Irishmen. They are providing religious support and, in some cases, leadership to the members of the Society. We want to destroy that link. I want you to focus on County Down. I take it you are familiar with these ministers?'

'Yes. I will see what I can do.'

'The Viscount wants you to concentrate on Reverend Steel Dickson, Reverend Archibald Warwick, the licentiate in Kircubbin Presbyterian Church and the Reverend James Porter from Greyabbey. Porter has been writing some very scathing articles about Viscount Castlereagh's family in the Northern Star.'

'I have read some of the articles. He is not very kind to you either.'

'Well let's not dwell on him. There is someone else I want you to look out for,' added the Reverend Cleland. 'Have you heard of any talk about an individual called Magennis?'

Johnston shook his head. 'No. I haven't.'

'He is the leader of the Defenders in mid Ulster. He recently signed a treaty with Henry Munro, a General in the United Irishmen. In this treaty they have agreed to do everything in their power to stop sectarian fighting between Catholics and Protestants in mid Ulster, and to try and get people to focus their energy on political reform instead.'

'I've heard about the treaty, but I didn't know about the rest.'

'I want you to find out everything you can about Magennis and this accord.'

'Why is that?'

'Because it would suit us if the treaty broke down, and sectarian fighting returned.'

'I will never really understand everything that's going on,' said Johnston with a shake of his head.

Reverend Cleland smiled at the comment. 'You don't need to. You just need to do everything in your power to ensure the safety of our country.'

Johnston stood up to leave.

'Before you go, there are some more things I need to discuss with you,' said Reverend Cleland.

'What are they?'

'First of all, thanks to you, we were very successful at the protest march in Bangor. We were able to arrest and remove ninety-five members of the United Irishmen from our streets. The courts did their part and the magistrates have exiled most of them to Van Diemen's Land and sent the rest into the navy or army. Well done.'

'Thank you.'

'However, we had a bit of a problem that day as well.'

'What was that?'

'Several prisoners we were holding in an old warehouse managed to escape. I'm sure you are familiar with the facts. I couldn't believe that someone would actually break in and help them getaway. That was very embarrassing for us, and I know it has given a huge propaganda boost to the United Irishmen. I'm quite sure you have heard about them?'

'Yes,' nodded Johnston. 'People were very pleased with what happened.'

'As well they might, but it makes us look foolish and incompetent. Thankfully we managed to recapture most of them, but we think there are a few who have avoided our attempts to identify and arrest them. I've already asked several other agents to help identify these people and where they live, but so far, I have heard nothing. I want you to get involved and see if you can locate them for me.'

'I understand',' said Johnston. 'What happened to those who were recaptured?'

The Reverend Cleland glanced down at his notes. 'They are dead. Unfortunately, they tried to escape again and were hung.'

'All of them?'

'Yes, all of them,' replied Reverend Cleland coldly.

'When did they appear in court? Did they have a trial?'

'No. There was no need. The army has the power to hang any prisoners who try to escape from custody.'

'Is that what will happen to the others if they are recaptured?'

Reverend Cleland looked up at him as he started to gather the paperwork lying in front of him and shuffled the sheets into a neat pile. 'Who knows, we shall have to wait and see David. Things are moving fast. I would be very grateful if you could find these people for us. Before you go, there is something else that has been playing on my mind over this last few weeks.'

126

Johnston waited.

'I understand your wife is pregnant.'

Johnston nodded his head. 'Yes, she is. How do you know that?'

'I make it my business to know everything about anyone who works for me,' replied Cleland. 'Are you a practicing Presbyterian?'

Johnston was stunned and surprised by the question. 'Yes, I am.'

Reverend Cleland shook his head. 'You should think about converting to the Church of Ireland. It would certainly open the door to a lot of opportunities for you and your family in the future.

'No. I couldn't do that. People in my community would never accept it. They would become suspicious of me. I think they are already watching everything I do.'

'Well, make sure you consider it.'

'I will, when all of this dies down.'

'Good, I knew you would see sense. Now come on, let me walk you out, I have a very important dinner appointment to go to.'

Chapter 13

As hundreds of young people rushed to join the United Irishmen, they demanded to be trained in how to use a pike so that they could take part in the revolution they believed was imminent. But before any recruit was assigned to an existing fighting unit, they had to complete an initial training programme consisting of educational classes, before any involvement in weapons training. In the Gransha district, Betsy was involved in teaching new recruits the values and principles of the Society of United Irishmen and explaining why the struggle for political reform was necessary and why they had to take up arms to achieve them. The second part of their training was designed to instil discipline in each recruit and teach them the importance of working together as a team. Ex-military officers were given the task of drilling the raw recruits in the skills of marching as a unit, repeating each manoeuvre until it was flawless, and they understood the importance of obeying orders.

Each infantry unit within the United Irishmen consisted of pikemen supported by a small number with muskets. Betsy did not want to be left out, so she was trained in how to use a pistol and a sword in hand to hand fighting, in preparation for engaging with the enemy.

As soon as each trainee completed their basic training, they were allocated to a fighting unit where they were presented with the weapon they would use in battle. For most this was a ten-foot pike. The soldiers in each of the fighting units were trained in how to carry the pike while they were marching and how to use it against the enemy during a battle. Each pike consisted of an eighteen-inch, metal spearhead that was securely attached to one end of an ash timber shaft. Some of the pike heads also had a metal hook that protruded from the base of the spearhead which was used to slash at the enemy infantry and to cut the leather reins on the cavalrymen's horses.

Most training took part in church halls or barns, but with the arrival of Spring all physical exercises were moved outside to the surrounding fields, where the focus was centred on how to fight in their units using various battle formations. These included how to carry out a pike charge; how to respond to a cavalry attack; and how to fight the enemy in narrow town streets and country lanes.

For the final part of their training, the individual pike units were combined into larger battle formations of up to eighty so that they could take part in mock battles with other infantry companies from various parts of Counties Down and Antrim.

As the infantry units worked towards the final phases of their training, the Reverend Steel Dickson was discovering that success can bring its own set of issues. In the past he had been able to rely on local blacksmiths to manufacture enough new pike heads to satisfy their needs, but the recent jump in new recruitment numbers, combined with a severe clamp down by the security forces on the activities of all local blacksmiths, meant there was a shortage of new pike heads. When Reverend Steel Dickson raised the matter at his leadership meetings it was agreed they would seek out alternative suppliers.

A few weeks later David Johnston informed the Reverend Steel Dickson that he had found a couple of blacksmiths operating a forge in a forest just outside Crossgar, in the southern part of the county, from whom they could purchase an additional fifty pike heads.

Reverend Steel Dickson asked Johnston to select some members to work out how they could collect the pike heads from the blacksmiths and transport them the twenty-two miles across country to a farm on the outskirts of the village of Donaghadee, from where they would be distributed to several United Irishmen companies.

Within a few days Johnston called his team together. They were all young men from the Gransha area. After he had outlined the problem to them and asked for suggestions it didn't take long before several ideas were put forward. They quickly agreed on one suggested by Richard McClure. He was due to go to a farm near Crossgar to collect a cartload of hay for Mr. Sloane, and as the farm wasn't too far from the forge, he proposed using his trip as a cover.

'It would be easy to hide the pike heads in the hay on my return journey,' he said.

'Carts loaded with hay are a normal sight at this time of the year,' said Johnston. 'And will not raise any suspicion.'

'I did a lot of work down there and I know the Crossgar area well,' said Brice Killen.

'Well then I think you should accompany Richard,' said Johnston. 'I think we have a plan.'

A couple of days later, Killen and McClure met Johnston at the Sloane farm to collect the horse and empty cart they were going to use. After receiving last minute instructions from Johnston about where to take the pike heads when they returned the pair set out to drive the twenty plus miles to the farm where they were to collect the hay. Although it was a warm day there was little traffic on the roads and they arrived at the farm without any incidents. Once the hay was loaded onto the cart, they headed to the blacksmith's forge for the pike heads. The roads were clear but when they reached the forest, they had to trek quite a long way along a narrow, bumpy lane into the woods. It was almost noon when the two weary men eventually stopped outside a small thatched cottage.

'Hello,' Killen called out to the two men sitting on chairs on either side of the front door of the building.

'Can we help you?' one of them shouted.

'We are here on a bit of business.'

'Who sent you?'

'The Reverend Steel Dickson.'

The men's attitude changed immediately. They both came running over.

'Good. We have been waiting for you. I'm Joe Higgins. I am the blacksmith, and this is Danny McCambridge, he owns the cottage. Come inside and we'll get you something to drink. I'm sure you are thirsty after your long journey.'

Killen and McClure jumped down off the cart and followed Higgins inside the cottage where they discovered a plateful of cheese sandwiches and a couple of glasses of milk had been set out for them.

'Eat away lads,' McCambridge said as he handed them the milk. 'What's the security situation like up your way?'

'Not so good,' replied Killen. 'Every day the soldiers are out and about searching homes around our way for weapons, and if they find any, they arrest the occupants and set fire to their houses. Dozens of people I know have been transported to Botany Bay for life.'

'It's not as bad as that down here yet, but every day we hear rumours about more troops moving into the area. We think it is going to get worse. People are very frightened.'

'It's the same where we live,' said McClure. 'But we are still getting lots of new recruits. That's why we need the pike heads.'

'That's good news. Come on and I'll show you where they are,' said Higgins opening a door at the rear of the cottage. 'The forge is out the back. I don't know how long we will be able to operate it though.'

Killen was still eating his sandwich as he followed the blacksmith. 'We're going to hide the pikes in the hay. They should be safe in there.'

McCambridge shrugged his shoulders. 'I don't see why not. Farmers are moving their hay around here every day. It is a common sight. You should be safe.'

Higgins opened two large doors that led into the forge. 'They are in there.'

'It's so dark,' said McClure.

'It's because the fire had gone out,' replied Higgins walking over to a pile of hessian sacks stacked up against one of the walls. He opened one of them and pulled out a pike head and handed it to McClure.

'This is excellent quality,' McClure said turning the metal pike in his hand and running his fingers along the blade.

'The rest are just as good. I take great pride in my work. You will not get any better.'

'I'm sure,' said McClure shoving the pike back in the sack. 'Let's get them loaded onto the cart.'

They lifted the sacks and carried them through the cottage and out to the cart. Killen quickly scooped out several holes in the hay and shoved the sacks inside pulling the straw back over them to make the load look as normal as possible.

'That's perfect,' said McCambridge when they finished loading the last sack. 'Sure, you wouldn't know anything was hidden in there.'

'Has there been any troop movement around here lately?' asked Killen.

Higgins shook his head. 'No, it's been very quiet. You should have no bother getting home.'

'Right, we'd better head off.'

'And thanks for the pikes,' added McClure as he climbed up into the driver's seat and took hold of the reins. 'They are very much appreciated.'

'Good luck boys,' said Higgins as Killen climbed onto the cart.

'Thanks,' shouted Killen as he settled himself into his seat for the long journey ahead.

When they left the forest, they were able to make good time and about an hour later they reached the outskirts of Saintfield. McClure glanced over at Killen who was fast asleep in the seat beside him and smiled. Everything was going to plan. The roads were quiet, just as they had predicted. He relaxed and focussed on the rhythm of the horse's hooves. He was almost asleep when he spotted some movement on the road up ahead. He leaned over and shook Killen.

'Wake up Brice,' he said.

Killen stirred. 'What's wrong,' he muttered.

'There are soldiers coming,' said McClure.

Killen lifted his head and saw two columns of mounted soldiers riding towards them. As he sat upright, he spotted white plumes on the sides of the rider's dark helmets and knew immediately they were horsemen from the notorious Ancient Britons Regiment. Even though the regiment had only arrived in Belfast a few weeks ago, Killen had heard several stories about how cruel and brutal they were, and how they tortured and murdered people they suspected of being members of the United Irishmen.

'What the…'

'It's the bloody Ancient Britons,' McClure muttered as the horsemen drew closer.

When the mounted soldiers were about fifty feet away from them, they stopped and the officer leading them trotted forward indicating he wanted McClure and Killen to stop their cart.

'Whoa,' said McClure pulling on the reins.

The officer rode up to them.

'Am I addressing Richard McClure and Brice Killen?' he asked in a strong English accent.

'Yes. Why do you ask?' said McClure.

'I want you to follow me,' said the cavalry officer as he moved his horse in front of them.

'Why, is there something wrong?' replied a worried McClure as he flicked the reins.

'Just do as I say,' called out the officer.

The other mounted soldiers formed themselves into two columns on either side of the cart and escorted them along the road.

'Is everything okay?' McClure asked the nearest soldier.

There was no answer.

As they rounded a bend in the road McClure spotted more mounted soldiers on the road ahead of them. When they drew close to the soldiers, the officer leading them, indicated to McClure that he wanted them to follow him through an open gate into a field.

'What do you think they are going to do?' whispered Killen.

'I don't know,' murmured McClure. 'But, if you get a chance, run for it. I don't like the look of this.'

As they passed through the gates McClure and Killen suddenly realised why they had been ordered off the road. In the middle of the field they could see a group of soldiers gathered around a large leafless tree and to their horror they were throwing ropes with a noose at one end over a couple of the branches.

The officer ordered McClure to stop the cart.

'Which one of you is Richard McClure?' he asked.

'I am,' replied McClure as he secured the reins. 'Why have you brought us in here?'

The officer ignored his question as he turned towards Killen. 'I take it you are Brice Killen?'

'Yes sir.'

'Would you both mind stepping down from the cart.'

'Why have you brought us here?' demanded McClure again.

'We just want to talk to you. Now would you please step down from the cart.'

McClure lifted his jacket and jumped down. Killen followed him. As soon as their feet touched the ground several soldiers rushed forward and grabbed hold of them.

'Hey, what are you doing?' shouted Killen as the soldiers began dragging and pushing him away from the cart.

The soldiers who had seized McClure did the same.

The officer smiled at the look of shock on McClure's face. 'You didn't think you would get away with it, did you?'

'Get away with what?' shouted McClure as the soldiers continued to drag and push him up the grassy slope towards the tree.

'We haven't done anything,' screamed Killen as he struggled to push the soldiers away from him. 'Let me go, why are you doing this?'

'We are going to hang you,' said the officer.

'Why?' screamed Killen as he continued to struggle. 'What have we done?'

'You escaped from lawful custody,' replied the officer.

'No, we didn't,' pleaded McClure. 'We are innocent, we have never been arrested in our lives. You have got the wrong people. Please you must listen to us, we are just farmhands doing our work.'

A crowd of locals from Saintfield gathered at the gate into the field and watched in silence as the two men were dragged towards the tree.

'Hang them,' ordered the officer when they reached the nooses that were dangling from the branches of the tree.

The crowd gasped as the nooses were placed over the heads of McClure and Killen and tightened around their necks. Some of the women screamed when the soldiers pulled at the ropes and lifted both men off the ground and high into the air. There were cries for mercy from some of the people in the crowd as they watched the jerking and convulsing movements of McClure and Killen's bodies as they struggled to breathe. The laughing soldiers tied the ropes around the thick trunk of the tree and stood around chatting as they waited for McClure and Killen to die. An officer ordered the rest of the soldiers to remove the hay from the cart and soon the hidden sacks of pike heads were uncovered and thrown out onto the ground.

After thirty minutes the officer rode over and checked the gently swaying bodies of McClure and Killen. Once he confirmed both were dead, he ordered his soldiers to remount and to take the sacks of pike heads with them as they rode away.

After the soldiers left the field the people watching from the gate rushed up to the tree. They quickly loosened the ropes and lowered the bodies of McClure and Killen to the ground where they tried to revive them. As they were working on them Reverend Ledlie Birch arrived. He helped to try and revive the men but after a few moments everyone stopped, declaring there was nothing more they could do. Reverend Birch arranged for an undertaker to take the bodies of McClure and Killen to their families in Gransha while he and another man drove the hay cart back to the farm.

When Reverend Ledlie Birch arrived at the Sloane farm, he quickly explained what had happened to the two boys.

'But why did the soldiers hang them?' asked Mrs Sloane.

Reverend Ledlie Birch shook his head. 'I don't know. We thought it was because they were caught smuggling pikes, but the people watching what was happening said the soldiers didn't search their cart until after they were hung.'

'What other reason could there be?'

'I'm not sure, but it's possible it was because Richard had freed Brice and the other boys after they were arrested at the protest march.'

'If that's true, do you think they will come for our Thomas?' asked Mrs Sloane.

'We can't wait to find out,' said her husband. 'We'll have to get him out of the country. He can go to our Harry's in America.'

'Where is Thomas now?' asked Reverend Ledlie Birch.

'He's out in the field bringing in the cows to be milked. He should be back shortly.'

As she spoke, they heard the latch on the door and Thomas walked into the room.

'Hello Reverend,' said Thomas. 'There's a man standing outside, is he with you?'

'Yes, we had to bring your cart back.'

'I thought Richard and Brice were using it today. Where are they?'

'The soldiers arrested them this morning,' said his mother.

'Why?' he exclaimed. 'When I saw them this morning, they were going to get some hay for us.'

'That's right,' said his father. 'They picked the hay up but were stopped by the army just outside Saintfield on their way back.'

'Why did they have to stop them, moving hay isn't a crime?'

'Richard and Brice were transporting some pike heads for us. They were using the hay as a cover,' said Reverend Ledlie Birch.

Thomas stared at him for a few moments. 'They didn't tell me that was what they were really doing.'

'They were under orders to tell no one. The army stopped them outside Saintfield and took them into a field and hung them. Both are dead.'

'Because of the pikes they were carrying?'

'We thought that was why, but we're not sure. There's a chance it was because they were part of the prison breakout in Bangor.'

Thomas sat down. 'So was I.'

'We were just talking about that,' said his father. 'If it is true it means you can't stay here any longer.'

'You'll have to go to America,' added his mother.

Thomas shook his head. 'I don't want to go there; this is my home. All my friends live here.'

'But you must go,' pleaded his mother. 'If you stay, you could end up being murdered like Richard and Brice.'

'But if the soldiers found a load of pike heads in the cart that would explain why they hung them. So, I don't have to leave.'

'The soldiers didn't search the cart until after they hung them,' said Reverend Ledlie Birch. 'They were waiting for them. Someone must have told them they would be travelling on that road and at that particular time.'

'But that means someone in the United Irishmen informed on them?'

The Reverend nodded his head. 'It is not safe for you to stay here. You must leave.'

'Please Thomas, for my sake,' pleaded his mother. 'Just go to America. When things calm down you can comeback. We will still be here and when you do you can take over the management of the farm. But, please don't stay here.'

Suddenly the door flew open and a very flustered man came rushing into the room.

'Soldiers are coming,' he managed to say as they heard many horse's hooves pounding on the cobbles outside.

Thomas's mother rushed to the window and looked out and saw mounted soldiers riding down the lane and into the farmyard. Each one of them was carrying a blazing torch.

'Quick Thomas,' she called out. 'Run out the back.'

Thomas ran out through the back door and into the nearest field. He kept on running staying close to the shadows along the hedgerow.

But some of the soldiers had already anticipated he might try to escape and were in the fields surrounding the farm. One of them spotted Thomas as soon as he opened the back door.

136

'Over here lads,' the mounted soldier called out as he spurred his horse and chased after him.

Thomas heard the soldier coming and climbed through the hawthorn hedge into the next field. As he ran along the hedgerow, he saw the torches of more horsemen and could hear them calling out to each other as they rode into the field, he was in. He tried to sprint to the other side of the field but when he was about halfway across, he realised they were closing in on him. He stopped and raised his hands. He could hear the thundering of horse's hooves in the darkness around him.

'Tally ho,' shouted the cavalrymen as they galloped towards Thomas.

As Thomas turned around to surrender, he glanced up and caught the glint of the cavalrymen's sword blades sparkling in the moonlight seconds before they came slicing down on him. The kill was over in a few bloody moments.

As Thomas's body lay motionless on the ground the cavalrymen tied a rope around his feet and dragged his lifeless body into the farmyard and dumped it at the feet of his distraught parents.

'Burn the farmhouse and the rest of the buildings,' shouted the officer as he tossed his blazing torch onto the thatched roof.

'You can't do that,' shouted Reverend Ledlie Birch at the officer. 'These people have done nothing wrong.'

The officer pulled a pistol from his holster. 'Step back sir. I have never killed a man of the cloth before, but if you continue to get in the way of my soldiers carrying out my orders I will not hesitate,' he shouted as the rest of the soldiers threw their burning torches onto the nearest building.

Soon every building on the farm was ablaze. But the soldiers were in no hurry to leave and sat in their saddles watching and cheering as the buildings went up in flames.

'Let this be a message to anyone who tries to defy the Ancient Britons,' shouted the officer. 'We take no prisoners.'

With that he spurred his horse and rode down the farm lane followed by the rest of his mounted soldiers.

A neighbour, Danny Malory, came running from his farm to see what was going on. He was stood by the gate as the soldiers rode out.

'Murderers,' he shouted at them.

The last soldier in the column pulled a pistol from his holster and as he rode past Malory, he shot him in the head. The officer laughed as he and his soldiers rode away leaving another dead body lying by the gate.

Chapter 14

Over the next few weeks the terrifying actions by soldiers of the Ancient Britons Regiment sent shockwaves throughout the county. Many people were too frightened to leave their homes, so when David Johnston rose early and told Martha he had to go into Bangor to meet the architect who was developing the plans for the modifications he wanted carried out on the farmhouse, she pleaded with him to postpone the trip. But he insisted he had to go.

When Johnston left the farmhouse and rode away, he wasn't happy for two reasons. The first was that Martha had recently gone against his wishes and brought her brother Robert to stay with them. When Martha heard that Robert might be in trouble because of what had happened to the other boys who had escaped from the warehouse she went immediately to the family home and offered him a haven at their farm. David had been reluctant to bring Robert to their house arguing that the soldiers might search their farm when they discovered Martha was Robert's sister. But Martha refused to listen, declaring this was an opportunity to heal the rift between her and her mother. She eventually put Robert up in the small room they kept in the main barn for the farmhands they hired during harvest time.

The second worry and real reason why he had to go out was that Reverend Cleland had sent a message last night ordering him to come to Belfast to see him at eight o'clock next morning.

'Why have you sent for me?' an upset Johnston demanded when he was ushered into Reverend Cleland's office. 'I had to lie to my wife about where I was going, it's very risky for me to be seen anywhere near here.'

'Calm down, David,' said Reverend Cleland. 'Sit down.'

'Why am I here, I have done everything you asked of me?'

The Reverend Cleland studied Johnston's face for a few moments before replying. 'But that's the problem David. You haven't been honest with me. Have you?'

'What do you mean?'

'When I asked you to get me the names of the people who escaped from the warehouse, I expected you to give me information on all of them.'

'Which I did,' replied Johnston. 'Your soldiers captured Brice Killen, Richard McClure, and Thomas Sloane. I also gave you a cart load of new pike heads. What more do you want from me?'

'But you didn't tell me everything,' shouted the Reverend Cleland. 'Did you?'

Johnston felt his face and neck go red. 'What do you mean?'

The Reverend Cleland stood up behind his desk. 'You did not tell me there was a fourth person.'

Johnston tried to look surprised. 'What do you mean a fourth person?'

'You didn't tell me about Robert Madison.'

Johnston stared back at him. 'I... I couldn't,' he whispered.

'Why not?' shouted the Reverend Cleland. 'Why couldn't you tell me about him?'

'Because he is my brother-in-law. My wife's brother,' pleaded Johnston as his eyes filled with tears. 'I couldn't do anything to hurt Martha. She's my whole life.'

Reverend Cleland walked around the desk and stood in front of Johnston. 'I control your life David. Don't ever lie to me again. Do you understand?'

Johnston nodded his head slightly as he looked up at him. 'But I could never do anything that would hurt Martha. You must understand that. She is my wife; she means everything to me.'

'But you must understand David,' said Reverend Cleland. 'Thousands of people will die in this war, and hundreds of thousands more will be injured and maimed. It is strong people like you and me who will survive. We must not show any weakness. So never, ever lie to me again. Do I make myself clear?'

Johnston lifted his hands and wiped tears from his face. 'Yes, I hear you,' he muttered. But as he spoke, he began to realise something was wrong.

'Why have you brought me here?'

The Reverend Cleland didn't answer and turned to walk back to the seat behind his desk.

Johnston stood up. 'Hold on, if you knew about Robert Madison, then you would have already known he was my wife's brother,' he said as he began to understand. 'And you would have known where he is... Oh my God, what have you done?'

Reverend Cleland glared at him. 'Never, ever lie to me again. I have to look after your welfare David.'

Johnston ran to the door. 'What have you fucking done?' he screamed as he pulled open the door and ran out.

Shortly after Johnston left the farmhouse Robert joined Martha in the kitchen for breakfast. They spent an hour or so enjoying cups of tea and reminiscing over old times when they heard the farm dogs out in the yard start barking. Martha went over to the window to check and almost dropped her cup when she saw several cavalrymen riding down the lane towards the farmhouse, the white plumes on the sides of their black helmets shimmering in the bright sunshine.

'Oh my God Robert, quick the soldiers are coming. Quick get into the bedroom and hide in the wardrobe where I showed you. I'll go outside and talk to them.'

As Robert ran into the bedroom Martha paused to compose herself before she opened the door and walked out to the farmyard. The officer in charge of the cavalrymen, pulled up in front of her.

'Lieutenant Howell of the Ancient Britons at your service,' the officer said in a clipped English accent. 'We are looking for Robert Madison. We believe he has been residing in these premises for the last few days.'

Martha took a deep breath wondering who had told them about Robert. 'I don't know what you are talking about. There is no one...'

'Oh, shut up woman,' snapped Lieutenant Howell. 'I know he is here.'

He turned in his saddle to face his men. 'He is in the house. Go and get him.'

Several of the soldiers dismounted and rushed past Martha. She went to follow them but was stopped by a couple of soldiers.

'You stay here with us,' said one of them as they caught hold of her arms.

Martha tried to push him away as she listened to the other soldiers running from room to room in the house.

Suddenly she heard one of them shout. 'We've got him.'

A few moments later Robert was bundled out from the farmhouse and pushed towards Lieutenant Howell.

'The little prat was hiding in the wardrobe,' sniggered the soldier.

The lieutenant looked down at Robert, before raising his head and gazing around him. After a few moments he pointed towards the large oak tree.

'That will do. Hang him from that tree.'

'No,' screamed Martha as she struggled to break free and grab hold of Robert. But the soldiers tightened their grip on her preventing her from moving.

When Robert realised what the soldiers were going to do, he looked back at Martha as they started pushing him out of the farmyard. He could hear Martha screaming as he struggled with the soldiers dragging him across the field. Once they reached the tree, one of the soldiers threw a rope with a noose on the end, over one of the branches. Another one caught the noose and quickly slipped it over Robert's head tightening it around his bare neck. The rest of the soldiers pulled on the rope until Robert was standing on his tiptoes. They stopped and looked over at Lieutenant Howell.

'Hang him,' shouted the lieutenant.

The soldiers quickly pulled the rope, lifting Robert's writhing body into the air, his legs flaying about as he struggled to breathe.

Martha became hysterical. She kicked and punched the soldiers holding onto her, but they were too strong, and she was unable to break free.

Lieutenant Howell guided his horse towards Martha. He stopped and looked down at her.

'I understand how you feel,' he said. 'He is your brother after all, but you should never have allowed him to join the United Irishmen. You can tell the rest of those bastards that we are coming for them. They're all going to hang.'

'Let him go,' screamed Martha.

'Make sure she gets a good view of her brother dying for the cause,' said Howell as he manoeuvred his horse out of her way.

One of the soldiers grabbed hold of Martha's face and forced her to watch the spasms and convulsions of Robert's dying body for the final minutes of his young life.

Martha wept when Robert's body eventually began to gently sway at the end of the rope.

Lieutenant Howell rode across the field to the oak tree and studied Robert's face for a few minutes.

'He's dead,' he called out to his soldiers. 'Mount up, we're finished here.'

One of the soldiers holding onto Martha punched her hard in the face and shoved her to the ground before quickly mounting his horse and riding off to join the lieutenant.

Despite feeling groggy from the punch Martha was able to drag herself into the kitchen and grab hold of a large knife and a small wooden stool before running across the field to the tree.

'Robert,' she sobbed as she climbed onto the stool and held onto his body as she frantically cut away at the rope just above his head. When she was about halfway through the remaining filaments suddenly snapped and they crashed to the ground. Martha tugged at the noose around Robert's neck until she was able to loosen it. But as she touched Robert's face, she realised there was nothing she could do. Her darling, fun loving brother was dead. Martha looked to the heavens and screamed, just before she fainted and collapsed beside his body.

'Martha. Martha,' someone repeated.

'What?' Martha mumbled, opening her eyes to see her neighbour Jessie Poulter gazing down at her.

'Are you okay Martha?' Jessie asked as she knelt beside her.

Martha shook her head as she sobbed. 'The soldiers murdered Robert. I tried to save him. But they were too strong for me.'

Jessie put her arms around her. 'You poor girl,' she said softly.

Martha sobbed as Jessie held her. 'I couldn't stop them Jessie.'

'There, there, I know,' said Jessie. 'Do you know where David is?'

'He's not here. He's in Bangor. He went there to see the architect.'

'Thank goodness,' said Jessie. 'I thought they might have hurt him as well.'

Martha struggled to her feet. 'Help me get Robert's body inside the house. He shouldn't be lying in a field like this,' she said as she put her arms around Robert's chest and lifted him. Jessie took hold of his legs. The two women carried the body to the farmhouse.

'We're not putting him on the floor,' said Martha once they were inside. 'Put him up on the kitchen table.'

After a struggle they finally managed to get Robert's body onto the table.

'I'll go and get some help,' said Jessie as Martha stared at the body. 'Will you be alright?'

Martha looked at her and nodded. 'The ghost of my brother is not going to harm me.'

Jessie left and ran back to her farm looking for Henry. She eventually found him in one of their fields.

'Henry,' she shouted. 'Come quick, the soldiers have been at the Johnston farm again, they've murdered Martha's brother.'

'What?' he shouted as he ran towards her.

'The soldiers have just been to the Johnston farm and found Martha's brother Robert hiding there. They took him out and hung him from the oak tree beside the house.'

'Where's Martha now?' he asked.

'She's still at the farm.'

'What about David?'

'He wasn't home. Martha said he had to do some business in Bangor. You need to go and see if you can find him. She said he was going to see their architect. I think his office is on the High Street, and will you see if you can get hold of Doctor Gilmore.'

'It sounds as though it is too late for a doctor.'

'Henry,' demanded Jessie. 'Until Robert is officially declared dead there will always be hope. Please, just go and get the doctor I'm worried about Martha and the baby she is carrying.'

Poulter realised he may have been too blunt. 'I'm sorry Jessie, I'll go and get him right away. You should go back to Martha and stay with her. I'll see you over there.'

While they were speaking David Johnston was forcing his horse to gallop as fast as it would go. He realised he had been tricked. Cleland had ordered him to come to Belfast to make sure he wasn't around when the soldiers went to the farm to arrest Robert. He was terrified of what they might do to Martha if she tried to protect her brother. When he turned off the main road onto the farm lane, he saw a rope hanging from the oak tree and an upturned stool lying underneath it.

The farmhouse looked deserted.

'Martha,' he shouted as he jumped down from his horse and ran inside. In the semi dark room, he saw Robert's body lying on the table, a rope lying on the floor beside it and his beloved Martha standing gently stroking Robert's hair.

'Martha,' he cried as he ran over and took her in his arms.

'I couldn't stop them,' she whispered. 'They were too strong for me.'

'Don't worry Martha, I'm here now.'

It had been a quiet day at Bangor market and after closing her stall Betsy decided she was going to quickly visit the shops on High Street to buy a few things before heading home. As she was checking how much money she had in her purse she heard a familiar voice.

'Hello Betsy.'

She looked up and was surprised to see a very smartly dressed Jenny Knox.

'Hi Jenny, you look as though you are going somewhere important.'

'I've just been with my solicitor to give him the keys to the farm. I'm going to America tonight to join Rachel. I've come to say goodbye.'

Betsy wasn't surprised by her news. 'I thought you might do that. I think you're doing the right thing.'

'Thank you. I did try to look after the farm on my own, but it was just becoming too much for me. I thought I'd found a good farm manager, but it turns out he wasn't, and rather than go through all the worry again I've decided to put the farm up for sale and take my chances in America with Rachel. My solicitor will be handling everything.'

'When do you leave?'

'My ship sails from Belfast harbour tonight. I have a carriage waiting for me out on the street.'

'Well thank you so much for coming to see me, come on I'll walk with you. I was going to go into town to buy a few things.'

When they reached Jenny's carriage, they hugged once again before she left.

As the carriage pulled away Betsy gave one last wave and called out.

'Give my love to Rachel when you see her, and please write to let me know how you are getting on.'

Betsy stood for a few moments and watched the carriage as it drove down the street. She felt sad. She was beginning to lose count of the number of close friends who had felt the need to leave Ireland in search of happiness in another country. She was jolted out of her gloom when a rather flustered looking Henry Poulter bumped into her.

'Sorry, it was my fault, I wasn't looking,' he said quickly.

'Are you alright?' Betsy asked.

'No, something terrible has happened. I'm looking for David Johnston. Have you seen him?'

'No, I haven't, why, what's wrong?'

'The soldiers were at his farm this morning and found Martha's brother Robert hiding there…They hung him from the oak tree.'

Betsy took a sharp breath. 'Oh my God. Is Martha alright?'

'Well Jessie's with her but she's in shock. I need to find David and tell him what has happened. He needs to get back to the farm and take care of Martha. Jessie said he was in Bangor to meet with their architect. She thinks their offices are somewhere on High Street, but I can't find them, and I have to find Doctor Gilmore as well and take him back to the Johnston farm.'

'I know where their office is,' said Betsy. 'I can go there if you want.'

'Would you please and tell David that Martha needs him back at the farm immediately.'

'Of course I will,' said Betsy.

'Thanks,' shouted Poulter as he rushed away. 'I'll see you at the Johnston farm.'

Betsy ran around to the architect's offices on High Street and went inside to the reception area where an elderly lady was sitting behind an imposing looking desk.

'Yes, can I help you?' she asked.

'Hello,' said Betsy. 'A friend of mine, Mr David Johnston, was due to come in today to see one of your architects and I was wondering if he was still here, there is an emergency back at his farm?'

'Do you know which architect he was coming to see?'

'No, I'm sorry I don't.'

The woman quickly checked through the paperwork lying in front of her. 'What did you say his name was?'

'David Johnston.'

146

'Ah, I remember him, he deals with Mr Redmond,' she said as she looked up from her paperwork. 'I'm sorry, but Mr Redmond has been on holiday for the last two weeks.'

'Would he have seen someone else?'

The woman shook her head. 'No. Mr Johnston did not have an appointment with any of our architects today. I've been sitting here all day and he hasn't been in.'

'Thank you,' said Betsy.

She went back to the market and collected her cart before heading home. She kept thinking about poor Robert and how terrifying it must have been for him and Martha when the soldiers arrived. She couldn't get the image of a hanging body out of her mind. When she arrived home, she saw George coming out of the house to help her off load the cart.

As he helped her down from the cart, he looked at her. 'Is everything alright, Betsy?' he asked.

'No George. I have heard some terrible news.'

'What has happened?'

'It's about Robert.'

'Why, what has he done now?'

'The soldiers caught him this morning. Robert is dead…'

'What do you mean he's dead?'

Betsy put her arms around George's shoulders. 'The soldiers found him hiding in the Johnston farm this morning. I'm sorry, but they hung him.'

George's body sagged into her arms as he started to weep. 'We thought he would be safe at Martha's; how did they know he was there?'

'I don't know George. Help me put this stuff away and we'll go over to the Johnston's. Maybe somebody there will know.'

About an hour later Betsy and George drove into the farmyard that was already packed with neighbours' horses and carts. After finding a space to leave theirs they walked over to the front door. Betsy paused in the open doorway. On the journey over she had been worried about this moment, but nothing in her imagination could have prepared her for the shock she felt when she saw Robert's body lying on the kitchen table with his distraught sister sitting alongside being comforted by the Reverend Porter and David. Betsy was relieved that he had arrived home.

Betsy forced herself to walk over to the table.

'Martha, I'm so sorry.'

Martha looked up and grasped hold of her hand. 'Oh Betsy, look what the soldiers did to our poor Robert. I tried to stop them. But there was nothing I could do. They knew he was hiding here. They just walked straight in and dragged him out. They put the noose around his neck and hung him. They made me watch until he was dead.'

Betsy put her arms around Martha and hugged her. 'I'm so sorry Martha. It must have been horrific. But at least they can't hurt him anymore. He is with the Lord now.'

A few moments later there was a noise at the door as Robert's mother arrived. The elderly woman looked calm and composed as she walked to the table and looked at her son's body.

'You told me Robert would be safe here,' she said.

'But there was nothing I could do.'

'I'm taking him home with me,' she said before turning to one of the men who had arrived with her. 'Will you please bring the coffin in.'

Martha went to say something to her, but David stopped her. 'Let her do what she wants,' he said.

A coffin was brought into the room by two men and set down on a couple of trestles. The men lifted Robert's body into it and secured the lid. The Reverend Porter then asked everyone to join him in prayer. A heavy silence descended on the room.

'Dear lord, please help the loved ones of Robert Madison in their hours of need. We ask that you accept his soul into your arms and care for him. And in those hearts that are filled with grief at his death, we ask that you instil in them the knowledge that eternal life is the gift you give to us all. Amen'

Betsy had been holding Martha's hand during the short prayer. She squeezed it gently as the men lifted the coffin and carried it outside to a waiting hearse. Martha's mother followed them out and boarded her carriage. Everyone watched in silence as the solemn procession left.

As Betsy was about to leave Henry Poulter joined her. 'Betsy, I need to apologise to you. I'm afraid I sent you on a bit of a wild goose chase this morning when I asked you to try and find David.'

'That's okay. It didn't take me very long. David must have had his dates mixed up.'

'Yes, that's what he told me. He had to go to Belfast to meet his accountant. Thanks for your help this morning.'

'Thank goodness your Jessie was here until David got back,' said Betsy as she beckoned George over indicating it was time for them to leave.

Chapter 15

As the government's initiative to disarm and destroy the United Irishmen gathered pace in Ulster, barbaric acts carried out by soldiers from the Ancient Britons and other regiments soon became an everyday occurrence. Betsy didn't realise the full extent of the savagery until the day she had to take some of her mother's linen cloth to an agent in Belfast.

'Don't forget, when you get to the Linen Market, make sure you deal with William Bracket and only him. He asked me to make this special order and promised to give me a good price for the cloth. I would go myself, but I can't leave the loom, I'm so far behind in my schedule.'

'Mum don't worry about it,' said Betsy. 'It's months since I've been to Belfast, I'm going to check out the shops I've heard they have just received the latest fashions from London, and I need a new blouse.'

'Right, but I wish you would take that green ribbon off your bonnet. I've heard about women being stopped and molested by soldiers because they were wearing something green.'

'I'll think about it mum,' said Betsy. 'Billy is meeting me outside the Linen Market, and he's going to take me to his favourite coffee shop. So, I won't be on my own.'

There was a gentle rain falling as Betsy and her mother loaded the last of the finished rolls of linen cloth onto the cart. Her journey through the countryside was quiet. There wasn't much traffic until she reached the outskirts of Belfast where she was stopped by soldiers at an army roadblock at the entrance onto the Long Bridge. However, she was not unduly delayed, and was soon on her way into the town. The first thing that struck her as she drove through the streets were the large numbers of soldiers milling around. Each street seemed to have its own army check point, and everywhere she looked she could see people being stopped and questioned by groups of intimidating looking soldiers.

When Betsy turned onto North Queen Street, she was horrified to see the body of a man hanging from a tree at the side of the road. There was a plaque around his neck saying he was a traitor and a member of the United Irishmen. But what shook Betsy most was how the people of Belfast casually walked past as though there was nothing hanging there at all.

Betsy had heard about the army searching people's homes for weapons and how they would set fire to the houses if they found any. But to see smashed pieces of furniture lying in the street outside the smoking ruins of someone's home truly brought home the reality of the cruelty. As she drove on, she was becoming quite nervous and was genuinely relieved when she eventually spotted Billy waiting for her outside the Linen Market.

'Hello, you,' he called out when she pulled up beside him.

He jumped up onto the cart to embrace her. 'I was beginning to think you had changed your mind.'

Betsy felt safe in his arms. 'No, I wouldn't do that. I was stopped by the army at a checkpoint on the other side of the Long Bridge. I didn't realise how bad it was in Belfast.'

'I should have warned you. The army has really clamped down. I saw them whipping a man on High Street yesterday. It was barbaric. There is no law and order in this country anymore. If the soldiers suspect anyone of supporting the United Irishmen, they have the power to stop and search them and do whatever they want. I saw a bunch of soldiers setting fire to a row of houses claiming their owners were United Irishmen. I have even heard rumours about women being raped. But I haven't seen anything like that myself.'

Billy glanced at Betsy's bonnet.

'That might be dangerous,' he said.

'What are you talking about?'

'The green ribbon on your bonnet.'

'Oh no, not you too?'

'I really think you should take the ribbon off. If we are stopped by the soldiers there is no telling what they might do.'

'No,' said Betsy firmly. 'The ribbon is staying where it is. They were on the bonnets when Gina and I bought them, and we agreed we weren't going to take them off. It's not a crime to wear green. Anyway, it's a woman's right to wear whatever colour she wants.'

Billy shrugged his shoulders. 'Alright Betsy, but I did warn you.'

They went inside the Linen Market and eventually found her mother's agent, William Bracket. She introduced herself to him.

'Ah, the daughter of the talented Mrs Gray,' said Bracket. 'I should have known you would be as beautiful as your mother. She makes the most exquisite fabric,' he continued, waving his hands around him. 'The finish is so beautiful. Where is it my darling?'

Betsy was slightly amused by Bracket's flamboyant behaviour. 'We'll go and get it. It's on the cart outside.'

'I'll be waiting here my dear.'

When they returned, Betsy showed Bracket her mother's material. He became even more excited as he ran his fingers over it.

'It's just as I imagined it would be. Your mother never lets me down. Tell her I will take another batch in four weeks' time. There is always a great demand for quality linen, and your mother produces the best. Here's the money we agreed.'

'Mum told me to check it,' said Betsy.

'That's fine.'

'Thank you very much,' replied Betsy quickly checking the amount before she and Billy left.

Billy took Betsy to his favourite coffee shop on High Street. She was very excited. This was going to be a real treat. She had only tasted coffee once before while on a trip to Belfast with her father many years ago. When they walked into the packed café the first thing Betsy noticed was the gentle buzz of conversation as Billy guided her over to a table, he had booked beside one of the large windows that looked out onto the busy street. A few moments later a waitress handed Betsy a menu saying she would be back to take their order shortly. Betsy studied the menu. There was a large variety of coffee and freshly made sandwiches and scones with jam and cream.

'I didn't know there would be such a choice,' said Betsy when the waitress returned. 'Please may I have a filtered coffee with some cream and sugar.'

'Of course,' replied the waitress. 'And would you like anything to eat with your coffee?'

'Yes please. I'll have a scone with cream and strawberry jam.'

'I'll have the same,' added Billy.

The waitress smiled as she took their order and left.

Betsy gazed around at the people in the packed café. 'It's wonderful. There is such a friendly atmosphere in here.'

'This is where the old Volunteers used to meet. It would be packed with old soldiers talking about their experiences in the army. It's where I first heard about the United Irishmen. I was having a conversation with several Volunteers and they told me about how they had stood against the Irish government and demanded changes in how the country was being governed. I remember being very impressed by their honesty, and their enthusiasm for change. Like me, most of them were Presbyterians and despised sectarianism in any shape or form and were adamant about the need for Catholic emancipation. As far as they were concerned Ireland would never be prosperous until everyone was treated the same. And when they asked me if I wanted to join the United Irishmen, I said yes immediately.'

The waitress returned carrying a tray with their order and expertly laid everything out on the table. Betsy was loving every minute of the experience. When the waitress left Betsy cut her scone and spread cream over one half, before topping it with strawberry jam. After pouring the coffee Betsy dropped a lump of sugar crystal into the cup along with a small amount of cream. She stirred the coffee for a few minutes, before lifting the cup to enjoy the aroma of fresh coffee.

As she took a sip of coffee she glanced out through the window and spotted Gina Russell on the other side of the street. She was surprised to see she was with Private Peter Carron. They were holding hands and looking very much in love. As Betsy watched she saw a group of drunken soldiers gather around them. One of them seemed to be saying something to Gina when he suddenly reached out and ripped Gina's bonnet from her head. Private Carron immediately grabbed hold of the drunk and tried to get the bonnet back. As they struggled more soldiers became involved and soon there was a free for all brawl as scores of soldiers punched and kicked each other.

Betsy and Billy quickly ran out and rescued Gina, taking her back with them into the coffee shop for safety. The mayhem on the street was getting worse before several mounted army officers arrived and began yelling at the fighting soldiers, ordering them to stop. When the scrapping eventually died down Gina ran out to look for Peter, but when she found him, an officer ordered her to stay back, informing her that Private Carron had been placed under arrest along with several other soldiers, including the drunks who had started the fight. When the military police arrived, they quickly took control and marched the arrested soldiers back to the barracks.

'So, how long have you been seeing Private Carron?' Betsy asked as they watched Peter being marched away.

'Not very long,' replied a tearful Gina. 'Do you remember when we were stopped at the army checkpoint and they ordered us to unload everything from the cart, and Peter helped us put it all back?'

'Yes, I remember thinking at the time that you two were getting rather friendly.'

Gina smiled at the thought. 'Well I literally bumped into him later that same day and he asked if he could see me again. I've been going out with him a couple of times a week since then.'

'Why didn't you mention it before?'

'Peter asked me not to tell anyone. Not even my best friend.'

'Why?'

Gina lowered her voice. 'Peter is a member of the United Irishmen. He said there are hundreds of them at the camp, and he thought it would be best if I didn't mention it to anyone.'

'What did the drunken soldier say to you?' asked Billy.

Gina looked down at the bonnet in her hand. 'He asked me why I had a green ribbon on it, just before he pulled it off my head. When Peter tried to get it back the fighting started. What do you think they will do to him?'

'He will be confined to barracks for a few days, but nothing more than that.' reassured Billy.

'I'd better be going,' said Gina.

'I'll give you a lift home,' said Betsy. 'You should stay here with us for a while. I think you could do with something to drink.'

They sat on for another hour or so before Betsy took Gina home with her.

When Betsy arrived home after dropping Gina off, she was surprised to see her mother standing at the farm door. She looked very worried.

'Have you seen George?' her mother asked.

'No. Why?'

'He hasn't come home yet. He should have been home hours ago.'

'Don't worry mum. I'm sure he will be alright.'.'

It was another two hours before they were relieved to hear the latch opening on the door as George walked in.

154

'What kept you?' his mother said as soon as he stepped through the open doorway.

George didn't answer her. He looked exhausted.

'What's wrong George?' asked Betsy when she noticed how upset he was.

'The soldiers came to our workshop today.'

'Did they hurt you?'

'No, I was out on a job with a couple of the lads.'

'What happened?'

'When we got back old Sam the cleaner told us that he had been working in the workshop with Daniel and Tommy when about a dozen soldiers rode into the yard and said they had evidence we were hiding pike shafts for the United Irishmen. Sam said the soldiers were from the same regiment as those who hung Robert and the other boys.'

'The Ancient Britons?'

'Yes, that's them. Sam said he recognised them from the white plumes on the sides of their helmets. They asked Daniel and Tommy where the pike shafts were being stored and when they said there were none, the soldiers started wrecking the place. They accused Daniel and Tommy of being in the United Irishmen and said if they didn't tell them were the shafts where they would torture them. It was ironic because they are the only people in our workplace who aren't members of the United Irishmen. Sam is ninety-five years old, Daniel doesn't belong to anything, and Tommy had just joined the Orange Order.'

'What did the soldiers do to them?' asked Betsy.

'Sam said an officer called Captain Swayne asked Tommy where the pike shafts were being stored, and when Tommy said he didn't know, Swayne pulled a piece of round paper from his bag. Sam said he knew immediately what he was going to do, because he had seen the same sort of thing before when he was in the army. Swayne poured oil onto the paper and rubbed some gunpowder into it. When the paper was covered in gunpowder, he wrapped it around Tommy's head and asked him again where the shafts were being stored. When Tommy said he didn't know, Swayne set the paper on fire. The gunpowder went up with a whoosh, setting Tommy's hair and the skin on his head on fire. Sam said the screams of Tommy were awful as he ran around the workshop trying to pull the burning paper from his head. And when Tommy tried to get out the door Swayne shot him in the back. Sam said he did the same thing to Daniel.'

George broke down and began to sob.

'Did they torture Sam?'

'No, Swayne told a couple of his soldiers to beat him up.'

'How is he?' his mother asked.

'He's badly shaken, he might be ninety-five years old, but he is very tough. We went and got his daughter and she took him home. Then we had to go and tell Tommy's parents he was dead. That was awful. There is no easy way to give bad news. And then we went to Daniel's house. His wife is expecting their third child. She is totally devastated.'

'I don't know how much more of this barbarity we can take,' said Betsy's mother. 'Every day there seems to be more terrible news. These soldiers are a law onto themselves. They are going to kill us all. How is it going to end?'

Chapter 16

At the Belfast headquarters of the Monaghan Militia, Colonel Charles Leslie, their colonel in chief, held an urgent meeting with his senior officers to discuss what had happened earlier that day. He was furious that the actions of a few soldiers had brought the reputation of the whole regiment into disrepute and seemed surprised when Lieutenant-Colonel Archibald Alsop, one of his senior officers, suggested the fighting may have something to do with the hold the United Irishmen had over some of their soldiers.

'What do you mean?' Colonel Leslie asked.

'For some time now, the rebels have been deliberately seeking out our men and filling their young heads with nonsense about how they can help bring about an egalitarian society in Ireland.'

'But why would they do that?' the perturbed Colonel enquired.

'The belief within the rebel's camp is that if there is an uprising a significant number of our soldiers will abandon the regiment and join them to fight against his majesty's forces.'

'But my soldiers have sworn an oath to the King.'

'Some of them have also sworn an oath to the United Irishmen.'

'How many men are we talking about?'

'I don't know, but my guess is that it could be in the hundreds.'

The colonel was taken back by the reply. 'Well we had better find out, and the quicker the better. I want the whole regiment on the parade ground.'

'But sir, it's quite late,' said Lieutenant-Colonel Alsop. 'Should we not wait until first thing in the morning?'

The colonel took a deep breath. 'If one has a boil it will fester if you do not seek to treat it immediately. The sooner we lance this one the quicker we will recover.'

The officers rushed away to carry out his orders, and twenty minutes later five hundred and sixty soldiers stood in the parade ground in front of the colonel.

'It has come to my attention following a disgraceful incident in Belfast today,' roared Colonel Leslie. 'That an organisation that wishes to destroy the King's rule in Ireland, has infiltrated this regiment. It has enticed several soldiers to swear an allegiance to them. I will remind everyone here that they have already sworn their loyalty to the King. No one in this regiment will be serving two masters. The government has decreed that anyone who takes the oath of the United Irishmen will be charged with treason and will face the death penalty.'

The colonel paused to take a deep breath and to allow his soldiers time to contemplate the severity of his words.

'Whereas I have no sympathy for anyone who has decided to join the enemy, I can understand how some of you may have made a mistake, and perhaps in the cold light of day you are beginning to regret your moment of weakness. I will therefore promise you this, if you admit to the error of your ways tonight, and solemnly reaffirm your loyalty to King George, I will personally seek a pardon for you, and you will be allowed to continue to serve within the Monaghan Militia for as long as you want. But, if you do not accept my offer, and if I subsequently discover that anyone serving in the Militia is also a member of the United Irishmen, I will not hesitate to have that individual shot for treason.'

Once again, the colonel paused for a few moments.

'I will seek a pardon for any soldier who has been influenced by members of the United Irishmen, and who has sworn their oath. If you have done this, I ask you to step forward now.'

The colonel waited, as he looked up and down the silent ranks. Suddenly a soldier in the front rank stepped forward. He was quickly followed by another as more and more soldiers followed him. The colonel lost count of the number of soldiers who had accepted his offer. When he was satisfied there were to be no more takers the colonel gave the order for those who stepped forward to march off to the side of the parade ground where his officers were waiting. There was a sharp sound of stamping boots on the hard ground as the soldiers marched from the parade ground. Once they had left the colonel thanked the remaining soldiers for their loyalty before dismissing them.

For the rest of the day and most of the night the soldiers who had stepped forward were questioned by senior officers to establish when they had joined the United Irishmen, why they had done so and who had administered the oath. Once the officers completed all the interviews, they had a meeting with Colonel Leslie.

'Well, how many where there?'

'One hundred soldiers admitted they were members of the United Irishmen,' replied Lieutenant-Colonel Alsop.

'My God. Have we been walking around with our eyes closed? Why did we not spot this before? Why did it take a damned fight in the street to bring this to our attention? How did the people in the United Irishmen manage to influence so many?'

'A wealthy businessman and some of his friends have been visiting the camp and plying the soldiers with free alcohol and filling their heads with radical thoughts.'

'Who is this gentleman?'

'A Mr David Jenkins. He owns several stores in Belfast.'

'Was he ever challenged or questioned when he came to the camp?'

'No sir.'

The colonel shook his head in disbelief. 'Very well. At least we now know how they did it. And what reason did the soldiers give for joining them?'

'Most of them said they wanted a better country for their families and children. A few mentioned putting an end to discrimination against Dissenters. And quite a few simply joined because their friends did.'

'That doesn't surprise me. Is that it?'

'In the main, yes,' replied Lieutenant-Colonel Alsop. 'There was no desire to destroy the country. It was quite the opposite in fact. I formed the opinion that most of the soldiers were rather naïve and idealistic in their view of the world.'

'Did any of them talk about a revolution, or a desire to overthrow the king?'

'No. There was no suggestion of any of that. Most of them talked about a wish for equality. The views of most of the soldiers were idealistic rather than rebellious.'

The colonel nodded in agreement. 'It always is until the killing starts. So, what are your conclusions?'

'We do not think many of the soldiers would desert the regiment to join the ranks of the United Irishmen. When we asked what they would do if there was an uprising most said they would stay loyal to the regiment. However, we have identified four soldiers we believe are the leaders, and who administered the oath to the other soldiers. They openly admitted they would fight alongside the rebels.'

'So, what are your recommendations?'

'The death penalty for the leaders. This is in line with current army policy,' said Lieutenant-Colonel Alsop.

'And what about the others?'

'We recommend a pardon for each one of them. When they were questioned, they recognised they had made a mistake. We believe a show of clemency towards them will encourage any other soldier who might find themselves in a similar position to come forward, but if not, to at least remain loyal to the regiment in the event of an uprising.'

'Very well. Thank you. This has been the lowest day for the regiment since we were formed, but we shall rise from these ashes. Thank you, gentlemen.'

Colonel Leslie left immediately and travelled down to Dublin Castle to seek a pardon for the ninety-six soldiers who had admitted membership of the United Irishmen. While he was away Lieutenant-Colonel Alsop organised a court martial for the four leaders.

A few days later while Betsy was delivering some groceries to one of her regular customers in Gransha village a very upset and distraught Gina came running down the street towards her.

'Betsy,' she called out. 'A friend of Peter's called in at the shop and gave me this,' she said holding a leaflet in her hand. 'They're going to kill Peter.'

'What are you talking about?'

'Here, read this, it's all in this General Bulletin the Colonel of the Monaghan Militia issued to his men yesterday. Peter's friend was given a copy when he went to the camp in Belfast.'

The pamphlet described how Privates Peter Carron, Daniel Gillan, William McKenna and Owen McKenna of the Monaghan Militia had been sentenced to death for being active members of the United Irishmen. The article described how the condemned men were to be transported from Belfast to the main camp in Blaris, where they were to be executed. The article claimed their deaths were to be a warning to other soldiers who may be contemplating switching their allegiance to the United Irishmen in the event of an uprising against the King.

'When is this happening?' asked Betsy.

'Today,' wept Gina. 'Will you take me to Blaris camp, they might allow me in to see Peter.'

'Of course, I will,' said Betsy.

The cold, damp weather reflected their mood as Betsy and Gina headed towards Blaris army camp. Shortly before twelve o'clock they joined a small crowd of relatives of the condemned soldiers who were asking if they could see their loved ones. The guards pushed them back to the side of the road telling them no one would be allowed into the camp.

A few minutes later Betsy and Gina saw the procession, that was bringing the soldiers from Belfast, marching down the road towards the camp. A mounted party consisting of the senior officers of the Monaghan Militia led a company of infantry soldiers into the camp. Behind them came a wagon carrying William and Owen McKenna. The two men were dressed in white shirts and trousers and were manacled to the seat of the cart. They were followed by another company of Monaghan Militia marching in front of a second wagon. This one carried Peter Carron and Daniel Gillan who were also dressed in white and manacled to their seats.

Gina cried out when she saw Peter. His head was bowed as though he was in prayer.

'Peter,' she called out.

To Betsy that one simple word was full of all the love and terror that Gina was going through as the wagon carrying the man she loved rolled passed.

Peter raised his head and looked towards her, the grief he was suffering plain to see in his eyes.

Gina collapsed into Betsy's arms.

The wagon continued through the gates followed by mounted troops from the Light Dragoons and to Betsy's horror a company of Ancient Britons.

Betsy and Gina watched as the procession came to a halt at the far end of the parade ground where a military band was playing The Dead March in Saul. They could see the four prisoners being ordered down from the wagons.

Peter was taken to one of four, six-foot tall wooden posts fixed to the ground and ordered to stand with his back to it. His arms were then tied behind the post.

The Monaghan Militia and the other soldiers were marched into position so that they were facing the condemned men.

Once everyone was in place Lieutenant-Colonel Alsop marched over to the prisoners and read out their punishment.

'Private Peter Carron, Private Daniel Gillan, Private William McKenna and Private Owen McKenna, you have been found guilty by a military court of coercing members of the Monaghan Militia into swearing an oath to the United Irishmen. Your sentence, for carrying out this act of treason is death by firing squad.'

The Lieutenant-Colonel turned and saluted Colonel Leslie who gave the order to proceed.

Betsy heard commands being shouted out and saw a dozen armed soldiers march from the side of a building and quickly line up facing the condemned men. As the commands continued, Betsy saw the soldiers in the firing squad raise their rifles and point them at the prisoners. She glanced at Peter Carron as a volley of shots rang out and saw his body being slammed against the post before slumping forward, held in suspension by the rope tied around the post. An officer stepped forward to check that each prisoner was dead. When he came to Peter, Betsy saw him take a step backwards and place his pistol against the side of Peter's head and pull the trigger.

When the officer was satisfied all four prisoners were dead, he returned to his position as more orders were bellowed out.

The slow beat of the mournful music and the sight of soldiers marching past the grotesque spectacle of the lifeless bodies of Peter and his friends dangling from the wooden posts added to the horror of their punishment.

Gina was distraught as Betsy tried to comfort her.

When the march pass was completed the bodies were cut down and thrown onto the back of a cart and taken away to be buried in an unmarked grave. Their obliteration complete.

Betsy helped Gina back to the cart, and as they headed home, she listened as Gina cried and talked about how much she loved Peter, and how they had planned to get married and go to live with his brother in New York.

The killing of the four soldiers had also affected the men's friends within the Monaghan Militia. They were furious at what had happened and needed something upon which to vent their anger. Two days after the executions a large group of Monaghan Militia soldiers marched into the offices of the Northern Star in Belfast and destroyed the printing presses. The damage they inflicted was so severe that the newspaper was never able to print again. Not only had the United Irishmen lost four loyal members but they had also lost one of their greatest assets.

Chapter 17

Throughout 1797 the killing and torture of suspected members of the United Irishmen in Ulster gathered pace as the army continued to wreak havoc among the Presbyterian population in their search for weapons. Any premises where they were found were burned to the ground, and the unfortunate families of the suspect thrown out onto the streets.

In the soldier's haste to disarm the United Irishmen, they carried out raids on the premises of citizens who would have classified themselves as loyalists and who would have had no connection whatsoever to the liberty men. The widespread destruction caused panic and anger amongst the general population and resulted in a swing in public opinion against the United Irishmen. People who, up until then, had been willing to tolerate their activities began to equate their existence with the pain and suffering they were experiencing.

The Irish government, sensing this backlash, began to recruit for several new Yeomanry and Militia units in Ulster, targeting specific areas that were traditionally seen as being loyal to the United Irishmen, appealing directly to local people to join them. All new volunteers were asked to swear an oath of allegiance to King George, and to declare that they were not or no longer were members of the Society of United Irishmen. Many were willing to do so to protect their families.

In some localities the opportunity to become a volunteer was restricted to those who were members of the local Orange Lodge, whilst in other districts a more liberal approach to applicants was applied, encouraging both Catholics and Protestants to enlist.

People who joined the part time army saw it as an opportunity to openly display their loyalty to the crown and the Irish government and began wearing their uniforms daily.

Betsy noticed this happening while she was tending her stall in Bangor market and served several men wearing the uniform of the Militia or Yeomanry companies they had recently joined. When she mentioned this new show of patriotism to them, they said that it was important they display their loyalty to King and country and hoped that if enough men did, the aggression by the army would stop and everything would go back to normal and the way it was before.

They clearly placed the blame for the army's aggression on the backs of the membership of the United Irishmen, and openly stated that if they didn't exist and there were no hidden weapons then the army would stop their searches.

Next market day while Betsy was setting up her stall in Bangor, John Agnew the owner of the stall beside hers, arrived wearing the uniform of one of the new yeoman companies.

'John, what have you done?' she declared when she went over to talk to him.

'Well, what do you think?' he said spreading his arms and spinning around to show her his new red jacket and white pantaloons. 'I'm now a sergeant in the Newtownards Yeomanry cavalry.'

'I must say you do look very smart. But why did you have to join up?'

Agnew stopped spinning and smiled at her. 'I wanted to secure a safe future for me and my family, and the only way I'm going to achieve that is by becoming a soldier, albeit a part time one.'

'I didn't know we were under threat. Who are you going to fight?'

Agnew answered with a shake of his head. 'You know where the threat is coming from Betsy. We must stop the forces of republicanism and popery from taking over the country. We have been talking about nothing else at our lodge meetings for the past few months, and we all agreed that we could no longer stand by and watch Ireland being destroyed by the United Irishmen.'

Betsy was shocked by his reply. 'But that's not true John, and you know it. The United Irishmen don't want to destroy Ireland. In fact, we want the complete opposite. We want to build a fairer society, that's all. You swore the same oath as me John, you know what it says. How is trying to form a brotherhood of affection wrong?'

Agnew picked up a box of potatoes and placed some of them on his stall. 'That was then Betsy, this is now. Everything has changed.'

'No, it hasn't, we still want to do away with religious barriers and elect a parliament that represents everyone. What is wrong with that?'

Agnew continued working on his display. 'We will never have a parliament that represents everyone because if you give Catholics the vote, Ireland will be ruled from Rome because their first loyalty is to the Pope. Our first loyalty is to the King. Catholics want the Protestants out of Ireland, but we are never going to leave… I know you are a good person Betsy, but can't you see, you are being used by people who hate Protestants and who will do everything in their power to destroy us?'

'I take it you are talking about the Defenders.'

'Yes, I am. Look, I know the leadership of the United Irishmen is predominantly Presbyterian and that the membership in Ulster is mainly Presbyterian, but your membership in the south of Ireland is largely Catholic. They are only using the Presbyterians to get what they want.'

'I don't agree with you John. Don't forget we have all taken the same oath, and that is to build a fair and just Ireland. We all want the same political reform. I know there will always be people who will try to exploit us for their own ends, but the vast majority of our members are not sectarian. All we want is a peaceful country. It is sectarianism that keeps the Irish government in power, that's why they continually try to exploit people's fears.'

'There is nothing wrong with the Irish government. It is the enemies of Ireland who are trying to destroy our way of life and our religion.'

'We are not enemies of Ireland John.'

'You may not be Betsy but your friends in the United Irishmen are. Did you know that a body was found in a shallow grave on the banks of the river Farset yesterday?'

Betsy shook her head, confused as to why John was bringing this into their conversation. 'No, I didn't. Why is that relevant?'

'It was the body of a young man who has been missing for the last few months. He had been shot in the head.'

'That's terrible,' said Betsy still unclear as to why he was bringing this up. 'I'm sure his family must have been going through hell.'

'I'm sure they were,' replied Agnew aggressively. 'The rumour is that he was a United Irishman and was murdered because he was an informer.'

Agnew stated the last word loudly and clearly.

Betsy shook her head sadly. She had heard the same rumours about how the government was offering people money for information about the United Irishmen, and that some of them had taken up the offer, but this was the first she had heard of anyone being accused. Dealing with the idea that there might be informers in the Society was something new to all the members. Most didn't believe any member would become an informer, claiming the idea was simply propaganda being spread by the government to try and destabilise the organisation. It was a tactic they had often used in the past. This was also the first time she had heard about someone being murdered for being an informer.

'Of course, you know who I'm talking about,' said Agnew assertively.

Betsy was shocked by the comment and how it was said, almost implying there was a possibility she was in some way complicit in the man's death.

'What's his name?' she asked with some trepidation.

'Oliver Garfield. The same young man I had to chase from your stall when he was making a nuisance of himself. Do you know what happened to him?'

Betsy was appalled by the question and noticed that Agnew had stopped tending his stall and was staring at her as though he was studying how she would react to his news.

'John that is a horrible thing to say,' declared Betsy. 'Of course, I have no idea why Oliver Garfield was killed. Why are you so sure he was murdered by the United Irishmen?'

Agnew shrugged his shoulders as though satisfied with her response. 'It's common knowledge that most of the senior members of the United Irishmen are informers,' said Agnew. 'I have actually heard that some were heard boasting about how much money the government was offering them for information. We think it is only a matter of time before the entire organisation collapses and some of the more forward-thinking members try to save themselves from prison or the noose. The government is gaining the upper hand, that's why we think the United Irishmen are to blame.'

Betsy was stunned by Agnew's frankness as she turned away and went back to her own stall.

'Be careful Betsy,' Agnew called. 'Things might be coming to a head soon. Just make sure you are on the winning side.'

Betsy tried to focus on her customers for the rest of the day. There were a few chats with Agnew but the intimacy and friendliness that had been there before had disappeared. Agnew's answers to her questions were short and clipped whenever Betsy tried to engage him in conversation. She was thankful when it was time to head back home. Later that evening she rode over to Billy's house to tell him about her conversation with Agnew.

'He practically accused me of being involved in Garfield's murder,' Betsy said as Billy showed her into the living room. 'I was so incensed and angry, but there was nothing I could do.'

Billy put his arm around her. 'I heard about a body being found but I didn't know it was Garfield's.'

'Did we have anything to do with it?' declared Betsy angrily.

Billy shook his head. 'I'm sure we didn't, but I don't know Betsy. There are always rumours going around about United Irishmen being involved in the assassination of suspected informers. I have even heard talk that there's an assassination squad in the United Irishmen. But I have never heard it being discussed at any of the meetings I have attended.'

'It's murder,' said Betsy furiously. 'I would never have agreed to become involved if I thought the United Irishmen were going to commit murder. I don't want my name associated with death squads or anything like that, and I'm sure I speak for many others.'

Billy could see that Betsy was furious. 'I think the same as you. We could talk all night about it Betsy but the truth is I don't know. Why don't we go and ask Reverend Steel Dickson if it is the policy of United Irishmen to kill informers?'

Betsy felt calmer and hugged Billy. 'I'm sorry for taking my anger out on you. You're right we should ask the Reverend if it is true.'

Later, when they arrived at the manse, Reverend Steel Dickson's housekeeper showed them into the study where the old preacher was preparing his sermon for next Sunday's service.

'Come in,' he said warmly when he saw who it was. 'Have a seat. It's good to see the pair of you.'

'Thank you,' said Billy as they sat down.

'So how can I help?'

Betsy took the lead. 'Are you aware that the body of a man called Oliver Garfield was found in a grave, in a field beside the river Farset. He had been shot in the head.'

'Yes. I heard about that. It's a terrible tragedy.'

'Did we kill him?' demanded Betsy.

'Pardon?'

'Is there an assassination squad in the United Irishmen?' asked Betsy.

The old man looked stunned by the bluntness of her questions.

Billy sensed his disquiet as he added. 'We have heard a rumour that the United Irishmen were involved in Garfield's murder and that he had been shot for being an informer. I have also heard other rumours about the United Irishmen being involved in the assassinations of suspected informers.'

The Reverend Steel Dickson relaxed into his armchair as he contemplated his reply.

'Let me answer your questions this way,' he said addressing them both. 'Do you remember when you first joined the Society of United Irishmen?'

'Yes,' they replied.

'One of the first actions every new member must do is to swear the Society's oath. Did you both do that?'

'Yes.'

'Good,' the old man said as he stood and walked over to a cabinet and pulled out one of the drawers from which he extracted a sheet of paper. 'I have a copy of the oath you both swore here,' he said coming back and sitting down with it.

Holding the sheet of paper in his hand he began to read.

'In the presence of God, I .... do voluntary declare.'

He stopped and looked up at them.

'Do you remember adding your name into the space?'

'Yes,' they replied.

'The first part of the oath you swore was to commit yourself to help build a better society in Ireland. And that is what we are all working towards. However, it is the second part of the oath that I believe may hold the answer to your questions. Can you remember what you said?'

Billy shook his head as he looked at Betsy.

'Yes,' she replied. 'I do further declare that neither hopes, fears, rewards or punishments shall ever induce me directly or indirectly, to inform, or give evidence against any member, or members, of this or similar societies, for any act or expression of theirs done or made individually or collectively in or out of this society, in pursuit of this obligation.'

The Reverend Steel Dickson smiled when Betsy finished. 'That's correct. Well done. I'm impressed Betsy. It is our belief that anyone who swears an oath to God, and who subsequently breaks that oath, will answer to God. There are over one hundred Presbyterian ministers involved in the United Irishmen and they along with the rest of the leadership will not countenance the harming or killing of anyone who breaks the oath they swore to God when they joined us, because we believe that those who transgress will have eternity to suffer for their treachery. So, to answer your question Betsy, we do not have assassination squads in the United Irishmen.'

'Thank you,' said Betsy.

'The Society of United Irishmen is an honourable association,' added the Reverend Steel Dickson. 'Our aims are simple and principled, and they are based upon the teachings of Christ. A few weeks ago, I warned everyone that the government would use dirty tricks to try and break the ties that bind us. And for the last six months we have been sorely tested by atrocity after atrocity carried out on our members by soldiers of the government in pursuit of a policy to disarm and destroy us. They have tried to get us to react. But we have stayed our hand and have not sought revenge. To my knowledge, Oliver Garfield has never been a member of the United Irishmen. We did not kill him. It is not our policy to commit murder, that is the way of the barbarian.'

'But if we didn't kill Garfield, who did?' asked Billy.

'I don't know,' sighed Reverend Steel Dickson. 'It is a question that has being weighing heavily on my mind. My understanding is that Garfield was shunned by most people in our community. And yet, someone is trying to position him as one of our members and implying that we murdered him because we discovered he was an informer. That doesn't add up. I think there is a more sinister motive behind his death.'

A couple of days later while Betsy was standing in a queue at the Ballycopeland flourmill waiting to buy a couple of bags of wholemeal, she overheard a conversation the mill owner was having with another customer.

'Did you hear about the body found near the river Farset the other day?'

'Yes,' replied the customer. 'Wasn't it terrible. They're saying it was a local man called Oliver Garfield. I went to school with his father, he was a God-fearing man.'

'I knew him well; he was a good man.'

'Oliver collected our rent,' said the customer. 'He used to call every week. We have a new man now.'

'I've heard a few bad stories about Oliver and some of the things he would get up to while he was collecting the rent money. They were not very complimentary I'm afraid. It sounds as though his behaviour might have caught up with him.'

'Is it true that he was shot?' asked the customer.

'That's what I heard. A bullet in the head. An assassination.'

The customer glanced around at Betsy. 'We shouldn't speak ill of the dead,' she said.

'No, you're right,' replied the miller handing the customer her change before picking up her bags of flour and following her out of the shop to her horse and cart.

One of the miller's assistants brought Betsy's bags of wholemeal over to the counter.

'Mr Lansbury didn't like Oliver very much,' she said softly. 'He used to come in here regularly. He was a terrible flirt. Lansbury thought he was a pest, but we thought he was all right. He was good for a laugh; it was just a bit of fun.'

Betsy smiled at her even though it would not be how she would have described Garfield's behaviour.

'When did you last see him?' she asked.

The assistant thought for a few moments. 'I think it was the day after the parade in Bangor, when a lot of people were arrested. He came in here to show off his new clothes. He was in a good mood and kept going on about London and how he was going to go and live there.'

'Do you think he meant it?'

'I'm not sure. He was always talking about the big things he was going to do with his life. When he didn't come around for a while, I thought it was because of the row he had with one of our customers.'

'Who did he have a row with?'

'Mr Johnston, he's one of our biggest customers.'

'Is that David Johnston?'

'Yes, that's him.'

'What happened?'

'Johnston was dropping off some bags of grain to be processed in the mill when Oliver walked in. As soon as Johnston saw him, he rushed over, grabbed hold of him and dragged him outside. I could hear Johnston shouting and accusing him of something.'

'What was it?'

'I don't know but Oliver kept saying, it wasn't him. He must have said that five or six times, but Johnston kept shouting at him.'

'And you are sure this was the day after the parade.'

'Yes. Anyway, Mr Lansbury heard them and came out from the mill and ordered Oliver to leave. He brought Johnston in here and gave him a glass of water. Johnston looked very angry and agitated.'

'Did he say why they were arguing?'

'No, he didn't mention it.'

Betsy could hear the miller returning.

'Thanks for that,' she said to the assistant as she gave her the money for her flour.

'Here let me help you with those,' said the miller picking up the bags and following her out to her pony and cart.

Later that night Betsy told Billy what the assistant had told her about Garfield and Johnston having an argument at the windmill and how she heard Garfield saying it wasn't him several times.

'Did she say what the argument was about?' he asked.

'No, she didn't know, but she was certain it happened on the day after the parade and would have been around the time everyone was looking for him.'

'I was talking to a friend of Garfield's today called Nat McKee and he told me something very interesting. I had asked him if he had heard anything about Garfield's death. He said he hadn't, but he told me about an incident that happened about a month ago when he was with Garfield. As they were walking past the Government Building's they bumped into two men coming out of one of the side doors. Nat said one of the men looked terrified when he saw Garfield and tried to hide his face with his hand. Later when Nat asked Garfield who the man was, he said it was David Johnston. Garfield said he was doing a lot of work for him and was being well paid.'

'Did Nat say who the other man was?'

Billy nodded. 'Yes, Johnston was with the Reverend Cleland.'

'The judge from his trial?'

'The very man.'

'But, why would Johnston be visiting him?'

'I don't know. That wasn't the only time Nat saw Johnston. He saw him running out of the Government Buildings on the day Robert was killed. Nat remembered the date because he knew Robert. And he knew that Johnston was married to his sister.'

'Was the Reverend Cleland with him?'

'Not that time. Johnston was alone. Nat said he looked as though something awful had just happened.'

'Maybe he had just heard about Robert's death.'

'Nat said it was around ten thirty. That was long before anyone had heard about what happened.'

'Maybe Cleland told Johnston that he knew were Robert was and the soldiers were going to arrest him?'

'I don't know. But there could be a link.'

'Is anyone in the United Irishmen looking into Garfield's death?'

'No there isn't,' replied Billy. 'Reverend Steel Dickson has asked Henry Poulter to set up an internal investigation team to carry out an enquiry into the deaths of Richard McClure, Brice Killen, Thomas Sloane and Robert Madison. He wants to know how the Ancient Britons knew where they would find the boys before they killed them.'

'Maybe we should ask them to include Garfield's murder?'

'I'll have a chat with Henry the next time I see him.'

A few days later Billy took a message to Henry Poulter from Reverend Steel Dickson describing the arrangements for a senior officers meeting later in the month. When he finished he decided to raise the question about Garfield's murder.

'I've heard you're leading a team enquiring into the deaths of Richard McClure and the other boys,' said Billy.

Poulter nodded his head. 'That's right, but we haven't had our first meeting yet. It's been very hard to find a date that suits everyone.'

'I was wondering if you had thought about including the murder of Oliver Garfield in your investigation.'

'Why would we do that?'

'I've heard a few things about him and David Johnston that sound very suspicious.'

'What have you heard?'

'Garfield was seen arguing with David Johnston at the Ballycopeland mill a few days before he went missing.'

'Anything else?'

'Johnston was seen coming out of the Government Buildings with the Reverend Cleland, and we know he is always trying to get people to spy on us. I was told that Johnston was seen running out of the Government Buildings on the day Robert was murdered.'

'Are you saying David is a spy?'

'Well don't you think it is too much of a coincidence.'

'But that might be all it is,' replied Poulter. 'David has already told me why he was in Belfast on the day Robert was killed, and we know that Garfield worked for him collecting rent. So, it's possible they were arguing about some work-related incident. As far as David being seen with Cleland is concerned, I'm sure there is a rational reason for it. Look, I have already spoken with Reverend Steel Dickson about Garfield's murder and we both think government agents were probably involved in his death. I will bear in mind everything you have told me but unless he asks me to include Garfield's murder, we won't be looking into it. Was there anything else?'

'No,' replied a deflated Billy. 'I just thought I would tell you what I know.'

'You did the right thing,' replied Poulter as he left. 'If you think of anything else please let me know.'

Chapter 18

David Johnston was also aware that a team comprising of senior officers, had been formed by the Reverend Steel Dickson to carry out an investigation into the deaths of Richard McClure and his friends. He knew that would happen and expected to be part of the team so was concerned when he wasn't called. The uncertainty about what was being discussed behind closed doors was beginning to get to him. He worried that everyone was whispering behind his back. His mistrust of his fellow officers was so severe that he was reluctant to engage in a conversation with any of them in case he said the wrong thing. And when he did talk to them, he would analyse every discussion, replaying every word that had been uttered, searching for any hidden meaning. It wasn't long until he felt it was safer not to say anything to anyone. This notion even extended to his relationship with his wife Martha.

'Is there something wrong David?' Martha asked as they were sitting down to their evening meal and he, as was becoming normal, sat facing her without saying a word.

'No,' he replied adding a shake of his head.

'But you have been like this for days. What is it?'

'Nothing,' he muttered staring at the food on his plate.

'Look at me David,' she demanded.

Johnston ignored her and continued to stare down at his plate.

'David, I'm your wife, I will not allow you to ignore me,' cried Martha as she pushed her meal away.

Johnston didn't move and kept his head bowed.

'Tell me what's wrong,' screamed Martha. 'You spend all day out in the fields and when you come in here you don't talk to me. You think more of your animals than you do of me. You just ignore me. But I have needs as well, and you are not fulfilling them. What have I done wrong? For God sake will you just look at me.'

Johnston threw his knife and fork down and stormed away from the table. 'Why don't you just leave me alone.'

But Martha was determined to find the cause behind her husband's behaviour. 'Come back here David,' she shouted. 'I have a right to know what is going on. Are you seeing someone else?'

Johnston stopped and turned around to look at her. 'How can you even think that.'

'Well, are you?' Martha screamed at him.

'No. Everything, I do is for you.'

'Then why won't you just talk to me. I'm your wife.'

Johnston's chin sunk to his chest. 'I've tried to do my best for everyone, but it is never enough.'

'Why do you say that?' demanded Martha. 'I have never complained about anything, but you won't let me in. I don't know what I have done wrong. Don't you love me anymore? Do you want me to leave?'

Johnston shook his head. 'No. You know I love you.'

'Then please come back to the table and talk to me David. Tell me what is wrong with you. Is it me?'

Johnston returned to the table and stood by Martha. 'No of course it's not. You have done nothing wrong Martha. You are the only good thing in my life. I would die if I lost you. It's just that everything seems to be building up against me.'

'Like what? Tell me what is worrying you. I thought the farm was going well. You said we made more money last year than ever before. Do you need to hire more farmhands?'

Johnston sat at the table. 'No,' he said as he shook his head.

'Are you worried the soldiers will come back? Is that it?'

'Yes,' said Johnston. 'They are burning houses all over the place, and people are being thrown out onto the streets to live like beggars.'

'But David, there is no reason for the soldiers to come back here.'

'But they might.'

'Why would they? They took your gun, they murdered Robert. There is nothing left.'

'There is something else... The Reverend Steel Dickson has formed a team to look into the death of Robert and the other boys and hasn't included me.'

Martha stood up and hugged David close to her. 'Is that what's been worrying you?' she said relieved she may have found a reason for her husband's strange behaviour. 'He probably didn't include you because you were too close to Robert. Please don't worry about that, I'm sure there is some simple reason. Why don't you go and tell the Reverend Steel Dickson about your concerns? You are a senior officer in the society. I'm sure he would understand. When he sees how upset you are, he will probably ask you to help the investigation.'

'But why didn't he ask me to join the team in the first place? I think they don't trust me.'

'Of course they do,' said Martha. 'Sure, didn't they all come out here to lift our potato crop when you were in prison. They have the greatest respect for you David, of course they trust you.'

Johnston put his arms around his wife's waist and held her tight. 'You're right Martha. I'll go and see the Reverend tonight.'

'Good,' said Martha holding him close.

Later that evening Johnston saddled his horse and waved to Martha who was reassured that he was on his way to see Reverend Steel Dickson to tell him about his concerns. But he had lied. David didn't go to the Reverend's house, he went Belfast instead, to where he knew he would find the Reverend Cleland.

'Come on in David,' said Reverend Cleland. 'To what do I owe this visit?'

Johnston pulled his cap from his head and walked into the sitting room. 'I need to talk to you about my safety. I think they suspect me of being a spy.'

'Who suspects you David?'

'Everyone in the United Irishmen.'

'Yes, but who specifically thinks you are a spy?'

'The Reverend Steel Dickson for one. He has formed a team to carry out an investigation into the deaths of the four lads involved in the jail break in Bangor and has excluded me. I should've been part of that team.'

'So, let me be clear, has anyone actually accused you of anything?'

'No, at least not to my face. But I should have been on that team. They must know I'm involved with you.'

'David, they don't know anything. Trust me, they don't.'

'How can you be so sure?'

'David you have to trust me on this. No one suspects you of being a spy. Steel Dickson is investigating the four deaths because the whole episode has made him look weak and foolish. He has to be seen to be doing something.'

'But it's me they will target. If it wasn't, why didn't they ask me to join them. You have to help me.'

The Reverend Cleland shook his head in despair. He had witnessed other agents of his lose their confidence and nerve before.

'David,' stated Reverend Cleland. 'I want you to stop thinking like this. You are not under any suspicion. Go home and relax.'

'How can I relax?' replied Johnston his eyes filling up, he felt close to tears. 'My wife is even asking me what is wrong. They all suspect me; you have to help me.'

'David, will you for goodness sake stop this moaning,' shouted Reverend Cleland. 'Just go home man and forget about them. If you don't stop behaving like a frightened animal, I'll have to put you back in prison where you belong.'

Johnston stopped whimpering and looked directly at him. 'But if you did that, they would definitely kill me.'

'Well then stop this stupid behaviour. Man up David, and stop acting like a frightened child.'

'But I....'

'Oh, for goodness sake shut up. Why don't you just stop this farce and go home. No one suspects you of anything.'

Johnston stood up. 'I'm sorry I wasted your time.'

'Now David I didn't say that,' said Reverend Cleland realising he may have been too blunt.

Johnston walked towards the door without looking back. 'I will not bother you again.'

'Where are you going?'

'I'm going home.'

'David, come back here.'

Johnston ignored him and walked out, closing the door behind him.

Reverend Cleland stared at the closed door for a few minutes before getting up and going into his study where he took a small notebook out of one of the drawers on his desk. He quickly wrote some brief notes about his meeting with Johnston and finished by adding that he didn't think Johnston's information could be trusted in future, and that it may be time to look at other ways to use him.

Martha noticed an immediate improvement in David's behaviour when he returned home. He seemed much more relaxed and told her he had a good conversation with Reverend Steel Dickson and was able to clear the air. He said the Reverend had even apologised to him and asked him to join the investigation team. Martha was relieved to hear this and was happy for him.

Over the next few days David was soon back to his usual self and began to talk about improvements to the farm and the approaching arrival of their baby.

Johnston was finding it relatively easy to act as though everything was normal, because it was giving him the time, he needed to work on a plan that would help him get out of his predicament. He wasn't surprised or flustered when Poulter mentioned to him that someone had seen him talking to Reverend Cleland outside the Government Building. He had remained calm and reminded Poulter he had already told him he had gone to Belfast to meet his accountant and afterwards went to the Government Buildings to see the land agency about purchasing a few more acres near his farm and had simply bumped into Cleland when he was leaving their offices. He felt good when Poulter seemed to accept his answer.

It was exactly three weeks after his last meeting with the Reverend Cleland that Johnston told Martha he was going into Belfast on business and would be home late. Martha said she would leave some ham and bread out for his supper as she was going over to Jessie Poulter's farm for a social evening with Betsy and a few friends.

Once Johnston completed his business in Belfast instead of going home, he made a detour to the court buildings in Newtownards where he knew the Reverend Cleland would be meeting with local magistrates to discuss their role in the current unrest. It was getting dark and after securing his horse he managed to find a hiding place close to an exit door he expected the Reverend Cleland to use. As he waited it began to rain adding to his feeling of isolation. After a while he spotted the Reverend's carriage pulling up a short distance from the doorway and a few minutes later the exit door opened. As the candlelight flooded out Johnston saw Reverend Cleland standing in the open doorway. He saw the Reverend pause when he saw it was raining and watched as he pulled his coat collar up around his neck before stepping out and walking towards his carriage.

Johnston stepped out of the shadows with his loaded flintlock pistol in his hand. The Reverend stopped and turned to see who it was. Johnston aimed his pistol and pulled the trigger.

Reverend Cleland saw a flash of gunpowder and heard a bullet whizz past his head.

As his would-be assassin turned to flee, Reverend Cleland pulled his own pistol from his belt and returned fire. He was sure he hit the man.

Johnston felt the smack of the bullet as it buried itself in his right shoulder forcing him to drop his pistol. He kept running as Reverend Cleland began shouting for the guards to come and help.

Johnston managed to reach his horse and climb into the saddle despite the searing pain in his shoulder. As he galloped away, he saw several Militia soldiers running down the street and quickly surround Reverend Cleland.

A few moments later a patrol of mounted Yeomen arrived.

'What's going on here?' shouted the officer in charge.

'Someone just tried to murder Reverend Cleland,' shouted one of the soldiers. 'He went that way.'

'Wait,' shouted the angry minister.

The officer wheeled his horse. 'Yes sir, Sergeant Agnew at your service.'

'Sergeant I recognised my assailant. He's a United Irishman called David Johnston.'

'David Johnston, the farmer from near Gransha?'

'Yes, that's him. I returned fire and I'm certain that I hit him in the back. He is wounded.'

Sergeant Agnew pulled his horse around. 'Come on men, I know where the gunman lives,' he shouted as he rode away.

Johnston was losing a lot of blood and was beginning to feel weak and lightheaded as he tried to force his horse to go faster. When he eventually reached the farmhouse, he almost fell out of the saddle and staggered into the warm kitchen.

'Martha,' he shouted as he slumped into a chair in front of the fireplace, his breathing heavy and laboured. 'Martha,' he whispered as his eyes closed and he passed out.

A few minutes later Sergeant Agnew and his patrol rode into the farmyard and dismounted. They gathered around Johnston's untethered horse standing outside the open doorway.

'David Johnston,' shouted the sergeant. 'This is Sergeant Agnew of the Newtownards Yeomen. We know what you attempted to do tonight. Come out with your hands up.'

The sergeant ordered his men to stand on either side of the doorway.

'Come out Johnston,' called Sergeant Agnew again as he indicated he wanted his men to rush into the farmhouse.

The house remained silent as the soldiers readied themselves for the charge. Sergeant Agnew gave the signal to move forward. Two of the soldiers rushed in through the doorway quickly followed by the rest of the patrol. They spotted the body of David Johnston slumped in a chair by the open hearth. One of the soldiers fired a shot and Johnston's head jerked backwards. The other soldiers ran over and checked to make sure he was dead.

'Search the rest of the house,' ordered Sergeant Agnew as he stood over the body.

With his pistol he moved the front of Johnston's jacket to one side exposing his bloody shirt.

'Reverend Cleland returned fire and hit the man who tried to kill him. I think we can safely assume we have killed the right man.'

'The house is clear,' shouted the soldiers.

'You know what our standing orders are, when we confirm someone is in the United Irishmen and is guilty of a crime against the state,' said Sergeant Agnew. 'Burn the house, burn everything. Let us make sure this time that this farm disappears from the face of the earth.'

'What about Johnston's body sir?'

'Tie it onto his horse. We'll take it back to the barracks with us. I'm sure Reverend Cleland would like confirmation his would be assassin is dead.'

Two soldiers carried Johnston's body outside while the rest of the patrol began to set fire to the farmhouse and the surrounding buildings. Soon everything was burning. Sergeant Agnew waited until every building was well alight before he ordered his men to mount up. He had learned from past mistakes that it takes a while for a fire to gain an unstoppable hold on a building. When he was satisfied everything was blazing, he ordered his patrol to move out taking Johnston's body with them.

Over at the Poulter farm, Martha was enjoying her evening with Betsy and her friends when a casual glance out the window caused her some concern.

'What's that red glow in the distance?'

Jessie and the other women turned around to look.

'It's too late for the sunset,' said Jessie as she walked over to the window.

'Oh my God,' she uttered when she realised what it signified.

'What's wrong Jessie?' asked Martha.

'There must be a fire at your farm.'

Martha ran over to the door and opened it. 'There's no one home. David has gone to a meeting in Belfast. We have to hurry.'

Betsy joined Martha in her buggy, while the other women climbed into Jessie's. They raced down the lane and onto the main road where they slowed down when they saw a troop of Yeoman riding towards them.

'They must have been at our farm,' said Martha. 'David was worried they would come back.'

The troops formed into a single line to pass them. At the rear of the riders Martha spotted David's horse with his body slung over the saddle.

'That's David,' she screamed as she stopped her horse and cart and ran over to the body.

'Get back,' ordered the soldier holding the reins of Johnston's horse.

'David,' Martha screamed as she lifted his head and saw the bullet wound.

'Get away from him,' ordered Sergeant Agnew as he came riding from the front.

'He's my husband,' screamed Martha.

Betsy recognised the sergeant. 'John it's her husband. You can't take him away.'

'David Johnston tried to murder the Reverend Cleland tonight. We have to take his body to Newtownards. You can collect it there. Now get back or you will be arrested.'

'You're not taking him anywhere,' shouted Martha as she felt a twinge of pain as her baby moved in her womb.

'Aaaaagh,' she screamed and collapsed to the ground.

'Ride on,' shouted Sergeant Agnew to his troop.

Betsy and the other women jumped down from their carts and ran to Martha's aid.

'My baby is coming,' shouted Martha. 'Help me.'

'We'll take you back to my house,' said Jessie as she helped Martha to her feet.

'Aaaaagh,' screamed Martha.

As Jessie helped her into her carriage Betsy jumped into Martha's.

'I'll go to her farm and see what I can save,' she shouted as she drove away.

Jessie quickly turned her cart around and headed back towards her farm. As they drove up the lane, she met Henry and some of the farmhands coming down.

'The soldiers have killed David Johnston, they said he tried to murder the Reverend Cleland. They've set fire to his farm. Betsy has gone to see what she can do. You had better get over there and help her. Martha's baby is coming we'll be staying here to look after her. Go on.'

Martha gave birth to a healthy baby boy not long after they managed to get her into the farmhouse.

When Betsy arrived at the Johnston farm every building was on fire. Despite everyone's efforts it quickly became obvious that this time nothing would be saved. It was almost dawn when Betsy finally gave up and went back to Jessie's farm. Martha was holding her son in her arms when Betsy walked in.

'There was nothing we could do,' said Betsy. 'The whole farmhouse and all the buildings have been completely destroyed.'

'Nothing at all?'

Betsy shook her head. 'I'm sorry.'

'Did you hear what they are saying about David?'

Betsy nodded her head. 'Yes. I did and I'm sorry, but it's true. Someone tried to shoot Reverend Cleland in Newtownards last night.'

'But David was in Belfast, it couldn't have been him.'

'Martha… The Reverend Cleland fired back and shot his assailant in the back as he ran away. There is no doubt Martha. David tried to kill him.'

'It is true Martha. I'm sorry,' said Jessie as she joined them. 'Henry is going to try to find out why David tried to kill him.'

'Did the United Irishmen order him to do it?' asked Martha.

'I've already asked Henry that Martha,' said Jessie. 'He is adamant they didn't. There was no reason to have him shot. David has done this on his own.'

Martha held her son close as she wept.

'Henry is going to Newtownards to get David's body and bring it back here. We will help you with the arrangements for his funeral.'

Martha began to sob. 'David always said he wanted to be buried beside the large oak tree on the farm.'

Jessie nodded her head. 'I will tell Henry that is where you want the grave to be dug. He will sort everything out. You can stay with us for as long as you like.'

'Thank you, Jessie. You and Henry have been so kind to me.'

The next day David Johnston's coffin arrived at the Poulter's farm and was carried into the farmhouse and placed on a table in the front room. Neighbours and friends arrived throughout the day bringing food and drinks with them for the wake. Most of them were curious as to why Johnston had tried to kill Cleland, but no one had the answer.

As rumours began to spread about the possibility of Johnston being a spy and being responsible for the deaths of the four young men many people told Martha they would not be coming to the funeral.

Betsy was never far from Martha's side and when she heard that Reverend Steel Dickson was thinking of staying away, she rode over to his home and reminded him of his promise to her, that he would not judge anyone. She told him it was his duty to support Martha and her new son no matter what he thought about Johnston's guilt.

On the day of the funeral there was a large turnout, and as the mourners gathered around the oak tree the Reverend Steel Dickson arrived to take the service. He began by describing all the good deeds that David Johnston had been involved in during his lifetime reminding the mourners that it was God who would ultimately decide on an individual's innocence or guilt.

As the funeral ceremony ended Martha's mother arrived and apologised for her behaviour and asked Martha if she and her grandson would like to come and live with her.

Chapter 19

Almost a year after his arrest, the date for the trial of William Orr was finally set for Monday 18th September 1797. Rumours about the weak evidence against him were common knowledge and many assumed Orr would be released once the case started. However, the Reverend Steel Dickson was not so sure. He was of the same opinion as Dr Drennan and was convinced Viscount Castlereagh and other government ministers were going to destroy Orr to deter people from joining the United Irishmen. He was also aware of another more sinister rumour that the British Government's longer-term aim was to form a union between the kingdoms of England, Scotland, Wales and Ireland and that they intended to use Orr's death to provoke a short, sharp, civil war with the United Irishmen. The British Government believed that once they defeated the United Irishmen the Irish politicians would agree to the new union, even though many were against the idea.

Reverend Steel Dickson had been planning to go to the trial himself but unfortunately, he had to attend to urgent family business in Scotland, and asked Billy if he would go in his place. Billy was honoured and when he told Betsy he was going she asked if she could go along with him. They arrived early in Carrickfergus on Monday morning and while Billy went to stable the horses, Betsy joined several people queuing outside the court building.

'Hello,' said one of the women in the line. 'Have you come far?'

'Not too far. I live in Gransha. It's a small village on the other side of the lough, near Bangor,' replied Betsy noticing the woman was pregnant. 'I left home just after six this morning. What about you?'

'About the same distance. I live over near Lough Neagh. May I ask why you decided to come today?'

Betsy was slightly surprised by the question. 'To show our support for William Orr. I've come with my boyfriend. He will be here in a few moments. We think it's appalling what the government is putting Mr Orr, and his family through. Let's hope the British legal system will finally show some sense and throw his case out, and let the poor man go home to his family. It's what everyone wants.'

'That's very honourable of you.'

'And what about you?'

'I'm here to support my husband.'

Betsy realised she was talking to Isabella Orr.

'I... I'm... sorry I didn't...'

'Please don't be,' said Isabella hurriedly. 'I'm sorry if I embarrassed you. It's good to know there are people out there who fully support William.'

'Oh, but we do, and I know hundreds of people who would have come here today if they only could. Are you here on your own?'

'No, William's brother, James and his father Samuel are with me.' With that she paused to introduce them.

'Pleased to meet you,',' said Betsy as she shook hands with both men. 'My name is Betsy Gray.'

'Hello Betsy,' said Samuel Orr. 'I heard what you said earlier, and may I say it is a pleasure to meet you.'

'My mother was going to join us,' said Isabella. 'But she is looking after our children. Let's hope their ordeal will be over soon. It has been very hard on them, not having William at home. They miss him terribly, but, as you said, hopefully the judge will realise this is all a mistake and let him come home with me tonight.'

As they chatted Billy joined them and to Betsy's surprise, they seemed to know each other.

'Hello Isabella,' he said. 'It's been a terrible time for you and your family but hopefully it will be over soon.'

'Thanks Billy, I have already met your charming girlfriend. Thank you for your support.'

Suddenly several armed soldiers appeared on the street as the doors into the court building were opened. Everyone entering was stopped and searched by more soldiers before they were allowed in.

'Will you sit with me?' Isabella said to Betsy. 'My in-laws are wonderful men, but it would be nice to have another woman beside me.'

'Of course, I will,' replied Betsy.

As they walked in Betsy was taken aback by the number of armed soldiers inside the building. It was obvious the authorities were prepared for any form of protest.

Once they reached the courtroom where the case was to be heard, Betsy and Billy sat beside Isabella. They could see William Orr's defence team sitting in their black robes as they studied several papers lying on the benches in front of them.

'The tall one is John Curran,' whispered Billy to Betsy. 'The other one is William Sampson. They are the best defence lawyers in Ireland. They will make sure William receives a fair trial. The man sitting to the right of the defence counsel is Thomas Kemmis. He is the crown prosecutor. The people around him are his legal team.'

Betsy glanced at them and saw that they were also concentrating on their paperwork. They appeared to be slightly nervous and on edge compared to the defence counsel.

Suddenly there was a hush in the court as a door opened and the prisoner, William Orr was marched in.

Betsy saw him briefly stop in the open doorway and gaze around the courtroom before stepping into the defendant's dock where he was surrounded by a body of armed soldiers.

This was the first time Betsy had seen the man everyone was talking about. William Orr was over six-foot-tall. He had a well-proportioned body and looked very confident as he walked into the dock. To Betsy his demeanour suggested strength and a certain gracefulness. He was wearing a blue coat over a patterned waistcoat and a white shirt with a green tie. He had black trousers and white silk stockings with thin blue stripes.

Betsy watched as he gazed around the faces of those in the courtroom and saw him smile when he spotted Isabella.

Betsy liked him immediately.

As Orr sat down, she watched his lively, dark brown eyes absorbing everything going on around him.

A few moments later there was another buzz when everyone rose to their feet as Judge Yelverton and Judge Chamberlaine walked in to take their seats.

When the courtroom settled, Judge Yelverton asked the prosecution to begin the case by presenting their evidence against William Orr.

Thomas Kemmis stood up and called for Private Hugh Wheatley of the Fifeshire Regiment of Fencibles to come to the witness stand.

Various voices called out Wheatley's name and eventually a rather nervous looking soldier entered the witness box. A court official asked him to place his hand on a bible. He swore that the evidence he was about to give was the truth, the whole truth and nothing but the truth.

Prosecutor Kemmis adjusted his robes before he addressed the witness. 'Private Wheatley will you tell the court how you first met the defendant William Orr.'

Private Wheatley took a deep breath and placed both hands on the horizontal metal bar in front of him and gripped it tightly as he tried to stop his body from shaking.

'Your honour, I had been on leave for a few days, visiting my family in Scotland. I was making my way back to Derry to join my regiment...'

'When was this?'

'It was on Monday the 25th April 1796. It was a very warm day and I decided to stop at a pub to quench my thirst. While I was having a drink, I was approached by several men who asked me if I would like to join the United Irishmen. I said I would.'

'Private Wheatley, why did you tell these men that you wanted to join the United Irishmen?'

'I didn't really want to your honour, but I was afraid they might harm me. And so, I pretended I was interested in what they were saying. I wanted to save my life.'

'What did the men do next?'

'We finished our drinks and left the pub. We walked up the road to a barn. When I walked in, I saw William Orr. He was chairing a meeting of several other men. The men I was with told him I wanted to join the United Irishmen. Orr asked me if I would be willing to promote the Society among my fellow soldiers. I told him I was. I did that because I was frightened what he might do to me.'

'After you agreed to this, what happened?'

'William Orr had a bible with him. He asked me to put my hand on it. When I did, he gave me a sheet of paper and asked me to read the words that were printed on it out loud with him. I did as he asked. When I finished, he congratulated me and told me I had just sworn the oath of the United Irishmen, and that I was now one of them. William Orr said that from now on I had to promise to keep the secrets of the Society. He said that the United Irishmen had enough armed men to get the political reforms they wanted, by force if they had to. He said if there was an uprising, I would have to show him where our weapons were stored. I had to desert the regiment and join them and the French soldiers when they invaded Ireland. I agreed to do everything William Orr asked me because I was afraid for my life.'

'No further questions,' said prosecutor Kemmis as he sat down.

Defence counsellor John Curran stood up to begin his cross examination of the witness.

'Private Wheatley, have you ever deserted from the army?'

'No sir, I have not,' replied Wheatly looking astonished by the suggestion. 'I may have been late getting back to the barracks after leave on a few occasions, but I have never deserted. I'm a loyal soldier.'

'Has anyone ever offered you money to desert?'

Wheatley paused for a few moments before answering. 'Well, yes sir. I met a man in a public house in Belfast once and he offered me money if I would leave the regiment and join the United Irishmen. But I refused.'

'Was that one of the times you were, as you say, late back after a spot of leave?'

'Yes, it was, but it was just a coincidence.'

'Have you ever expressed your dislike of the army to anyone Private Wheatley?'

'No sir... Unless it was to someone, I suspected of being a member of the United Irishmen.'

'Private Wheatley, were you drunk when you first enlisted in the Army?'

Wheatley seemed surprised by the question.

'Erm... I might have had a drink or two on that day in question,' he replied wondering who the lawyer had been talking to, because everyone knew he had been so drunk when he enlisted that he didn't know what day it was, and when he sobered up and realised what he had done he had tried to desert.

'Have you not told several people that you hate your life as a soldier Private Wheatley. And did you not tell them that you wanted to desert?'

'No sir, I did not. I don't recall saying those words to anyone unless I was trying to trick them.'

'Private Wheatley what date did your leave end on?'

Wheatly coughed a couple of times. 'I can't remember. I think it was that Monday.'

Defence counsellor Curran lifted a sheet of paper. 'I have an army instruction here that says your leave expired on Saturday 23rd April. I put it to you Private Wheatley that you were late in returning from your leave and you made this story up to save yourself?'

'I did not. I was on my way back when William Orr made me join the United Irishmen.'

'No further questions.'

Private Wheatley looked around for guidance as to what to do next before one of the court officials ushered him away.

Prosecutor Kemmis stood up and called for Private John Lindsay, his second witness, to come to the stand.

A few moments later a thin, gaunt looking man in a rather unkempt uniform marched into the courtroom and entered the witness box. The court official asked him to place his hand on the bible. He did as he was told and like Private Wheatley before him swore to tell the truth and only the truth.

'Private Lindsay, can you please tell the court how you first met the defendant, William Orr.'

It was quite clear to Betsy that Private Lindsay looked very uncomfortable. He seemed nervous and uneasy as he began to speak in a very low whisper.

'I was with...'

'Speak up private,' ordered Judge Yelverton. 'I need to be able to hear what you have to say.'

Private Lindsay cleared his throat and began again. 'I met Private Wheatley on the boat that was bringing us both back after a short spell of leave in Scotland. As we were walking back to our barracks in Londonderry, we stopped at a public house to have a drink. It was a very warm day. While we were sitting in the bar we were approached by a group of local men. After a few drinks they asked us if we would like to join the United Irishmen. I said no, but Private Wheatley said he would. And so, we were invited to join them in a nearby barn. When we went there, I saw William Orr talking to several men. After a while I saw him take Private Wheatley to one side and administer the United Irishmen's oath to him.'

'Thank you,' said prosecutor Kemmis.

Defence counsellor Curran stood up.

'Before we start Private Lindsay, I would just like to remind you that you are under oath to tell the truth and nothing but the truth to the court.'

'Yes sir. I know. I will.'

'You say you saw William Orr administer the United Irishmen's oath to Private Wheatley. Is that true?'

'Yes sir.'

'Did you actually hear Private Wheatley swear the oath?'

Private Lindsay swallowed deeply before he answered. 'No sir, I did not.'

'Do you know what Private Wheatley said while he was talking to William Orr?'

'No sir, I do not.'

Defence counsellor Curran paused and looked over at the members of the jury. 'So how do you know that Private Wheatley swore the United Irishmen's oath?'

'I know he did because Private Wheatley told me he had taken the oath.'

'When did he tell you this?' asked Defence counsellor Curran while looking at the members of the jury.

Private Lindsay cleared his throat. 'He told me a few hours later that he had sworn the United Irishmen's oath with William Orr.'

'He told you a few hours later?'

Private Lindsay nodded his head vigorously in agreement. 'Yes, that's right. He told me when we went to the magistrate's house.'

'To the magistrate's house? And is that when you found out that Private Wheatley had sworn the oath of the United Irishmen?'

'Yes sir.'

'Why did you decide to go to the magistrate's house?'

'We were worried that we would be charged again for getting back to the barracks late and Private Wheatley thought that if we told someone in authority what had happened that we would be safe.'

'What happened when you arrived at the magistrates.'

'Magistrate McCartney asked us for our statements. That's when I heard Private Wheatley say he had taken the oath.'

'Did you give Magistrate McCartney a statement in which you stated that you heard William Orr administer the oath of the United Irishmen to Private Wheatley?'

'No sir, I did not. I told the magistrate that I had seen Private Wheatley and William Orr talking. It was Private Wheatley who said that he swore the oath.'

'So, let us be clear on this Private Lindsay. Did you give a statement to Magistrate McCartney that you heard William Orr administer the oath of the United Irishmen to Private Wheatley?'

'No sir, I did not.'

'Did you hear Private Wheatley swear the oath of the United Irishmen?'

'No, I did not. But I was in the room when Private Wheatley said he did, and I saw him talking to William Orr. But I don't know what they were saying to each other.'

'So, you are unable to tell the court what they were talking about?'

'No. That's right, sir.'

Defence counsellor Curran addressed Judge Yelverton directly. 'Your honour, I move we dismiss any evidence given by Private Lindsay as being completely immaterial. He has admitted he doesn't know what William Orr and Private Wheatley were discussing, and it wasn't until after he left the meeting that he was told it was the United Irishmen's oath.'

Judge Yelverton looked at Judge Chamberlaine and shrugged his shoulders before agreeing with the defence counsellor and asked Private Lindsay to leave the stand.

Defence counsellor Curran continued. 'My Lords, given the lack of evidence we have heard this morning from both of the prosecutors witnesses I ask that the case against our client be dismissed. When William Orr was arrested almost a year ago, he was charged with High Treason. May I remind your lordships that anyone who is charged with High Treason has certain rights, which include the need to have the full charges laid out against him, and to have at least two viable witnesses who can testify against him. However, at the Lent assizes, earlier this year, our client was arraigned on a different indictment. This new charge was framed under the Insurrection Act for administering unlawful oaths to which he pleaded not guilty. The need for two witnesses is not a requirement under the Insurrection Act. My Lords, I believe the original charge brought against my client is unfounded and therefore this case against him should be dismissed.'

Judge Yelverton and Judge Chamberlaine deliberated for a few minutes.

'Mr Curran your objection is overruled. The case will continue,' said Judge Yelverton.

Prosecutor Kemmis stood up and called another witness.

John Wilson, the owner of a public house near the barracks of the Fifeshire Fencibles Regiment in Londonderry was called to testify for Private Wheatley's character. However, under cross examination Curran was able to quickly establish that Mr. Wilson wasn't really that well acquainted with Private Wheatley at all and asked that his evidence be dismissed.

Betsy noticed that even though there were several officers of the Fifeshire Fencibles present in court, none of them were called to give evidence as to the good character of Private Wheatley or Private Lindsay.

Once John Wilson left the courtroom, prosecutor Kemmis declared they had no more witnesses to call and proceeded to sum up the evidence against William Orr.

'Members of the jury, today you heard Private Wheatley describe how the defendant William Orr forced him into joining the United Irishmen and how he asked him to commit treason for the same organisation. You also heard from Private Wheatley that, the defendant, William Orr openly declared his intention to work with a French invasion army to overthrow the legitimate government here in Ireland. You heard how William Orr tried to ensure Private Wheatley's commitment to these treasonable acts by having him swear the illegal oath of the United Irishmen. An activity that is unlawful under the Insurrection Act. You have heard the defence counsel try to besmirch the reputation of Private Wheatley, but I leave it to your good judgement to consider the credit due to this honourable witness. Members of the jury, after having listened to the damning evidence against the defendant, I say there is only one verdict you can deliver and find William Orr guilty as charged.'

When prosecutor Kemmis finished he sat down.

Betsy was expecting William Orr's defence team to sum up their view of the evidence and was surprised when Judge Yelverton proceeded to remind the jury that if they found William Orr guilty of administering the United Irishmen's oath to a serving member of his majesty's forces he would be obliged under the Insurrection Act to sentence him to death by hanging. He then asked the jury to retire to consider their verdict.

As the jury members filed out of the courtroom Betsy could feel an air of optimism in those watching from the public gallery and she assumed the jury would quickly reappear and return a verdict of not guilty.

'I don't see how they could convict William on the evidence we saw today,' said Isabella. 'They never had a case against him. They should have set my poor husband free months ago.'

'I agree,' said Billy. 'He was initially charged with committing High Treason but when the prosecution studied the witness statements, they must have realised they didn't have two witnesses and so there was no case to answer.'

'When they realised they only had Private Wheatley's testimony, and even that sounded very unconvincing,' said Betsy. 'Someone must have decided to charge William under the Insurrection Act.'

'The case against William is non-existent,' said Orr's father. 'The jury shouldn't be out for too long.'

A man, sitting behind them leaned over to add. 'They should have released him when they realised their mistake.'

'That's right,' agreed Betsy. 'It was cruel of them to keep William in prison and away from his family.'

'Aye, you're right,' agreed the man.

About an hour later the court administrative officer announced the court was adjourned and would reconvene at nine o'clock tomorrow morning, depending upon the jury reaching a decision.

'Have you somewhere to stay for the night?' asked Isabella as the courtroom began to empty.

'No, we weren't expecting this. We'll have to go home and come back in the morning.'

'We are staying with my aunt here in Carrickfergus, you are welcome to stay with us if you like. She has plenty of spare rooms.'

'Thank you, Isabella that would be very kind.'

Betsy spent a restless night during which she got very little sleep. She kept thinking about the case and what might happen to William Orr. She was relieved when they eventually left the house in the morning and walked back to the courthouse. Once again everyone stood when Judge Yelverton and Judge Chamberlaine entered and took their seats.

A few moments later members of the jury entered the courtroom. There were gasps of astonishment from people sitting in the public gallery as they watched the men stagger to their seats because it was obvious to everyone that a significant number of them were drunk or were suffering from hangovers.

Once they were all seated the clerk of the court stood up.

'Members of the jury, have you reached a verdict?'

A sad, elderly looking juryman stood up. 'My Lord, I am the foreman of the jury, and we would like to know if we would be allowed to reach a qualified verdict. We have discussed the case long and hard and we were wondering if we could find the defendant guilty of administering an unlawful oath, but we would like to ask your lordships that you would spare the defendant's life.'

Judge Yelverton shook his head. 'No, you may not. The only verdict this court will accept from the jury is one of guilty or not guilty.'

There was a hush as Judge Yelverton looked towards the clerk of the court, who once again posed his question.

'Members of the jury, have you agreed upon a verdict?'

The foreman of the jury shook his head and sat down. The courtroom was silent for a long time until the clerk of the court repeated his question. Once again, the foreman of the jury stood to answer. Betsy thought the poor man looked distressed and was finding it difficult to speak.

'I'm sorry your honour, but we have not been able to reach a verdict upon which we can all agree. We can do no more and therefore we leave the defendant in your lordship's hands. His fate is at your lordship's mercy.'

There was a stir around the court as Betsy and everyone else tried to comprehend the consequences of what was happening.

'Quiet in the courtroom,' ordered Judge Yelverton. 'Gentlemen of the jury, I'm afraid I cannot accept that reply as your judgement. You must return to your deliberations and reconsider your verdict. I repeat, I can only accept a verdict of guilty or not guilty.'

Once again, the members of the jury filed out of the courtroom to reconsider their verdict. The judges also left the court while everyone else, including Betsy and Billy remained seated. About an hour later the court was back in session as the jury returned.

The clerk of the court stood and once again asked, 'Members of the jury, have you agreed upon a verdict?'

The foreman of the jury rose to his feet. 'No, we have not been able to reach a verdict.'

There were loud gasps from members of the public. Betsy could feel Isabella tense beside her. She took hold of her hand and gently squeezed it reassuringly.

'Quiet in the court,' bellowed a frustrated Judge Yelverton. 'Gentlemen, there is only one verdict I will accept from the jury and that is either guilty or not guilty. Now go back and make your decision.'

Once again, the jury left the court but this time they did not deliberate for very long and within fifteen minutes they indicated they were ready to return.

When the judges took their seats the clerk of the court asked the jury if they had finally reached a verdict. The foreman of the jury stood but did not answer immediately.

After a few awkward moments another member of the jury called out. 'Will you please stop all this nonsense and tell the judge that we have found the prisoner guilty.'

With this intervention the foreman seemed to resign himself to the jury's decision.

'We, the jury, find the prisoner guilty, with a recommendation to have his life spared.'

As the foreman of the jury handed a note to the clerk of the court to give to Judge Yelverton many of the people sitting in the public gallery stood and began shouting, 'Shame on you.'

Betsy glanced at Isabella and saw there were tears in her eyes. She heard her whisper, 'I love you,' as she stared at William Orr.

Betsy glanced at Orr and saw him nod his head and smile. She was sure he seemed to stand taller in the dock. Orr slowly lifted his right hand and straightened his green necktie as he waited for the noise to die down and for Judge Yelverton to speak.

'Quiet in the court,' he ordered before he looked down and read the note from the jury. 'I will consider your verdict for clemency. This court is now adjourned until two o'clock this afternoon. Clear the courthouse.'

The soldiers quickly escorted Orr from the dock as others began ushering everyone else out of the building.

'What happens now?' Betsy asked Billy as they left the courthouse.

'Judge Yelverton will consult with Camden the Lord Lieutenant of Ireland to consider the jury's recommendation and will pronounce his decision this afternoon.'

'The evidence against him is farcical, surely the judge must accept their recommendation for clemency,' said Betsy.

Orr's father shook his head wearily. 'I don't know Betsy; we must prepare ourselves for the worst.'

No one felt like eating any lunch and shortly after two o'clock the doors were reopened. They took their seats as William Orr was escorted back into the dock. A few moments later Judge Yelverton and Judge Chamberlaine returned. The courtroom was silent as Judge Yelverton turned to William Orr to pronounce the decision of the court.

'The request for clemency has been denied. It is therefore my duty to pronounce the sentence of the court.'

Defence counsellor Curran stood up.

'My Lord may I have your permission to address the court on behalf of my client before you pronounce sentence?'

'Of course, you may,' replied Judge Yelverton.

'My Lord, I ask that this judgement be put aside as I have been reliably informed several members of the jury have stated that large quantities of alcohol was brought into the room where they were deliberating their decision last night subsequently a significant number of jury members became inebriated during their discussions and proceeded to threaten other members with violence if they did not find the defendant guilty.'

Judge Yelverton quickly declared against his legal argument announcing that any statements by the members of the jury would not be permitted to influence any action by the court as they were calculated to throw discredit upon the verdict and could therefore not be the foundation of any motion to the court.

Defence counsellor Curran stood up and held up three affidavits made by members of the jury in which they stated they had witnessed other members being drunk and had been threatened by them. When Curran began to read one of the statements to the court, he was interrupted by Judge Chamberlaine and ordered to stop on the grounds that the remarks were insensitive towards the jury.

A dejected Curran sat down saying he had no more appeals to offer.

Judge Yelverton looked directly at William Orr. 'It is my duty to pronounce the sentence of the court...' However, as he tried to continue, he began coughing and had to stop on several occasions to clear his throat. 'William Orr... you have been found guilty of administering the illegal oath... of the United Irishmen... to a serving soldier of his majesty's forces... in which you enticed him to commit acts of treason against his majesty....' His voice became weaker until it was almost inaudible.

There was a long awkward pause before the judge finally regained his composure.

'You will be taken to the place from whence you came... from thence to the common place of execution... the gallows... there to be hung by the neck... until you are dead.'

A silence continued after Judge Yelverton finished speaking and with everyone's eyes on him, the judge slowly lowered his head into his hands and began to weep, his sobbing clearly audible throughout the courtroom. No one moved or made a sound as they watched Judge Yelverton in his distressed state. His sobbing went on for almost ten minutes before he was able to raise his head.

'May I speak, your Lordship?' William Orr said when he saw the judge look at him.

Judge Yelverton nodded his head.

'My Lord, the jury has convicted me of being a criminal. But my own heart tells me their conviction is a lie, and that I'm not a criminal. If they have found me wrongly, it is worse for them than for me. For I can forgive them. I'm not afraid to die. I wish to say only one thing and that is to declare upon this awful occasion and in the presence of God, that the evidence against me was grossly and wickedly perjured.'

William turned and smiled at Isabela before he left the dock to be escorted back to his prison cell by several soldiers.

As Judge Yelverton and Judge Chamberlaine left the courtroom everyone in the public gallery began shouting abuse at them and the other court officials.

'Isabella, I'm so sorry,' said Betsy as the soldiers began ordering them out of the courtroom.

'Thank you,' she whispered as they held each other close.

'We will appeal,' said William Orr's father. 'They cannot get away with this.'

The soldiers gathered round them and ushered them from the court building.

'Thank you for being here,' said Isabella. 'We must not give up. This is so wrong. I'm going to see if they will let me see William.'

'Good luck' said Betsy.

Over the next few days William Orr's family and friends quickly mounted several appeals against the decision but each one came to nothing, and a week after his trial the authorities announced that William Orr was to be hung on Saturday the 7th of October 1797.

This was cancelled at the last minute, raising everyone's hopes, and for a while it looked like his appeal was going to succeed. But their hopes were dashed when the decision of Judge Yelverton was ratified by the Irish government and a new date of the 14th of October was set for Orr's execution.

Betsy and Billy kept in touch with Isabella while the appeals were going on and were with her at her farm in Farranshane when the final appeal was rejected, and the new date was set.

'They say I can take the children to the jail to see him. The jailers are so kind, if it was up to them, they would let him go. But we seem to be caught in some government conspiracy, it's as though they are using William as a pawn in a much bigger political game.'

'How are you coping?' asked Betsy.

'I have discovered that my body can only take so much grief and I can weep no more, I feel as though the whole world is crushing the breath out of me. That's when I must rest here and think about my love. There are days when I imagine I can hear him speaking to me and I turn around to look for him, but he is never there. Sometimes I waken in the middle of the night and I'm sure I can feel him lying beside me, his breathing gentle and rhythmic. If it wasn't for my faith in our lord Jesus Christ, I don't know how I could get through these terrible days. I'm so glad I shared those few short years with William. Everyone is telling me to stay here on Saturday, but how can I do that. How can I stay here when the only man I have ever loved will be taken from me forever?'

Early on the morning of Saturday the 14th October 1797, Betsy and Billy joined Isabella and a small group of William Orr's close family and friends outside the gates of Carrickfergus prison. The authorities had been expecting thousands of spectators and had lined the half mile route from the prison to the field at Gallows Green, on the main Belfast Road, where the hanging would take place, with hundreds of armed soldiers from Carrickfergus Castle and Belfast. However, to show their disgust at the decision of the court the baulk of the population stayed away in protest.

At precisely eight thirty the prison gates opened and a carriage carrying William Orr and two Presbyterian ministers, Reverend Hill and Reverend Stavely came out with an armed guard marching on either side.

Isabella waved at William as he passed by before she and the rest of the small group began walking behind the carriage. Throughout the journey Betsy could hear both ministers deep in prayer and as the grieving procession drew near to Gallows Green the Reverend Hill began reading an extract from the bible.

'...For I have heard the slander of many; fear was on every side; while they took counsel together against me, they devised to take my life away. But I trusted in thee, Lord; I said, thou art my God. My times are in thy hand; deliver me from the hand of mine enemies, and from them that persecute me. Make thy face to shine upon thy servant; save me for thy mercy's sake. Let me not be ashamed, O Lord; for I have called upon thee; let the wicked be ashamed, and let them be silent in the grave...'

Reverend Hill was still reading the passage when the carriage turned off the road and into the field at Gallows Green. At the end of the field there stood three ancient granite pillars which local people called the Three Sisters. They had been erected in a triangular formation so that when wooden beams were spanned from pillar to pillar three condemned criminals could be hung at the same time. A single rope, with a noose at the end, was suspended from one of the beams.

As the solemn cortege approached the pillars Betsy felt Isabella become tense.

'I cannot do this,' she said. 'I cannot watch my husband being murdered.'

One of the men walking beside her said quietly. 'There is a house across the road. You can go there.'

'I'll come with you,' said Betsy, and together they turned around and began walking through the ranks of the waiting soldiers. As they left, they could hear Reverend Savage reading the final passage from his bible.

'…O grave, where is thy victory? The sting of death is sin, and the strength of sin is the law. But thanks be to God, which giveth us the victory through our Lord Jesus Christ. Therefore, my beloved brethren, be ye steadfast, immoveable, always abounding in the work of the Lord, forasmuch as ye know that your labour is not in vain in the Lord.'

When Betsy and Isabella finally reached the house on the other side of the road, the front door was quickly opened by a young woman who directed them to a neatly furnished room at the rear of the house. Betsy sat down beside Isabella on a large sofa.

'Thank you, Betsy,' said Isabella as she grasped her hand.

They sat in silence.

A large grandfather clock sitting in the hallway began to chime the hour. Isabella tensed, her fingers gripping tightly on Betsy's wrist with each strike until the echoes of the last one died away.

'It's over,' whispered Isabella. As an intense silence filled the room her eyes glistened, and tears began to run down her face.

Sometime later there was a sudden commotion in the hallway outside. Betsy stood up as the door was flung open and several men rushed in carrying William Orr's body which they placed on the large table and a doctor began to examine him. For a few moments there was hope, but that was dashed when the doctor sadly shook his head.

'It is no good, William's neck is broken.'

Isabela stood beside the body.

'Tell me what happened,' she asked as she gently held one of her husband's hands.

'When the carriage stopped by the pillars,' said Reverend Hill. 'William stood up to address everyone. He reminded them he was an innocent man, and that he loved you and his children and that it would be them who will suffer most because he had been found guilty by the evidence of a liar and a corrupt court system. He shook our hands before walking up the steps onto the scaffold where the executor was waiting. Just before he died, William called out. "I'm no traitor. I die for a persecuted country. Great Jehovah receive my soul. I die in the true faith of a Presbyterian." William was a truly brave man right to the end.'

'Thank you,' said Isabella. 'You have been wonderful friends. I don't know what I would have done without your help.'

Isabella was not permitted to organise a formal funeral to bury her husband's remains as he had died a criminal, and so after a short service his body was carried from the house and placed on a bed of straw in an open cart to begin the journey to his final resting place. The army were under strict orders to stop any show of support or mourning as the cart travelled through the countryside, but despite their best efforts soon every road was packed with people waiting to show their last respects to a man they viewed as a martyr for his religion and Ireland. Some people were so overcome with emotion they would rush over to the open cart and kiss it like it was some holy relic. The slow, painful, journey continued along the country roads, through the small, packed townland of Straid, until the cortege reached the meeting house in the middle of Ballynure village. Here they stopped for the night. William Orr's body was carried inside the hall where it was dressed and placed in a coffin and his wake held. Food was provided for the thousands of mourners who arrived throughout the night to pay their last respects.

In the morning the coffin was loaded onto a black hearse, behind a large black Clydesdale horse. When the soldiers saw all the trappings of a formal funeral being assembled, they tried to prevent the hearse from leaving the village, but the sheer numbers of mourners forced them to stand aside. The roads ahead were already packed with thousands of grieving people as the cortege finally set off. Despite being harassed all the time by the soldiers, the mourners in the solemn procession managed to maintain their dignity as they passed through the town of Ballyclare, along crowded country lanes towards his final resting place in a graveyard at Castle Upton, just outside the town of Templepatrick.

When the cortege reached Castle Upton the hearse turned off the main road and onto a long narrow, tree lined lane. When it reached the end of the lane the driver stopped, and six mourners slid the coffin from the back of the hearse onto their shoulders and carried it into the walled graveyard before stopping beside an open grave. The soldiers climbed onto the walls surrounding the graveyard and continued their harassment, mocking the mourners, and waving flags with ERIN GO BRAY crudely written on them while braying like donkeys.

The undertakers stood at either end of the coffin and lowered it down onto two planks that spanned the open grave. Reverend Hill then led the mourners in the final service before the coffin was gently lowered into the grave of Ally Orr, William's favourite sister.

Reverend Hill sprinkled soil onto the coffin saying, 'Ashes to ashes, dust to dust. I'm the resurrection and the life, saith the Lord. He that believes in me, though he were dead, yet shall he live. Whosoever lives and believes in me shall never die.'

No marker was allowed to be added to the existing headstone because William Orr had died a convicted criminal.

As the Reverend Steel Dickson stood by the graveside, he could see the hurt in the eyes of those around him. He knew it wasn't just over the murder of William Orr, but the effects of the government's war of attrition that was beginning to take its toll on them. Some had personally experienced the violence of the militia, while many knew of someone who did. Reverend Steel Dickson's senior officers were telling him that most of the companies were on their knees, but none had suggested it was time to surrender and quit. As he looked down into the open grave Reverend Steel Dickson decided it was time to fight back, to show the government that the United Irishmen were still a force to be reckoned with.

Three weeks later on a dry, sunny November weekend, one thousand armed members of the North Down, United Irishmen gathered on the shores of Strangford Lough to demonstrate their prowess on the battlefield.

The pikemen were lined up in four rows, standing one behind the other as Sergeant Major White quickly inspected them.

'Pikemen,' he bellowed at the top of his voice. 'Pikemen. Attention.'

One thousand pikemen snapped to attention. The razor-sharp blades of their pikes glistening in the bright sunshine.

'Pikemen,' bellowed out Sergeant Major White. 'Pikemen. Move into battle formation.'

There was a sudden clatter of noise as two hundred and fifty pikemen in the front row lowered their pikes to a horizontal level. The second row held their pikes horizontally at shoulder height, in between the men in front. While the third and fourth rows raised their pikes in readiness to fill any gaps that came in the ranks in front of them.

'Pikemen. Pikemen will move forward at a slow march… By the left,' hollered the Sergeant Major.

There was a loud grunt as one thousand pikemen stepped forward in unison.

'Left… right… left…,' called Sergeant Major White, dictating the speed at which the rows would move.

Slowly the tempo began to pick up, and as the body of men gained momentum the sergeant major yelled at the top of his voice.

'Pikemen. Pikemen charge.'

All one thousand pikemen immediately roared, 'Remember Orr' as they rushed their wall of steel towards an imaginary enemy at the far end of the field.

Watching from the safety of the side lines Betsy thought the charge was formidable and imagined how frightened the enemy would feel as they came charging towards them.

With the charge over, the pikemen moved on to practice different formations in smaller groups of up to eighty men. Betsy and the other members formed support teams to practice hand to hand combat using their swords and daggers.

When the training was finished Reverend Steel Dickson gathered everyone around him.

'For the last few months the Irish government and their henchmen have been forging a war against the United Irishmen, but it has been particularly brutal here in Ulster. Their intention is to destroy our will to fight but they forgot one thing. We will never surrender.'

A great roar went up from the pikemen.

'Our resolve is buried deep in our hearts. When the time comes, and it will be soon, we will prove our willingness to fight. When you leave this field tonight go home and prepare for war. When we march into battle, we will let everyone know that we have not forgotten what they did to William Orr.'

With a mighty shout the pikemen once again roared their approval. 'Remember Orr.'

As the main body of pikemen started to break up Henry Poulter called the Gransha unit together.

'I would like to thank you all for coming here today and showing everyone just how skilled and dedicated you are as a fighting unit. But there is someone who has been working extremely hard to help bring this company up to battle readiness. We all know how difficult the last six months have been, but through it all this individual has managed to keep every one of you together, no matter what hurdles were placed in the way. It is therefore my honour and pleasure to present this specially made sword, in recognition of all the hard work she has done to help get this company of pikemen to battle readiness. Betsy if you would please step forward.'

Everyone clapped and cheered as an embarrassed Betsy walked over to him.

'This sword was made especially for you by the best blacksmith in the county, and it is my honour to present you with it.'

Poulter extended the handle of the sword towards Betsy. She reached out and took hold of it, pulling the blade from the scabbard. The sword felt light and well balanced in her hand as she held it aloft.

'Thank you, Henry,' she said, as the crowd loudly roared.

'Remember Orr.'

Chapter 20

The Lord Lieutenant of Ireland, the Earl of Camden, sat down with his nephew Viscount Castlereagh in Dublin at a small dinner party on New Year's Eve as 1797 drew to a close. After a pleasant meal the gentlemen moved to the library to enjoy their cigars and brandy.

'Tell me about Ulster,' said Camden.

'I think we can conclude that General Lake's mission to disarm the United Irishmen has been very successful. We were expecting a violent reaction from them when William Orr was found guilty, but the response was rather muted. I suspect the old fox, Reverend Steel Dickson had something to do with that. There were a few protests, but there was no sign of the armed rebellion we had anticipated.'

'I heard that there was a very large turnout of mourners for his funeral.'

'There was. Senior officers have been chastised for not being more forceful in preventing the gathering, but they said there were simply too many.'

'I've heard Wolfe Tone has been very active in Paris again, preaching freedom for his fellow countrymen and pressing for another French invasion force. Unfortunately, the French still view Ireland as the weak point in our defences and as far as we can establish, they are still determined to take advantage of the political unrest we have here. London's current belief is that if the French were able to land an army in support of an uprising by the United Irishmen there is a high probability our forces would be unable to contain them. We would have to sue for peace. That would result in Britain having a hostile country only a few miles from our shores, just waiting for any of our enemies to exploit. We could never allow that to happen. We would be in a very weak military position. Therefore, we must do everything in our power to prevent the French and the United Irishmen from coming together.'

'I agree. That's why we are shifting our focus to the southern counties, particularly in and around Dublin. Our intelligence sources indicate that is where the United Irishmen expect the uprising to begin.'

'Have they set a date?'

'No, a few speculative dates have been mentioned, but personally I think their leadership would want the revolt to be launched sometime around May or June, when the good weather arrives, and before the men have to return to their farms to bring in the harvests.'

'So, what are our plans?'

'General Lake is moving his troops to the southern counties, with a remit to disarm and disrupt the activities of the United Irishmen. Just as his soldiers did in Ulster.'

'I heard a few members of parliament complaining about what they did up there.'

'Well his tactics may be distasteful to some but at least we know they work. We only have to look at what he achieved to see proof of that. They carried out over one hundred thousand raids on homes of people who were suspected of being members of the United Irishmen. They captured over eighty thousand pikes along with seventy thousand guns. They disrupted supply routes, by destroying blacksmiths premises and breaking up organised gangs who had been stealing guns and young saplings from houses and estates around the province. Those weapons would have been used to kill soldiers in an uprising. I agree, that on some occasions the soldiers may have been overzealous, but the deterrent effect their actions have had on the rest of the population is excellent. When people saw thousands of their neighbours being tortured and thrown out onto the street and watched their homes being set on fire because they were associated with the United Irishmen, they quickly realised that it was safer to be with us, rather than against us. General Lake's soldiers have done an excellent job and have destroyed the capability of the United Irishmen in Ulster to wage war against us. I will be recommending he is rewarded for his industry, because when the French assault force anchored in Bantry Bay last December we were restricted in how many soldiers we could send from Ulster to stop them.'

'I agree. What is the current situation in Ulster?'

'General Nugent is taking over command of the troops there and if the French attempt another invasion, he will be able to send his best troops to wherever they land on the Irish coast. To make sure he has enough manpower to do this, we are running a recruitment campaign to raise new Yeomanry support groups in Ulster. We tried to do something similar earlier this year, but it wasn't very successful. However, we managed to get a positive response from members of the Orange Order in mid Ulster and since then several new Orange lodges have been established. There are now over twenty thousand Orangemen in Ulster. To tap into this expansion, we're going to announce another drive for new recruits in January and we will be giving priority to anyone who is a member of the Orange Order. We anticipate raising a force of at least five thousand men this time.'

'I understand there is a growing animosity between Orangemen and United Irishmen.'

'That's correct. This is something that we have been encouraging because it's in our interests to fuel that hostility. We have been declaring that the fight for liberty by the United Irishmen is a charade to cover up a popish plot to kick the protestants out of Ireland and establish a Catholic state. If we can drive a deep enough wedge between the loyalist Orangemen and the republican United Irishmen, we'll see the end of rebellion in Ireland.'

'Good. I was talking with Pitt a few days ago. He is still keen to bring forward the union.'

'So am I,' said Viscount Castlereagh. 'But we cannot do it while the United Irishmen exist. One of their prime aims is for Ireland to have its own parliament, where elected Irishmen can make their own laws without interference from Britain. We cannot allow that to happen for state security reasons. But if we push too hard for the union before we have sorted out the concerns of the current members of the Irish Parliament we could lose. We could find ourselves in the ludicrous position of having Dublin MP's siding with the United Irishmen. To win we must do this in stages. The first step is to destroy the United Irishmen. The second is to cajole, bribe, threaten, whatever, the Irish MP's to vote for a union. I believe we can buy enough of them to secure a majority, but it will take time. I have already begun discussions with several of them about this and I am discovering how an offer of a large state pension or a peerage can lower the high morals of these fine, upstanding gentlemen.'

'Pitt is also keen for us to move forward on Catholic emancipation.'

'As we agreed before, we must tread carefully with this. It would be a mistake to try and introduce legislation on this subject through the current Irish parliament. The MP's would never accept it, because their Lords and masters know that the Catholic vote would change the profile of parliament and they would lose their privileges and power. Our strategy is still to form a new union between England, Scotland, Wales and Ireland with the four nations having their own elected representation in Westminster. Once this has been achieved we can proceed with Catholic emancipation because the Irish Catholics will have become a minority within a protestant dominated United Kingdom, and any fears protestants may have about popish plots will disappear and the large estates of the gentry will remain safe.'

Camden raised his glass. 'Here's to a successful new year and the demise of the United Irishmen.'

Chapter 21

Betsy's mother finished setting the kitchen table in preparation for a meal to celebrate Betsy's twentieth birthday early on the afternoon of Saturday, the 6th January 1798. Normally, she would have arranged a party for such an occasion as this in the evening and in the village hall, but because of the curfew, people were reluctant to travel too far from their home at night in case they were challenged by any marauding soldiers in the search for United Irishmen and their weapons.

One of the first guests to arrive was Martha Johnston and her baby son, David.

'Oh, he looks so like his father,' said Betsy's mother as she picked the baby up and held him in her arms.

Martha smiled weakly and nodded. Any mention of her husband still caused her pain.

Betsy recognised the hurt in her face and put her arms around her.

'It will be all right,' she whispered.

'I'll be fine,' said Martha handing Betsy a small parcel. 'Happy birthday. I'm afraid it's not much, but I haven't been able to get the farm sorted out yet. I should have a new manager starting in a few weeks' time. The last few months have been very hard.'

'Thank you for your gift Martha, that's very kind,' said Betsy placing the present beside the others on the kitchen table while George went to answer another knock at the door.

'Hi Gina,' he said. 'Come in.'

Gina Russell looked very happy and was smiling as she stepped into the room.

'Hello everyone. It's been such a long time. And a special big hello to our birthday girl.'

'Thank you,' said Betsy as Gina handed her a gift. 'Can I get you something to drink?'

'I'll have some lemon water, please.'

While Betsy was getting Gina a drink Billy arrived with a bottle of wine.

'Happy Birthday,' he said kissing Betsy softly on the cheek.

Jessie Poulter was the last guest to arrive.

'Thank you all for coming,' said Betsy. 'Please have a seat at the table, we've prepared some party food.'

As everyone gathered around the table there was a knock at the door.

'Hello,' said the man when Betsy opened it. 'I'm looking for Elizabeth Gray.'

'That's me.'

'I have a letter for you.'

Betsy stared at her name and address on the envelope.

'Who is it?' her mother called.

'It's the postman. He has just given me a letter.'

'A letter?'

'Who is it from?' called George.

Betsy closed the door and turned the letter over.

'It's from Jenny Knox,' said Betsy walking back to the table where she picked up a knife and broke the wax seal and unfolded the single sheet of paper. 'I can't believe this came all the way from America.

'What does it say? Is Jenny well?' asked a curious Gina.

'Oh, I'm sorry,' said Betsy. 'Yes, Jenny says she is in good health, despite the long sea journey. When she arrived in Philadelphia she stayed with Rachel and Hugh for a few weeks before moving into her own house. She describes it as being detached, with four bedrooms, two reception rooms, a large kitchen and an enormous well-maintained garden with a beautiful lawn and wonderful flowers and shrubs.'

'My, that sounds wonderful,' said Betsy's mother.

Betsy continued reading. 'The first thing I noticed when I arrived in America was the pleasing sense of freedom everywhere, I went.'

'Does she say what she means by that?' asked Gina. 'I have heard other people say the same thing.'

'Hold on,' replied Betsy as she began to read aloud from the letter. 'In Ireland I was so used to being governed by politicians who don't really care about me. Their main aim was to further their own pockets. Whereas, here in America ordinary people are treated the same as the very rich, everyone has the same opportunities. People don't care about my religion. The government is elected by the people and are answerable to the people. Any policies a politician tries to introduce must be good for the majority, otherwise they will not get it through the parliament. Hugh is so taken with the politics over here that he has joined a political party and is actively canvassing for a politician called Thomas Jefferson to become President of America.'

Betsy looked up from the letter. 'Imagine that, being able to vote on who will be the President of America...'

'It is so different to here,' said Martha sadly. 'Our government wants to divide us into republican or loyalist. Protestant or Catholic.'

'By dividing us they rule us,' said Billy. 'I read recently that Thomas Jefferson was involved in writing The Declaration of Independence for America. In it he described how important it was for every man to have individual rights and freedoms. He also said the American people must have the right to worship as they choose, but to keep religion out of politics. Reverend Steel Dickson told me that the thinking behind a lot of the new ideas being adopted by America came from an Ulster Presbyterian minister who was born near here, in Saintfield. He is called Francis Hutcheson, and once taught philosophy to Presbyterian ministers at Glasgow University. He was the one who declared the best action to follow is that which secures the greatest happiness for the greatest numbers. The Reverend told me he also argued that victims of unjust regimes have the right to rebel. He said that it is because of Hutcheson's influence so many Presbyterian ministers are actively supporting the drive for political reform.'

'I'm going to America when I finish my apprenticeship,' said George. 'Mum says we have more relations living in America than we have in Ireland. My aunt Mary said I can stay with her until I get my own place sorted out. She said there is always plenty of work and America is crying out for skilled people like me. This place has changed so much since Robert died. I can't wait to leave.'

Betsy noticed the sad look on her mother's face as she returned to reading Jenny's letter. 'I have opened a clothes shop in Philadelphia, in partnership with a businessman I met on the sea journey over to America. Our business is very profitable, and we are planning to expand and open more outlets in the city soon.'

'I always knew there was more to Jenny,' said Gina. 'I'm so glad the move has worked out well for her.'

'Ah, hold on,' said Betsy excitedly. 'Rachel and Hugh are expecting their first baby in June. Isn't that wonderful.'

'A new baby,' exclaimed Gina. 'How exciting, just think of the opportunities that little child will have compared to here.'

'Will you please give my love to everyone back home, especially Gina, Martha, and Jessie. Tell them I love them all so much. And if they ever want to come to Philadelphia there will always be a room in my home for them. Bye for now. Love Jenny.'

Everyone was silent as Betsy folded the letter.

After a few moments Gina said. 'I have some good news as well. A few months ago, I met a wonderful man. He's called David McCartney. He's English and was over here on business. He has asked me to marry him and live with him in Liverpool. I have said yes.'

'That's wonderful,' said Betsy's mother. 'When's the big day?'

'The wedding will be in July, in Liverpool. David is from a big family and it would be impossible for all of them to come here. There is only me and father, so we are going over there.'

'Well I hope we are going to have a big party before you go,' said Betsy.

'Of course, and you are all invited.'

'It's so good to have something pleasant to look forward to after all the bad news there's been lately,' said Betsy.

'Talking about news,' said Billy. 'Has anyone read an article in the Newsletter recently in which William Orr was supposed to have confessed he was guilty as charged?'

'I read that,' replied Jessie. 'But I didn't believe a word of it.'

'And you were right not to,' said Billy taking a sheet of paper from his jacket pocket. 'Because it's a fake. I was in Belfast yesterday and bought a copy of William Orr's last declaration. In it he makes it quite clear that he has never said he was guilty. He claims the article was an attempt to ruin his character.'

'Poor man,' said Betsy. 'The government is not satisfied with taking his life and destroying his family, but they want to ruin his reputation as a God-fearing man as well.'

'William Orr did not deserve to die.' said Billy. 'He was an honest man, who simply wanted everyone to be treated as an equal.'

'I think,' said Jessie. 'His death has brought everyone closer together.'

Betsy nodded in agreement. 'Some people were beginning to lose heart. I think they stopped believing it was possible to get the political reforms we need. But since William's death everything has changed.'

'That's right,' agreed Billy. 'The government was winning the propaganda war, but I don't think they will be able to stop an uprising now.'

'Neither do I,' added Jessie. 'I was talking to one of our elderly parishioners the other day and he told me he was working in his field one day when a party of Ancient Britons rode passed. When he stopped to watch them, he saw one of the soldiers raise his rifle and point it at him.'

There was a sharp intake of breath from Gina. 'Oh, the poor man, what did he do?'

'Nothing. He told me he straightened up and stared back at the soldier.'

'Was he not frightened?'

'He said he wasn't. He refused to be intimated by them and said he wished he had a pike in his hands rather than the reins of his horse.'

'What happened?'

'The soldier didn't fire.'

'The old man's defiant action describes how people are feeling at the moment,' said Betsy. 'They are angry. He is a proud man, and they are trying to take our dignity away. Everywhere I go people ask me, when are we going to fight back. But I tell them, not yet. Hopefully we will not have to wait much longer.'

Billy raised his glass.

'Remember Orr.'

'Is there any news about Isabella Orr?' asked Martha.

Billy shook his head wearily. 'I'm afraid it's not good. The day after William was buried soldiers arrived at her farm in Farranshane and told her she had to leave. They gave her fifteen minutes to get the children out and to gather what clothes she needed before they set fire to the farmhouse. She had to flee to her parents' home on the other side of Lough Neagh.'

'That's terrible. And what about her children?'

'They're safe. Their education and welfare are being looked after by the Masonic Lodge.'

214

'There will be no justice in this land until these soldiers are confined to barracks and all of the corrupt politicians are removed from office,' added Martha.

'That will not happen until we take control,' said Betsy.

Chapter 22

On the last Saturday in January Billy called at the farm just after eight in the morning. He and Betsy had been invited to a meeting in the small town of Ballynahinch where the County Down leadership of the United Irishmen were gathering to hear some significant news.

'I'm looking forward to letting Sandy stretch his legs,' said Betsy as she tightened the saddle around his girth. 'He has been cooped up in the stables all week because of this snow.'

'At least the roads are clear,' said Billy. 'And we have plenty of time to get there. The meeting is not until eleven o'clock.'

'Come on let's go,' said Betsy as she climbed into the saddle. They trotted down the lane and out onto the main road.

'What's the meeting about?' asked Betsy.

'I don't know but it is something big. All of the senior officers are under strict orders to be there.'

'Must be important.'

'We'll find out soon,' said Billy. 'I had a long chat with Henry Poulter last night about his investigation into Robert's death.'

'Has he finished it?'

'Yes, he has. He said they ended up combining two investigations into one.'

'Do you think that's what this meeting is about?'

'No. Their conclusions are too sensitive. There are no plans to make them public.'

'What do you mean?'

'Well, do you remember Henry's team had been set up initially to carry out an investigation into the deaths of Richard, Brice, Thomas and Robert, because Reverend Steel Dickson wanted to know how come the Ancient Britons knew where to find them…'

'…Yes, and then we asked Henry to include Oliver Garfield's murder because we thought there might be a link between his death and David Johnston, but he said we hadn't enough evidence.'

'I think he might've said that to put us off. But they did investigate Garfield's murder. I'll come back to that in a minute. Their main conclusion is that David Johnston was working as a spy for the Reverend Cleland.'

216

'Oh my God,' said Betsy. 'I didn't really want to hear that. Poor Martha. Imagine how she's going to feel when she finds out.'

'She won't. She has been through enough. They're not going to go public with any of this. And you must never say anything to her.'

'No, I wouldn't but what did they discover?'

'Henry said there is no doubt that it was Johnston who told the Reverend Cleland about the movements of Richard McClure and Brice Killen, and where to find Thomas Sloane. It was his information that was used by the Ancient Britons to capture and hang the three of them.'

'Has this news been shared with their families?'

'I don't know. And we will not be saying anything to them.'

'What about Robert's murder?'

'His death is a bit more complicated. Henry's team discovered that Garfield was spying for the Reverend Cleland. They believe it was him who told Cleland that Robert was hiding on Johnston's farm, but for some reason Cleland didn't try to have him arrested immediately.'

'Maybe he was trying to protect Johnston?'

'That's what Henry thinks.'

'But why did Cleland change his mind. He could have just let Robert go. Afterall he was still getting information from David. By hiding Robert on his farm, he must have known it would make David look even more trustworthy to the United Irishmen.'

'But Cleland couldn't let Robert go free. Everyone knew he was one of the escapees, so it was only a matter of time before he had to order his death. Henry reckons Cleland sent for Johnston that day so that he would be in Belfast when the Ancient Britons went to the farm. When Johnston discovered what Cleland had done, he decided to kill him, but his attempt to shoot him missed. Cleland fired back, and wounded Johnston, he immediately recognised him and that's why the soldiers were able to go straight to his farm and kill him.'

'But who murdered Garfield?'

'Garfield was blackmailing Johnston. He must have realised that Johnston was an informer when he saw him and Cleland together outside the Government Buildings. Johnston couldn't take a chance on Garfield saying anything to the United Irishmen...'

'So, it was David Johnston who murdered Garfield.'

'Yes. That was Henry's conclusion. Johnston must have lured him to a meeting and shot him probably hoping the United Irishmen would be blamed.'

'Poor Martha.'

'Poulter said Martha is completely innocent, she was unaware of her husband's activities. As far as Reverend Steel Dickson and the rest of the leadership are concerned the investigation is over and will not be mentioned again.'

'I suppose that's something,' said Betsy. 'People, outside the families involved, will soon forget it ever happened.'

'That's right Betsy. And if anyone asks us about it, as far as we're concerned the case is closed.'

It was almost ten forty-five when they rode into Ballynahinch and after stabling their horses went to find a seat in the already packed hall. A few minutes later the doors were closed, and the meeting started. The Reverend Steel Dickson, Reverend Sinclar, Reverend Bailey Warden and Reverend Ledlie Birch walked onto the stage and sat down behind a table.

'Welcome everyone,' declared Reverend Steel Dickson from a sitting position. He paused for a few moments until everyone was quiet. 'We have invited you here to update you on what happened at a recent meeting I attended in Dublin. I beg you not to discuss anything you hear today with anyone outside this hall. Government spies and their agents will be desperate to hear what I'm about to tell you. Remember, this is top secret…. I and several senior officers from the Society recently attended a meeting in Dublin that was chaired by Lord Edward Fitzgerald in his role as the head of the military committee for the Society of United Irishmen. At the meeting Lord Fitzgerald informed us that the date for the uprising has been set for Wednesday the 23rd of May 1798.'

There were loud gasps of astonishment from several people in the audience as the Reverend continued.

'Dublin will rise first, including any bordering counties to prevent British reinforcements from getting into the city. The rest of the country will rise on the same day. We in County Down will take to the streets at the same time with the objective of engaging the Yeomanry and Militia regiments in the county to prevent them from being sent to Dublin.'

The Reverend paused momentarily allowing the information to sink in before he continued.

'Many of us thought this day would never come, but soon we will be able to sweep away this government and the corruption we have endured for decades.'

'Are the French coming to help us?' asked Henry Poulter.

The Reverend shook his head. 'No, we will be on our own. The time has come for us to stand up for ourselves and fight.'

'But we don't have enough guns and cannons to take on the British army.'

'Almost eighty percent of the British soldiers in Ireland are Irishmen. Several thousand of them have already sworn an oath to our cause. We believe that once the fighting starts in Dublin large numbers of them will cross over to our side.'

'I agree,' added Reverend Sinclar. 'If we are to win the hearts and minds of the people, our uprising must be carried out by Irishmen. If we are seen to be inviting foreign armies onto our soil the British will use it as propaganda against us. We have over one hundred thousand trained fighters in the United Irishmen. Once the Irish government realise the strength of feeling against them, they will resign, and the British government will sue for peace just as they did in America.'

'But the Irish government is actively recruiting new yeomanry and militia units as we speak. They are telling anyone who joins them that they are needed to fight against a popish plot the United Irishmen are hatching with Catholic members of the Defenders. I have spoken to dozens of the recruits and they are convinced we are in cahoots with agents of Pope Pius to destroy their Protestant way of life.'

'It is propaganda. We know what the Irish government is up to,' said Reverend Steel Dickson. 'They're trying to drive a wedge between us. It is up to you and me to make sure everyone understands that this is not a sectarian plot, and that we oppose all acts of religious bigotry. I want all of you who are in positions of leadership, to make sure the people you are responsible for understand that. From now on government agents will be watching our every move. They will be looking for anything they can use against us. It is up to us to make sure we do nothing that will discredit our task. Does everyone understand?'

'Yes,' came back the collective response.

'Thank you. Reverend Sinclar will explain some of the specific actions we would like you all to take over the coming weeks.'

Sinclar stood up. 'We think discipline will be a major factor in how we conduct ourselves in any forthcoming confrontations with soldiers of the British Army. I know your men don't like the drills and the marching you have been putting them through, but they help instil the discipline they will need once they take to the battlefield. The new men the British are recruiting will have no idea what to expect when they come under fire from our musketeers or confront large numbers of pikemen. We must be prepared to use that fear to our advantage. That's why discipline is so important... We also need to build up our stocks of weapons rifles, cannons, pistols, and bullets. We need you to tell your people to look for opportunities where we might acquire any of these... Our blacksmiths are producing hundreds of new pike blades every week, but more saplings for the pike shafts are required. Send out teams to gather these from the woods and forests in your areas. If anyone needs help or advice about how to go about any of this, please come and see me after the meeting.'

'Now you know what you have to do,' said Reverend Steel Dickson. 'We will meet again in three weeks' time when we will discuss the provisions each fighter should bring with them once the fighting starts. Don't forget to step up your training. Discipline will be crucial once the battle begins. Thank you.'

After Reverend Birch said a prayer to close the meeting everyone began discussing what they needed to do.

Over the next few weeks it quickly became apparent to the general population that there was an upsurge in illegal activities by the United Irishmen as they prepared for an uprising.

One of the outcomes of this was an increase in the friction between members of the public and supporters of the United Irishmen. This was something Reverend Steel Dickson was acutely aware of and kept reassuring his leadership team that although he did not enjoy ordering the activities, it was vital to be well armed if they were to win against soldiers of the British army.

The meetings quickly changed format to include training in drilling, battle formations and how to use a pike in close combat. Raiding parties were formed to break into houses where guns and gunpowder were stored. Teams were sent to chop down young saplings for pike blades, while others stripped lead from the roofs of houses and commercial buildings. The lead was cut into small, square slabs and farmed out to other members to be melted down and turned into bullets using cast iron moulds and smelting dishes the blacksmiths were producing in their hundreds.

One night Billy arrived at Betsy's farm carrying a bag full of implements for making bullets.

'The boys in Bangor managed to get hold of a dozen rifles the other night,' he said as he set the tools on the table. 'But we have very few bullets for them. We have all been asked to make some.'

'What's that you've brought with you?'

'It's a smelting dish,' said Billy showing her the eighteen-inch piece of wood with a small cast-iron dish on the end. 'I put a piece of lead in it and place the dish in the fire.'

He set it down and picked up what looked like a pair of pliers with a round bulbus mould at the end.

'This is my bullet mould,' he said tentatively. 'Apparently I pour the molten lead into this small hole and the bullet is formed inside the mould.'

'Have you done this before?' asked Betsy.

'No, not yet' he replied sheepishly. 'But seemingly it's a very simple operation.'

'Here let me show you. I've been making bullets for my pistol for some time.'

Betsy took a piece of lead and placed it into the cast iron dish. She placed the dish on top of the glowing embers in the turf fire, making sure the wooden stick did not catch alight. When the lead melted, she quickly lifted the dish and poured the molten liquid into the small opening on the bullet mould. After a few seconds she scrapped the hardened excess lead from around the hole and opened the mould to reveal a perfectly shaped round bullet. She dropped it onto a towel.

'Our first bullet,' said Billy.

'How many are you expected to make?'

'They want as many as possible. At least a hundred a week.'

'There are other things we could be doing in front of the fire,' whispered Betsy as she leaned over and kissed Billy.

Chapter 23

A few days later, while Betsy was on her way to the market, she was surprised to see how many men in Bangor were wearing the red jacket of the new Yeomanry force. It was something fellow stall owner John Agnew later commented on when she met him.

'Have you heard the news,' he said to her as she was setting up her stall. 'Castlereagh has introduced Martial Law.'

'I didn't know that, when did this happen?'

'Last Tuesday. He is going all out to crush the United Irishmen. Are you still involved with them?'

Betsy continued putting out her goods. 'The government has to reform John. People are still being deprived of their rights. Nothing has changed.'

'But can't you see Betsy, an armed struggle would be pointless. Castlereagh is recruiting a whole new army here in Ulster.'

'I take it you are referring to the Yeomanry I saw in Bangor this morning?'

'Yes, he has called for a force of over five thousand and is asking the members of the Orange Order to join him. Thousands are volunteering, we think it will be oversubscribed. All we talk about at our lodge meetings is the link between the United Irishmen and the popish plots to take over Ireland.'

'You know that's not true; we are against any sectarianism. As far as we are concerned religion should not come into politics. Look at what happened in France after the revolution, the cardinals lost their influence over the French government, and in America religion doesn't come into the political process. That's what we want for the people here.'

'I know you do, but I don't think others do. They think you are too close to militant Catholics. Why on earth did you have to involve the Defenders? It looks as though you are in cahoots with them.'

'They want to change the political system in Ireland, just as we do. The United Irishmen are non-sectarian. Our aim is to reform the Irish parliament and make it more answerable to the people. What's wrong with that?'

'But if you give Catholics the vote, they will introduce policies that will destroy our way of life. Our rights will be taken away. We talk about nothing else at our lodge meetings.'

'That fear is there because of the way the present political system has been running this country for the last hundred years. An elite set of aristocratic protestants have ruled Ireland in such a way that leaves most of its citizens living in poverty. We believe that if you trust all of the people, you will create a better and fairer society for everyone.'

'How can you trust the Catholics when they murdered your ancestors in 1641?'

'And the Catholics will argue that we did the same to their ancestors on some other date. We have to stop that sort of thinking. We can't alter the past, but we can change what we do today. That's what will decide what our future looks like. It's up to us.'

'If the truth be told Betsy, the Catholics want us out of Ireland. And if you continue down this road, I'm truly afraid for your safety.'

'We have to make a stand against sectarianism. If we don't these injustices will continue.'

'Take this as a warning from a friend Betsy. If the United Irishmen take to the streets they will be destroyed. These new part time soldiers are itching for a fight. They're armed with cannons and rifles; the United Irishmen have pikes. Are you mad? You may as well fight with bows and arrows. There will only be one winner. The United Irishmen will be slaughtered. I'm begging you Betsy, please tell your friends to give up the struggle. Things will get better, but you must trust Camden and Castlereagh.'

'I can't do that John. Too many of my friends have been murdered by the politicians you're asking me to trust. If we are forced into a fight, I will stand shoulder to shoulder with my people.'

John shook his head. 'I wish you well Betsy Grey. I may not be around for a while. There is some talk about us being called up for full time duty now that General Nugent has taken over command of the forces in Ulster.'

'What happened to General Lake?'

'He has been moved to Wexford.'

'I hope his soldiers are not as cruel to the people down there as they have been to us.'

'They were only trying to prevent a war.'

Betsy stopped what she was doing and turned to glare at Agnew. 'Don't tell me you think they were trying to prevent a war by torturing, killing and burning Presbyterian families out of their homes. Their methods will not prevent a war, if anything they have provoked a strong desire for one. General Lake's soldiers have left a legacy of fear and hatred alongside a longing for revenge. They have left us no alternative but to make sure no one can ever do anything like that to us again.'

Betsy turned away leaving Agnew stunned by her angry outburst.

Later that night Betsy was surprised when Billy arrived unexpectedly at the farm. He was almost breathless as he jumped down from his horse and rushed into the farmhouse. She was about to greet him when he gushed out his news.

'The Dublin Leadership has been arrested.'

'What!'

'They were holding a meeting in a public house in Dublin last night when troops burst in and arrested every one of them. They're all in prison.'

'What about Lord Fitzgerald?'

'He wasn't there, thank goodness. He has issued a statement saying they were betrayed.'

'What about the uprising?'

'It goes ahead. They're going to swear in a new leadership team as quickly as they can.'

'Do we have to do anything?'

'No, we are to go ahead as normal. Nothing changes.'

'Have you heard about the new reserve forces Castlereagh is calling up?'

'Yes. I heard he is looking for about five thousand men and is deliberately targeting Orange Lodges. It's causing turmoil across the county. I've heard that some of our people have applied to join. It could cause us a few problems.'

'I suppose it all depends on what happens in the first few days of the uprising. If enough people and soldiers come out to join the revolution; no army will be big enough to stop us.'

'You're right. And that's the plan. Those first few days will be crucial'

While they were talking Betsy heard a carriage arrive in the yard outside. Betsy looked out to see it was Martha Johnston and baby David.

'Martha,' said Betsy going out to meet her. 'It is so nice to see you and this wonderful little bundle of joy,' reaching into the carriage to lift baby David out. 'Come inside, Billy is here.'

'I'm glad the two of you are here, because I need to talk to both of you.'

'Certainly, come in I've some fresh tea on the boil.'

Inside the farmhouse Betsy continued nursing the baby while Billy poured three cups of freshly brewed tea.

'Thanks Billy,' said Martha as she took a sip before setting her cup on the kitchen table. 'It's still a bit warm for me. I'll let it cool for a while.'

'So, what did you want to talk to us about?' asked Betsy.

'I've heard a date has been set for the uprising, and I want to volunteer.'

'What do you mean?' asked Billy. 'I haven't heard of any date.'

'Please don't play games with me,' said Martha placing her hands around her warm cup. 'I want to fight alongside you and Betsy in the uprising. I don't know the actual date, but I know it will be soon. Everyone is talking about it. And I want to fight in that battle.'

'But what about your son?' asked Betsy. 'What will happen to him if you are captured or killed?'

'It is because of him that I want to fight. My husband has been branded an informer…'

'We never called him that,' said Billy.

Martha glanced at him. 'People don't always have to use words. I can tell by the way they are treating me, and I don't want my son to experience those feelings of shame.'

'But you have done nothing to be ashamed of Martha.'

'David was my husband, and what he did reflects on me.'

'But it doesn't Martha.'

'I should have seen the signs and been there to help him. David must have thought he was doing the right thing, because all he cared about was us. His family, me and our unborn baby. I have to make things right in my own mind.'

'But I still don't see how putting your life at risk could benefit your son?'

Martha lifted her cup and drank some tea. 'When David is older people will talk about the uprising by the United Irishmen and how their bravery brought changes to our way of life. I want him to be able to say his mother fought alongside them.'

Billy shook his head. 'What you are asking is impossible. Our members have been spending years preparing for this moment. With no disrespect Martha you have not. You would not only be a danger to yourself but to those around you. We cannot allow you to take part.'

'Please,' whispered Martha. 'I'm begging you.'

'No. It is not possible.'

Martha began to weep. 'Please.'

'You can come and work with me,' said Betsy. 'We need fighting men for the front ranks and we also need people supporting them. They are no less important because an army is made up of thousands of essential parts.'

'Thank you, Betsy.'

'But you can't bring baby David with you.'

'I know. I've already made arrangements for him to be looked after. I will not let you down.'

Later, after Martha had gone home Billy asked Betsy why she had agreed to let Martha join her.

'Because when I looked into her eyes, I saw myself and generations of Irish women who were expected to simply obey their men and have no say in what was going to happen to them and their loved ones. Martha is just like me. She wants to influence her future and shape it the way she wants, for her and her children. I could not say no.'

Betsy was tending her stall at Bangor market on Monday the 21st of May, just two days before the uprising was due to start when she noticed a buzz spreading amongst the shoppers and other stall holders.

'What's going on?' she shouted over to a stallholder.

'I don't know.'

A man running past held up a newspaper he was carrying and pointed to the headlines.

'Lord Fitzgerald has been captured in Dublin,' he called out. 'The government is asking for peace talks. There will be no uprising.'

Betsy ran over to where the daily newspapers were being sold and bought a copy of the Newsletter. The article on the front page described how Lord Fitzgerald had been captured on the previous Saturday, explaining how he had tried to escape but had been wounded and was quickly overpowered before being thrown into prison. Betsy's heart sank as she read the article.

'There will be no uprising now,' a stallholder called over. 'There is going to be peace, thank God.'

Betsy didn't stay long at the market and left around noon to head back to the farm. After unloading the cart, she saddled Sandy and rode over to the Reverend Steel Dickson's house to find out what was going on. When she was shown into the study, she wasn't surprised to find several people were already there, including Billy. Everyone wanted to know what was happening.

After a few minutes the Reverend Steel Dickson joined them.

'As you can imagine my news is a bit sketchy, but I understand someone betrayed Lord Fitzgerald to the authorities and when they went to apprehend him, there was a struggle in which Fitzgerald managed to stab one of his attackers before being shot himself. He is in prison. There was an emergency meeting of the leadership yesterday and they have confirmed the uprising will still go ahead on Wednesday morning as planned.'

'But everywhere I go people are telling me it has been cancelled,' said one of the commanders from a company in Downpatrick. My members are totally confused.'

Reverend Steel Dickson seemed frustrated by the man's attitude. 'All wars are fought in a fog of confusion. It is up to us to provide leadership and guidance to our members. This is just a setback. There will be more. Wars are not fought on a friendly basis.'

'So, do we still tell our people to gather on Wednesday morning?' Betsy asked.

'No, not yet, my orders are that we have to wait until we get the signal confirming Dublin has risen.'

'And what will that be?'

'All mail coaches throughout Ireland will be stopped,' replied Reverend Steel Dickson. 'When that happens, the whole country will rise up as one.'

'But what happens if the mail coach is not stopped on Wednesday?'

'Then we have to wait until they are. It is important that all our companies across Ireland take to the streets at the same time so that the British army is overwhelmed by the sheer size of our rebellion. They will have to stay in their barracks and negotiate a settlement and the minimum amount of blood will be spilled.'

The Reverend continued to answer questions for the next hour, constantly trying to reassure everyone that the uprising would still go ahead. He finished by telling them to go back and tell their people to continue their preparations.

'All we can do now is wait,' said Betsy as she and Billy rode back to the farm.

Chapter 24

On the morning of Wednesday 23th of May, Betsy waited, expecting to hear a knock at the door telling her the uprising had started, and that she was ordered to go to the village hall where the rest of the members were gathering. But no one came. As George prepared to go to work, he asked her what he should do, but all Betsy could say was what Reverend Steel Dickson had told her.

'We have to wait.'

It was late in the afternoon when a neighbour told her that something was happening in Dublin. The news was sketchy, but there was enough to understand that a revolt by the United Irishmen in the city had been quickly suppressed and several people had been arrested and thrown in jail.

Later that night more news arrived. The uprising had spread to counties outside Dublin and was rife in County Wexford. But to Betsy's disappointment there was still nothing about the United Irishmen being called out in any of the northern counties.

On Thursday Betsy heard a rumour that the British troops were struggling to contain the revolt in Wexford. But there was still no news from any northern county. It wasn't until the following Tuesday that Reverend Steel Dickson and his leadership team were called to a meeting of the Ulster Provisional Council. Betsy joined Billy in the hall and after a few minutes it became quite apparent that the existing leadership were confused about what to do.

'The Dublin uprising has failed,' said the chairman of the meeting. 'That was a crucial element in our plan.'

'Then we need a new plan,' said a young man called Henry Joy McCracken. 'The focus has shifted from Dublin to Wexford. We knew the start of the rebellion would be difficult, but I still believe people will rally to our cause if we take to the battlefield in support of our colleagues in Wexford.'

'But we might not get enough members to come out,' said the chairman.

'We will, we just have to believe in ourselves,' said McCracken. 'William Orr died for our cause, and if we don't support the people of Wexford thousands more will. It is our duty to take to the streets and fight.'

'But no other counties have risen.'

'Then, it is up to us to provide the leadership to the rest of the country and bring our people out onto the streets. Others will follow when they hear we have taken control of our towns and counties. They will join us, but we must fight.'

'I can't support that. It would be a foolish act.'

Henry Joy McCracken and several men stormed up to the front of the hall. 'Then sir, I propose that you step aside and allow those who are prepared to fight, to lead.'

'I second that,' called out another man.

'Here, here,' shouted most of the people in the hall. 'Stand down, stand down.'

With most of the delegates calling for the current leadership to leave and for the election of a new leadership team the chairman recognised he was beaten. He resigned and walked away from the table.

Henry Joy McCracken was voted in as the new leader and a new plan for the following week was quickly devised and agreed. This time the uprising would begin simultaneously in Counties Antrim and Down on Thursday the 7th of June.

After the meeting, Reverend Steel Dickson gathered his team around him. 'Now that a new date is agreed, go back to your members and prepare them for war. Remember Orr.'

Over the next few days Reverend Steel Dickson met with several of his commanding officers. A meeting was arranged in Ballynahinch on Monday 4th of June to finalise their plans. As Reverend Steel Dickson walked through Ballynahinch to the meeting he was suddenly surrounded by several soldiers. He was arrested and taken to a prison in Belfast.

When news of his seizure reached the hall where the United Irishmen were gathering Reverend David Warden quickly assumed command and confirmed the uprising would still go ahead on Thursday morning. The officers quickly dispersed and went back to their members to prepare them for the revolution.

Betsy rose at five o'clock on Thursday. She had barely slept, lying awake most of the night thinking about what the next few days would bring. Everything had come down to this moment. She knelt by her bed and prayed to God for guidance.

As she passed George's bedroom, she knocked the door.

'I'm getting dressed,' he called out. 'I'll be out in a minute.'

Betsy carried on to the kitchen where her mother had set the table for breakfast.

'I'm sorry if I woke you,' Betsy said.

'You didn't. I was awake. I've made some porridge. There are packs of food for you and George to take with you. You said everyone was told to bring enough cheese and bread for three days.'

'That's how long they think we will be away.''

'I've added a few apples and a couple of bottles of water.'

'Thank you, mum,' said Betsy as she sat down and ladled porridge into a bowl.

'Morning,' said George as he entered the kitchen. 'You shouldn't have got up mum, we could've seen ourselves out.'

'Come here you,' she said throwing her arms around his shoulders. 'I have to make sure my big son is well fed and ready for the next few days. I've made you some porridge.'

George sat down at the table and let his mother ladle porridge into a bowl for him.

'Where have you to meet the others?' she asked.

'Henry Poulter has told everyone to gather at the church hall at six o'clock. We should be going soon.'

'I know,' said her mother her eyes glistening with tears.

'Mum we will be fine.' said George. 'Don't cry.'

'I know, I'll be alright... it's just I've been dreading this moment. I knew it would come one day... There were times I prayed we would be spared all of this, but I fear God is looking somewhere else today... Promise me you'll look after each other. I don't know what I would do if anything happened to either of you.'

Betsy put her arms around her mother and hugged her. 'Of course, we will. We'll be safe mum. You wait and see. The whole country will rise up and the government will have to sue for peace. No one will be hurt.'

'Please God you're right,' said her mother as she followed them out to the barn where George pulled his pike from a stack of straw. The metal blade sharp and gleaming from constant honing and polishing.

Betsy went over to a corner and pulled up a couple of floorboards and lifted out a sack containing her sword and pistol. Both weapons were well oiled and gleaming as she tucked them into her belt.

'Look after each other,' her mother called out as they walked down the lane. When they reached the main road, they stopped and waved back at her before heading to the church hall.

They were not the first to arrive. Several men stood chatting by the entrance. Their sharpened pikes held casually in their hands. From inside the hall Betsy could hear drumbeats and the shrill notes of fifers as members of the company's small band practiced a marching tune. George left to go and speak to his friends while Betsy went inside. She found Jessie Poulter. She was keeping a record of those who turned up.

'Nearly all here,' Jessie said as she put a tick by Betsy's name.

'Our George is outside.'

'Good, only a couple more. We should have a full turnout. Did you see John Gracie or Patrick McKay on your way over?'

'No, I didn't, but they are always the last ones to arrive. Is Billy here?'

'Yes, I saw him earlier, I think he is outside with the pikemen. Will you take these green ribbons with you and hand them out?'

Betsy pulled one of the ribbons from the bundle and tied it around her bonnet. She gave the rest of them away and went outside to find Billy. He was talking to the pikemen about tactics on the battlefield. He was wearing a green coat, over a white cotton shirt, with brown linen breeches, dark blue leggings and highly polished black shoes. She thought he looked very handsome in his officers' uniform.

'My you look smart,' said Betsy as she joined him. 'Every bit the officer and gentleman.'

Billy smiled. 'Why thank you Betsy,' he replied as he bowed. 'I'm always at your service.'

'Here I have the perfect item for you,' said Betsy placing the green ribbon around his neck and tying it like a necktie. 'Now you are complete.'

'Thank you.'

'Have you heard anything?'

'Yes. I was talking to a messenger who was on his way to a leadership meeting in Downpatrick. According to him, Larne,

232

Glenarm, Carrickfergus, Ballymoney, Toombridge and dozens of other towns in County Antrim have risen. Henry Joy McCracken has an army of about ten thousand following him. They're marching on Antrim Town and Ballymena; and should gain control of them today.'

'What about County Down?'

'It is the same here. Bangor and Holywood have risen, as have the rest of the companies on the coast from Millisle to Portaferry. So far, there has been very little fighting and no casualties have been reported.'

'Thank God. What are we going to do today?'

'We've been ordered to march to Donaghadee where we will join more companies from the peninsula. Our first objective is to take control of Donaghadee harbour in case the British try to land reinforcements.'

'Betsy,' called out a familiar voice.

Betsy turned around to see Gina walking towards her.

'What are you doing here?'

'I wouldn't miss this for anything,' said Gina. 'Did you think I was going to let you go on your own. I had to come and look after you.'

Betsy put her arms around her friend. 'You fool, I love you so much.'

A few minutes later Martha arrived with Patrick McKay.

'Well it's finally happening,' she said as Henry Poulter appeared in the doorway.

Henry was wearing a long green jacket over a brown waistcoat and brown britches with black glossy boots. The uniform of a General in the army of the United Irishmen. He also had a dark hat with a green and yellow plume that had been secured to one side by a green ribbon.

'It is time to go. Assemble in the hall please?'

Once everyone had lined up, Sergeant Major John White ordered them to stand to attention. There was a loud stamping of feet and pikes as one hundred and twenty pikemen obeyed the order.

Henry Poulter walked to the front of the hall.

'Today marks a turning point in all of our lives. When you leave this hall, you will become part of an army fighting for Ireland's freedom. You have been preparing for this moment for months. You have nothing to fear. With God on your side no one will be able to stop you until you are triumphant. Are you ready for war?' boomed Poulter.

'Yes sir,' everyone roared.

'Your task today is to secure the harbour at Donaghadee… Sergeant Major White,' called Poulter. 'Let's go.'

'Attention…' barked Sergeant Major White. 'The Company will about turn on my command… About turn.'

The pikemen turned as one.

'On my command rows one and two will follow the fifes and drums from the hall.'

The double doors at the entrance were opened and four men with fifes began playing as two men with side drums set the beat.

'March,' roared the sergeant major. 'Left… Right… Left… Right…'

Soon the hall emptied as the pikemen, riflemen and the rest of the support teams of the Gransha company of United Irishmen marched along the road towards Donaghadee. Their rebellion had started. At the front of the column Henry Poulter ordered the band to play The Marseillaise.

As they marched through the village of Cotton people came out of their houses to wave and cheer them on. There was a carnival atmosphere. Whole families began to follow them, dancing and singing at the rear of the marchers. More people joined as they continued along the long, straight road towards Donaghadee, eventually swelling their numbers to several hundred.

When they reached the outskirts of the small port Henry Poulter called a halt to consult with his scouts for a few moments before they set of again. A few minutes later the small army reached the shoreline. As they headed towards the harbour the marchers saw a ship in the harbour. Its decks packed full of people. They could see sailors scurrying around unfurling the rigging as the ship slowly pulled away from the quayside.

'There go the rich, running away to Scotland,' said Gina. 'They'll stay there until all this is over.'

The marchers watched the sailors unfurling more of the sails as the ship navigated towards the deeper waters outside the harbour.

As the column of United Irishmen continued their march through the streets of Donaghadee the local people came out of their homes to clap and cheer as they passed by.

'Hurray for the patriots,' called one old lady.

Henry Poulter sent some of the pikemen to the harbour while the main column was ordered to turn right and march up a gentle hill on the edge of the village leading to a large, flat expanse of grassy land where they were ordered to stop.

'We will make camp here,' called out Henry Poulter.

Within a few minutes the marchers dispersed, searching for somewhere to rest on the grass and eat some of the food they had brought with them.

Betsy, Jessie, Gina and Martha found a spot close to a large oak tree that would give them some shade and spread their food out on the grass.

'I never thought I would be doing anything like this,' said Jessie. 'I was always taught to obey the law and here I am, defying the government.'

'I'm the same,' said Betsy. 'I've never done anything like this either. But I must say it feels as though we're on a church outing. Most of our congregation is here. It's ever so strange.'

'I know what you mean,' said Gina. 'I'm actually enjoying this comradery. I can remember the first time we went to a meeting of United Irishmen. We were so frightened and shy.'

'We even wondered if the man on the door would let us in, let alone that anyone would listen to our opinions,' said Betsy.

'Yes, I remember that,' added Gina. 'And when we did get in, we discovered everyone was in the same boat as us.'

'That's right,' said Betsy. 'Because what surprised me most that night, was that everyone was struggling with the same issues and experiencing the same hardships.'

'Yes,' said Jessie. 'All we did was talk about how badly we were being treated. I never envisaged doing anything like this though. To say I'm rebelling against the people who govern the country feels surreal. I still have to pinch myself.'

'I'm the same. I think change happens in gradual steps for all of us,' said Gina. 'I joined the United Irishmen. I took part in discussions and activities. I kept secrets. I saw soldiers doing things that appalled me and made me even more angry and so I agreed to do things that would normally horrify me. I broke the law. Each step I took altered my principles of right and wrong. The question I keep asking myself is, will I be able to take the next step and kill someone?'

'That's why we are here,' replied Martha.

'Let's hope we don't have to,' said Jessie. 'I don't know if I could live with the death of someone on my conscience.'

'I don't know what I would do either,' said Betsy.

They were interrupted by the arrival of Billy. 'You're all looking very serious,' he said as he joined them. 'What are you talking about?'

'Just discussing how we ended up here,' said Betsy. 'We were saying that when we first joined the United Irishmen none of us ever thought we would be marching into battle one day. Back then it was just a protest group, but now we have weapons and are part of an army on the march.'

'I agree. When I discussed this with Reverend Steel Dickson he always ended with a quote from the bible and would say, sometimes the only way to keep sinful people from doing great harm to the innocent is by going to war.'

'I wish he was here now,' said Betsy.

'So do I,' added Billy.

'Have you heard what's happening?' asked Gina.

'Some of our men are searching houses in the village. We had reports of soldiers seen hiding in them and someone claims he saw a couple of soldiers down by the harbour. We have been searching down there but didn't find them. Henry is looking for volunteers to stay and guard the port when we leave.'

'When are we going?'

'Tomorrow morning. This is one of the main rallying points for the other companies on the peninsula. We're expecting reinforcements to arrive from Millisle, Groomsport and Carrowdore soon.'

'Where are we going to?'

'We are going to a camp near Saintfield. That's where the people from north Down will be congregating.'

Once word spread that they would be staying overnight several people went down to the shoreline to search for driftwood. They brought it back and lit fires to cook their food and make hot drinks. As darkness fell, they sat around the fires chatting.

Betsy and her friends were joined by a couple of the fifers. Soon everyone in the field was singing along as the musicians played hymns and a few folk songs. The singing continued long into the night until the music eventually stopped, and people lay back on the cool grass to sleep. Soon the whole campsite was quiet. As Betsy stared up at the stars in the clear, dark sky she thought about her father and wondered how he would have reacted to her lying in the middle of a field surrounded by a revolutionary army.

Next morning as Betsy woke from her sleep to another warm, sunny day, she became aware of people moving around her.

'What time is it?' she heard someone ask.

'It's five-thirty.'

'Everyone waken up,' roared the familiar voice of Sergeant Major John White. 'It's time to go.'

'Come on Gina, time to get up,' said Martha as she gently shook her shoulder.

'It's alright, I'm awake,' replied Gina softly. 'I was just having a wonderful dream about David.'

'What did he say to you when you told him you were going to fight with the United Irishmen?' asked Betsy.

Gina looked rather sheepishly at her. 'Nothing. He doesn't know. He thinks I'm visiting my mother, which was true until I heard about this.'

'I hope he understands.'

'I once tried to explain to him what the United Irishmen were trying to achieve. He could understand Ireland being independent of Britain, and treating everyone as an equal, but he didn't think it would work here because of the religious hatred.'

'That's why we must do this,' said Martha. 'We have to show everyone that there is another way.'

'Come on girls,' said Jessie joining them. 'Time to go. It's going to be breakfast on the go this morning I'm afraid, we have a long walk ahead of us.'

Around them, pikemen began to group together in their individual platoons before lining up to wait on the order to leave. There was a lot of shouting of orders in what appeared to be a very chaotic manner as different groups began to leave the field. It took the sergeant major about fifteen minutes of yelling and hollering to empty the field and to get everyone into some semblance of order on the road.

Just like the previous day, people came out of their homes to wave and cheer as they passed by. It was a long march on a very warm day. There were frequent stops to allow for rest, and by the time they reached the camp at Oughley Hill on the outskirts of Saintfield at seven o'clock that night, most of the one thousand marchers were totally exhausted. All they wanted to do was to find somewhere to sleep.

Chapter 25

Next morning Betsy awoke, to find that several thousand more had arrived to join them during the night.

Someone told Gina there were over ten thousand in the camp, and more were on their way.

'I hope it is not to long before we engage with the British,' said George as he arrived with Billy looking for his breakfast. 'They're saying the soldiers are still in their barracks. Let's hope they come out soon.'

'You always were impatient,' said Betsy. 'I'm sure you will get your fill of fighting when it comes. Anyway, I don't want that to happen, I want the British to sue for peace when they see how many people are involved.'

'I was told the turnout has been the same in County Antrim,' added Billy. 'I've heard more are expected to join us when we reach Ballynahinch.'

As they were talking a man stopped beside them. 'Excuse me but are you Betsy Gray?' he asked.

'Yes, I am. Who wants to know?'

'I'm sorry, allow me to introduce myself. I'm the Reverend Ledlie Birch, Presbyterian minister here in Saintfield. I heard the Gransha company had arrived last night. I just wanted to say that I knew your father Daniel well. We used to attend the same meetings of the United Irishmen and had many good debates about politics. He was a wonderful man.'

'Thank you,' replied Betsy. 'This is George, my brother.'

'Hello George, you're the image of your father. He would be very proud of the pair of you.'

'When did you meet my father?' asked Betsy curious to know, as she wasn't aware, he had been a member of the United Irishmen and she had never heard him mention a minister from Saintfield.

'I first met him about six years ago, when we formed a company of United Irishmen here in Saintfield. We were the first company in County Down. Your father was one of the first men to join.'

'He never mentioned being in the United Irishmen,' said George.

'Oh yes I can assure you he was. But he had to stop coming to the meetings and concentrate on his farm, it was just too far for him to travel,' said the Reverend.

'I'm quite shocked,' said Betsy. 'Father never mentioned being a member.'

'Well, I just wanted to tell you how much I enjoyed the debates I had with him. He was a very interesting man. I particularly remember his views on the rights of minorities. He would maintain that democracy is not just about satisfying the physical and social needs of the majority of the people, but also how the state treats minority groups in the society. He would argue that the ill-treatment of people in those groups is merely sowing the seeds of future revolutions.'

'Yes, I often heard him saying that,' said Betsy. 'He was a great believer in democracy. But I didn't know he had been a member of the Society. I'm beginning to wonder what else I didn't know about him.'

'Hello,' said Martha arriving with two jugs of water. 'When I was over at the stream people were talking about a massacre in County Wexford. Is that true Reverend?'

The minister slowly nodded his head. 'Yes, I'm afraid it is.'

'What happened?' asked Betsy.

'I haven't all the details yet, but my understanding is that a barn containing loyalist civilians, was set on fire killing everyone inside. None escaped.'

Betsy felt physically sick. 'If they were civilians, that means there must have been women and children in the barn.'

The Reverend nodded. 'Yes, I'm afraid there were. All I can say is that the people who carried out this heinous act do not represent the Society of United Irishmen that you and I are part of. These killers will be brought to trial to face murder charges. These are the acts of barbarians not Christians.'

'But it happened,' cried a distraught Betsy. 'And they did it in our name, how can we say we want to make life better for everyone, when something so terrible happens?'

'War is awful Betsy. War releases the evil in mankind. All we can do is try to make sure nothing like that happens again.'

While the Reverend was speaking Betsy became aware that other people were also talking about the massacre at Scullabogue. She could see a look of disgust in their faces. Reverend Birch saw their reaction and stood up to address the people gathered around them.

'I would like to say something about what happened in County Wexford a few days ago. It's true that one hundred civilian loyalists; men, women and children, who were being held prisoners in a barn, in a small village called Scullabogue, were murdered by members of the Wexford United Irishmen. The people who had been left to guard them set fire to the barn killing all one hundred prisoners.'

There were cries of shame and disgust from those sitting nearby.

'I and the rest of the leadership of the United Irishmen,' continued Reverend Birch. 'Utterly condemn the murder of these innocent people. We are totally against the harming of prisoners. Something which the British forces have failed to do on several occasions. We vow to you, that when the fighting is over, we will do everything in our power to bring to justice the perpetrators of acts such as took place at Scullabogue. Any prisoners captured by us will always be treated with dignity and respect. Anyone found guilty of abusing a prisoner will be severely punished.'

'The question we should be asking ourselves is why are we not shocked that this has happened?' said a man in the crowd.

'I don't understand,' said a woman sitting nearby.

The man continued. 'Our history is full of examples of acts of intolerance and bigotry that are fuelled by religious hatred, which means when we hear about the massacre in Scullabogue, we are not so surprised. And if we were brutally honest with ourselves, we may even say we have been expecting to hear something like this.'

'That's a good point,' said Reverend Birch. 'Which makes it even more important that we are successful in our quest to build a new Ireland. An Ireland where all men are equal, and everyone has access to the same opportunities no matter what religion they are. An Ireland where there is no poverty, no unemployment, no intolerance. If we lived in such a society now, there would be no atrocities like Scullabogue. My friends, hatred and intolerance run deep in our society and our enemies will try to use what happened at Scullabogue against us, but we must be strong, resolute, and unforgiving in the pursuit of a new Ireland. That's all we can do.'

'Time will tell,' said the man.

After breakfast small teams left the camp to go and search for food and to see if they could find any more weapons in the nearby houses and farms. It was around ten o'clock when those in the camp were suddenly stunned by a very loud explosion. Some ran to gather their weapons thinking a British force had arrived and were firing their cannons at them.

As Betsy stood up and looked around her, she saw a large cloud of smoke rising into the sky not too far from the camp.

'What was that?' asked Gina.

'It sounded like a gunpowder explosion,' replied a man standing close by. 'I think some of our people went off in that direction looking for houses that may be storing weapons. It might involve them. I hope everyone is safe.'

About fifteen minutes later Betsy saw a group of men coming into the camp. George was with them. He looked very upset as he ran over to her.

'What happened George, are you alright?'

'Did you hear the explosion?'

'Yes, someone said it might be gunpowder.'

'It was. We were sent out to search for weapons, and as we were walking along the Lisburn Road, we saw a large crowd of men gathering outside one of the houses. It was a big place, two storeys high, with a slated roof. When we got closer, we could see that the windows in the house had been barricaded from the inside. The men standing outside were shouting at the people to come out and bring their guns with them. One of the boys with us was from Saintfield and he reckoned a family of eight lived in the house. The next thing we heard were several gunshots coming from the people inside the house. I think a couple of our people were wounded. Our men began firing back. There was a lot more shouting and then we saw a man at the back of the house. He climbed up a ladder and managed to get onto the roof. He removed some of the slate tiles and threw a burning torch into the roof space...'

By now a small crowd had gathered around them and everyone was listening intently to George as he continued.

'...The men on the ground were shouting at the family to come out. They kept telling them the house was on fire, but every time they went near the house the people inside fired their guns at them. Within a few minutes' flames were shooting out of the roof and the man who had climbed up there had to jump to save his life. The fire spread very quickly throughout the rest of the house. We could hear the people inside screaming. We were all shouting for them to open the front door and come out. Suddenly there was a massive explosion. The force blew me off my feet. The fire must have reached where the gunpowder was being stored and it blew up. The whole house was completely destroyed. Everyone inside was killed. There was nothing left of them. If only they had come out.'

'Did anyone know the family?' asked Betsy.

'I heard it was owned by people called McKee,' replied George.

'I know them,' said an elderly man. 'The house was owned by Hugh McKee. He was the head of a large family and was very unpopular around here. He has been a thorn in the side of the United Irishmen for a long time. He was always boasting about his loyalism and accusing the United Irishmen of being popish traitors. Last year he accused twelve of Saintfield's leading United Irishmen of attacking his home. They were all arrested on his word and put on trial, but were acquitted. That didn't stop McKee. He was always boasting about the arsenal of weapons he kept in the house. He must have stored a large amount of gunpowder as well for his guns. The gunpowder must have exploded when the house was set on fire, although that's not what the British will say happened, they will accuse us of murdering a family of loyalists.'

'But we didn't,' replied George. 'I was there. It was an accident.'

'We should not have attacked them,' said Betsy. 'The Reverend Birch said war releases the evil in mankind. I think there is more to it than that. We are an army. Look around you. The soldiers you see are ordinary people who have come here to fight against tyranny. They are not here to impose another version of it upon someone else. They do not want to kill people for the sake of it. Or to seek revenge for a slight they or their ancestors experienced in the past. I fear their willingness to fight for liberty is being used as a cover by a few evil men to satisfy their own ungodly bloodlust at places like Scullabogue and now the McKee household. But, because these people say they are on our side, we look in the other direction, we make excuses for them, or even worse we do nothing... But we should turn our backs on them. We should shun them. The word of God and the laws of the land are the glue that holds our society together and if we desert them, we will abandon our very

243

civilisation. We must unconditionally condemn acts of needless violence and bring the culprits to justice at the earliest opportunity. Otherwise, we will become no better than mindless beasts and will turn Ireland into a moral wilderness for generations to come. There must be no more acts like this.'

A few hours later while Betsy was sitting in the camp on Oughley Hill with Billy, Gina and Martha, she watched as a horseman came galloping towards the entrance.

'Make way, make way,' he was yelling frantically as he rode up to the guards barring his way. 'Let me pass, I have important news for General Munro about the British.'

The guards stood back to allow him through.

'What is that about?' asked Billy.

'I don't know, but something is going on,' replied Betsy as she watched the man manoeuvre his horse through the throngs of people in the camp towards a tented area where General Munro and his senior officers were based.

The horseman's arrival was causing quite a stir, as more and more people stood up to see what was going on.

When the rider reached the tents, Betsy saw him leap from his horse and rush over to a group of men.

'Where is General Munro?' he demanded. 'I must speak with him.'

'He is at a meeting,' replied one of the men. 'In that tent over there.'

Betsy saw the man rush over to the tent and speak to a guard outside it. A few moments later General Munro and a couple of his men stepped out to greet him.

'What news do you bring?' the General asked.

The man was panting heavily. 'Sir, my name is Colin Edwards. I'm part of Captain Murray's scouting party. We were sent out this morning to monitor the movements of any British troops in the area. Captain Murray sent me back to report to you that a large British force, led by Colonel Stapylton of the York Fencibles, left their headquarters in Comber barracks shortly after one o'clock this afternoon and is on its way here.'

'What size of a force?'

'Colonel Stapylton has a military force of fifty Newtownards Yeoman cavalry, two hundred and seventy York Fencible light infantry and fifty Newtownards Yeoman infantry. He is also bringing two cannons with him. There are several civilians travelling with the Colonel. Captain Murray believes at least two of the civilians are magistrates.'

'Stapylton must be bringing them with him so that he can administer punishment immediately to any United Irishman he believes they are going to capture. Where is this force now?'

'We tracked Colonel Stapylton and his army to make sure they were heading towards Saintfield. I left as they were approaching the outskirts of Ballygowan. They will be here in just over an hours' time.'

General Munro quickly called for the rest of his generals to join him in his tent. Betsy saw a couple of men rush over when he asked for anyone with local knowledge to join them.

Inside the tent the men debated various battle options before settling on a plan on how they would attack Colonel Stapylton's army. Once all the details had been agreed the men quickly dispersed to inform their various companies about their plan.

Henry Poulter called Betsy and the rest of the Gransha officers together to explain their role in the upcoming battle.

As they circled around him Poulter spread a map out on the grass. 'A British force of 370, comprised of soldiers and cavalry, along with two cannons is currently about four miles away on the outskirts of Ballygowan, marching towards us.'

Poulter pointed at the map. 'For about three and a half miles the road they are travelling on is surrounded by open countryside. However, about a quarter of a mile from Saintfield the road enters a densely wooded area and remains like that until it reaches the bridge here,' he said indicating the bridge on the edge of the village. 'We will ambush them along this half mile stretch of road in the woods. We will conceal our musketeers behind these trees and bushes along the road here,' he added pointing to a stretch of road leading back from the bridge to the beginning of the wooded area. 'They will be supported by pikemen hidden in the trees behind. Four companies of pikemen will be in position in Doran's Wood on the south side of the road, here,' he continued, indicating on the map.

'That's a long stretch of road, what will be the signal to attack?' asked Billy.

'Good question. Colonel Stapylton always rides at the front of his soldiers. By the time he reaches the bridge, we believe most, if not all, of the soldiers in the column will be inside the wooded area. When Stapylton reaches the bridge one of our snipers will shoot him. That gunshot will be the signal for all our musketeers to open fire on the rest of the soldiers in the column. Once that happens a company of pikemen will move out of Doran's Wood to block the bridge preventing any soldiers from escaping into the village. At the same time, three companies of pikemen on the northside of the road will leave the trees and attack the rear of the column and capture the two cannons. They will also block the road to prevent any soldiers from retreating. We will be part of that assault. We will be positioned here,' he said indicating a spot near the top of a hill on the north side of the road. 'Our primary task is to block the road. We will commence the attack on my order. Does everyone understand?'

'Yes sir,' they replied.

'Good, let's go.'

Within minutes the Gransha pikemen and hundreds of others filed out of the camp on Oughley Hill to march to their assigned positions.

Chapter 26

Colonel Stapylton was enjoying the sunshine and the warm afternoon as he rode at the head of his troops along the Comber road towards Saintfield. He was a man who liked to confront any issues, so when news broke of a rebellion by the United Irishmen, he assumed he would soon be called into action. But no orders arrived. Instead he found himself sitting in his office idly wasting time and becoming frustrated. So, when he heard that a large group of rebels were seen gathering in a field just outside the village of Saintfield he decided he would go and confront them.

The journey so far had been fairly quiet, the only thing of note was that his men had spotted some riders following them. He assumed they were scouts for the United Irishmen. However, given the size of his force he saw no reason to feel concerned. When he reached a farmhouse, about a quarter of a mile outside Saintfield, he ordered his men to stop. He knew the countryside well and was familiar with the next part of the road.

'Captain Chetwynd,' he said. 'The road between here and Saintfield meanders through a heavily wooded area with thick bushes on either side. It would be an ideal spot for an ambush. The land on the right is very steep and hilly, while that to our left is soft and marshy. It would be difficult manoeuvring horses or cannons on it. Send a couple of scouts forward as far as the bridge just before the village.'

Captain Chetwynd turned to two cavalrymen. 'I need you to check out the road ahead,' he said. 'Ride as far as the bridge and make sure that everything is clear, and then come back immediately and report to me. Do you understand?'

'Yes sir.'

As the scouts headed off, Colonel Stapylton and the rest of the cavalry dismounted while Captain Chetwynd ordered the infantry to stand down and to get some rest.

'Do you think we'll find anyone?' said one of the scouts as soon as they were out of earshot of the captain.

'I don't know. There are supposed to be thousands of United Irishmen on the march, but I haven't seen any of them so far.'

'Maybe they've moved on to another village?'

The two men slowed their horses as the trees and bushes on either side of the road began to thicken.

'You take the left; I'll check this side.'

'These bushes are so thick it would be impossible to see if anyone was hiding behind them.'

'Just keep checking anyway. You heard what the Colonel said, he thinks this would be an ideal spot for an ambush.'

'Have you ever been caught in an ambush?'

'No, and I don't intend to be. Keep looking and stop talking.'

'Well, I can't see any signs that anyone has been through here lately.'

'Look out for any broken branches or footprints that might give us a clue.'

'The ground looks as hard as a rock.... It hasn't rained here for.... What was that?'

'What was what?' said the cavalryman pulling up his horse.

'Listen....'

The two riders tried to concentrate on the noises coming from the woods around them.

'I can't hear anything. What did you hear?'

'It sounded like someone coughing.'

'It was probably a fox.... Come on there is nothing there.'

'My horse is very nervous. Do you think she can sense danger?'

'You're making her edgy. It's your fear she's picking up.'

'I'm not nervous, I'm sure I heard something back there, that was all.'

The men rode on.

'So, have you any family living down here?'

'I've a cousin who lives near here, but I never see him. The last I heard he was in the United Irishmen.'

'Sure, we all have someone who is a member of the Society. I think my youngest brother might be a liberty man. I hope he's at home and hasn't come down here to fight.'

'My wife and I were thinking about retiring and buying a farm somewhere near here. I quite like the idea of becoming a gentleman farmer.'

'There is no such thing as a gentleman farmer. Farming is a tough way of life. You have to be born into it.'

'Well, we still might give it a try. I like the outdoor life.'

'There's the bridge up ahead?' said one of them after they had been riding for about ten minutes.

'Yes. That's it. That's where the captain told us to turn. I think we can see into the village from up there.'

A few minutes later they reached the bridge.

'It all looks very peaceful,' said the cavalryman when they stopped.

'It looks normal enough to me. Somebody said there were fifteen thousand United Irishmen in a field somewhere near Saintfield. I don't think any of them are around here.'

'I agree, there's nothing here.'

'Come on, let's get back. We don't want to keep the colonel waiting. He can be a bit impatient.'

Back at the farmhouse Captain Chetwynd was standing in the middle of the road waiting for his scouts to reappear. After a few moments he saw the men riding towards him.

'Here they come sir,' called one of the soldiers.

'Well did you see anything suspicious?' demanded the Captain.

'No sir. We checked as far as the bridge. The road ahead is clear. The village looks very quiet.'

'Right, mount up,' ordered Colonel Stapylton. 'We'll establish our headquarters in Saintfield village and send scouts out to check the surrounding area. The United Irishmen must have a camp close by. We'll soon find the buggers and send them packing.'

The cavalrymen and soldiers quickly reformed as the drummer boys at the front of the column set the marching pace with the beat of their drums.

In the woods over one thousand musketeers and pikemen lay hidden amongst the bushes and trees on either side of the road. They too were listening to the marching drumbeat. The air was thick and heavy. The pikemen were watchful and nervous. The musketeers were on heightened alert as they listened to the distant thump… thump… thump… thump of the drumbeat as it slowly became louder and louder. Suddenly they heard the snorting of the cavalrymen's horses and the stamping of the infantrymen's marching boots. The musketeers began to sweat. Their muskets felt slippery in their hands. The drumbeat became louder. They could hear the soldiers laughing and the livery rattling on the horses. They could see red and white uniforms through the green leaves as they passed. They listened to the voices of the soldiers talking to each other. Tension increased as the musketeers strained to hear the first killing shot.

From her vantage point, high up on the top of the hill, Betsy watched as the soldiers at the front of the column disappeared into the wooded area. She could hear the drummer boy's steady drumbeat. When about half of the column was inside the wooded area Betsy was startled by the loud 'crack' of a single musket shot. This was immediately followed by a huge barrage of explosions as hundreds of musketeers fired their weapons into the soldiers in front of them at point blank range.

'They've fired too early,' exclaimed one of the pikeman standing beside Betsy as she saw the soldiers at the rear of the column stop when they realised, they had been ambushed.

Deep in the woods, at the front of the column Colonel Stapylton was yelling at his men to retreat. But as he and the rest of his cavalry tried to turn their horses, they crashed into the crowded ranks of infantry directly behind them. In the melee the Reverend Robert Mortimer of Comber died instantly from a bullet wound. As the soldiers rushed to find cover the musketeers continued firing at them from behind the hedges. As more soldiers fell the screams of the wounded drowned out the orders of the officers. In a desperate attempt to escape the onslaught several soldiers managed to crash through the bushes and into the woods where they began vicious hand to hand fighting with the musketeers and pikemen. One pikeman, an ex-soldier would later describe the fighting as the most brutal he had ever witnessed.

At the rear of the column the officers ordered the gunners to get their cannons off the road and into an open field from where they could bring their firepower into action.

Up on the hill Henry Poulter stood in front of his pikemen.

'Everyone get ready,' he yelled. 'Prepare your pikes. We're about to attack. Remember your training. Trust each other and we will succeed. When you go over the brow of the hill, you'll see the soldiers below. They are trying to set up their cannons. Our objective is to capture those cannons. On the sergeant major's order, we will move forward.'

'Pikemen,' bellowed Sergeant Major White. 'Pikemen attention.'

Three hundred pikemen, standing in rows, stood to attention. Betsy was behind the third row with her pistol and sword in her hands.

'Pikemen,' roared Sergeant Major White. 'Pikemen. Move into battle formation.'

There was a sudden clatter of noise as the pikemen in the front row lowered their pike blades to a horizontal level. The second row held their pikes horizontally at shoulder height in between the men in front of them.

'Pikemen…. Pikemen will move forward at a slow march… By the left,' hollered Sergeant Major White.

There was a loud grunt as the first row stepped forward, followed by the second and third rows.

'Left… right… left…,' called Sergeant Major White. 'Let the row in front of you dictate your pace.'

When the pikemen walked over the summit of the hill their tempo picked up as they headed down the hill towards the soldiers who were desperately trying to get their cannons into position.

When the pikemen were about halfway down the hill Sergeant Major White yelled at the top of his voice.

'Pikemen…. Pikemen charge.'

'Remember Orr,' roared three hundred men as they ran down the hill towards the soldiers.

At the rear of the charge Betsy could see the British officers ordering the infantry around the cannons to fire their rifles at the pikemen. She heard several shots and saw men in the front line collapse. Their place quickly taken by men from the second row. The attack never faltered, and as the soldiers struggled to reload their rifles the front line of pikemen were upon them. Within seconds the soldiers and pikemen were engaged in brutal hand to hand fighting. No quarter was given on either side.

Betsy was directly behind Billy and George when the front row of the pikemen smashed into the soldiers lined up some way from the cannons, and with their slashing pikes it looked like they were going to win. At one point during the battle Betsy saw an officer lunge at Billy with his sword, she quickly pointed her pistol at him but as she fired, she was jostled by the surging pikemen around her. When she was able to look back the officer had disappeared, and Billy was struggling with another soldier. Above the confusion Betsy heard a British officer ordering his men to disengage and very quickly the soldiers pulled back exposing the pikemen to the cannons behind them. Suddenly there were two massive explosions as both cannons were fired sending their loads of grapeshot into the attacking pikemen. As the grapeshot burst open deadly steel balls decimated the pikemen, killing dozens of them instantly. Scores more fell to the ground as the shrapnel ripped their bodies apart. Before the rest of the pikemen were able to regroup the gunners quickly reloaded the cannons and fired again and again into their ranks killing and maiming hundreds more. In the confusion Betsy heard the order for the pikemen to withdraw.

As the gunners continued firing their cannons the pikemen began to quickly disengage. Betsy followed the Gransha pikemen when they ran into the woods and began scrambling up through the trees and bushes as they made their way back up the hill. Once they reached the summit, they stopped and carried out a quick headcount and were relieved to find that most of their unit had survived unscathed, but other companies were not so lucky. Hundreds had been killed or badly maimed as they tried to run back up the open slopes of the hill to escape.

With the attack repulsed the officers turned their cannons to try and support the soldiers fighting in the woods where most of their casualties were happening, but because of the topography they were unable to offer much help. As the fighting continued on the road and nearby woods dozens of soldiers from the York Fencible light infantry tried to escape the onslaught by running down into the marshy ground beside the river. When six of them suddenly found themselves surrounded by dozens of angry pikemen they expected to die but were surprised when the leader of the pikemen stepped forward and reassured them they would not be harmed if they surrendered. After a brief standoff the soldiers eventually laid down their arms and were escorted to a house in Saintfield where they were held prisoners.

Colonel Stapylton eventually managed to extract his cavalry and infantry from the ambush. As he gathered his troops around the cannons, he was informed that three of his senior officers, Captain Chetwynd, Lieutenant Unite and Ensign Sparks had been killed and one hundred and twenty of his infantry were either dead, wounded or missing. Given the loss of so many officers and men, and the overwhelming numbers of musketeers and pikemen facing them Colonel Stapylton decided to withdraw and head back to Comber.

As the soldiers began to retreat General Munro ordered several men to follow them to make sure it wasn't a trick. They soon discovered Colonel Stapylton had abandoned five of his wounded soldiers at the farm where they had first stopped. The men summoned one of their own doctors from within the ranks of the United Irishmen to treat the soldiers' wounds before transporting them to the camp at Oughley Hill where they were reunited with the six other prisoners from the house at Saintfield.

The scene after the battle was one of total devastation with hundreds of dead bodies lying where they had fallen. Hundreds more wounded, their clothes soaked in blood and in agony and distress, begged and pleaded for someone to come and help them.

As Betsy gazed down the hill at the bodies scattered over the grassy slopes below her, she spotted Jessie carefully making her way through the carnage.

'Jessie,' she called out.

Jessie looked up at her. 'Oh Betsy, I can't find Henry. Do you know where he is?'

Betsy felt her heart skip a beat. 'The last time I saw him was when we attacked the cannon.'

'Where was that?'

'Come on, I'll take you there.'

Jessie followed Betsy down the hill, stepping over scores of dead bodies until they reached the spot where the cannons had been.

'This is where I last saw him,' she said as they began looking closely at the broken bodies lying around them. '

'Oh my God,' whispered Jessie as she ran over to one of the men lying face down on the blood-soaked grass. She had found Henry. She knelt beside him praying he was still alive. But as soon as she saw the gaping wound on the side of his head, she knew he was dead. Jessie began to weep as she cradled his body.

Betsy knelt and put her arms around Jessie.

'I'm so sorry.'

Tears flowed down Jessie's face as she continued to embrace Henry's body.

'I knew something was wrong when he didn't come back to the camp to tell me how the battle had gone. Were you with him at the end?'

'Henry led the charge down the hill towards the cannons. But we didn't get there in time and they were able to set them up and fire at us. Dozens of men fell around me. But we had been told not to stop. Henry must have been one of them. He would have died instantly. There was nothing anyone could have done.'

'I know.'

A few minutes later Billy and a couple of men joined them.

'I'm so sorry Jessie,' he said when he saw Henry's body.

'Thank you, Billy. I don't want to leave Henry here. I want to take him home with me. The farm was his pride and joy. It meant everything to him. He would want to be buried in the soil he loved so much.'

'I know he would,' said Billy.

'Henry brought our stallion with him. It's back at the camp. I want to take Henry's body back to the farm on the horse and bury him there.'

'I'll get a stretcher,' said one of the men. 'We'll take him back to the camp.'

While the men went to find a stretcher, Betsy walked back to where she had fired at the officer. She was still unsure whether she had hit him or not. As she stood amongst the dead, she realised that places and landmarks can look so different during the heat of battle. As she looked around at the dead soldiers, she suddenly recognised the officer she had tried to kill. She went over and stood by his body. With the multiple wounds on his body it was difficult to say how he had died.

'Are you alright?' Billy asked.

'Yes,' she replied. 'I fired my pistol at that officer lying over there but I don't know if I hit him or not. He was about to kill you.'

'Are you worried you might have killed him?'

'I'm not sure. I know it was kill or be killed during the battle, but that doesn't make it right. There must be a better way of sorting out our problems. Why are we so quick to fight?'

'I don't know the answer to that Betsy. But I do know we just have to keep going until the end. Maybe then we can do something different.'

'Do you remember fighting at this spot?'

Billy looked around and shook his head. 'No, I don't. To be honest Betsy I can't remember very much about the battle, I was so scared and just desperate to stay alive. The whole clash is just a blur to me. I can remember running down the hill towards the soldiers and praying I wouldn't get shot and then I was swinging my pike like a madman, trying to hit any soldier close to me. Everything seemed to be happening at once. And after the first cannon shots, I just wanted to get away. I remember running towards the trees in the woods, that's about it. Maybe you did kill the officer and saved my life, but we will never know.'

'You're right. What's done is done. We can't change anything now.'

They were interrupted by one of the men 'We've got a stretcher, are you coming?'

Betsy and Billy helped carry Henry's body back to the camp where Gina and Martha managed to get a waterproof sheet to wrap his body in and tie it securely onto the horse.

'Thank you,' said Jessie when they finished.

'Why don't you wait until morning,' said Gina. 'It might be safer.'

'No, I'll be fine. I know this part of the country. I grew up not too far from here.'

Martha put her arms around Jessie and hugged her. 'I'm so sorry. None of us ever thought anything like this would happen. You take care now. We'll come and see you when this is over.'

The pikemen and musketeers from the Gransha company gathered around to offer Jessie their sympathies. As she prepared to leave, they lined up to form a guard of honour for their fallen commanding officer.

Jessie led the stallion through the pikemen. 'Thank you,' she said.

General Munro quickly organised stretcher parties to begin gathering the wounded from the battlefield to bring them back to the camp where they were tended in a makeshift field hospital by a team of doctors, ably aided by Gina and Martha.

As news of the battle spread, grieving families from farms and villages in County Down began arriving throughout the rest of the day and most of the night to search amongst the dead for their loved ones and take them home for burial.

Next morning Billy and George along with several other men were given the task of gathering the bodies of United Irishmen that had not been claimed and burying them in a mass grave close to the Presbyterian Church in Saintfield. While others buried the dead British soldiers in another mass grave on a small piece of land close to the bridge on the outskirts of the village.

Betsy went with Gina and Martha to the field hospital to help tend the wounded. It was while she was changing the bandages on one patient that she overheard a conversation between two United Irishmen sitting outside the tent. She was quite shocked when she realised, they were talking about killing the soldiers they had captured the previous day.

'It is not right that we have to look after them,' she heard one say.

'I agree, I don't understand why we don't just kill them, after all that's what they would do to us if we were taken prisoner.'

'That's right. I heard that the soldiers were ordered not to take any prisoners and when some of our men offered to lay down their arms, they were butchered.'

'We should do that to our prisoners...'

Betsy quickly finished changing the bandage and went outside to confront the men. But they had already left.

'Did you see two men standing here a few minutes ago?' she asked the women sitting nearby.

'I'm afraid people are walking by here all the time,' offered one of them. 'We didn't notice them.'

'Do you know where the British prisoners are being held?' she asked.

'I think they are keeping them by the hedges over there,' said the woman pointing to the far corner of the camp.

'Right, thanks,' said Betsy.

Betsy walked over to where the woman had been pointing. Several wagons were lined up along the hedgerow and a cordon of several armed musketeers and pikemen stood guard around them. Betsy spoke to one of them.

'Is this where the prisoners are being held?'

'Yes. Why do you want to know?'

'I was working in the hospital when I overheard two men talking about killing the prisoners and I thought I should warn you.'

'You need to tell General McCambridge. He's the big man standing over there.'

Betsy went over and introduced herself and told the General what she had overheard.

'Thank you, Betsy. I know that General Munro is aware of that sentiment and I can reassure you that we will make sure our prisoners are safe.'

As Betsy turned to leave General McCambridge called her back.

'Hold on, did you say you're called Betsy Gray?'

'Yes. Why?'

'One of our wounded prisoners was asking earlier if there was a Betsy Gray in the camp.'

'What's his name?'

'He's called John Agnew. He's serving with the Newtownards Yeomanry cavalry.'

'I know John. He has a stall beside me at Bangor market. How is he?'

'Not very good I'm afraid. He has a bullet wound in his stomach. The last time I saw him he was delirious.'

'Could I see him?'

McCambridge glanced around him briefly. 'I'm not supposed to let anyone near them. But on this occasion…. Come with me.'

Betsy followed McCambridge to one of the covered wagons.

'He's in there.'

Betsy climbed into the back of the wagon. There were four soldiers lying in the cramped space. She quickly found Agnew.

'John,' she said. 'Can you hear me?'

Agnew opened his eyes.

'Betsy? Is that really you?'

'Yes John. I've come to see how you are.'

'I'm lucky to be alive. I was directly behind Colonel Stapylton when we were ambushed. I was shot in the stomach. Your doctors think I'll make it. They've been very good. Were you involved in the ambush?'

'You know I can't answer that John.'

'How many soldiers died?'

'I can't say John.'

257

'Do you know what is going to happen to us?'

'General Munro has given strict orders that you are to be well looked after. He will probably trade you for some of our prisoners later.'

Agnew lowered his voice. 'Betsy be careful. It's going to get worse for you. They're bringing troops over from England, Scotland and Wales. They are amassing a vast army. There's still time for you to get out. You know my feelings about what you are trying to do. Please go home Betsy.'

'I can't John. There was no other way. We had to make a stand. The government was doing everything it could to destroy us. They left us with no choice. It's better to die fighting than waiting to be murdered in your home.'

Agnew started coughing. 'Take care Betsy. I hope I'll see you tending your stall in Bangor market one day.'

'Let's hope that's not too far away. Bye John.'

Betsy climbed out of the wagon and re-joined McCambridge.

'Thank you for letting me see John. He has been a good friend for several years.'

McCambridge walked back to the security perimeter with her. 'They're not all bad. Rest assured we'll look after them. They'll be good bargaining chips when we're trying to get some of our people released.'

Betsy thanked him and went back to the field hospital.

Around noon she joined Billy and George for some lunch.

'We lost two hundred men yesterday,' said George. 'Most of their bodies have been taken back to their homes for burial. We buried the rest of them in a big pit. It was horrible I've never seen anything like it in my life and I hope I never see another one. I was talking to a man from another team, he told me that they buried fifty-six soldiers in a grave near the bridge.'

'I was at the field hospital with Martha and Gina all morning,' said Betsy. 'There's over a hundred wounded being treated there.'

'I heard our musketeers fired too early,' said George.

'That's what I thought,' said Betsy.

'Apparently the man who fired the first shot slipped and his gun went off accidently,' said Billy. 'Unfortunately, everyone then thought the shot was the signal to fire. The front of the column hadn't reached the bridge by then and it meant the gunners at the rear were able to take their cannons into the fields beside the road and set them up. It was the cannon fire that caused most of our casualties.'

'I don't understand why everyone I speak to is treating the battle as a victory,' said Martha. 'It certainly doesn't feel like one to me. Oh, it's true the British had to retreat, and we managed to capture eleven of their soldiers, but we have lost over three hundred, either killed or wounded. In my books that's too high a price to pay for a victory.'

'That's the way of war,' said Billy.

During the rest of that day and night as word of their triumph over the British army spread throughout the county, hundreds of new recruits began arriving at the camp on Oughley Hill.

Next morning, with overcrowding in the camp becoming a problem, General Munro decided to move everyone to a much larger camp at Creevy Rocks on the other side of Saintfield.

As soon as the Gransha company received the order to move they gathered around Betsy.

'Ever since Henry died the men have been talking about who they want to lead us,' said Sergeant Major White. 'They want you to do that Betsy.'

'Yes, that's right,' said one of the pikemen. 'We want you to lead us from now on Betsy.'

'But I can't do that,' she replied. 'The leader has always been a man.'

'The men don't care about that,' said the Sergeant Major. 'We want you to be our leader.'

'Come on Betsy, you can do it,' said the pikeman.

'Yes, you can,' said another. 'You've been training with us from the start. You know every move and formation as well as any of us. We want you to be in charge. We trust you.'

Betsy looked around at the men's faces. She had known them all her life.

'You're the one they want Betsy,' said Billy. 'They always come to you for help. They know you'll never let them down. You must say yes.'

Betsy felt overwhelmed. She hadn't been expecting anything like this.

'I would be honoured to take on the challenge, but with certain conditions,' she replied slowly.

'What do you want?' someone called out.

'There will be times, as we witnessed recently, when we will lose our close friends. When that happens it's important that we stick together, and never give up. Will you do that for me?'

'Yes,' they shouted.

'Every musketeer must make sure his musket is clean and well-oiled. Every pikemen must keep his blade razor sharp and always close at hand. Will you do that for me?'

'Yes,' they shouted.

'When we engage the enemy in battle everyone must trust each other and obey every order they receive. Will you do these things for me?'

'Yes,' roared the men of the Gransha company.

'Thank you,' smiled Betsy.

Betsy led the Gransha company of pikemen and musketeers out of the camp. When they reached the bridge on the outskirts of Saintfield village they paused to pay their respects to the fallen United Irishmen and British soldiers.

Later that day after they set up their camp at Creevy Rocks, Betsy was called to meeting with General Munro and his other senior officers.

'Welcome,' said the General as they gathered around him. 'I've just received an update on how the uprising is progressing. The British garrison in Newtownards has been forced to retreat to their barracks in Belfast. United Irishmen are in control of Bangor, Holywood, and Conlig. Our next objective will be to consolidate our hold over the rest of the county.'

'Any news about County Antrim?'

'Yes. A Committee of Public Safety has been established in Ballymena and United Irishmen control Larne, Islandmagee, Glenarm and all along the County Antrim coast. The British garrison at Randalstown has surrendered to us.'

'I heard we were defeated at Antrim,' said one of the officers.

'Yes, I'm sorry to say that's true,' said Munro sadly. 'After heavy fighting in Antrim town, Henry Joy McCracken had to withdraw his forces to prevent further losses. My latest news is that he is regrouping them and hopes to be able to reengage with the enemy soon, but it's not looking good. I've received reports of the British army burning hundreds of farms and cottages around Antrim town and the surrounding districts. It's therefore very important that we continue our good work here and give heart to the United Irishmen in County Antrim.'

'What about in the rest of Ireland?'

'United Irishmen forces continue to tighten their grip in Wexford and in a few other counties in the south. However, Dublin is calm, but we are expecting them to rise any day.'

'Have any of the soldiers from the Militia regiments come over to us yet?' asked John Sanderson, one of the commanders.

'The short answer is no. A few individual soldiers have left their regiments and joined us. You can see them around the camp, but there is no word about any large-scale desertions taking place anywhere to date.'

'But they were an integral part of our strategy,' retorted Sanderson. 'Without their arms and skills, we don't stand a chance.'

'We have enough weapons,' replied General Munro. 'And if we keep our nerve and engage the British soldiers on our terms, we will have nothing to fear. The people will eventually come out and join us when they see we are winning.'

'What about the French, are they coming?'

'What do you mean?' asked Munro.

'I heard a French fleet was sailing here with thousands of rifles and dozens of cannons for us. Is that true?'

Munro looked around the rest of his officers. 'Well, has anyone else heard the French are coming to our aide?'

No one answered.

'There's your answer,' said Munro. 'They're not coming. We don't need them. We can fight on our own.'

'But if the French don't come and if the Militia soldiers stay loyal to their regiments where are we going to get the extra rifles and cannons that we so desperately need?'

'No, we mustn't think that way, as long as we keep mobile and don't allow ourselves to be drawn into confrontations in open fields with the British, we will be stronger than them in street fighting and close combat. We always knew that it would be difficult in the beginning but with each success more people will come and join us. Look what happened after our victory at Saintfield. More than two thousand men have joined us since then. Those are the sort of close-range battles we have to engage in until we become stronger.'

'But that strategy can only last for a short time. Major General Nugent is amassing a large army to move against us and if we don't find more weapons soon, particularly cannons, we will be destroyed.'

'Then it is up to us to get more,' said Betsy.

'That's right,' said General Munro. 'Our search parties are scouring the countryside for weapons as we speak. We'll soon have a fighting force in excess of ten thousand men and to make sure we are an effective fighting unit; I need every one of you to maintain discipline within your company. For the rest of the day the order is for each company to practice street battle formations and prepare your pikemen and musketeers for the next battle. It's best if we concentrate on the effectiveness of our own units and not worry ourselves with how the fighting is going in other parts of the country. War is complicated. Our enemies are constantly spreading false information and rumours to try and demoralise us. Concentrate on our objectives and if we are successful, we will become a beacon for everyone else in the country to follow.'

Betsy spent the next few hours with the Gransha company honing the men's skills in small battle formations for manoeuvring their way around narrow town streets and country lanes; and training in close hand to hand fighting.

By the next morning the numbers in the camp had swollen again just as General Munro had predicted. And when asked why they had come to join most of the newcomers gave the victory at Saintfield as the reason.

While Betsy and Billy were eating their lunchtime meal, they heard a loud cheer coming from one section of the camp. They stood up along with several others to see what was happening and spotted a large column of pikemen and musketeers marching towards the camp entrance.

'Who are they?' asked Betsy as she watched the men enter the camp.

'They're the Defenders from mid-Ulster,' answered Billy. 'That's Magennis at the front of the column. I was wondering when they were going to show up.'

'Which one is Magennis?'

'The tall, muscular man, with the black hat. Come on, I'll introduce you to him.'

They followed the column as Magennis led his men into the heart of the camp. He ordered them to halt when they reached General Munro standing outside his tent.

'Good afternoon General Munro,' said Magennis. 'I told you I'd bring my men once the fighting started.'

'Thank you. I'm afraid we have few facilities on the camp, but we don't intend staying here much longer. We'll be moving to another camp much closer to Ballynahinch.'

'Congratulations on your victory at Saintfield,' said Magennis after he had dismissed his men. 'You certainly sent shock waves throughout the whole country. My men couldn't wait to join you once they heard about it.'

'It's the way we have to fight in the future. The British will try to draw us into open conflict, but we don't have the weapons yet with which to compete. Our only option is to fight them in the streets of our towns and cities.'

'I agree. Until the majority of the population come out and join us it will be tough going. But I do believe we can succeed.'

'How many men have you brought with you?' asked General Munro.

'I've brought just over seven hundred of my best men. I saw a lot of women and children in the camp when we marched through. How many fighting men do you actually have?'

'Our numbers are increasing every hour. We'll have about ten thousand here over the next couple of days.'

'We're going to need all the men we can get, because I heard it didn't go well at Antrim.'

'That's right. Henry Joy is trying to regroup as we speak and is thinking of bringing his forces down here to join us.'

'What about the men in the Militia who promised to leave their barracks and bring their weapons with them; how many of them have joined you?'

'I'm afraid that has not happened yet. A few serving soldiers have joined us, but the desertions are not on the scale we were anticipating.'

'We've been hearing similar stories from other counties. My understanding is that a lot of soldiers are waiting to see which way the fighting goes. If it looks like we're going to win, they'll come out and join us.'

Later that Sunday evening the foraging parties returned to the camp bringing more weapons and food with them. The air was still warm as the night drew in and many turned their thoughts to their loved ones. Betsy lay in Billy's arms as the glow from the cooking fires began to dim. From nearby Betsy heard the strong voice of one of the line singers from a Presbyterian church begin to sing, *'Amazing grace. How sweet the sound.'* Soon thousands of people throughout the camp were singing along.

'That saved a wretch like me.
I once was lost, but now am found;
Was blind, but now I see.
'Twas grace that taught my heart to fear,
And grace my fears relieved;
How precious did that grace appear
The hour I first believed.
Through many dangers, toils and snares
I have already come;
'Tis grace hath brought me safe thus far,
And grace will lead me home.'

As the singing died out, darkness fell, and the camp became silent.

Throughout the night Betsy was aware of horsemen coming and going all the time and was not surprised when she was invited to an early morning briefing by General Munro. This time there were too many company commanders to fit into the General's tent, so the meeting was held in the open air.

'We've been receiving intelligence reports that reinforcements from England have been arriving in Belfast over the weekend. It looks like Major General Nugent is amassing an army in the city. We expect him to leave Belfast soon and try to seek a confrontation with us. There was another British force of around one thousand stationed in Ballynahinch, but our reports are that this has now moved to secure Downpatrick. We can only assume Major General Nugent must have thought we were going to attack the town. It would also appear that Colonel Stapylton has been ordered to take his force back to Comber.'

'It sounds as though they are going to try and surround us?' said one of the officers.

'It's too early to say. If we can defeat Major General Nugent's army the other smaller ones will fall. As I said to you yesterday, it is important that we choose where to fight, and in a landscape that suits us. That's why I have decided to set up our defences in and around Ballynahinch. General Townsend will take a scouting force of two hundred and fifty to establish our first position in Ballynahinch and check out the other locations we intend to use. The rest of us will continue our preparations to move to Ballynahinch this afternoon.'

As the meeting broke up General Townsend asked Betsy and two other company commanders to stay behind.

'We've been given the task of rooting out any British soldiers from Ballynahinch. As far as I know General Stewart has left a small force behind to guard the town. We have to deal with them and prepare several locations for when the rest of our army arrives later today. We'll be leaving in twenty minutes. Any questions?'

There were none.

After the briefing Betsy went back to prepare the Gransha company and fifteen minutes later they joined General Townsend and the rest of his force on the march to Ballynahinch.

Chapter 27

As Betsy and the United Irishmen marched into the outskirts of Ballynahinch local people came out of their houses to wave and cheer them. When they reached the town square they were confronted by an appalling sight. Two bodies were hanging from a rough scaffold that had been erected in the middle of the square. General Townsend ordered the men's bodies to be cut down immediately, and a medic to try and revive them, but after a few minutes he indicated there was nothing he could do and pronounced both dead.

'Does anyone know what happened?' said General Townsend to some of the local people who had begun to gather around.

A distressed woman stepped forward. 'The soldiers hung them just before you arrived.'

'What was their crime?' asked the General.

'They said the man on the right was a liberty man, and that this is what they were going to do to anyone who sympathises with the organisation.'

'And what about the other man?'

'He's my husband. He tried to save his friend.'

By this time more local people had gathered around the bodies.

'The soldiers were laughing when they hung them,' said a man. 'They said they would be back for the rest of us.'

'Don't worry, if they come back, we'll be waiting for them,' declared General Townsend. 'We'll not let them do anything like this to you again.'

'I pray that you do,' replied the man as he helped a group of men lift the two bodies and begin carrying them from the square.

'We'll take care of them,' said the sobbing woman as she followed them.

General Townsend ordered the United Irishmen to stand to attention until the cortege had left.

'Okay, you all know what you have to do,' said the General. 'Check the locations you were given and report back as soon as you can. I don't think we'll find anymore soldiers here.'

The United Irishmen quickly split into small groups and headed off in different directions. Betsy ordered a section of the Gransha company to follow her as she headed to the main entrance of the large Montalto estate belonging to Lord Moira. After forcing the gates open, they marched down the long drive, passing through a heavily wooded area until they reached the large Montalto house where Betsy gathered everyone around her.

'Our orders are to search the house and estate. General Munro wants to use it as our main camp. We have to make sure it's safe for the rest of our army arriving later today.'

Betsy divided the men into small groups, telling each of them what she wanted them to do. As they headed off, Billy hammered on the large door of the house. A few moments later it was opened by a rather nervous looking butler.

'Yes, can I help you?'

'We are requisitioning this house for the army of the United Irishmen,' declared Billy.

The butler stared at him. 'But you can't. Lord Moira is not at home.'

Billy glanced at Betsy before pushing his way past the man. 'We do not need his lordships approval.'

'Stop, you can't come in…' said the butler.

'I would like to reassure you that we will not damage anything in the house,' said Betsy as she and four pikemen joined Billy in the hallway. 'Are there any British soldiers here or on the estate?'

Before the terrified butler could reply a stern looking man came rushing into the hallway.

'What the hell do you think you are doing?' he demanded. 'Jenkins, who are these people?'

'They say they are with the United Irishmen,' replied the butler. 'I could not stop them.'

'I'm ordering you to leave immediately,' demanded the man.

Billy lowered his pike. 'I'm ordering you to step back. We're not leaving. This house now belongs to the army of the United Irishmen. And we'll be staying here for as long as we like.'

The man recoiled in fear. 'We've no weapons here. Lord Moira gave strict instructions to have them all removed months ago. There's nothing here for you.'

'That's for us to decide. We'll be using this house and the rest of the estate as a campsite for our army. I would advise you and the rest of the staff to leave immediately. Now, are there any soldiers here, or anywhere else on the estate?'

'No,' declared the man. 'There are no guests staying here at present.'

'Then you won't mind if we search the house,' said Betsy as she turned to the other pikemen. 'Make sure you don't damage anything and report back here as soon as you're finished.'

Five minutes later the pikemen declared the house was safe. When the rest of the men returned and reported the estate was also safe Betsy and Billy rushed to the square to report back to General Townsend. They were still in the square a couple of hours later when General Munro arrived at the head of a long column of thousands of United Irishmen.

As each new company arrived General Townsend and his team directed them to the campsite they had been allocated on either Bell's Hill, Windmill Hill, Montalto Estate, or other locations around Ballynahinch.

As more of his army arrived General Munro ordered barricades to be constructed on every road into the town. While all this was going on scouts were constantly coming and going, updating Munro and his officers on what the British were doing.

Later that night Betsy, Billy, George, Gina and Martha went back to the Montalto estate to join the rest of the Gransha company at their campsite nestled in amongst the trees. As they gathered around the campfire their conversation quickly turned to the forth coming battle.

'Tell us what's happening Betsy,' said Gina.

'The latest information I have is that Major General Nugent is expected to move against us soon. Our men have spotted his scouts watching our every move ever since we left Creevy Rocks.'

'How many soldiers do you think he will be bringing with him?'

'I don't know, but it will be in the thousands this time. There is another British army just south of us in Downpatrick. They're still there and haven't moved.'

'I'm glad General Munro is in charge, at least he seems to know what he is doing.'

'Yes,' agreed Billy. 'We have the whole town sealed off. And this time we'll have our own cannons.'

'Where did we get them from?' asked George.

'The Bangor men took six of them from a frigate berthed in Bangor harbour, and the boys from Lisburn managed to get two more. They might not be as big as some of the British guns but at least we will be able to fire back.'

'I've been waiting for this for a long time,' said George. 'I feel so excited.'

'I agree,' said Betsy. 'The Irish government couldn't defeat us with their corrupt judges, their torture, their illegal hangings and their cruel deportations. Soon we'll defeat them on the battlefield. And after we do, we'll march to the houses of parliament in Dublin and set up our own government that will become a beacon of light for all oppressed people in the world.'

Next morning, shortly before ten o'clock, Betsy and Billy left the campsite for a meeting with General Munro in a hotel near the town square. The room was packed with officers when they arrived.

'Good morning everyone,' said the General. 'First the news from outside the county. Fighting continues in County Wexford with no substantial breakthrough being predicted. I'm afraid it's not good news from County Antrim. After Henry Joy McCracken's defeat at Antrim town his troops scattered all over the county. We believe some of them, including Henry Joy, may be trying to make their way here, to join us. Other towns in the county continue to hold out but I don't know for how much longer. We need a substantial victory to give our people something positive to focus on otherwise the uprising will soon collapse...'

While General Munro was speaking there was a bustle at the front door of the hotel seconds before a flustered looking man came barging into the room.

'Sir, I'm Captain Robinson I bring urgent news of the British army movements.'

General Munro remained calm as he looked up at the new arrival.

'Very well Captain, you'd better tell us what you know.'

'My scouts have been monitoring the movements of three British armies in the county. I have just received reports that Major General Nugent left Belfast this morning at the head of two thousand soldiers in an army that includes the Monaghan Militia, the Fifeshire Fencible Infantry and the Twenty-Second Dragoons.'

'What direction is he heading?'

'There is no doubt he is coming here. Nugent also has eight heavy cannons with him, which means he will have to keep to the main roads. A company of engineers have been trying to delay him and have managed to destroy a few bridges but that will only slow him down. We believe they will be here sometime this afternoon.'

There were a few gasps in the room.

'Is there any news of Lieutenant Colonel Stewart and his army?' asked General Munro.

'Yes sir. Lieutenant Colonel Stewart and his army left Downpatrick this morning. They are also heading in this direction. They will be here this afternoon.'

'What of Colonel Stapylton?'

'Colonel Stapylton moved his army from Belfast to their barracks in Comber yesterday. They are still there.'

'That's very interesting. Keep an eye on Stapylton,' said General Munro as he turned to his officers. 'Now we know. It looks like they are going to try and surround us. Our outer defences are in place. All we can do now is wait. Any questions?'

'I have one,' said Betsy.

'Go ahead,' said General Munro.

'On my way over here I noticed an awful lot of young children in the camp and on the streets. It looks like whole families have joined us. I saw the terrible damage cannon shot can do to grown men, we should send the children and their mothers and other non-combatants home before the fighting starts.'

'I've brought my wife and my two daughters with me,' said one of the officers. 'I was going to send them home when it looked like we were going to be attacked.'

'I also have my family with me,' added another. 'I thought it would be safe for them to remain in the camp while we were away fighting.'

'We don't know how the battle will go,' added another officer. 'The British army could attack us on three different fronts and bombard our camps with their cannon. We just don't know what they're going to do. I agree with Betsy, I think all the women and children and other non-combatants should be sent home immediately.'

'I'm here to fight,' declared Betsy. 'As are dozens of other women. This is our cause as well. We will not leave.'

'I'm sorry Betsy, I didn't mean to include you in my remarks,' said the officer quickly. 'I was talking about the mothers, wives, sisters and servants who came to the camp to see what was happening and have no intentions of being involved. I recognise there are women here who want to fight, and I'll be proud to stand beside every one of them.'

'Does anyone else want to comment?' asked General Munro.

'Yes,' replied General Townsend. 'We must send them home. Warfare is the most terrifying experience anyone of us will ever go through. When we arrived yesterday, we found two men hanging from a makeshift scaffold in the square. That's what the soldiers say they're going to do to any United Irishmen and their sympathisers. We must not give them the opportunity of extending that horror to our children.'

General Munro looked around his officers before he spoke. 'General Townsend is right. Our fighters must be focussed on the enemy and not worrying about what is happening to their loved ones. We'll begin the evacuation of the children and their mothers along with other non-combatants from our camps immediately. Let the guards on the barricades know of our decision. Go back to your companies and make sure this is carried out as quickly as possible. When you're finished get back to your posts and prepare for whatever the British soldiers throw at us.'

Over the next few hours, many hundreds of people streamed out of the various camps as General Munro's orders were carried out. When the local inhabitants saw them leave they also evacuated their homes, piling their furniture and belongings onto carts before heading out of town.

Later that afternoon, while Betsy and the Gransha company were on guard duty at a barricade just below the Windmill, on the main road from Saintfield, they spotted several men running towards them. They looked terrified. Betsy rushed out to speak to them.

'Where have you come from?'

'We were part of the rear-guard on Creevy Rocks. Our orders were to keep a lookout for any troop movements,' said one of them as he tried to catch his breath. 'It all started around eleven o'clock this morning...There was smoke everywhere. It looked like the whole countryside was on fire...'

271

'Then we saw the soldiers,' said another man. 'There are thousands of them. They're setting fire to every farmhouse and building in their way.'

'When they reached Saintfield,' said the first man. 'We saw them rushing from house to house....'

'The whole village is ablaze,' blurted another.

'And when they spotted us on Creevy Rock they tried to surround us.'

'We were lucky to escape.'

'Anyone they caught they killed right away.'

'They're hanging people from every branch they can find.'

'They're coming this way.'

'They'll show you no mercy.'

'Betsy, look at the sky,' shouted George.

Betsy looked up to see dark grey smoke bellowing into the sky from dozens of fires on the horizon. More farms burst into flames as she watched.

'Look. There's smoke over there as well,' shouted George pointing to the right of them where dark, grey smoke bellowed into a cloudless sky.

Suddenly they heard the boom of a single cannon shot coming from the Saintfield direction. This was answered almost immediately by two cannon shots from their right.

'What was that?' said Betsy.

'Major General Nugent and Lieutenant Colonel Stewart are communicating with each other,' said Sergeant Major White. 'They'll be combining their forces soon. It won't be long before they mount an attack.'

Betsy turned to the men from Creevy Rock. 'You'd better report to General Munro and tell him what's happening. Do you know where Ednavady Hill is?'

'I do,' replied one of the men. 'I live here.'

'That's where General Munro is based. Go straight there and tell him everything.'

The panic stricken men raced off to deliver the fearful news.

Sergeant Major White turned to a couple of the Gransha pikemen. 'Do you see that hill over there?'

'Yes sir.'

'I want you to set up an observation post and watch for soldiers. As soon as you see any signs of them come back to me immediately. Do not wait. Do you understand?'

'Yes sir.'

'Off you go.'

'What do you think their tactics will be?' asked Betsy.

'We have Major General Nugent marching towards our positions on the left and Lieutenant Colonel Stewart's army coming towards us on our right, both armies will try to meet up before they mount an attack. While they are apart Nugent will be anxious that we will be able to attack him from the side.'

The waiting continued for over an hour. With the tension increasing they saw more farmhouses being set alight. Suddenly the two men on the observation post stood up and began signalling frantically before running down the hill.

'They must have spotted some soldiers,' said Betsy. Within minutes the two breathless pikemen rushed up to Sergeant Major White.

'There are hundreds of soldiers advancing through the fields towards our pikemen on Bell's hill.'

'What about on our right?' asked Sergeant Major White. 'What's happening with Lieutenant Colonel Stewart's army?'

'Nothing. We didn't see any soldiers over there.'

Suddenly they heard a roar behind them as a thousand pikemen came marching up the road from the town square.

'General Munro has ordered us forward,' shouted General Townsend. 'We're going to attack Nugent's left flank. Are you with us?'

The Gransha company joined the pikemen as they marched along Windmill Road towards the exposed left flank of Major General Nugent's advancing soldiers. After a few moments they stopped to observe through the hedges, the rows of soldiers in the fields below. Just as they prepared to get into battle formation, they came under fire from Lieutenant Colonel Stewart's soldiers arriving on their right.

General Townsend knew he had no option but to give the order to withdraw. As the pikemen ran back to the barricades the musketeers positioned on Windmill Hill began firing on the soldiers giving the pikemen enough cover to escape.

With his left flank now protected Major General Nugent ordered his infantry to resume the attack on the United Irishmen on Bell's Hill. With only a few musketeers to protect them the pikemen were soon ordered to withdraw into the town. The British soldiers moved onto Bell's Hill and began concentrating their cannon fire on the musketeers on the steep slopes of Windmill Hill opposite and on the pikemen assembling in the streets of Ballynahinch.

With the town now being bombarded by heavy cannon fire the number of casualties soon began to mount up, however, because the musketeers on Windmill Hill were so well dug in their losses were relatively light and they were able to keep the British infantry pinned down.

General Munro watched this unfold from his camp on Ednavady Hill. He was aware that Lieutenant Colonel Stewart was attempting to manoeuvre his soldiers to surround the musketeers on Windmill Hill.

'This is not good,' he said to one of his aides. 'The worst thing we can do at this stage is to divide our forces. Give the order to withdraw from the town centre and from Windmill Hill. We will concentrate our troops here in the Montalto estate and draw the British soldiers into the streets of Ballynahinch. Then when we counterattack, we will have the upper hand.'

Runners were sent out immediately to convey the General's orders.

Betsy was standing at the barricades on Windmill Hill Road with Sergeant Major White when the order to withdraw arrived.

'What do you make of this John?' she asked.

'It's a strategic withdrawal. General Munro knows we have no chance of defeating the British infantry in open warfare. We must draw them into the narrow streets of the town to give our pikemen the upper hand. General Munro is doing the right thing. He's winning the tactical battle.'

Sergeant Major White gave the order to leave the barricade and marched his men down the street into the town square where the pikemen were gathering.

'I wonder where Gina is?' said Betsy when they reached the square.

'I thought she was with Martha?'

274

'No, Martha stayed to help at the camp, Gina came down with me this morning, she said they were planning to set up a new hospital in the town. The last time I saw her was here, in the square.'

'Do you know where the hospital is?' asked George.

'Hold on, I'll see if I can find out,' said Billy.

He returned minutes later. 'They're using the King George hotel. It's somewhere on the square.'

They quickly found the hotel. It was packed with wounded men, some lying on makeshift beds, while others lay on the floor. It didn't take them long to find Gina.

'Oh Betsy,' exclaimed Gina when she saw them. 'I hope you haven't brought us more wounded; Mary and I can barely cope with what we have.'

'No, I haven't Gina, we've been told to withdraw from the town and go back to the camp in the Montalto estate. Everyone is leaving. You and Mary need to get out of here.'

Gina looked around her. 'But we can't leave these men, if we leave, the soldiers will kill them.'

'How many wounded are there?' asked Betsy.

'There are about thirty,' said Gina.

'Can they walk?'

'Some of them might be able to, but there are a few who can't.'

'Are there any doctors here?'

'No, the surgeons were here this morning to advise us what to do, but they had to go back to Montalto to operate on more wounded up there. There's no one else.'

'Look, we need to evacuate everyone. George, go back to the square and get as many men as you can to come and help us,' ordered Betsy.

While George ran back to the square, Betsy and Gina began to organise the wounded, quickly mustering together those who could walk. There were ten of them. They left with Billy and Mary as George returned with a large group of men.

'Right, listen up everyone,' shouted Betsy. 'We need to carry these wounded men back to the camp in Montalto, and we need to do it now before the soldiers come.'

George helped the men quickly sort themselves into pairs and to decide which patient they were going to take. The wounded on stretchers were lifted and carried out of the hotel. For some, the only way was to lift them onto the back of one of the men and carry them that way. About fifteen minutes later the hotel was almost empty. As Betsy checked each of the rooms, she found Gina moping the brow of a very sick looking young boy.

'He's only fourteen Betsy. A cannon ball ripped off his right arm. The surgeons stitched him up and said not to move him for a couple of days. He will die if we move him.'

'There's no option Gina, we have to take him with us.'

'Maybe if I was here the soldiers wouldn't harm him if I pleaded with them.'

Betsy shook her head at her friend's suggestion. 'You can't do that Gina. They would kill you both. Come on we must lift him and get out of here. The square is almost empty. Everyone has left. It's up to you and me.'

The young boy groaned as Gina tried to lift him. 'Mum is that you mum. Mum help me,' he said deliriously.

'We can't just lift him. We need a stretcher.'

Betsy went over to one of the windows and ripped the curtain rail from the wall. She did the same at another window.

'Help me make a stretcher with these poles and one of the curtains.'

When they finished, they gently eased the groaning boy onto their makeshift stretcher.

'Quick, let's go,' said Betsy.

The square was empty when they left the hotel.

'Come on Gina we need to hurry, the soldiers will be here soon.'

As they ran through the square Betsy spotted redcoats in the side streets and urged Gina to run faster. Suddenly she heard gun shots coming from the far end of the square as a couple of British soldiers fired at them.

'Halt,' one called out.

'Keep running Gina,' Betsy shouted.

One of the soldiers started running after them as the other soldier fired again. His shot shattered the glass in a shop window close to Betsy.

'Stop or I'll shoot to kill the next time,' the soldier shouted.

'Don't stop Gina,' screamed Betsy.

The other soldier was gaining on them, but just as he was about to grab hold of Gina there was another shot and he stumbled to the ground.

'Over this way,' shouted Billy, as the musketeers he had brought back with him fired at the other soldier.

As Betsy and Gina ran with the stretcher the shooting intensified forcing them to stop and duck behind a small wall. As they crouched down, Betsy was convinced she was going to die.

Suddenly she saw George appear with more musketeers. They quickly took up their firing positions and were able to provide enough cover to allow Betsy and Gina to escape from the square and run down the road towards Bridge Street. Even though more soldiers began arriving in the square, they were prevented from following them by the heavy fire from the musketeers.

When Betsy and Gina arrived at the barricades by the gates into the Montalto estate they handed the wounded boy over to two men who carried the stretcher to Montalto house where a temporary casualty unit had been set up. Gina stayed with the boy, while Betsy went to Munro's headquarters on Ednavady Hill to find General Townsend and let him know that she had organised the evacuation of the wounded.

'Well done Betsy,' General Townsend said. 'Those men would have surely died.'

As he was talking General Munro arrived and asked for an update.

'The whole town has been evacuated,' replied General Townsend. 'We've left a dozen snipers to harass and keep the soldiers on their toes. Nearly all the pikemen are back on the estate, there are just a few stragglers left, but they should be back soon.'

'What about the musketeers on Windmill Hill?'

'They should be here by now.'

'If that's true, why are they still firing on the soldiers below them?'

General Townsend looked over towards Windmill Hill. 'I don't understand, I know they received your order to leave. I'll send another message ordering a withdrawal immediately to the Montalto estate.'

'What happens next?' asked an officer.

'Once Nugent realises our troops have pulled out of Ballynahinch and left Windmill Hill, I believe he will secure the town and occupy the hill. He will move his cannons forward and begin firing on the Montalto estate, while at the same time reinforcing Colonel Stewart's army on our right, with the intention of attacking us on two fronts.'

'Will we have to improve our defences?'

'No, that will not be necessary, because before Colonel Nugent is able to put his plan into action it is my intention to attack.

'Where will you do that?'

'At his weakest point… in the narrow streets of Ballynahinch. I will use my pikemen to destroy his infantry and capture his cannon, before swinging around and attacking Colonel Stewart's army and defeating them. If my plan works, we will then march south and join forces with the United Irishmen in Wexford, and together we will smash General Lake's army.'

'The British will have to sue for peace.'

'Exactly, and we will be victorious.'

Thirty minutes later the messenger returned from Windmill Hill.

'Sir. The musketeers are refusing to leave the hill. General McCance said they are taking few casualties because of their strong position and are able to keep the soldiers pinned down. He respectfully requests to be allowed to stay on the hill and hold his strong position.'

Everyone expected General Munro to react angrily. But he didn't.

'Go back and tell General McCance I understand his concerns about protecting the hill,' he replied calmly. 'Tell him if they continue to stay where they are, we will be defeated because maintaining an armed presence on Windmill Hill is no longer of any strategic importance to us and our ability to defeat the British army. Tell General McCance I urgently request him to withdraw his musketeers immediately.'

The young runner nodded his head. 'Yes sir.'

'Make sure you give him all of my message,' said the General. 'He should be in no doubt that if he remains on the hill we will be defeated.'

When the runner left Munro began studying the maps spread out on the table before him. 'We will have one chance and one chance only to win this battle,' he said. 'And if we take it, people will look back at this moment as the turning point in the whole revolution.'

General Townsend left the tent and went outside to look over at Windmill Hill. He could see the musketeers firing at the soldiers below, and craters being gouged out of the earth around them as the British replied with cannon fire. After a few moments the rate of musket fire gradually decreased. The withdrawal had begun. He watched the musketeers running down the hill into the town. Soon the firing stopped completely. A few minutes later he spotted a few redcoats and then the British soldiers could be seen swarming all over the hill. Once the capture had been completed General Townsend noticed a crowd of soldiers gathering around one of the windmill's sails.

'What are the soldiers doing over there?' he asked those standing around him.

'It looks like they've captured someone,' said a pikeman.

'They're tying him to the sail,' said another.

There were gasps of horror when they realised the full extent of what the soldiers were doing to the unfortunate individual.

'Oh my God, they're going to hang him.'

They watched as the man's flailing body was winched high in the air.

Townsend then saw General McCance, who had been in command of the musketeers on Windmill Hill, storm into Munro's tent. It was quite apparent from his aggressive body language that he was furious at being ordered down from the hill and he was heard shouting.

'You should've left us there. We were keeping the British pinned down. They would never have beaten us.'

'They didn't need to,' replied General Munro calmly. 'All they had to do was to surround you and wait until you ran out of ammunition, by which time we would have lost the battle.'

As he was speaking General Townsend stormed into the tent. 'Who did you leave behind?' he demanded.

'What are you talking about?'

General Townsend dragged McCance out of the tent and pointed at the hill.

'Look,' he demanded. 'That's one of your men dangling at the end of a rope on the windmill. That's what I'm talking about. So, why did you leave him behind?'

'Oh my God,' said McCance when he saw the body. 'It's Captain Hugh McCullough, his men were providing cover fire while the rest of us escaped. I thought everyone had managed to get away.'

'It was your duty to make sure they did,' said Townsend.

'Alright, that's enough,' said General Munro from the tent entrance. 'Stewart's soldiers are threatening our right flank; get your musketeers over there as quickly as you can and await on my orders.'

Pikemen guarding the walls around the perimeter of the Montalto estate could hear the soldiers laughing and jeering in the town as they broke into shops and public houses, plundering whatever they could find, and harassing any of the locals who had decided to stay.

At six o'clock Major General Nugent ordered his cannons to begin firing into the Montalto estate. Many of the United Irishmen were forced to seek shelter wherever they could as red-hot cannon balls smashed their way through anything in their path.

It was during one barrage that Gina was almost killed. She had been nursing the wounded at the front of Montalto House when a cannon ball smashed into the wall just above her head showering her with pieces of broken masonry.

Betsy rushed down to the house to see how Gina was and followed Martha up the stairs to one of the large bedrooms where she found her lying on top of the bed.

Gina opened her eyes when she heard them come in.

'Thank God you are alive,' said Betsy. 'I was so worried when I heard a cannonball almost hit you. What happened?'

'I was working outside, changing a dressing on a wound when I heard a roaring noise and instinctively ducked down just as a cannonball smashed into the wall where my head would have been. I was completely covered in pieces of broken masonry. There's still some of it embedded in my hair. I must look a right mess.'

Suddenly the tension that had been building inside Betsy was released as she and Martha began to laugh.

'Don't laugh at me,' cried Gina before she too began to laugh. 'But my hair is a mess.'

As the three of them continued laughing Betsy put her arms around Gina and hugged her close.

The bombardment continued for another few hours until nine o'clock when Major General Nugent decided to save his ammunition for another day and ordered a cessation.

When the firing stopped General Munro sent Captain William Rogers into the town with two scouts to assess Nugent's defences. When they returned around eleven o'clock General Munro called a meeting of all his senior officers.

'Well Captain, tell us what you found?'

'Soldiers from the Monaghan Militia have taken over the town, or should I say they have broken into the public houses and other drinking establishments and would appear to be in a very intoxicated state. They seem to be more interested in fighting amongst themselves and consuming as much liquor as they can steal, than in securing the streets of the town against an attack.'

'So, what about their defences?'

'There are none sir,' replied Captain Rogers. 'In fact, most of the soldiers we saw appear to be drunk, and if they are not already in a deep stupor they soon will be. The Militia are behaving more like a drunken mob than a regiment of trained soldiers.'

'What about the cannons, has Nugent moved any of them into the town?'

'We didn't come across any but there was a lot of activity in and around Nugent's headquarters on Windmill Hill.'

'We should take advantage of the Militia's disarray and attack them,' said General Magennis. 'It sounds as though they will be too drunk to offer us any resistance.'

'I agree,' added another officer. 'This is a golden opportunity for us to retake the town and destroy a large part of Nugent's infantry and get more guns.'

Other officers began voicing their support. Most of them agreed it would be foolish to miss the chance of an easy victory and were becoming quite excited about the thought of inflicting another defeat on the British army.

Betsy noticed General Munro had remained quiet and that he stayed that way until the conversations gradually died down.

'Thank you for the suggestion,' said General Munro. 'But I have to disagree. To attack now would be a big mistake.'

'But if we go now, most of the Militia soldiers will be asleep or too drunk to fight. We will easily defeat them. Victory will be ours. We could then move on and attack Nugent's headquarters on Windmill Hill.'

'It certainly looks that way, but we would soon be right back to square one.'

'How would we? We would've gained the advantage by attacking and destroying the Monaghan Militia.'

General Munro shook his head. 'No, we wouldn't. There's no doubt we would destroy part of the Militia, but because Nugent still has the baulk of his army and all of his cannons outside the town, he would quickly resume a bombardment of our men in the town. We wouldn't have enough additional weapons to retaliate and would eventually lose the battle.'

'So, what are you planning to do?' asked Magennis.

'We wait.'

Betsy could see the disappointment in the officer's faces, but General Munro wasn't to be deterred.

'Major General Nugent has brought his army here for a fight,' he said. 'He will consider our retreat from Windmill Hill and from the town as a sign of weakness. He will be eager to try and finish us off. My belief is that he will use the darkness to build up his forces in the town and will attack us from there. He will also order Colonel Stewart to attack us from the right. The position of Colonel Stapylton's army is key to all of this. They have not moved and are still in their barracks at Comber which means Major General Nugent has left us an escape route to the north.'

'Why would he do that?' asked Betsy.

'Major General Nugent will believe that once he starts attacking us from the town and on our right flank, he will encourage a significant number of our men to think about retreating, and once they become aware of an escape route to the north, they will take it. Once the discipline in our ranks breaks down more men will join them. That's when Nugent will release his dragoons to wipe us out.'

'So, what do we do?'

'I want Major General Nugent to believe in his plan... We will start evacuating the wounded and the soldiers we are holding prisoner through this route. Nugent will see people on the roads going north and think his plan is working. If anyone else wishes to go with them they are free to do so...'

'You've talked about Nugent's plans, what are ours?' asked an officer.

'To attack when Nugent believes he is at his strongest.'

'But how are we going to do that?'

'As soon as this meeting ends, I want General Warden to take two thousand pikemen and musketeers to reinforce General Magennis's defences on our right flank. Your initial role will be to slow down the advance of Stewart's army. Let me explain why,' said the General as he pointed to the large map on the table.

'At three-thirty am, General Townsend will leave the Montalto estate with a force of two thousand pikemen and musketeers via the Church on Church Street and attack Nugent's infantry facing them at the bottom of the street. At the same time, I will lead the rest of the pikemen and musketeers out through the main entrance and onto Bridge Street. We will attack the same infantry at the junction of Bridge Street and Church Street. They will not be able to withstand a two-pronged attack and will be forced to retreat back up High Street and into the town square. We will follow them and push them out of the square up towards Nugent's Headquarters on Windmill Hill. Our priority will be to capture as many of Nugent's cannons as possible. Once we have secured the hill we will swing around and attack Stewart's army on his right flank. Stewart will be trapped in a pincer movement between us and General Warden and General Magennis's force. Victory will be ours.'

'What about Nugent's cavalry. If he believes his infantry is under pressure, he will send them in.'

'As long as our pikemen maintain their formations I don't believe Nugent has that option. We've trained our men how to repel a cavalry charge. If Nugent is foolish enough to order them to attack the pikemen in the streets we will destroy them. We have the advantage if we fight them in the streets, but if we pull back and allow them to bombard us with cannon from long range, they will destroy us. This will be our only chance for victory and the opportunity to capture some much-needed cannons and rifles for the next battle in Wexford. If there are no more questions General Armlet will tell you when and where you have to assemble your men.'

The officers quickly dispersed over the estate to prepare their units for the battle ahead.

Betsy returned to her Gransha company and ordered them to gather around as she told them about General Munro's plans.

'We must be ready to leave here at three am,' she said. 'Most of Nugent's infantry will still be moving into their positions in the town streets at that time. We will be part of the main attacking force.'

Betsy could sense everyone's apprehension. 'When we gathered in the hall at Gransha, just before we marched to Donaghadee Henry spoke to us and said that we were about to become part of an army fighting for Ireland's freedom. Do you remember?'

'Yes,' murmured a few.

'And do you remember the last words Henry spoke just before he led us into battle at Saintfield?'

'Yes,' a few more replied.

'What were they?'

'Remember Orr.'

'That's right. When William Orr was standing on the scaffold waiting to die, he declared to the world that he was no traitor and that he was about to die for a persecuted country. William Orr and Henry Poulter gave their lives for our freedom. With their martyred souls marching beside us and with God on our side we have nothing to fear. No one can stop us. We will be victorious. Are you ready to fight?' shouted Betsy.

'Yes,' everyone roared. 'Remember Orr.'

It was shortly after midnight before the camp settled down. There was not much chat as people lay with their thoughts. There was only an occasional musket shot from the town to remind everyone of what was ahead of them.

Billy sat down beside Betsy.

'This is it Betsy. The moment we have been waiting for. All the talking and dreaming is over. Tomorrow we will be facing the biggest challenge of our lives. Do you remember the first time we met?'

'Yes, I do, it was at David Johnston's farm when we all went there to pick his potato crop.'

'But that wasn't the first time I saw you. I was on the roof of the house putting the flames out. I looked up and through the smoke I saw this beautiful woman with her hair blowing in the wind, riding into the farmyard below me. I couldn't take my eyes off you. It was love at first sight.'

'The first time I saw you I was passing buckets of water up to the people fighting the fire. I looked up and I saw this very handsome man on the roof. I remember looking at you and you turned around smiled and waved at me.'

'That moment changed my whole life,' Billy whispered. 'I couldn't stop thinking about you. When we went to the Johnston farm to dig their crop of potatoes, I saw you arrive and asked for you to be in my group. I was going to ask you if I could see you again, but I lost my nerve. And when we left the farm, I felt so down because I'd lost my chance of seeing you again. But when you opened the door on your farm, I couldn't believe it and I was determined not to mess up my second chance.'

On the campsite next to them a lone voice began to sing.
'The Lord's my Shepherd, I'll not want.
He makes me down to lie,
In pastures green; he leadeth me,
The quiet waters by....

'I'm so glad you didn't,' said Betsy as she nestled into his arms while the man continued singing.

At three-fifteen am, in the quiet of the night, various companies of United Irishmen began to gather at their allocated positions. The Gransha company joined General Munro at the main exit gates. Betsy was surprised when she saw Martha and Gina with pikes in their hands.

'I thought you were going with the wounded?'

'We're coming with you,' said Martha. 'This is more important.'

'Stay close to me at all times then,' said Betsy. 'We support the pikemen. They are used to fighting in their formations.'

While the pikemen and musketeers were checking their weapons in preparation for the attack they suddenly heard several loud booms of cannon fire coming from the other side of the town, seconds later red-hot cannon balls smashed through the trees and people around them.

'Steady,' shouted General Munro to his nervous warriors. 'We attack in fifteen minutes.'

'Look,' shouted someone near the gates. 'The town is on fire.'

'The soldiers are burning the houses,' shouted someone else.

Betsy rushed forward to look at the town and saw several fires. The sky above Ballynahinch glowed in the dark. As she watched more houses went up in flames.

'Why are they burning the town?' someone shouted as they waited on the order to go forward.

'They're burning the houses of our supporters.'

'They're trying to frighten us.'

'Why don't we attack now?'

'The Monaghan Militia have gone mad.'

As the cannon fire continued and the number of houses on fire increased, General Munro walked up to the gates. He turned around to face the expectant ranks of his army and pulled his sword from its scabbard, holding it high above his head.

'United Irishmen, today the eyes of the world are upon us. Let them know that we will never surrender to oppression. We march into battle with the spirits of our dead martyrs by our sides and the prayers and hopes of all free Irish people in our hearts. Today we will demonstrate by our courage and sacrifice, the supreme heights to which it is possible for human nature to aspire. Our aim is not victory today, but freedom for ever.'

General Munro turned to face the enemy.

'Remember Orr,' he shouted as he led the pikemen and musketeers out through the gates and onto Bridge Street. The companies of pikemen quickly assembled into their battle formations and marched towards the waiting British soldiers at the junction of Bridge Street and Church Street. Several companies of pikemen and musketeers broke away to run down side streets.

At the same time General Townsend led his army through the graveyard of a small church about half a mile away, out onto Church Street where they turned left and advanced towards the infantry at the end of Bridge Street.

The Monaghan Militia became aware they were about to be attacked when they heard a roar from the thousands of pikemen bearing down on them from two different directions.

In anticipation of an attack from the Montalto estate, Major General Nugent had placed two of his cannons facing the main entrance on Bridge Street, and as the pikemen charged towards them the soldiers fired grape shot killing and maiming many of them.

As men around her faltered Betsy kept urging them forward towards the cannons that the soldiers were trying to reload. The pikemen jumped over the meagre defences around the guns and began to engage in fierce hand to hand fighting eventually forcing the soldiers to leave the cannons and retreat towards the town square.

The pikemen cheered as they followed the soldiers into the square where a feeble attempt was made to regroup, but with more pikemen pouring into the square from the adjoining streets and attacking them from all sides, the soldiers were forced to pull back. Once again, they tried again to regroup at the exit from the square onto Windmill Street, but without cannon to support them they were forced backwards.

Major General Nugent on seeing that his infantry was beginning to buckle ordered his mounted Dragoons to attack. The cavalry charged down Windmill Street towards the advancing pikemen but just as Munro had predicted they were no match for the pikemen. Their tight formations soon defeated the horsemen and they quickly dispersed.

When he saw the Dragoons retreating General Munro could sense victory.

On the top of Windmill Hill, Major General Nugent watched his infantry being pushed back further and further. When he saw that they were on the verge of breaking he ordered an immediate retreat. A bugler sounded the signal for the infantry to disengage and they immediately started retreating away from the pikeman up Windmill Hill towards Major Colonel Nugent's headquarters.

The pikemen at the front of the attack were taken aback and confused when they heard the bugle and saw the soldiers running away from them. As their forward motion stopped the pikemen looked at each other.

'What's going on,' Betsy called out. 'Why have we stopped?'

'I don't know,' said Billy.

'The soldiers have run away?' shouted a pikeman.

'Why are they doing that?'

'Have they gone to get reinforcements?'

'Have they more cannons up there?'

'Is it a trap?'

'Someone said they are bringing in reinforcements,' someone shouted.

'They're going to fire their cannons on us.'

'We'll be sitting ducks.'

'We've been tricked.'

'Retreat back to the square.'

'It's a trap.'

'Stay where you are,' shouted Sergeant Major White as some of his pikemen turned and began heading back towards the town square.

'But there are reinforcements coming?' shouted one of the pikemen.

'There are no reinforcements,' shouted the Sergeant Major. 'The soldiers have been ordered to retreat. We have to keep advancing.'

But the pikemen's formation had begun to break up and as the men in the front ranks turned around to see what was happening more men began making their way back towards the town square.

'Get back in your positions,' shouted Sergeant Major White.

But the United Irishmen were no longer heeding him, and when they saw more of their friends leaving and heading back towards the square, they decided to follow.

'Get back into your formations,' yelled Sergeant Major White as the pikemen ran past him. 'We're winning the fight.'

But panic had spread like wildfire and soon hundreds of pikemen had turned around and were fleeing down the many side streets.

From his vantage spot on the top of Windmill Hill, Major General Nugent suddenly realised the sound of his bugler had caused confusion in the ranks of the pikemen and quickly ordered an immediate attack by his frustrated Dragoons and his retreating soldiers.

With his ranks in complete disarray Sergeant Major White finally gave the order to withdraw and when the pikemen saw the Dragoons charging towards them the sense of panic increased and the retreat quickly turned into a rout. Martha was knocked over in the confusion. Betsy and Gina quickly ran over to her but as they helped her to her feet Betsy saw a couple of Dragoons riding directly towards them.

'Come on Martha, we have to go,' begged Betsy.

'I'll be alright,' said Martha in a daze after her fall.

'Quick head to the alley,' said Betsy as she and Gina put their arms around her and were ushered down the narrow laneway by Sergeant Major White.

As they ran Betsy could hear the Dragoons chasing after them. The thunder of the horse's hoof beats getting louder and louder in the confines of the narrow laneway. Just when she thought they were about to be killed several pikemen including Billy and George stepped out in front of them. As they ran through them, they raised their pikes and charged. The Dragoons tried to turn their horses in the narrow laneway while trying to ward off the pike blades with their sabres. But they were hopeless against the long pikes and after a few seconds the bloodied bodies of the dead Dragoons crashed to the ground.

Gina and Betsy stopped to try and recover their breath.

'I thought you were dead,' said Billy when he ran over and held Betsy.

'Martha was knocked down and we had to help her.'

'We must keep going,' said Sergeant Major White.

'George has been hurt,' shouted one of the pikemen.

Betsy turned and saw him lying on the ground. She ran over asking, 'What's wrong?'

'It's my foot. One of the horses stood on it. I think it might be broken.'

Gina removed his shoe and sock as Martha quickly examined his foot. 'I don't think anything is broken but it's badly bruised. Come on, lean on us.'

'We need to get out of here,' shouted Sergeant Major White.

With Betsy on one side and Gina on the other George managed to somehow hobble down the lane to Bridge Street and back to the entrance gates into the Montalto estate where General Munro was addressing several hundred confused and frightened pikemen.

'What happened?' asked one.

'We were so close to victory,' said General Munro. 'But we were let down by a stupid mistake. Just as we were about to annihilate Nugent's soldiers on Windmill Hill Street, he ordered his bugler to sound the retreat. But when his soldiers stopped fighting and started running away from us some of our pikemen mistakenly thought the bugler was calling for reinforcements. Some of them, fearing they had been led into a trap, turned around and began running towards the square causing panic. This quickly spread throughout the rest of the pikemen and there was nothing we could do to stop them all from retreating. What happened to you on our right flank General Warden?'

'It was just as bad. When Colonel Stewart's army attacked, we tried to contain them as ordered,' said General Warden. 'But they were too strong for us.'

'They had too many cannons and rifles,' added General Magennis. 'They decimated our ranks. We had to retreat. I'm afraid his soldiers will be here soon.'

'The battle is lost. This is my last order to you,' said General Munro. 'Colonel Stapylton's army has not moved from their barracks in Comber. There is still an escape route to the north. Go home. Go back to your families and tell them about the courage you saw in Ballynahinch today. Tell them how you saw brave men die. Tell them we did not let them down. May God go with you.'

When he finished the pikemen began throwing their pikes away and gathering in small groups to discuss the best route home. The Gransha men gathered around Betsy.

'Which way will we go?' they asked.

'General Munro said we should head north,' said Betsy.

'I know a safe way,' said Billy. 'I used to come down here for my work. It's best to head towards Lisburn first, then towards Newtownards and home.'

'But we can't go in one large group,' said Betsy. 'The soldiers will be guarding the roads and the dragoons will be everywhere. Get yourselves into smaller groups and then split up. Keep to the fields and hedgerows. Stay off the main roads. We'll meet again, when we're all home. Good luck.'

The men quickly formed into small groups and began heading off in different directions.

Betsy's group comprised of Gina, Martha, George and Billy. As they were about to leave Betsy saw Sergeant Major White standing on his own.

'Are you coming?' she asked.

'No, I would only be a burden. I will try to make my own way home.'

'No, you can't do that,' said Martha. 'You're coming with us.'

'Yes, come on John,' said Gina. 'We're not leaving you.'

'Alright and thanks.'

'Good,' said Betsy.

'There are some people I know in Lisburn,' said Billy. 'If we can make it there, they'll put us up for a few days until everything calms down.'

George's injury slowed them down, and they were among the last to leave the Montalto Estate. When they reached the outskirts of the town, they could hear the yells and whoops of the soldiers as they hunted for pikemen, and the screams of anyone they captured.

They stayed off the roads. Walking along the edges of fields and staying close to the hedgerows. Hiding when they saw any soldiers nearby. The damage to George's foot was more serious than Martha had originally thought, and so they had to stop frequently as his pain became worse. In the end they made more progress as Billy and Sergeant Major White took turns to carry George on their backs. It was almost noon when they stopped for a rest, before setting off again making their way around the edge of a very large field thick with yellow gorse. They stopped when they realised, they were going to have to cross a road to get to the next field. It had a steep slope that led up to a coppice on top of a hill. As they lay in the hedgerow, they listened to several groups of Dragoons and foot soldiers pass by on the road.

'We can't stay here for very long,' said Sergeant Major White. 'It's only a matter of time before they find us. We'd be safer in the woods on the top of that hill. There's a lane on the other side of the hill that will take us most of the way to Lisburn.'

'We need to be sure there're no soldiers around,' said Betsy. 'We'll be very exposed on the road, and as we're making our way up that hill, even if we stick to the hedgerow.'

'Martha, Gina and I will go first,' said Sergeant Major White. 'When we get to the top of the hill, we'll give you a signal when it's safe for you to follow.'

'Yes, alright,' said Betsy. 'But be careful, this place is swarming with soldiers.'

Sergeant Major White crept through a small hole in the hedgerow followed by Martha and Gina. After checking everything was clear they ran across the road and climbed a gate into the field. They paused for a few moments before making their way to the row of hedges on the edge of the field. After making sure all was clear they ran along the hedgerow to the top of the hill and into the woods. Once they were in the safety of the trees they stopped. Everything was quiet. Martha went back to the edge of the wood and looked down the hill to where Betsy and Billy were hiding with George. After one final check to make sure there were no soldiers or cavalrymen anywhere on the road, she waved for them to come up.

Betsy and Billy helped George through the same small hole in the hedgerow and across the road. After climbing the gate they helped him hobble along the bottom of the field to the hedge. While Martha was watching their progress, she was distracted by a brief flash of sunlight coming from a few hundred yards down the road. She stood up to see what it was and to her horror saw several soldiers coming towards them. Martha tried to get Betsy's attention, but she and Billy were concentrating on helping George up the hill. Martha could hear the soldiers talking to each other. She prayed that her friends would reach the top of the hill before the soldiers spotted them. Just when she thought they were safe she saw the soldiers appear at the bottom of the hill. They were deeply engrossed in an argument, but as the last soldier walked past the gate, he glanced up the hill.

'Stop,' he shouted as he ran over to the gate.

The rest of the soldiers followed and clambered over the gate and began running up the hill.

When Billy saw the soldiers, he looked at Betsy.

'Run Betsy,' he shouted.

Betsy looked down at the soldiers. 'Come on George,' she urged, lifting him slightly as she tried to encourage him to move quicker. But it was no use and they were quickly surrounded.

'Put your hands up,' the small corporal demanded.

'Don't shoot' pleaded Billy as they raised their hands.

'Where have you come from?' the corporal asked.

'We work on a farm near Saintfield,' said Billy. 'We were sent down here to collect some sheep for the farmer, but my friend hurt his foot and so we are taking him back to the farm for treatment.'

'I don't believe you,' shouted the corporal. 'You were at Ballynahinch with the rebels.'

'No, we weren't,' said Betsy. 'We're farm workers. We only arrived this morning.'

'You're a liar. You were fighting with the United Irishmen.'

'We weren't,' said Billy. 'I promise you; we're telling the truth. We work on a farm near Saintfield. We were sent down here to collect half a dozen sheep for our boss.'

'Empty your pockets,' ordered the corporal.

'But I'm telling you the truth,' pleaded Billy.

'Do as I say,' shouted the corporal.

Billy pulled a white hanky, a couple of coins and a small piece of food from his pockets.

'That's all I have,' he said.

'Empty yours,' the corporal shouted at George.

George pulled out some coins from his jacket pockets and showed them to the corporal.

'Empty your trouser pockets?'

'There is nothing there.'

'Pull them inside out,' ordered the corporal.

'George put his hands into his trouser pockets, and as he pulled them out a green ribbon fell to the ground.

The corporal stooped down and picked it up.

'You are murdering bastards,' he shouted. 'You're popish rebels.'

The soldiers cocked their rifles.

'Don't shoot,' Betsy shouted positioning herself in front of Billy and George. 'They've done nothing wrong.'

The corporal pointed his pistol at Betsy's head. 'What's your name?'

'I'm Betsy Gray. This is my brother George. And this is my fiancé William Boal. We've done nothing wrong.'

'Were you at Ballynahinch?'

'Yes. We were,' Betsy declared. 'We're prisoners of war. It would be illegal to shoot us.'

'You're rebels,' declared the corporal. 'You've no rights.'

'Hold on Corporal. Maybe she's right. We should take them back to headquarters and let the sergeant deal with them,' said one of the soldiers.

'Shut up,' shouted the corporal. 'They're all part of a popish plot to destroy this country.'

'No, we're not,' said George.

'Shut your mouth,' screamed the corporal. 'Get on your knees.'

'We're prisoners of war,' said Betsy as Billy helped George to get down on his knees. 'You must not harm us.'

'You too,' the corporal shouted at Betsy.

'Corporal don't you think...' started the soldier

'Shut up... You will carry out my orders,' shouted the corporal at the soldier as Betsy turned to face Billy and George before kneeling down.

George started to weep. 'Please let us live,' he begged.

Betsy looked at him. 'Be brave George,' she whispered.

'I love you Betsy,' said Billy.

'On my count,' shouted the corporal as the soldiers pointed their rifles at the kneeling figures.

'Three... Two... One...'

'I love you,' said Betsy as the soldiers fired their rifles.

As Betsy fell forward, she threw her arms around the bodies of Billy and George.

'Come on there must be more of them around here,' said the corporal as he began walking back down the hill towards the road.

'What about searching the woods?' said one of the soldiers.

'What for?' snapped the corporal. 'If there were any more in there they would have fled by now. Come on. Leave the thinking to me. We'll have a better chance of finding more on the road. These people have to learn that they cannot take up arms against the king.'

Martha, Gina and Sergeant Major White lay listening to the corporal ranting as the soldiers left the field. When they eventually felt it was safe, they looked over the brow of the hill and saw the three bodies lying on top of each other. As they were talking about what they were going to do they heard a farmer arrive to investigate what all the shooting had been about.

'Who are you?' asked the farmer when he saw them walking out of the woods.

'We're friends of theirs,' said Gina pointing to the bodies.

'Were they with the United Irishmen?'

'Yes. Will you help us.'

'What do you want from me?'

'We can't leave their bodies here, will you help us bury them?'

'Yes,' he replied sadly. 'There's a small grassy clearing in the middle of the woods, we can bury them there.'

While the farmer went to get spades, Gina, Martha and Sergeant Major White carried the bodies into the woods.

'We want to bury them together,' said Martha when the farmer returned.

'That's okay,' he replied as he and Sergeant Major White started to dig.

After they buried Betsy, Billy and George, the farmer hammered a small wooden cross he had brought back with him into the ground at the head of the grave.

Gina took a piece of paper from her pocket and pinned it to the cross. On it she had written: *A Dream Rests Here.*

Betsy's friends took two more days to reach the safety of their homes. Martha went back to the farm where she raised her son, while Gina eventually married and moved to Liverpool. Sergeant Major White was arrested and after a short trial he was hung.

General Munro was captured as he tried to escape from Ballynahinch. He was court martialled and was hung outside his home in Lisburn. The Reverend Steel Dickson remained in prison for another five years before being released. The Reverend Porter was tried and hung outside his church in Greyabbey. The Reverend Archibald Warwick was tried and hung outside his parish hall in Kircubbin. The Reverend Robert Gowdy was tried and hung in Newtownards. Other Presbyterian ministers who had participated in the uprising were imprisoned or exiled to America. Thousands of United Irishmen from counties Antrim and Down were hung, imprisoned, flogged, or deported.

A French force did finally arrive in late August and were defeated by the British army.

By the end of 1798 the British Government had begun a process to create a new political entity in which the Irish parliament would be incorporated into Westminster. On the 1st January 1801 a new sovereign state called the United Kingdom of Great Britain and Ireland was formed.

Printed in Great Britain
by Amazon